Jack Curtis was born in Devonshire. He now divides his time between London and a remote valley in the West Country. His acclaimed first novel, *Crows' Parliament*, is also available from Corgi Books.

GLORY

'Extra-strong, sinuous writing here cements Curtis' stature as one of the finest stylists in the thriller field'
Kirkus Reviews

'In the world of suspense literature it is rare to find a work which has so much of the classic about it. With *Glory*, Jack Curtis has raised the genre and the expectations of his audience to a new state'
New England Review of Books

GLORY

JACK CURTIS

CORGI BOOKS

GLORY
A CORGI BOOK 0 552 13517 8

Originally published in Great Britain by Bantam Press,
a division of Transworld Publishers Ltd.

PRINTING HISTORY
Bantam Press edition published 1989
Corgi edition published 1990

This book is set in 10/11 pt. Palatino
by Goodfellow & Egan, Cambridge

Corgi Books are published by Transworld Publishers Ltd.,
61–63 Uxbridge Road, Ealing, London W5 5SA, in Australia by
Transworld Publishers (Australia) Pty. Ltd., 15–23 Helles Avenue,
Moorebank, NSW 2170, and in New Zealand by Transworld
Publishers (N.Z.) Ltd., Cnr. Moselle and Waipareira Avenues,
Henderson, Auckland.

Printed and bound in Great Britain by
BPCC Hazell Books
Aylesbury, Bucks, England
Member of BPCC Ltd.

For Lizzie

GLORY

PART ONE

1

The woman walked into the bedroom barefoot, her summer dress unzipped to the small of her back. She looked thoughtful. She pushed off the shoulder-straps of the dress and let it fall to the floor, then stepped out of it and walked to a small writing-desk in order to make an entry in her diary. She paused, looking at what she'd written as if it didn't quite make sense to her. After a moment she moved back to the centre of the room, reaching towards the small of her back with both hands.

When the man saw her make that gesture, he almost gasped. The idiosyncratic pose of a woman about to unhook her brassiere; it never failed to produce a rush of lust in him – the hands nimble and practised on the clasp, the back slightly arched, the elbows akimbo. He'd been fifteen when he first saw it. He remembered now the shock and excitement of the moment. He had lain on his narrow bed, and the girl had walked towards him, smiling, naked apart from that one garment, her hands going back in that casual secretive way. The girl had been his sister.

The woman shrugged out of the bra and let it drop; then, without pausing, stripped off her panties and walked past the window to the wardrobe. Strong bands of sunlight filtered through the slats of a venetian blind. Her copper-coloured hair shone in the glow. As she opened the wardrobe door, the man had to step to one side to avoid it. He moved to the centre of the room, but she removed a towelling robe and

11

turned almost at once and crossed to her dressing-table. He was directly in her path. If he hadn't moved quickly, she would have cannoned into him; as it was, she passed so close that he caught the scent of her body, a warm tang like the smell of tea, and could see tiny droplets of perspiration caught in the fine hairs at the corner of her mouth.

She threw the robe on the bed and sat down before her dressing-table mirror, sweeping her hair back from her face and tucking it behind her ears; then she opened a jar of cleanser, took a cotton-wool ball from a glass pot and began to take off her make-up.

She was slim and startlingly pretty. As she wiped the cream across her eyelid, bringing the cotton-wool away stained with pale eye-shadow, she leaned forward slightly as if communing with her own reflection, and her breasts swung clear of her ribcage, finding a perfect globular shape. Two thin creases developed across her taut stomach just above the neat sprout of hair in her lap.

The man walked behind her to look at the way her waist narrowed then flared at the hip – a shape made more pronounced because she was sitting down; then he ducked slightly to find his own reflection in the glass. The mirror-image of his face seemed to lodge on her shoulder. He wanted her very badly, but there was nothing he could do about that.

She got up and brushed by him again. This time he was backed up to the bed; he stumbled against it and sat down, watching her as she left the room. He thought: I guessed she would be as beautiful as that without her clothes.

After a few minutes he followed her, almost tripping on the shoes that she'd kicked off in the hallway. She was in the bathroom. The bath had been running and was almost full. A cloud of foam lay on the surface of the water. She turned off the taps. The day was hot, just as every day that month had been hot, so she had

12

run a cool bath and there was little steam in the room – just a slight fogging on one or two of the mirror-tiles that covered one wall.

As he came into the bathroom she was bending to test the water, and her body seemed all angles and planes; then she straightened up, extending the motion to stretch, raising her hands above her head and going up on tiptoe, and it was ovals and perpendiculars. The man looked at himself in the mirror-tiles. Like the woman, he was slim, but he was much darker. He had the black hair and blue eyes of the Celt. He looked past his own image at the reflection of the woman getting into the bath and went on watching her that way for a while because he wanted also to be able to see himself.

She sank down into the fragrant suds until only her head was visible, displacing a little billow of foam that rose against the back of the bathtub like a white cushion, and for a short while just lay there, soaking. The man looked at the woman's reflection, then at his own, then back at hers; he was trembling. As he turned round, she moved slightly, spreading her knees and lifting them a little so that the layer of foam shifted on the backwash, dividing, here and there, into small islets. Her hand appeared in one of the patches of greenish water and she began to stroke herself between the legs. She wasn't serious about it, though, and stopped after a few moments.

The man thought again of his sister, and how the family would sit round in that cavernous drawing-room in the evenings, Father, in *Father's* chair, reading the paper word by laborious word, only his legs and hands visible, Mother at the end of the sofa nearest the floor-lamp, head bent over some darning. His sister would be in the second armchair with her feet tucked up, her full skirt billowing over the seat. Now and then, he would glance up from his position on the floor, and catch her eye. She might look back at him, seeming almost angry, and he'd go back to his book;

13

but sometimes she would smile very slightly, and he would know that her hand had gone under her skirt, at the back where it was out of sight, that her fingers were moving under her thigh, that she was naked beneath the skirt. Her body would ease upwards, fractionally, as her finger found the place and then she would look directly at him, never taking her eyes from his face, her expression almost stony until the moment came when her lips parted, just fractionally, showing her teeth, and a blush of red showed on her neck. He would sit on the floor, his gaze fixed on her, while father turned the pages of his paper and mother's needle went deftly, nip and tuck.

The woman raised an arm from the bath and stroked it with the suds. The man went to the bath and stood over her. She seemed to give up on the notion of washing herself and lay there gazing at the ceiling. Her eyes closed briefly, then closed for a little longer. It had been a long day. She liked her job, but it was by no means trouble-free, and this week had been a tough one; a series of small foul-ups had culminated in a fairly major foul-up. Remembering it, her face took on that thoughtful expression again.

Ah well, the man thought, enough of this. He reached down and put a hand on the woman's throat. She looked startled and puzzled at the same time, as someone might who wakes in a strange place and can't get her bearings. Then the man straightened his arm and bore down, pushing her head under the water. Her long legs rose, threshing, from the bath and her hands came up to grab and wrestle, but it was no good. In a wet bathtub there's no purchase, nothing to give leverage. She fought as hard as she could. At one time her face came close to the surface, just below the skin of the green water that was killing her, her features stretched in a rictus of desperation and distress, but he sent her deeper.

Her legs were flailing, knocking the sides of the tub; her ankle whacked against the handbasin, but she didn't notice the pain; one heel cracked a mirror-tile. She tried to buck herself upright, but he held her, using all the strength in that one arm to keep her shoulders down, and her legs began to make big convulsive movements, splashing into the bath, then rising stiffly before crashing back again. He could feel her shaking, the vibrations coming up to him like the weight and movement you feel when there's a big fish on the line, but you can't see it yet. Then she was still.

The man held her for a while, patiently, looking straight ahead at the dimpled glass of the bathroom window. Patterns of light trickled round the corrugations like water finding its lowest level. He could hear traffic passing in the street at the front of the house. At one point the telephone rang in her living-room. He continued to hold her down, still gazing at the window, his face vacant, waiting for the task to be finished, like someone taking a temperature. Finally, he released her and, without looking at her again, went straight back to the bedroom. Less than ten minutes later, he was in the street.

The woman's flat seemed unnaturally silent and still, as if the air had become fixed and the furniture somehow gained more weight; as if household objects – the stereo, the dishwasher, the food-processor – had spontaneously broken and would never work again. It was the silence and stillness of death.

The woman lay motionless under the water, one leg crooked over the side of the bath, her hair spread and floating like weed, her eyes wide open. The phone rang again, making the fixity of everything more pronounced. After ten rings it stopped, and the silence was like dust-sheets and bare floors and windows boarded over.

*

It would have been difficult for someone watching what had happened to understand those moments in the bedroom and bathroom when she had brushed past the man, almost walking into him, going to and fro between wardrobe and desk and dressing-table, then taking her make-up off before passing him again and going out into the hallway. She had turned off the taps and tested the water and touched herself that way; and there hadn't been a moment when she'd looked in his direction and showed recognition, not a moment when she'd smiled or spoken. At times, it had seemed that she expected to be able to walk straight through him. She had done the things she'd done like someone completely alone.

The watcher, had there been one, might have supposed her to be blind, but that would have been a foolish thought. The blind are more sensitive than the rest of us to another, unexpected presence somewhere in their territory.

The woman wasn't blind.

She simply hadn't known that the man was there.

2

When John Deacon looked up, he saw the ocean. He had walked along the cliffs for about five miles, conscious at first of the sound of the surf, though after a while the endless roar had become something he no longer heard – a backdrop for his thoughts. It comforted him even though he'd forgotten it was there. The sun was hot, but there was a brisk inshore blow and the breakers were forming well out to sea, rolling in to clout the little bay that had been his destination. Deacon had slipped and slithered down an almost vertical cliff-path that led to the fifty-foot sickle-shaped beach. He'd done it by instinct, still lost in his thoughts, and had plodded to the far side of the stretch of sand to get to the rock where he liked to sit. For better than thirty minutes, he'd lodged there, never once raising his eyes. Now he looked up and saw the ocean, and regarded it calmly like someone who knew all about its power but didn't have to be afraid.

A year, he thought, a year since I was here with Maggie. The admission stung him, as he had known it would, but he didn't turn aside from it. A year – and a day very like this one. There had been a heatwave, as there is now. We brought a picnic: salami and cheese, a salad, wine, and butter on a dish and a chequered tablecloth, because Maggie had delightfully fixed ideas about how a picnic should look. We ate and slept and swam. It got dark, but still we didn't go home. The night was warm. The sea-breeze was warm. The sand

17

and the rocks had retained the sun's heat. We lay and listened to the surf, or talked to each other in low voices, and we made love and we watched the sun come up. That's what happened. Not something else. That. Don't pretend it wasn't good; it was. It was terrific. Don't pretend you can get it back; you can't.

Like a man preparing to pick up a weight that went to the limit of what he could lift, Deacon turned his mind to a thing he wanted to forget. The day after the picnic, he had left for London. Maggie had driven him to the station. 'The weather's so good,' she'd said. 'I'll be back in three days; four at the most.'

Deacon would have given anything to have stayed with her, but the fine weather was a matter of indifference to London's criminals, who went on mugging and raping, robbing and swindling, just as office workers were obliged to get to their desks each morning. It was their job. It was Deacon's job to try to stop them; or, at least, to catch them after the event. While he and Maggie had been listening to the sea and gently taking each other's clothes off, four men had broken into a bullion warehouse near the London docks and removed the equivalent of half a million pounds. It wasn't clear how they had done this, since the place was fitted with sensors that would have detected fly-shit. Unsurprisingly, some of Deacon's colleagues concluded that the men had organized some inside help, but the theories didn't go much further than that. The two security guards who patrolled the warehouse and its surrounds had been ruled out as suspects, since both had been blown almost in half by blasts from an over-and-under shotgun.

That morning, a copper from the local force had driven to Deacon's house on the beach and told him that he was to leave Cornwall by the next train and not bother stopping at his London flat before reporting in. He commiserated with Deacon, mentioning the exceptional weather.

18

Deacon said: 'Shit!'

Maggie had already gone to the bedroom to pack for him.

The four men were eventually caught, along with the warehouse stock clerk who had given them the circuit-plan for the alarms, but it wasn't Deacon who caught them. Four days after his arrival in London – just four days, as she'd said – he was sitting in his flat drinking a slow Scotch and waiting for Maggie to arrive. He knew she'd come. She would never have stayed longer without letting him know, and it was seven o'clock, so she must, he figured, be on her way. Cornwall was a five-hour drive in the BMW. She would have left at two-thirty as she always did. Deacon had bought two lamb chops and made a salad.

The phone went, and he smiled. She'd stopped for petrol. In a moment he'd hear her say, 'I'm almost there; put something on ice,' and he'd make a joke of that. When he lifted the phone, he didn't say the number or 'Hello'; he said 'Hi!'

The voice on the phone was a man's. It told him that Maggie was dead.

A creamy lip of foam sluiced the rock Deacon was perched on, then retreated and sank into the sand. Christ, he thought, it's so big. So big a burden. I've got to carry it for ever. A year; but he hadn't been carrying the burden for that long. It was a new thing to him. He hadn't been able to pick it up, or look at it, or even acknowledge it was there. That avoidance hadn't been an easy thing to achieve, nor had it been a wise thing to do. But booze had made it possible. After the daze of the arrangements, the funeral, the *busy* time, Deacon had stayed drunk for a month. That way he could make the mind-pictures blur; he could deaden the obsession that brought him back again and again to a scene he hadn't witnessed, but could invent, endlessly, and did at three in the morning, at noon, at five in the afternoon, any time *any time*, but mostly at three in the morning.

Maggie driving, handling the big car with her usual assurance; listening to a tape, maybe. . . . What? . . . Mozart, or Bach, or one of their collections of seventies rock music. Christ, it didn't matter. Why did that *matter* so damn much? The sun-roof open, the windows down to catch a breeze; wearing that striped skirt and a blue T-shirt, driving barefoot, sand still between her toes, a dusting of it on the car floor. Then a truck jack-knifing, the rear end coming through the barrier, Maggie in the fast lane, of course, of course that's where she'd be, and no time to do anything. Then the car ramming the trailer that had wound up broadside across the central reservation. The chaos of movement, Maggie slamming forward and back, the car spinning and moving across the lanes into the paths of other cars.

How long? How long for her to die? Was it the truck or one of the other cars? Whichever it was had killed her. No, not just killed her. It had taken her head off. Deacon remembered the skirt and the blue T-shirt and the granules of sand between her toes. Insane that something as fragile as the sand should still be there. Where her head was separated from her body, they had put a frill, like a chorister's collar.

He had stayed drunk for a month. When, finally, he'd sobered up, he'd realized that was a mistake, so he'd stayed drunk for another month. Then another. Phil Mayhew had come round to tell him that he'd lost his job. Already he'd been given more leeway than should be allowed. He had refused to go out, except for a drink, wouldn't talk to anyone, wouldn't answer the phone. They'd put him down as a hopeless case.

Deacon had poured himself another Scotch and advised Mayhew that he didn't give a flying fuck about the job. Mayhew had run his hand through his hair and given every impression of a man who didn't know what to do or what to say. Eventually, and not at all unkindly, he'd remarked that at least Deacon would be OK for money. Deacon took this to be a sardonic reference to the fact that Maggie had been rich – which she had – and that Deacon would be glad to have her money. Mayhew was one of his closest friends. Deacon had tried to hit him, but was too drunk to stand.

It went on that way for better than six months. Deacon learned to regard hangovers as a natural hazard and memory-lapses as allies. He paid little or no attention to his life. Bills that weren't settled by the bank were left unpaid. Had it not been for the loyalty and concern of Phil Mayhew, Deacon would have gone through winter without heat or light. Christmas had been a nightmare; he'd spent it holed up in bed, thick with whisky and self-pity. Maggie's money – and Mayhew had been right about that, there was a lot of it – was less a benefit to Deacon than a burden. The need for a job might well have forced sobriety on him, and with sobriety the ability to come to terms with what had happened. As it was, Deacon could have stayed drunk for years – or until the booze finished him off.

One morning in early spring, something happened that pulled him around. He had woken to the hammering headache and incipient nausea that had become pretty much second nature. The flat stank of stale Scotch and cigarette smoke. It was about seven o'clock and still dark, so he'd reached out to switch on the bedside lamp and had dragged down a half-full glass of whisky that splashed over his chest and on to the tangled bedclothes. Cursing and near-blind, he'd stumbled out of bed and into the bathroom to throw up.

It wasn't until he'd got back to the bedroom that he'd realized there was a girl in his bed. He wasn't too surprised. It had happened before, and the only problem for Deacon in that sort of meaningless encounter was the business of getting rid of whatever-their-names-were the next morning without fuss and as quickly as possible. This girl – whatever her name was – had continued to sleep through his accident with the glass and his foul-mouthed departure from the room.

Deacon watched her a minute. His getting out of bed had hauled the sheets down to her waist and he could see, between her breasts, what was either a birthmark or a stain. Her dark hair was long and veiled half her face but didn't entirely hide a complexion that was blotchy with drink. Because she was sleeping on her back, her arms at her sides, she resembled an effigy. Her mouth was slightly open, and she'd made a tiny noise with each exhaled breath, a just-audible whimper that Deacon, for some reason, found frightening. He'd let her lie and gone to the kitchen to make coffee, spiked with a shot of Scotch.

She'd taken another three hours to wake – so long that Deacon had almost forgotten she was there. His flat was at the top of a three-storey Victorian house, and from his kitchen window he could look out over the rooftops of a nearby Georgian crescent to a tree-lined avenue and beyond that to the greenness of the local park. During the time it took for the girl to wake, he'd perched on a stool and looked at the roofs, the trees and the sky, only moving to make more coffee or to splash another slug of whisky into his cup. He had started to count the birds that flew between his window and the plane tree at the end of the garden, but after a while he forgot to. Terrible imaginings – the crash, the moments that had led to Maggie's death – began to plague him. Worse than his inventions, though, were the memories that came, one by one, out of the past like a series of tiny playlets, clear in every detail, each action, each remark, each gesture. Precise vignettes depicting happiness, love, fulfilment and precious secret things. They were inescapable and agonizing; only drink could efface them.

22

He'd heard a noise that, at first, he'd taken to be the whine of some piece of small machinery: a distant chainsaw, perhaps, or a drill being operated somewhere else in the house. Then he'd realized it was coming from the bedroom. He'd walked down the hallway and opened the door. The girl was crouched, naked, in a corner, her face to the wall. She was keening, a soft unearthly sound that seemed to come from some deep and inexhaustible well of misery. Deacon had turned her, and she'd looked up at him, her mouth open, her face shining with tears. Her expression hadn't changed, and she'd kept making the noise. He'd spoken, but his words had changed nothing. He'd wanted to say her name, but didn't know what it was. She had remained there, her mouth open and wet, her eyes wide with incomprehension. It was as if her distress were too great even for her properly to understand. In the end he'd left her and gone back to the kitchen. He'd been trembling. It wasn't that the girl was upset – he'd faced recrimination and regret before on a number of other mornings when he'd woken to find that he wasn't alone; but this wasn't the tongue-lashing or frosty silence that, on other occasions, he'd traded for indifference or half-forgotten bad behaviour. This was something eerie; something broken inside.

He had gone back to his stool, not knowing what to do, too ill and too bound up with his own anguish to care much. But the sound the girl made had unnerved him, and he'd been glad when it stopped. He'd heard her bare feet on the hallway's wooden floor, and the bathroom door had opened and closed. For a short while, he'd made an effort to remember the details of the previous night, but nothing much would come back to him: a few pubs, then a club after that. Thinking through it, he'd heard a glass break in the bathroom – his tooth-mug, perhaps – and that gave his memory a purchase on something that had happened in the

23

club. . . . Someone falling . . . broken glass . . . himself, maybe. And he remembered something of the girl: a green dress and diamanté chandelier earrings that flashed in the smoky gloom of the place. He'd been able to remember nothing of what they had said to one another, or of how they'd got back to his flat. As he'd looked out, pondering these things, a ring dove had flown past the window. Deacon had poured another cup of coffee and added another tot. Suddenly the place seemed very quiet, and he'd wondered if she might have come out of the bathroom and left without his noticing it. Then he'd remembered the sound of the glass breaking.

The lock on the bathroom door was just a small bolt, and he'd been able to kick it off easily. The girl wasn't dead: there hadn't been time for that, but she'd fainted and there was a hell of a lot of blood. Deacon thought he would never forget the look on the hospital doctor's face when he'd had to say that he didn't know the girl's name, or what her address was, or who in the world might care whether she lived or died. It had been necessary for him to go back to his flat, along with a young copper who had checked Deacon out with Phil Mayhew. They had searched through the girl's bag and found an address-book. The look that had been on the doctor's face had also been on the face of the young policeman.

The incident had sullied Deacon, but it had also made him angry – principally with himself; and the anger was enough to change things. He hadn't stopped drinking, but he no longer allowed the habit to incapacitate him. This left him with a new problem: what to do instead of being drunk. He only knew one thing, and that was police work, so he'd used some of Maggie's money, some *more* of Maggie's money, to open an enquiry agency. It had given him no real sense of purpose. It wasn't some sort of new start. It was something to do. He'd rented an office in a reasonably smart neighbourhood and, working alone, had begun to take on the tasks that pay an enquiry agent's salary: debt-collecting, divorce work, custody cases.

He'd spend his days tracking down debtors or tailing erring husband and wives. He didn't care for the work, but it got him up in the mornings. It also occupied his mind, and that was important. He filled his days with the particulars of jobs that were tiresome or distasteful and had always known that eventually he'd have to stop doing that.

One evening, two months or so earlier, he'd been going from room to room in his flat, a little drunk and proposing to get somewhat drunker before going to bed. He had just completed a particularly unpleasant tug-of-love case that had seemed to hurt everyone involved – not least the child – and had left a vile taste in Deacon's mouth. He'd wound up in the room that Maggie had used as a study. Her books were in there, the ones she read and reread, together with a sound system and their collection of records. And the photographs.

It was a reflex action. He'd sat on the floor and taken one of the albums from its shelf. Himself and Maggie; endless permutations. Summer and winter, spring and autumn; on holiday, in parks, at Christmas, on birthdays. An hour later, he had still been sitting in the same position, surrounded by the albums. Next morning, he'd driven to the beach-house, opened the place up, aired it, cleaned it, and begun to exorcize the ghosts.

The light began to fade, bringing mauve shadows to declivities in the rocks. Deacon sat on until darkness seeped into ocean and sky and he could only see what was nearest to him, then walked back to the path that led up the cliff. When he gained the top, he turned, taking the breeze on his face and listening for a moment to the endless rhythms of the sea.

She's dead, he said to himself. Maggie is dead, and I'll never see her again. He shouldered the pain, as he knew he must, and began to walk with it back to the house they had both loved so much.

26

3

There was a shadow that resembled a chess knight, the arched neck, the long head flaring slightly where the nostrils would be.

There was a shadow that seemed to be a bird in flight, the outstretched wings lofted and spread at the tips, the head ducked between them as if the bird were looking down at a long plain where its prey scuttled and browsed.

There was a shadow that he thought of as a creature playing a flute, the head turned away so that only the flat nose and pointy chin remained of the profile, but the instrument could be seen together with the bent elbow and part of the forearm.

And on the wall directly opposite the chair in which he sat was the shadow that looked like the sheela-na-gig. He remembered seeing her for the first time – that grotesque dynamic little figure – carved in stone under the eaves of a Saxon church. A fertility symbol. She had survived the weather, survived Cromwell, survived the outrage of prim Victorian clergymen, one of whom had tried to take a cold-chisel and mallet to her and had been stopped by villagers who still believed, as if it were a race-memory, that the harvest would fail if she were destroyed.

She was ugly so that the word lost its meaning: a smooth bald polyp head like that of a massive tadpole, stick arms that reached around a slick slug-like torso a third the size of her head, the bandy frog's legs jacked back to her shoulders. Her hands were gripping the lips of her massive sex and wrenching them apart: a cavern between her skinny thighs, a great bag of darkness that offered fruiting and ripeness and decay and death.

The dim lighting was low to the floor and always cast those shadows. Elaine liked to keep it that way. She had chosen the basement as her territory, leaving him the rest of the house. Even on a bright day the room was dark, and she encouraged that; the bamboo blinds were always drawn, the lamps always necessary. She lived in twilight.

He had known that she would be out when he got back, but wouldn't mind if he went to the room to wait for her. He got up and went to a shelf by the fireplace. Among her strange trophies was a small framed photograph. He peered at it without picking it up. There she was, ten years younger but looking just as she did now: the pale oval face, the black hair and blue eyes that were a family trademark.

She would be pleased, because he had brought her back a keepsake. He made a small space for it on the shelf and left it there, wondering excitedly how long it would be before she noticed it. He imagined her coming into the room, silently, speechlessly, as she always did, then finding the gift and turning to him with that slow smile that always fired his growing desire. He would tell her about the woman, giving it to her just as she would want it, moment by slow moment, from the instant when he followed the woman into her flat, slipping past the half-open front door, up to the closing of that same door as he stepped into the street half an hour later.

Elaine would make him backtrack to tell some parts again, urging him to miss nothing, wondering whether he hadn't perhaps forgotten some tiny thrilling detail, some perfect grace-note. She would sit in the armchair opposite his, and as he told the story her hand would go behind her back as she eased her body slightly upward, and he would know what her fingers were doing under the full skirt. And then he'd finish the story. And then they could begin.

'Elaine,' he whispered. He went back to the armchair and stared up at the shadow of the sheela-na-gig. 'Don't be long. Hurry. Hurry back.'

4

It was a strange thing – you couldn't have said how it had happened, or why it seemed that way – but the silence in the woman's flat had become more profound. The place had bedded down in silence. As if moss had grown there, coating the wainscot and spreading along the roof-beams. As if cupboards had already begun to moulder. As if all the bits and pieces of the woman's day-to-day life had begun to root.

She lay in the bath, one leg hooked over the side, her sodden lungs keeping the rest of her body under the surface. She appeared to have put on a little weight – the effect of the water beginning to make her swell. On her leg, where she had clouted the handbasin and the mirror-tile, the bruises were a livid red and purple. The rest of her skin had a puffy pork-fat look, dead white and oddly greasy. Her hair floated, arrayed about her flaxen face like a child's drawing of the sun's rays. The foam had long since dissipated, and she was plain to see beneath the green water, like some creature trapped in the Arctic ice, preserved there by centuries of permafrost. Because her self had gone, her nakedness had no meaning; it was the nakedness of animals.

When Laura Scott unlocked the door and entered the apartment, she sensed the silence.

Normally she would have gone straight to her room, dumped her bag on the bed and begun to unpack. She so hated routine tasks that the only way of keeping endless muddle out of her life was to deal with that sort of trivial job at once. It only took three or four days of inattention to detail to leave her with mountains of dishes in the sink, unopened mail, littered surfaces, and a room strewn with discarded clothes and drifts of paper that seemed to come from nowhere. And since, like Laura, Kate had a natural tendency towards slobbishness they'd made a deal about tidiness.

The stillness was tangible. A dead chill. Laura dropped her bag in the hallway and went through into the living-room. She called: 'Kate!' A pause, then: 'Katie!' Her voice came back to her, loud and unexpected, like a tree falling in a frozen forest. Although she could see no reason for it, she felt a sudden small rush of panic.

The kitchen, where nothing was out of place; then back into the living-room, the cushions fluffed, the blinds drawn; Katie's bedroom – her clothes in a pile on the bed. She looked on the mantelpiece for a note. She checked the pad by the telephone. She went back to her own room, unzipped her bag and began to transfer clothes to her wardrobes and drawers.

She took the small satchel containing her toothbrush and toothpaste, her shampoo and her deodorant, and went into the bathroom.

5

Christ, Deacon thought, only a month away from London and the damn place produces culture-shock.

During his time at the house on the beach, he'd seen nobody. Now he was surrounded by nobodies; the streets and stores and parks were full of them. He sat in a traffic jam in the Goldhawk Road, and on all sides there were nobodies behind the wheels of cars, edging forward a couple of feet at a time like an army taking ground by stealth.

It took him a further twenty minutes to cover the half-mile to his flat. When he got in, he knew he needed a drink. He also knew he wasn't going to get one. Before leaving for Cornwall, he'd poured his supply of booze down the sink. He was dry now. 'Enough's enough,' he'd said as the last bottle emptied out.

He stood in the middle of the living-room floor and looked round. Out loud, he said: 'What now?' The light on his answering machine was blinking. He didn't count the blinks, but registered that there were many. Clients, of course. Husbands with cheating wives, wives with faithless husbands. Enough's enough. He flipped the switch to 'Play' but didn't bother to arm himself with a pad and pen. He wasn't going to call any of those people back. He half-listened to the catalogue of woe, thinking mostly about the drink he wasn't drinking. The tenth message had been running for a few seconds before he rewound the tape and started it again.

'Hello. My name's Laura Scott. I don't know if you'll remember me. I was a friend of Maggie's. I came to a party at your place in . . . ah . . . early last summer. Do you remember? Look, would you call me? I need to talk to someone . . . I need advice, really, and I thought you might be able to help.' She gave the number twice, suddenly efficient in dealing with that part of her call. During the rest of it, her voice had been uncertain: a little shaky.

He called the number she'd given and was answered on the second ring. She sounded much the same. 'It's John Deacon,' he said. 'I picked up your message.'

'Oh, yes. That was—'

'I've been away. I just got back. You didn't say when—'

'Three days ago. Three or four. Look, is it all right?'

'Yes, of course. I mean, what's the problem?' She was silent. 'Is there a problem?'

'Could I come round?' she asked. 'Are you still at the same place?'

'Yes,' Deacon said. 'Fine.'

'I could. . . . Is it OK to come now?'

He said: 'Sure. Come now.' He was almost able to put a face with the name. A tall girl, he remembered, pretty, heavy blonde hair. He tried to make the features assemble, but the recollection wasn't strong enough for that. He wondered what the problem was: a finance company getting set to issue writs, or a husband who took more business trips than credulity would allow? It didn't matter. He was through with all that. He didn't want to see Laura – what was it? – Scott in order to tell her the worst and take her fee. He wanted to see her because she had known Maggie.

'I can be there in about thirty minutes,' she said. 'Is that too soon?'

He'd been right – tall and pretty and blonde; and

33

when he opened the door to her he remembered her face at once. He remembered the party, too, and Maggie introducing her. 'We were at university together. We lost touch. Laura has been working in Paris; she called me just a couple of days ago.' Maggie had seemed delighted by the renewed friendship; she loved surprises of that sort. After that, she'd tell him, from time to time; 'I'm seeing Laura tonight. I won't be late.' She liked to have friends of her own – little areas where she and Deacon didn't do everything as a couple. He liked it, too. Tandem marriages were claustrophobic.

He put her on the sofa, then retreated a short way towards the kitchen. 'I can't offer you a drink, I'm afraid.'

'Coffee,' she told him. 'Fine.'

He was pouring some beans into the grinder when she appeared at the kitchen door. 'I'm sorry,' she said. 'After Maggie died, I wasn't sure. . . .'

'No,' he said. 'It's not as if we were friends. Don't worry.'

'It was so awful. I sent some flowers to. . . .'

'Did you?' he said. 'That was kind.' Then, because it might have seemed rude: 'I didn't really know much about what was going on – who phoned or sent messages. You know. . . .' He flipped the switch on the grinder, forcing a silence between them as the machine roared.

'Afterwards, I thought I should have made contact – something.'

He smiled at her and shook his head. 'Really . . . I wasn't in any shape. Don't feel bad about it.' For no reason, he added: 'It was just a few people.'

'What?'

'At the funeral. There didn't seem any point – you know.'

'Oh. Yes.'

All at once, she seemed to be on the point of tears,

34

and he mistakenly thought that she was thinking of Maggie, of the almost-empty church, of the brilliant sunshine and hard blue sky, and the flowers wilting in the heat as the coffin was lowered into the baked earth. Then he realized how foolish he was being. Those were *his* thoughts; hers were something much more immediate.

'Oh, God,' she said, 'I'm sorry,' and covered her face briefly with her hands.

She was able to hold up the tears while she told him the bald facts. She spoke in short sprints, wanting to get the important details out, breaking her sentences midway as if to gain breath for the next rush. But when she started to describe how she had gone into the bathroom she couldn't get through it and began to sob. He told her to stop, and finished making the coffee, then took her back into the living-room. He poured coffee and waited.

'Damn!' she said; then: 'I'm sorry. There's been no one. . . .'

He said: 'Look, it's OK. Take your time.'

She got up and simply stood for a moment, like someone trying to remember what it was she'd meant to do. Then she said: 'The bathroom's through here, isn't it?'

When she came back, she told him the rest and he listened carefully. Finally, he asked: 'This was a week ago.'

Laura nodded. 'Last Monday. They say she died on Friday. I'd been away for the weekend. Some friends of mine have a place in Norfolk.'

'You work at the same place, as well as sharing. . . .'

'At the bank. Yes. It's how we met. Kate needed a place; I needed a flatmate to help with costs.'

'And you saw her last—?'

'At about midday.' She was positive. 'Kate had a meeting after lunch. I left early to beat the traffic.'

'You didn't go back to your flat?'

Laura shook her head. 'Took my bag when I left that morning. Paid a king's ransom to park the car until three-thirty. Drove straight to Norfolk.'

'And left there on Monday morning.'

'Yes. Up early to beat the incoming commuters. Put the car in the same ruinously expensive garage. Did a day's work. Then home.'

'But . . . ah. . . .'

'Kate.'

'Kate wasn't there that morning. At the bank.'

'I was simply told that she hadn't turned up. It didn't seem odd. She might have been feeling ill; on the other hand, it was another glorious day.'

'Would that have been like her – just taking the day off?'

Laura paused. 'Sometimes. Sometimes not. You don't have a drink?'

'I've been away for a month.' He shrugged. 'I just got back.'

'It's OK,' she said. 'I don't drink that much really.'

'Neither do I.' He paused. 'Tell me about the police. What happened.'

'They came. The ambulance came. There seemed to be quite a lot of them. One of them asked me questions while some others were in the bathroom. They went round the flat looking at things and making notes. They told me it was – ' she searched for the phrase – 'a death under suspicious circumstances?' Deacon nodded. 'The questions were . . . where'd I'd been, when I'd last seen her, how we came to know one another. The kind of thing you've asked. After a while they took Katie away.' She shuddered. 'They left the water in the bath.' Because she was remembering, she stopped talking for a moment. 'Have you got a cigarette?'

Deacon gave her one, and lit it for her. She held it in the flame too long, then puffed at it anxiously. She said: 'I don't smoke much, either.'

'What then?' he asked.

'There were people to tell.'

'Her parents,' he guessed.

Laura shook her head. 'Couldn't. I just couldn't. The police did it. I had to speak to them later; that was bad enough.'

'OK,' said Deacon. 'Now the bit that worries you. The police came back—'

'A few times—'

'And asked more questions.'

'Not just that. I mean, they *did* ask questions, some they'd asked before. That's not the point. By this stage, I'd had some time. . . . I stayed at a friend's place that first night, but I knew I'd have to go back eventually. I started to take some of Kate's things out of the wardrobes – you know, just began to put her stuff together. There were a couple of things I couldn't understand. I told the police—'

'Who?'

She thought for a moment. 'A man called D'Arblay. Inspector?'

'Probably.'

'He didn't . . . none of them seemed very interested. They'd started asking me if she had been depressed lately. Split up with a boyfriend, been having trouble at work – things like that.'

'And?'

'Well, no. She wasn't seeing anyone special. The job's as tough and sometimes as tiresome as any other, but I know that in general she enjoyed it. I don't think life was wine and roses for Kate, not particularly, but it wasn't sackcloth and ashes, either. About middling, I suspect. Like for the rest of us. She certainly wasn't depressed. Anyway—'

'It seemed a stupid notion. If that's what they were suggesting.'

'Well, apart from anything else, I couldn't take

seriously the idea of someone committing suicide in that way.'

'It's been done.'

'Not in a bath?'

'I meant shallow water. I was thinking of the effort required. I imagine they asked you about drugs.'

'Yes.'

Deacon raised his eyebrows.

'No. There was no question of anything like that.'

'No. Well, the post-mortem would have answered that question. If they didn't persist with it, then I guess there was nothing to find.' He waited for her response, then asked: 'Was there?' She looked confused. 'The inquest,' he prompted.

'Oh. No, nothing was said about drugs. I'd have been surprised if there had been.'

'So,' Deacon said. 'Accidental death.'

'They were saying that before the inquest. It's what they said to me.'

'The police.'

'Yes.'

'You didn't believe it.'

'I told them things. They didn't seem to want to know. It was as if they'd made their minds up. No, not quite that.' She reached over and poured more coffee into their cups; her preoccupation with what she was saying made her sufficiently absent-minded to play the role of hostess. 'It was more that they'd decided what it would be. Not reached a conclusion based on what they'd found. A decision.'

'Tell me what you told them.'

Laura put her cup down on a nearby coffee-table and switched around a few of the objects that stood on it – a cigarette-case, a wooden box-calendar, a small ebony statuette – aligning them in a row as if they represented her thoughts as she marshalled them. 'You know how it is when. . . .' She broke off and made a new start. 'OK – one thing was perfectly

38

straightforward: an object had been stolen from the flat.'

'What was it?'

'An African sculpture. A woman – about a foot high. Kate bought it from a street-trader in New York a year or so ago. She kept it in her bedroom. It wasn't expensive. I think she paid about thirty dollars for it. But it was one of her favourite pieces. After I'd. . . . On the second day, when I was getting her clothes and so forth together, I noticed it had gone.'

'When had you seen it last?'

'I don't know. It was always there.'

'She could have sold it, given it away. . . .'

'Yes, the police said that: how could I be sure it had been stolen. She wouldn't have done that – sold it, or whatever. It should have been in her room.'

'All right,' Deacon conceded. 'A stolen sculpture.'

'The other things are harder. They're to do with what you know about someone. They only make sense if you're prepared to believe that you can detect people by their habits.'

'Yes,' Deacon said. The presence of Maggie in a room, in a house; the way she hated evenness, the feathers she would collect on country walks slotted into a glass like a bouquet, the bracelets and necklaces that dangled from her over-full jewellery-box.

Laura continued: 'She'd run a bath, and she'd got undressed in the bedroom; she almost always took a bath when she arrived home. Her clothes were in a pile on the bed – folded up. She simply never did that. She was a slob – both of us; we used to laugh about it. We agreed to be tidy in the parts of the flat we shared – tidy for *us* anyway. But in our own rooms it didn't matter. The neat pile of clothes, it just wasn't. . . . It was like finding steak in a vegetarian's fridge. I'd simply never seen it before. It reminded me of when I was a child and would discover that my mother had relented and tidied my room for me. It meant . . . a foreign presence, simple as that. The police weren't impressed. At first, I thought I could see why – I mean, it's a slender enough notion. But then . . . it wasn't something I'd simply reported as seeming odd. I knew damn well that Katie wouldn't have done it, and I told them so.'

'OK,' Deacon said. 'What else?'

'Her diary was on the desk in her room. I looked at it. She didn't use it as a sort of journal or anything like that. She didn't even write appointments out in full. She used some kind of personal shorthand. Anyway; she'd written something in on the Thursday, then crossed it out and transferred it to the Monday – the day I found her. The pen was still on the diary. It was a question mark, then the word "trace".'

'Meaning?'

'Who knows? The police took away the clothes that were on the bed, together with some papers from her desk, and the diary. The clothes and the papers came back, but not the diary. They say they can't find it.'

'You didn't believe them?'

'For some reason, no, I didn't.'

'That was all?'

'No.' Laura lowered her eyes for a moment and interlaced the fingers of both hands, the knuckles whitening as if she were gripping something for support. When she looked up, her eyes didn't meet Deacon's. She looked past his shoulder. She spoke slowly at first; what she was describing might have been projected on the far wall.

'I went into the bathroom. I saw Kate. At first, just her leg. Then I went a little closer and saw her under the water. It was like being pushed backwards. I suppose I'd begun to faint. I sat down on the floor. I don't remember sitting down, but I remember being on the floor. I couldn't get up. I sat there and cried. I could still see her leg.' She stopped. Deacon didn't prompt her. 'Eventually, I phoned the police. After

40

that I went back into the bathroom. OK. . . .' She paused again. Deacon knew that she was viewing the scene in her mind's eye, and that it wasn't an easy thing to do. A truck jack-knifing; the car going at it broadside. Which was worse – seeing it and remembering, or not seeing it and inventing?

'OK. . . .' Laura tapped her own knee with her clasped hands. 'I tried going along with the police theory to see how that might have happened. What would it be? Getting into or out of the bath, Kate slipped, fell backwards, struck her head, was unconscious or semi-conscious for a while, and drowned. Well, I suppose that happens; I mean, you hear about old people having accidents of that sort. If you think about it, though, it must be bloody difficult to do. I got in and out of the bath a few times – you know, testing the theory. I made the assumption that most people do it in the same way. Well, basically, you bend over and put a hand on the side of the tub, cock a leg over, turn slightly and follow it with the other leg. First, you're bending, and when you're in you're sort of crouching with your heels under your haunches. Then you sit down. When you're getting out, you reverse the process – first crouch, then a hand on the side and get out. You have to be bending as you do it – the action demands it, unless you're going to stand straight up and step to the side. I tried that. It feels completely unnatural. I'd never really thought about how I get out of the bath, but I'm sure I've never done it that way.

'The point is – it's easy to say "She slipped and banged her head while getting out of the bath" – it sounds likely enough. If you run through the actions that would have led up to it, then it seems impossible.' She had been rehearsing a theory, and her voice had become less hesitant. It grew slower again as she began to assemble the picture of what she'd seen.

'Kate's leg, her right leg, was hanging over the side of the bath. It was bruised. The theory was that she'd

41

knocked it against the side of the tub or the handbasin when she fell. All right, suppose she had. But it was bruised in three or four places. The bruises' – she searched for a way of saying it – 'showed up. Do you know—?'

'Yes,' Deacon said.

'A mirror-tile was cracked. I couldn't put that together with the fall. It could have been done some other way, I guess, but it was low and over the end of the bath.'

'So you—'

'I didn't—'

They spoke together. Deacon lifted a hand, indicating that she should continue.

'I didn't stand there making a note of these things; not at the time. . . . But they must have been registering. I remembered them, bit by bit, afterwards.'

Deacon interrupted. 'When the police began to talk about accidental death.'

'What? Oh, yes.' She had been thinking of what she was about to say – something more difficult to describe than bruises and a cracked mirror-tile. 'It was eerie – Kate lying there, everything else so normal, you know, the things in the place all looking so ordinary. But I felt something – something else there. It was like walking into a room just after someone's been slapped. It's silly. It doesn't mean anything, I know. There was a feeling of energy; of violence. As if it had left a pattern in the air.' She shook her head. 'It sounds ridiculous now that I've said it out loud. But it *was* there. Afterwards, it made me feel ill to think of it.'

'No,' Deacon said. 'No, it's the most believable thing you've said.'

Laura got up and walked to one of the open windows. The unbroken blue of the sky had begun to dim slightly as evening came on, but the air was still warm and the wooden sill, when she leaned on it, was warm, too. The weather had been that way for six weeks or more, and showed no signs of breaking. The country had taken on Mediterranean habits. Tables and chairs had appeared outside restaurants, people jostled in pub gardens, you could hear conversation and music wherever you were. Somewhere nearby someone was playing a violin, trying the same passage over and over again, clearly displeased with it.

'Everything's so damn *sunny*,' she said angrily. 'I wish to Christ it would rain.'

Deacon said: 'I'm not a policeman now – had you heard that?'

'I don't think I'd be telling you this if you were.' She turned round. 'Yes, I'd heard that.'

'Did you hear why?'

'No.' She waited. 'Why?'

He didn't answer her. 'I've been running an enquiry agency.'

'I hadn't heard that.'

'It's not what it sounds. You don't have to be able to throw your fedora on to the hatstand every morning. You don't have to wait around until the silhouette of some smouldering redhead appears on the glass of your office door. You don't conscientiously have to avoid streets that don't qualify as mean.'

'What does it involve?' She was smiling.

'Chasing debts; sitting outside flats where people are doing things that are going to make other people unhappy when they get to hear about it.'

'They get to hear about it from you.'

'Yes.'

'Not good.'

'No. That's why I've decided not to do it any more.'

Neither of them spoke for a while. Finally Deacon asked: 'Why me?'

Laura shook her head. 'Someone had to know. I

remembered that you used to be a copper. I remembered that it surprised me when I met you.'

'Did it?'

Laura shrugged and looked a trifle embarrassed. 'You seemed too bright.' Deacon laughed. 'I'm sorry.'

'You think I don't know what you mean?' He laughed again. 'Don't be sorry.'

'I suppose . . . I wondered if you might at least be able to tell me why I was being ignored. What that might signify. Maybe you'd be able to ask someone.'

'You think Kate was murdered.'

'I can't. . . .' She frowned. 'Yes. The answer's yes. But at the same time, when I think of that – when you say it: "Kate was murdered" – it doesn't seem possible. It doesn't make sense.'

'And it frightens you.'

'Yes. It frightens me.'

He got up and joined her by the window. Together they looked out at the trees and the elegant upper storeys of nearby houses. 'Leave me to think about it,' he said. 'I'll call you.'

'Will you?' She appeared anxious.

Deacon nodded. 'Yes. Apart from anything else, I'd like to see you again.' Laura turned to look at him, but he didn't meet her gaze. 'Because of Maggie.'

'I don't understand.'

He didn't reply for a while. They were standing close to one another, and Laura could see the muscles flexing in his jaw. Twice he opened his mouth to speak, then closed it again. She realized he was about to say something that was difficult, maybe even dangerous, for him to own up to. She wasn't at all sure that she wanted to hear it, but it was too late to avoid that now.

'Maggie and I were married for three years,' Deacon told her. 'And she's been dead for a year. It's not long, is it? Three years isn't long.' He wasn't asking for an answer. 'You know when people say: "I lost my wife; I lost my husband" – I always rather sneered at that sort of euphemism. It seemed a joke.'

'Carelessness,' Laura said. She wanted to clear her throat, and the word came out huskily.

'What? Oh – yes; that sort of thing . . . a joke. But it's not; that's what it's like. The times you had together, the times you would have had, the things you didn't know – hadn't told one another, hadn't shared. Lost.' The way he said it, the word sounded indescribably bleak. 'In a way, I feel that some of what I lost was knowing Maggie. *Coming* to know her. It would help me to talk about her. To someone who knew her. Someone who knew her before I did. Does that—?'

'Yes,' Laura said. 'OK.' She had spoken quickly because she didn't want to hear any more.

He went back to where they'd been sitting and began to busy himself with the coffee-cups, stacking them and taking them through to the kitchen. She heard him running the taps over the sink.

She looked around the room. Everything was tidy: nothing rumpled or out of place. It wasn't a fussy neatness; there was nothing prim or sad about it. She hadn't noticed it before, but now she saw that it was the kind of furious energetic order that stands just on the brink of chaos.

6

The pub was an outpost. The streets surrounding it
were dowdy, lined with featureless small houses most
of which seemed to keep thin curtains drawn all day.
If the people who lived there came and went, they
seemed to manage to do that without being seen. The
pocket-handkerchief gardens were neither cared for
nor wild and overgrown, as if there was something
mean in the air and in the soil; something that stunted
growth. The only things that appeared to have taken
root were the cars, many of them up on blocks behind
the scabrous planking that fenced off the tiny plots.
There were so few signs of life that the houses would
have appeared vacant at first glance; but there was a
tension about the streets that belied that. Mute and
shuttered, the houses resembled the faces of refugees.

A dozen streets to the south lay a prosperous area of
spacious houses and flats, broad pavings and leafy
cultivated squares. The cars parked in the 'residents-
only' bays were sleek and seemed to be never quite
switched off. As often as not, the men who washed
and polished the cars didn't own them. In those
streets, the windows were open. You could hear
laughter and the murmur of conversation and music
played at a modest level; the orchestration of wealth.

To the north, fewer streets away, was the ghetto.
The people from the leafy squares never went up
there. They wouldn't have given the ghetto a thought
from one day to the next, were it not for the fact that
now and then someone would come home to find a

window broken or the door kicked in. The television would be gone, and the video-recorder, together with any loose cash and whatever jewellery the lady of the house might have owned.

'Kids', the police would say, and they would be right. The ghetto's serious criminals wouldn't bother with that kind of penny-ante stuff. The kids were nimble and fast and they didn't work the area close to home often enough to establish any pattern, nor did they waste time trashing a place, though now and then they would take a few minutes out to urinate on the beds. Most often it was over in five minutes or less. Arrests were unusual. The people who had been robbed would spend a few days feeling edgy. The insurance companies would pay.

You couldn't call the area that lay between the two factions neutral ground. 'Neutral' sounds safe. It was no man's land.

Deacon walked into the pub and saw Phil Mayhew almost at once. Mayhew would have been easy enough to spot under most circumstances. He was tall – over six feet – and his build was broad, though he carried no extra weight. Also, he was the only person in the place sitting on his own. The other drinkers there knew Mayhew, and knew what he did, and no one would share his table unless there was some business to transact. There were two drinks on the table, one of them an untouched whisky. Deacon went to the bar, bought a bottle of Perrier, then walked over to Mayhew's table. He sat down and set the whisky to one side, then took a packet of cigarettes from his pocket. Mayhew looked at the drink, then back at Deacon as he lit a cigarette.

'That's an extremely dangerous habit,' he said.

'No shit,' said Deacon. 'They didn't tell me that.'

Mayhew smiled. He worked out in a gym three times a week and played squash on the intervening days. He didn't smoke; he drank only wine and beer, and that sparingly. These activities had never failed to provoke wryness in Deacon. 'How are you, John?' he asked.

Deacon nodded. 'Fine,' he said. Then: 'I went down to Cornwall. Cleaning house.'

'It was time.'

'Yes, it was.'

There was a silence between them. Deacon looked round the pub. 'Nothing changes,' he observed.

'Sorry?' Mayhew had been thinking of something else.

Deacon gestured. 'The halt and the lame.'

'What did you expect – a victory for social work and aftercare?' Mayhew snorted, then looked thoughtful. 'There's a tall guy over there playing pool – bad teeth and Cologne that clears your sinuses – who knows something that I want to know. He was seen sharing a motor with three blokes last week: sharp suits and low foreheads. It's likely they'd just driven the same route as a wages-van.'

Deacon didn't turn to look. 'Will he tell you?'

'Oh, yes. Sooner or later. Possibly after the event. I don't care that much.' Mayhew sipped his beer. 'Well, John. Car registration or warning off?'

The two men had been friends for eight years. When Deacon had started to operate privately, he'd gone to Mayhew for information now and then. A quick rifle through the police computer would marry a name and address to a car parked too often, and for too long, outside a certain address; and if the name happened to be an important one it was sometimes possible to solve the problem with a semi-official whisper in the ear of the wayward VIP. The process provided a handy dossier for Special Branch, who liked to keep tabs on the seamier doings of prominent citizens. It was surprising how quickly people could be persuaded to toe the line when confronted with

48

half-forgotten moments from the past. Deacon's advantage, apart from getting the information in the first place, was that cases would often solve themselves. Men who had been enjoying a little action on the side would suddenly become dutiful husbands again; suspicious wives would chide themselves for their doubts and pay Deacon off. Frequently, the women would become embarrassed or hostile, seeing in Deacon a symbol of the fear and danger that had kept them awake at night. They were glad to have back the safe world that had seemed at risk. They were glad to have been wrong. Deacon would deliver his reports and take the hastily written cheques. He'd wondered from time to time how the payments might have been explained when the bank statements arrived. A dress designer, perhaps; or a tennis coach.

'No more of that,' Deacon said. 'I'm through with that.'

'Yes, well. . . .' Mayhew looked at him appraisingly. 'I can't say I'm surprised.' He paused. 'You weren't thinking of coming back to coppering' – Deacon shook his head – 'because I don't think they'd have you.' He pointed at Deacon's drink. 'Despite the designer water.'

'And I wouldn't have them. Despite the murderous hours and the lousy pay.'

Mayhew grinned. 'How are you really, John?'

Deacon lit another cigarette. After a moment, he said: 'Injured but still functioning.'

'It's been a year.' Mayhew's voice was soft, as if he were speaking to himself.

'I know.' Deacon hefted a shoulder. 'So what?'

Mayhew's gaze shifted to a point further off in the room. The pool-player was leaving. Mayhew watched him to the door until the man turned, feeling the stare, and Mayhew got the glance of complicity that he'd been waiting for. After the door had closed, he smiled briefly and said: 'He'll keep.' Then: 'Well, what is it, then? You called during business hours.'

'Last Thursday week – the fifteenth – a girl called Katherine Lorimer died on your patch. Suspicious circumstances. Katie Lorimer.'

'Yes.'

'Yes, what?'

'Yes, I heard about it. It wasn't my shout.'

'No. D'Arblay.'

'That's right.'

'Inspector D'Arblay.' Deacon's tone was rueful.

'Well, if you kiss arse long enough, that's what you get – promotion and bad breath.' Mayhew chuckled. 'I expect his mother's proud.'

'When I worked with him, D'Arblay couldn't have *found* an arse – least of all his own.'

'His homing instinct started to function,' observed Mayhew. 'What about her?'

'She drowned in the bath.'

Mayhew nodded. 'That's what I heard. And?'

'Some sleuthing was done. Forensic were at the girl's flat for a while. Eventually it was written off as an accidental death.'

'Go on. . . .'

'Was it?'

Mayhew looked at Deacon, trying to read his expression. 'I've heard no different. Is there a doubt?'

'That's what I'm asking you.'

Mayhew looked thoughtful. 'It certainly caused no ripples in my pond. There was an inquest, wasn't there?'

'There was.' Deacon anticipated the next question. 'Accidental death,' he said.

Mayhew shrugged: *There you are, then.* Out loud, he said: 'Who's asking?'

'Do you know a girl called Laura Scott?'

'A friend of Maggie's, no? Gossipy evenings at the Turkish baths.'

'That's right. She shared a flat with Lorimer. In fact she found the body.'

'Ah.' Mayhew took another small sip from his glass. 'I imagine she was upset.' Deacon smiled. 'I imagine she was bloody hysterical.'

'She found her bad dream for the next couple of decades,' Deacon agreed, 'but I don't think it softened her brain, if that's what you're implying.'

'You know how it is, John; it's better if there's someone to blame. A drama is easier to handle than a tragedy.' Mayhew looked up, his eyes on the door. Then he picked up his drink, hiding a brief half-smile behind its rim. 'More interesting, too.'

'He's back,' Deacon concluded.

'Yes. His friends left a minute ago. He'd've been waiting for that.'

'I can go,' Deacon offered. 'He'll be edgy. Wanting to get it done.'

'Let the fucker sweat,' Mayhew said. 'He'll keep.'

'You might lose him.'

'Not now.' Mayhew could barely keep the grin off his face. 'He's made the choice and he knows I know that. He's committed.'

'Do I know him?' Deacon asked.

'No. He's a new face. Not long since arrived from Glasgow, with a price on his head. There are one or two psychopaths up there who'd like to talk to him about a bullion job that didn't quite go as planned. He's beginning to think he might be safe under my wing.'

'Will he?'

Mayhew raised his eyebrows. 'Give me a break. His days are numbered. But he'll be useful until his friends find him.' His gaze flickered away briefly to where the man sat on a bar-stool, his face dipping towards a pint of ale; then he looked back at Deacon. 'What on earth makes her think it's anything else?'

'If I told you, you'd laugh.'

51

'Then, don't tell me. I thought you said you weren't doing it any more – the enquiry agency.'

'I'm not. She phoned me because she needed someone to tell and remembered that I used to be a copper. She phoned because she'd known Maggie.'

'And you.'

'No, not really. We'd met a couple of times. She was Maggie's friend.'

'OK. She called you and said, "I think my friend's been topped by the Mafia, but the police won't have it," and you said—'

'It's real enough to her, Phil.' There was a flash of irritation in Deacon's voice.

'You're the one who said her theories would make me laugh.' Mayhew paused. 'But there's something . . . yes?' His voice grew sepulchral. '*Clues.*'

Deacon couldn't help but laugh. He held up a hand in mock-deference. 'Something,' he said. 'Not much.'

'Why are you bothering?'

It was on the tip of Deacon's tongue to tell the truth; to say that it was a way of getting closer to Maggie; that he wanted to talk to Laura Scott about the Maggie he hadn't known, the teenage Maggie, the student, the young woman who had gone to parties, been taken punting on the Cherwell, collected her BA in cap and gown. He wanted to know about her ambitions then, her enthusiasms, even her lovers. The world before they met. . . . A past that was lost to him, just as the future was lost. Maybe he could gain a little, just a little, of that past. A little more of Maggie.

In the event, he said: 'Maybe I can convince her that there's nothing to worry about. Would that be such a bad thing?'

It was Mayhew's turn for deference. 'You're right.' He nodded. Then: 'Is there something? Even if I do laugh, I ought to know – if I'm going to poke about a bit; which is what you want me to do, I imagine.'

The neatly piled clothes, the sense of violence in the

place like dark air-currents: they weren't the kind of thing a policeman would give much credence to – especially Phil Mayhew. Deacon said: 'How easy is it to drown in the bath?'

'Coke,' Mayhew wanted to know, 'speed, Mandies, a nice joint after a long day at the office?'

'None of that.'

'Booze?'

'No.'

'Who says so?'

'The inquest says so.'

Mayhew thought for a while. 'I don't know. It must happen. Most accidents are domestic, aren't they? You're getting in or out, you slip, your head whacks the side of the bath. It only takes a moment to drown. A dessert-spoon of water will do it. I guess this girl was just unlucky. It happens to some; others get away with it. Metabolism – you know? She had a weak skull. One guy can withstand beatings, torture, years in a bloody gulag or whatever. Another will be walking down the road, a car backfires – *boom* – heart attack.'

'I know,' Deacon said. 'There was something missing from the flat where Katherine Lorimer died. An African sculpture in wood – so high.' Deacon held his palm some twelve inches above the table.

'The Scott girl told you this?'

'Yes.'

'It was hers?'

'Lorimer's.'

'When did Scott last see it?'

'I thought you'd ask that.'

Mayhew looked at Deacon askance. 'For Christ's sake, John.'

'I know, I know.' Deacon thumbed another cigarette from his packet. 'She seemed pretty certain.'

'A light-fingered copper, you think.'

'It's possible.'

53

Mayhew laughed. 'Not very. The lads in my squad don't have much of a taste for *objets d'art*. The odd video or two, maybe, or what's left in the drinks-cabinet. She sold it; gave it away—'

Deacon interrupted. 'I've said all that.'

Mayhew sighed. 'OK, OK. I'll sniff the wind. I expect to smell nothing more than the lingering farts of wild geese.'

Deacon chuckled. The chuckle became a full-blooded laugh. 'You're a bloody tonic, Mayhew.'

The other man smiled back. 'You look better than you have for a long time. Life goes on, John.'

'So it seems,' Deacon conceded.

Mayhew shifted in his chair: a gentle hint. 'I'll call you.'

'OK.'

'It was good to see you. Don't stay locked up.'

Deacon crushed out his cigarette and got up. When he turned to leave, the man at the bar looked over sharply, then away again. A tall man, thin, with sparse ginger hair and a sanding of stubble on his cheeks. Deacon passed him on his way to the door. Mayhew was right; the cheap Cologne smelt like something scorched.

Everyone was wearing as little as possible. The heat was dry and light, as if the air was fizzing with sparkling particles. It was the sort of heat that made your hair crackle and fly. Hyde Park looked as if it had taken a direct hit from a neutron bomb. The grass was strewn with inert near-naked bodies, and everywhere there was music, borne up by the thermals from dozens of radios and cassette-players. As soon as you walked through the force-field of one bass beat, you slammed into the next.

None of the bodies spread-eagled on the grass twitched a foot or slapped a hand on the ground to keep time. Willing victims of the sun, they lay doggo, at ground level, just below the warp and shimmer of the heat-haze. The usual pallor of English skin had been replaced by variegated tones of brown, glistening under oil. The girls looked toasty and delicious. Deacon noticed that he was noticing this for the first time for a long time.

When he got to the horse-track that circled the park, he paused to let a rider go by – a girl dressed incongruously in jodhpurs, hard hat and bikini top. The effect was startlingly erotic; she looked as if she had started to undress. The horse was a big bright chestnut, better than sixteen hands, crabbing, giving little hops, a root-system of enlarged veins on its neck and withers. It was eager to go, feeling speed in every muscle and already looking far beyond the confines of the park. The energy possessed by both rider and mount was like an explosion that had already happened and was fighting to emerge. The girl looked wholly confident, hands low, her body a perfect vertical from dropped heel to shoulder. She held the horse in a moment longer, then shortened rein fractionally and tapped him behind the girth with her boot. The horse took two sudden bounds before settling to a pace much faster than the park authorities would have liked.

Maggie riding on the beach. Maggie setting off for a hack across Bodmin Moor. Maggie on a morning so cold it made your teeth ache, circling among other riders at the local meet, dressed in black coat and bowler and hair-net. Although an American, she had always ridden English-style, even at home in Massachusetts. *Especially* at home in Massachusetts: the Henderson family was old money; it looked east, towards its English origins; frontiers were for refugees and vulgar opportunists.

Deacon's mind went back to the day of Maggie's funeral. Her father and her brother looking like misfits in the tiny Cornish graveyard – seven-hundred-dollar suits, club ties and careful haircuts. Peter Henderson's wife had died the previous year; now he stood at his daughter's graveside, his face like rock.

Afterwards, Maggie's brother, Edward, had walked with Deacon half a mile along the cliffs. He was a tall man, broad across the shoulders like a swimmer, his brown hair dusted through with the grey of early middle age. He and Deacon hadn't met often, but they had instinctively taken to one another. Deacon detected something in the other man of the adventurer: someone who would take risks, but tend to be on the side of the angels. His father's semi-retirement had effectively put Edward in charge of the family firm, though there was nothing about him of corporate pomposity.

They had walked in file along the narrow dusty path that stretched off towards a distant blue headland. Neither spoke, but they hadn't felt oppressed by the silence. The tide had been at the full, waves flopping into rock-hollows at the base of the cliff – a series of flat slaps.

Finally, Edward had said: 'I don't think Father and I exchanged more than a dozen words on the flight. Now here I am with you, and I still can't think of a damn thing to say.' Deacon had liked him for that. Edward was ten years older than his sister, but still looked a lot like her.

On their way back, Deacon had stopped near a vantage-point that Maggie had always liked.

'As soon as we'd arrive,' he explained, 'she would come up here, while I unpacked.' Edward had stood for a moment, looking out at the sea. Then he'd taken the signet ring from his little finger and hurled it far out. It glistened in the sunlight, then Deacon lost sight of it against the blue of the ocean and the blue of the sky. Edward had said: 'Why did I do that? I don't know why in hell I did that.'

*   *   *

The music in the park was also the music in the streets. The weather had moved people's lives out of doors. It was untypical, bizarre almost, and in an odd way made Deacon feel uncomfortable. In part, it was the English climate that made the English secretive and withdrawn. Expansiveness didn't suit them; they lacked the vocabulary for it.

Laura had been expecting him. When he pressed her doorbell, she buzzed him in without using the entryphone. He climbed a flight of stairs and looked for the number. Her front door was slightly ajar. She heard him close it and called out to him. He went in the direction of her voice and found her in the kitchen, talking on the telephone.

'Yes,' she said, 'yes . . . at six o'clock. That's fine.' She gave her address, then her phone number; at the same time she gestured towards an opened bottle of wine and some glasses on a Welsh dresser. Deacon poured one glass and gave it to her, then found some orange juice in the fridge and filled a second glass with that.

When Laura hung up the phone, she said: 'An estate agent. I might . . . I'm thinking about selling the place.' She looked at his glass. 'Don't you drink at all?'

'No,' Deacon told her.

She sipped her wine. 'I've been here five years. I like the place – always have. I don't think I can live in it now.' She paused. 'Did you see him? Ah. . . .' She waved a hand, trying to recall the name.

'Phil Mayhew.'

'Right.'

'Yes, I did. Nothing. I didn't think there would be. He'll check. He doesn't expect to find anything.'

'Do you?'

Deacon smiled. 'He suspects you of being . . . over-imaginative.'

A question got to her lip, but no further. Instead, she asked another.

57

'What will he do?'

'Look at the crime-sheet: the report. Ask the people you met.'

'Inspector D'Arblay.'

'I doubt it. Forensic probably.' He set his glass down on the kitchen table. 'Can I look round?'

'Sure.' Laura started towards the door.

'No.' Deacon stopped her. 'On my own.'

She waited in the kitchen while he went from room to room, checking his progress from the sounds he made, from doors opening and closing. There was a tension about the silences that made her edgy. She felt a little as if she were being frisked. After about ten minutes, she heard him go into the bathroom.

It must happen every day, Deacon thought. London is full of old houses. Every day hundreds of people must go into rooms where someone has died. Rooms where they entertain friends, rooms where they sit alone watching television and eating fast food from the carton, rooms where they work late on projects brought home from the office, rooms where they lie in bed and look at the same ceiling, the same walls, the same view of the sky that a dying person saw.

The old houses had, for the most part, been converted into flats. Bedrooms had become kitchens, dining-rooms or studies. Those who lived in top-floor flats were probably occupying a space that had been all bedrooms. Thousands of old houses, tens of thousands of rooms. How many deaths? Millions. Every day people ate and slept and talked, worked and cooked and made love in rooms where people had died. If you didn't know about the deaths, it didn't matter.

Deacon looked at the cracked mirror-tile, then at his own reflection, then beyond that to the bath behind him. He tried to see the girl as Laura had described her to him, her leg hooked over the side of the bath, her body seeming to be suspended in the clear water.

Along with the image, he conjured the stillness in the room as the body had lain there, stillness that was not peaceable, but came from an awful absence.

When he went back into the kitchen, Laura was pouring herself more wine. She raised the glass to her lips and paused, looking at him over the rim. 'And?' she asked.

'No. Nothing. I wasn't really looking. The police have been here, you've been living here. I doubt there was anything to be found, but if there was it's gone now. I just wanted to get a feel of the place.'

'The police went round the flat a couple of times – windows, the front door.'

'Yes, they would have. Looking for forced entry. Obviously they didn't. . . .'

'I don't understand. . . .' She broke off and moved towards the door. 'Let's go in here.' Deacon followed her through to the living-room and took one of the two big armchairs. Laura perched on the sofa. She frowned. 'If there was someone—'

'You're beginning to doubt it?'

'No.' She shook her head. 'No. But it's how he got in here. . . .'

'How did I get in here?'

'What?'

'You didn't use the entryphone to check on who was coming up here. You – what? – heard the buzzer, pressed the release for the street-door, opened your own front door, then went back to the phone.'

'I knew it was you; I was expecting you.'

'You *thought* it was me – assumed it.' Deacon lit a cigarette. 'Have you heard of the Boston Strangler?' Laura nodded. 'Do you know how he got access to his victims? I'll tell you: he rang their doorbells.'

'Just like you did.'

'Just like that.'

Laura looked at him for a moment, then went to the kitchen and came back with an ashtray and put it down on a table close to Deacon's elbow. Then she rummaged in her handbag and came up with a small blue inhaler, held it to her mouth and took a sharp breath as she pressed the plunger.

'It's not so much that people are gullible,' Deacon went on, 'more that they're not looking for it. Why should they be? They're living their lives, dealing with the day-to-day problems of work and bills and a leaky roof, or whatever. Someone arrives at the door saying that he's delivering a package. Why not believe it? They're simply not expecting a normal day to turn into a nightmare. After all, you—'

Laura broke in. 'I let you in. And I'm telling you that I believe Kate was murdered in this flat just a few days ago.'

Deacon shrugged. 'Perhaps you should have been warier. But if I'd said I was the meter-reader you'd probably have let me in. People do. Don't feel bad about it. As a rule, people believe what they're told. Why not? A few years back, a girl was telephoned by a man who asked to speak to her flatmate. She told him the other girl wasn't there – that she was visiting her parents, then attending a three-day television convention. The guy said that was a great shame because he was only in town for a day and the flatmate – I can't remember – Mary, let's say – was an old friend and he'd been looking forward to taking her out to dinner. The first girl, whose name I *can* remember – Hilary – agreed that it was a shame, and chatted to the guy for a few minutes. He asked after Mary's parents – was her father recovered from his illness, how was Mary's career in television going, that sort of thing – then suggested that since he was at a loose end, and a stranger to London, maybe Hilary would have dinner with him. Well, she was at a loose end, too, and the guy sounded pleasant. She went. They had a terrific evening. He was entertaining and good company. Eventually, he took her home in a cab and she invited him to come in for a nightcap. In he went; drank a brandy and a couple of cups of coffee; then he left.'

'I'm waiting,' Laura said.

'Before he left – as he was standing at the door in fact – he said: "I've enjoyed this evening; but you're very foolish. And lucky. I don't know Mary. I've never met her. I picked the name at random from the phone-book. It was the fifth I tried."'

Laura looked at Deacon, expecting more. She said: 'What did he do?'

'He left.'

'He didn't hurt her?'

'That wasn't the kick. Not for this guy at any rate. In one sense, he was right: Hilary *had* been lucky. I don't suppose you could have called the guy entirely sane, but he wasn't there to rape her or kill her. It's likely that he thought about it, but it seemed that simply having the power to do that was enough. Or it was on that occasion anyway. In six months' time, in a year – who knows? It was a grown-up version of what kids do when they follow someone home.'

'This was . . . you knew her? Hilary?'

'No. She reported it. I was the cop she spoke to.'

'I don't see how he could carry it off.'

'It's easy.'

'But he knew things. The other girl's parents and so forth.'

Deacon lit another cigarette, then glanced at the inhaler that Laura had put on the arm of the sofa. 'Does smoking bother you? What is it? Asthma?'

'No,' she said. 'Yes, it's asthma. Not the cigarettes, though: the weather. The pollen count's been through the roof for weeks. Don't worry.'

'He didn't know things,' Deacon pointed out. 'She told him things. Mary was visiting her parents – plural. So he knows they're both alive. She's on her way to a conference, so it's probable that her parents live fairly close to the venue. Not so? OK, then they've

61

moved, or it's someone else's parents who live there. As long as you talk about someone, it's assumed you know them. Does she still wear her hair long? It's fifty-fifty. If "yes", you sound as if you know her. If "no", then you knew her when she did. He asks whether her father's recovered from some illness. Most people get ill. It's a better than even bet that Mary's father had some health problems at some time. In fact a detail like that can make it seem that you know the family better than the person you're talking to. All con-men know that technique. You listen, glean information, then feed it back. People hear something from you that seems to establish your credentials. The truth is that they gave you that information earlier in the conversation.'

'Are you telling me that you think Kate was . . . that it was just random? A crazy?'

Deacon sighed. 'Because you phoned me . . . because you knew Maggie . . . because you believe what you believe, I'm asking a few questions of a cynical and amused copper with other things on his mind. Because he's a friend of mine, he'll ask fewer questions of other coppers who are even less interested. I don't know whether or not Kate was killed by someone. Maybe she slipped in the bath. *You're* the one who's sure. You *know* that the stolen sculpture and the tidy clothes mean something. I don't.'

'Do you think they *might*?'

'Yes, I think they might.'

'But . . .' she prompted.

'But I don't, in fact, think it was a crazy. Assuming there *was* someone.'

'No?'

'No.'

He didn't offer more, so she thought it through for a brief while. Finally, she said: 'Because it wouldn't – if it was a crazy – it wouldn't have looked like an accident.'

Deacon nodded.

62

'What, then?'

'Someone she knew. Or, taking the case of Hilary, someone she thought she knew. Someone with a package to deliver. But it's really not that important.'

'It's not—' Laura wasn't sure what he meant. Maybe his friend Mayhew wasn't the only person to think her – what had he said? – over-imaginative. She met Deacon's gaze, and could see that, again, he was prompting a response in her. After a moment, she said: 'It's why.'

'Yes,' Deacon said. 'It's why.'

The sky had been flawlessly blue all day. Now it was gathering a deeper, plangent colour, soaking up the dusk. Laura went to the window and looked out at the darkening silhouette of houses and more-distant tower-blocks. They were honeycombed with light.

Deacon left her to her thoughts for a few minutes. Then he said: 'Tell me about the job.'

'The bank?' Laura went back to the sofa. 'I went to work there a year ago. Kate had been in the job a while before that. We're programmers. Kate's also the DBA.' Before he could ask she said: 'Database administrator. Troubleshooter, if you like.' She hadn't noticed that she'd spoken of Kate as if her friend were still alive.

'What do you do?'

Laura shrugged. 'Write programs.'

'Yes.' Deacon smiled. 'That doesn't mean much to me.'

'Oh. Well . . . whatever they want.' She hesitated, trying to think of a quick explanation. 'It's as if lots of people wanted to do the same calculation time after time, but each with different figures. A program does all the work for them. It's a matrix. They enter their information in the right way; the computer gives them the answer. All it means is that the computer knows what the user wants; the program tells it that.'

'What are the programs for?'

'Like I say – anything. From international exchange deals to annual profits. Even down to directors' expenses as a percentage of turnover. Computers will do whatever you tell them to do. In idle moments, most programmers use them as word-processors – write letters to friends, that sort of thing.'

'Is the work confidential?'

'What do you—?'

'Sensitive. Secret. Closely guarded from competitors.'

She pondered. 'No. Nothing I can think of. No, quite the opposite, in a way. Once a programmer has perfected a program it's made available to everyone in the place. That's the whole point; my work, Kate's, the work of other programmers, all goes into the public file eventually. It's the service we're there to provide.' She could tell what he was thinking. 'There's nothing to *kill* for. I mean, the stuff I write – people outside banking would have no use for it, people inside banking would have their own programs.' She laughed. 'Most of them much superior to mine, I expect.'

'If you're right about Kate's death,' Deacon told her, 'there's got to be a *why*.'

'I *am* right.' There was a sudden shrillness in Laura's voice: the sound of a woman beginning to doubt her own instincts.

'All right. Let's try something else. Most murders are domestic: at least in the sense that they're committed by someone the victim knows. I asked you about Kate's boyfriends.'

'Yes.'

'You said there was no one in particular.'

'There wasn't.'

'She stayed in every night. She watched the soaps. She slept alone.'

Laura smiled. 'Not quite that.'

'Who, then?'

64

'She had friends, of course.' Laura shrugged. 'There's a guy called Rupert Lawson — an ex really. Well, they were on and off.'

'Why?'

'That's the way he wanted it.'

'And Kate?'

'I don't know whether she loved him; if she didn't, you'd have to call it heavy liking. They saw each other now and then — he called the shots. I think Kate was resigned to that. She knew it wasn't going anywhere. She stood little chance against Rupert's real passion — he's putting together his first million.' She lifted a hand, palm outermost. 'Really, he's just an ageing yuppie. He might be guilty of wounding currencies from ambush, but I'm sure that's as far as it goes.'

'Ageing?'

'Thirty-two, -three. Geriatric by City-spiv standards. They're mostly burned-out cases by their late twenties.'

'Do you have his address?' Deacon asked.

'You're wasting your time.' None the less, Laura went to a bureau and fetched her address-book.

'No, I'm not; or if I am, then it's necessary to waste it.' Deacon watched while she copied out the address. 'It's like looking round your flat — a feel of things. Who knows what Rupert might have to say?' She handed him a sheet of paper. 'Imagine I were a policeman. Imagine I believed what you believe. Assume for a moment that I do. . . .' He glanced at the address, then folded the paper and put it in his pocket. 'Rupert would be on the list of people to see. You think he's a waste of time. There's no such category. Example. A guy called Donald Blake was found dead in his kitchen. He'd been preparing food with a butcher's knife. Well, someone had set about jointing and carving Donald. The whole room was striped with blood. There was blood on the ceiling.' He paused, remembering it. 'Nothing had been stolen. There was

65

no apparent motive. No sign of forced entry. We saw dozens of people: parents, brothers, sisters, neighbours . . . nothing. Then someone remarked that Donald had recently received a letter from an aunt he hadn't seen for years. No one in the family had seen her for years.'

'She was a waste of time,' Laura guessed.

'That's right. We got round to her eventually. Do you know what she said?' Deacon smiled mirthlessly. 'She said: "I never liked him as a child."'

7

This one was different. This one was better than the first.

The things he'd felt when he'd been with Kate Lorimer had all been new to him; exciting and new. This time anticipation made everything keener. Elaine had told him that it would be. They had sat in her basement room, Elaine curled up in the armchair while he sat close to her on the floor, and he had given every detail of the time he'd spent in Kate's flat. Now and then Elaine would make him backtrack to describe some moment again, or would ask him questions: about how Kate had looked when undressing but not knowing she could be seen; about the way his reflection and hers appeared side by side in the dressing-table mirror; about how he felt as her face went under the water and her body heaved beneath his hand.

The memory of those things, and of Elaine's gathering excitement in the shadowy room, made him breathless. This time, as he entered the hallway and walked on into a large, light, expensively furnished drawing-room, the hairs on his forearms and on the nape of his neck rose like hackles and his skin tingled.

The woman had been shopping during the afternoon. Then she'd kept an early-evening appointment. He had judged to within ten minutes when she would arrive home. He'd watched from his car as she climbed out of the taxi, burdened with carrier-bags bearing designer names. Now she tossed the bags on to the sofa and went directly to the kitchen. He lounged in the doorway while she stocked an ice-bucket and took a bottle of tonic water from the fridge, then went before her, back to the drawing-room. She filled a tall glass with ice, and poured a liberal shot of gin. The flat was in a very exclusive cul-de-sac; there was no noise from traffic or passers-by. He could hear the sharp popping of the ice as the warm gin trickled over it.

She eased her sandals off, toe to heel, then sat on the sofa next to the clutter of packages, putting her feet up on a glass-topped coffee-table, and took a slug of the gin. Using the big toe of her right foot, she eased up the lid of a small mahogany box that stood on the glass-topped table. It contained cigarettes. She looked at them for a short while – long enough to take a couple more large sips of gin – then reached forward, took one, and lit it with a nearby table-lighter, rapidly, as if trying to outdistance second thoughts.

Tut-tut, he thought. Back-slider.

The woman smoked and drank her gin. She appeared to have no interest in her purchases: the indifference of the wealthy. Charge-account ennui. He sat across the room from her, taking in the expensive and discreet antiques: an Italian short sideboard that looked eighteenth century, a Poussin over the marble mantelpiece. There was plenty of time. The woman's husband was away on a business trip until after the weekend. It was clear that she intended to spend the evening alone. She might, he supposed, cook herself a light meal. Perhaps she would listen to music for a while.

He was happy enough to sit with her. He liked the silence because it reminded him of the silence in his parents' house when he and Elaine were children.

On the table was a recently published novel, with an embossed invitation-card acting as bookmark. The woman picked it up and took it with her to the drinks-trolley, where she replenished her gin, then returned to the sofa and lay full-length on it, propped up on the bank of cushions. She nudged the packages aside with one foot and began to read. After a moment, her hand went out to the cigarette-box. She felt for the lighter without taking her eyes from the page.

No hurry, he thought. There's no hurry. He savoured the passing minutes. He noted details that Elaine would want to hear about. He watched the woman's face, almost blank in repose, smoke wafting from her narrow nostrils. No hurry. But he wanted his hands on her. Oh, God, he wanted that. The sudden thought of it was like a clout in the small of the back.

And, sooner or later, it would occur to her that she'd like to take a bath.

The phone stopped after the second ring as Deacon's answering machine picked up the call. At first he was inclined to let it run, then relented and lifted the receiver. 'I'm here,' he said, speaking over his own recorded voice. 'Just a minute.' He switched the tape off and said: 'Hello?'

'I always suspect those things,' Laura said. 'Once you'd need a secretary who could say "He's in a meeting". Now the whole world can be incommunicado.'

'I sometimes wish it were.'

'Listen,' she said, 'I've thought of something. Katie's diary. The word "trace".'

'I remember.'

'After . . . when I went back to work, I was told that the computer had stopped that Thursday: the day before she died. You recall I told you that Kate was DBA. She was called on to solve the problem. It was pretty much the last thing she did before she went home. I was thinking about that. Apparently the capacity was used up.'

'What?'

'Computers don't possess limitless capacity.' She looked for a way of explaining. 'Imagine it as lots of pigeon-holes.'

'OK.'

'They were all full.'

'Why?'

'Why, indeed. That's what I've been asking myself. Then I thought back to that entry in Kate's diary.' She hesitated. 'I gather that you don't know anything much about programming: about computers in general.'

'Only that they're taking over the known world.'

'Aha. Well, no, they're not. The people who use them might. Or the people who tell them what to do. It's like . . . you've heard the phrase "Garbage in, garbage out"?'

'Yes.'

'Computers are just high-speed idiots. Theirs not to reason why, et cetera. If you get a bill for zero pounds and ignore it, then get a reminder telling you that unless you pay zero pounds the Gas Board will disconnect your supply, it's because the computer hasn't been told that zero pounds doesn't require a response.'

'Two idiots, then.'

'Exactly. A programmer and a computer. The difference is that the programmer can realize that it's a nonsense to send someone a bill for zero amount. The computer will just go on doing it until it's told not to.'

'I understand.'

'OK. Say I'm writing a program. I want the computer to be able to perform a certain function – to perform it for everyone who wants to use the program – but I also want it to go about it in the most efficient way. So I set about the business of creating that program, and to some degree I do that by trial and error.'

'You're making it up as you go along.'

'If you like. Yes. Anyway, I do all that in my personal file.'

'What's that?'

'Imagine a locked filing-cabinet full of my notes. Only I have the key. It's a PIN-word. No one knows it but me. I type it into the computer, and it knows it's me; then it lets me into my personal file. The locked cabinet. When I've perfected the program, it can go into "public" and everyone makes use of it. But to make sure it's perfect – or as perfect as I know how to make it – I'll put a trace on.'

'All right. "Trace" – that's what was written in the diary. What does it do?'

'It tells me whether or not the software components are effective.'

'Try baby-talk.'

'It does what I've asked it to do; but it also writes a little book about how it's done it. Then it puts the little book on a shelf . . . in a pigeon-hole if you like.' There was a silence on the line. 'Oh, Christ. . . .' She paused for thought. 'Suppose I've asked you to go shopping for me. You're to go to the baker, the butcher and the greengrocer. You come back with a loaf of bread, lamb chops and some potatoes, so I know you've done what I wanted. What I don't know is whether you did it the most efficient way. Maybe you bought the potatoes first, then carried them to the other shops which are further from home. So I ask you; you tell me. If you got it wrong, I tell you to do it a more efficient way next time. That's a trace.'

'Thank you.'

'You asked for it. Now, I've never known it happen, but I've heard about it. . . . Maybe the company is pushed for a certain program. The programmer's being told to hurry with it. Other programs are backed up, waiting to be worked on. The programmer releases the program to the public file. But she forgets to wipe the trace.'

'The computer goes on doing it.'

'Exactly. Every time a user summons that program and works with it, the computer runs a trace. Every time. Eventually the system clogs. It's written zillions of traces and stuffed the pigeon-holes with them.'

'So Kate guessed this. Hence "trace" in her diary.'

'No. She guessed it all right. She also solved the problem – she cleared the system before she went home.'

'Then, what—?'

'The word had a question mark after it. My supposition is that she'd probably been curious about the trace. So would I have been in her place. She'd more than likely have pulled a copy to take a look.'

'There was something wrong with the program.'

'No. That would have shown up earlier; it wouldn't have been doing what was required of it.'

'There was something wrong with the trace.'

'In a manner of speaking. I mean, I'm guessing here; there wouldn't have been something wrong exactly. It would have been a while since Kate had written the program. She'd only be able to remember the bare outlines of what was required. So if there had been something wasteful or inefficient she wouldn't have picked it up. No – if the trace looked odd, then it must have been glaringly obvious.'

'Like what?'

'Like something that shouldn't have been there.'

'Try again.'

'The baker, the butcher. . . .'

'Yes, OK.'

'You're a robot. I've told you to go to those shops. Each time you come back with the bread and so forth. That's OK; you're doing what I've told you to do. You do it for me, you do it for anyone else who asks you. But someone else has told you to make another stop – at the bookie's, let's say. So you do that. Every time you make that shopping trip, you also stop off and lay a bet, because some other person has told you to. What do I know? Only that you come back with the shopping. How would I ever know, unless. . . .' She invited Deacon to complete the sentence.

'Unless you asked me,' he said.

'Unless, by chance, some time after the program was written, handed over to public and forgotten, I happened to see a trace that should have been erased long before. Someone has altered your instructions. You're making this extra stop at the bookie's. What that person doesn't know is that I've forgotten to tell you to stop reporting on how you do what you do.'

'Why couldn't it simply have meant that Kate had looked at the trace and discovered some flaw in her own work?'

'You're missing the point. She'd have done that – checked for inefficiencies before releasing the program. She simply forgot to take the trace off. If it puzzled her when she saw it again, then it must have been because there was some errant factor. Not a mistake. Something foreign. I've been thinking about this for two hours or more. You said that it wasn't a crazy. If Kate was murdered. So I started to look for a reason. Isn't that what policemen do? Look for a motive? The aunt you told me about – who killed Donald Whatever-his-name was. She must have had a *motive*.'

'No,' Deacon told her. 'She was a crazy.'

Soon, soon, soon. He felt calm but powerful, like something finely tuned.

The woman had eaten some fruit. She'd had a few more drinks. She had put down her book and taken the packages into her bedroom. It was sumptuous: walk-in wardrobes, thick carpeting, costly rugs and, best of all, a wall of mirrors. She took her clothes off and stood in the middle of the room, turning before the vast reflecting surface to view herself full-on, in profile, looking over her own shoulder, stiffening her leg then pointing a toe like a ballerina, and the man moved with her, their images passing and merging, touching and drifting away. She was blonde; her body pale. He watched her fair head and his dark head as they drew together, then drew apart.

Because she thought she was alone, the woman's movements – the turnings, the profiles, the elegant movements of her limbs – extended to become a slow wafting dance prompted by gin and privacy. She circled her arms; she spun, still looking back at herself, then bent her knees and rounded on her own reflection, straightening up and lifting her arms above her head. The man partnered her, turning and bending and stretching as if they were rehearsing a *pas de deux* – her white and gold, his darkness, perfectly matched. If he closed his eyes, he could see the auditorium behind the mirrors, the rapt audience; he could hear the silence that the dance imposed. He lofted his arms so that they seemed to lie on hers, all four extended like a double crucifix.

Our *danse macabre*, he thought. How step-perfect we are; how the camera loves us.

The woman's face smiled back at him. Then she stopped and took one of the dresses from its bag; she bunched it and pushed her head through, then lofted her arms and the oyster-coloured silk dribbled down her body like a flow of water, catching at her breast and hip as a stream might on a smooth boulder, then pouring suddenly to her ankles. She looked for the briefest moment, then stripped it off again and walked past him into the wings.

On stage alone, he took his bow, breathing heavily, his bright blue eyes glowing with pleasure. From somewhere beyond the drawing-room, he could hear the bath-taps running.

8

They arrived each evening before the sky had begun to lose its light and stayed on until deepest dusk: swallows, circling between the big plane tree and Deacon's window, their high-pitched screaming fading and growing and fading as they flashed round in a tight sixty-metre circle like Wall of Death riders. Every day he watched them: the flickering sickle-shaped wings, the compact dark bodies perfectly built for their mad aeronautics. Hour after hour, they swooped and banked and shrieked like hysterics rigid with energy.

He had spent the whole day in his flat, holed up like a hermit in his cell. He had gone from wardrobe to wardrobe. Maggie's top-coats, jackets, windcheaters; her winter and summer dresses, her evening-gowns; her elegant shoes, her sandals, sneakers, espadrilles; her belts looped over the hanger-rail; her jeans, linen trousers, shorts. Then the drawers: sweaters, blouses, plaid work-shirts, scarves, underclothes. He had filled three tea-chests and nailed them shut. There was more, though; much more. In a hat-box he'd found a bundle of letters that he'd preserved but thought he might never read. Her jewellery. Her perfumes. Her pens and headed notepaper: *From Margaret Deacon*. It seemed endless.

When Laura arrived, he took her to the window to look at the swallows. He felt light and faintly feverish, as if the soles of his feet were not quite touching the floor. He left her to watch and went through to the kitchen. When she joined him, he was shredding a lettuce into the salad-spinner. 'I didn't go out today,' he said. 'I thought. . . . Is a tuna salad OK?'

'Fine.' Laura had taken a bottle of wine from her shoulder-bag. 'I brought this. I assumed you wouldn't have any.' He didn't answer. 'You're on the wagon, aren't you?'

'That's right.'

'How long?'

'Not long.'

'How bad?'

Deacon laughed. 'I think that depends on your point of view. I was being it; other people were looking at it. It was less than amusing for me, so I imagine others found it a bit of a pain in the arse, too.' For some reason, the waspishness in his voice saddened her.

'I'm sorry,' she said. 'I couldn't help but notice.'

'No. . . .' He shook his head, and his tone softened. A day spent packing Maggie's things had put him in need of a drink. 'No – I don't. . . . To tell you the truth, there's a lot of it that I don't remember. What I do remember, I'd like to forget, but mustn't. If I did' – he mimed taking a drink – 'nothing to be afraid of.'

'Really?' she asked. 'Really afraid?'

'It's a very high cliff. You can fall forever.' He opened a drawer and took out a corkscrew. 'I'll smoke,' he said, 'you drink.' He held the corkscrew out to her. It was clear that he didn't want to open the bottle. His next remark came quickly: a businesslike diversion. 'If there's something to find – if what you spoke about on the phone last night has any substance – how would we find it?'

It was what Laura was there to discuss. It put them back on a firm footing and allowed Laura to find a glass and pour herself some wine without having to feel apologetic. She liked him for that.

'In theory we can't,' she told him. 'Only Kate can

look at the programs she wrote or the traces she devised. Users can execute a program once it's gone to the public file, but they don't see it. Only the programmer has "read, write and execute" access.'

'And Kate's dead.'

'Yes, well. . . .' Laura sipped her wine. 'The computer doesn't know that.'

'Go on.' He was slicing tomatoes, his head bowed over his work.

'Kate hasn't been replaced yet. So far as I know, she hasn't been closed down as a programmer. Let's say I sit at her VDU. I type in "Kate Lorimer". The computer says hello to me and asks me for my PIN-word. I type that in. As far as the computer's concerned, I'm Kate.'

'Do you know—?'

She interrupted. 'Her PIN-word. No. But I know what sort of word it is. Kate was a fan of horse-racing. She used to go to Newbury and Sandown Park quite a lot. Always video'd the classics. She told me once that she used the names of horses – you change the PIN-word from time to time. When she mentioned it, I think she was using Shergar. It wouldn't be that now.'

'Wasn't the word supposed to be a secret?'

'No. Yes, strictly speaking, I suppose. No one cares really.'

'Did she like to bet?'

'Yes.' Laura looked puzzled. 'Now and then.'

'It could be the last horse that won for her.'

'Ah. I suppose it could.'

'OK.' Deacon took oil and vinegar from a shelf. 'The computer believes you're Kate. Then what?'

'Well, the trace *files* have been wiped – Kate cleared the computer that evening. But I could look at her work – whatever she had in public and personal. I could look for the trace itself.'

'Would you find what she found? Supposing there was something odd.'

'Oh, yes, I imagine so. We do pretty much the same sort of work. I'd spot an oddity.'

'Can you do it?'

'What? I'm a programmer. Of course I can do it.'

'I mean safely.'

'Oh. Yes. People stay after office hours: overtime. The security officers come round and the cleaners, but no one who matters. I'll avoid Thursday. The manager always works late on that day. His queenly and socially responsible wife goes to some committee meeting or other; he makes a point of being visibly virtuous; he also makes a point of letting everyone know that he *dines* at his *club*. He's a creep.'

'This is ready.' Deacon carried the food into the living-room. Two places were laid at the dining-table; one wine-glass, one water-glass. Before sitting down, he went to a bookshelf and removed two large volumes, then found a notepad and pen. 'These might help,' he said.

'What's that?'

'Maggie had one leg of a hurdler called Solomon's Glory. It even used to win from time to time.' He reflected. 'I suppose it's mine now. I hadn't thought of that. Anyway, this is *Timeform*.' He tapped the books. 'A bible in racing circles. One's for the flat, the other for hurdlers and chasers.' He started to leaf through. 'I'll jot down the classics winners and Grand National winners for the last couple of years. Try those for the PIN-word.'

'OK.' Laura looked at him and smiled. 'You're thinking that it's all a bit thin.'

He shook his head. 'No. You've been following your instinct from the beginning. If anything, your persistence has made me feel that you're probably right – that there is more to Kate's death than a domestic accident. Instinct rarely leads people astray for so long.'

'You trust it.'

78

'Always have.'

They ate in silence for a while. There was an edginess between them that, until now, hadn't had the time to grow. Both knew its source; and both had known that at some point it would appear. Just beyond the window, the swallows circled and screamed.

Laura said: 'Why hadn't it occurred to you – that you owned part of a racehorse?'

Deacon smiled. It was a tactful question, oblique enough to give him a lead if he wanted to take it, but also allowing him to duck the issue. 'After Maggie died . . .' he said, then stopped.

'You don't have to—'

'No, it's not that.' He put his fork down. 'It's the phrase: I've said it, or thought it, countless times. Just then, it sounded like an indulgence. It sounded stale. I suppose I'd pretty much divided life into "with Maggie" and "after Maggie". Well . . . if I'm honest, I guess that's still true. Of course, there's also "before Maggie", though that didn't seem to count for much once we'd met. I'd come to believe that I lacked the talent for happiness, or that I was one of those people destined not to get his share. One way or another, I'd got used to the notion. I was never wretchedly unhappy: nothing so glamorous. Bully of a father; indifferent mother; good at school but didn't like it. Later on, I spent a lot of time working and not much playing. Had a few relationships that were nice enough, except that I could never quite work out what they were supposed to be *for*. "Acquaintanceships with sex" would about sum them up. Sounds like an extended whine, doesn't it?'

'Well, it certainly sounds *extended*.'

Deacon laughed. 'Yes. Don't misunderstand. I wasn't resentful. I didn't give much thought to the way I was spending my life, really. I was conscious of the fact that it was a bit dull, perhaps.'

'Then Maggie.'

'Then Maggie,' he confirmed.

'How on earth did you meet her?'

'Yes – how can that have happened? It's desperately unlikely, isn't it?'

A wryness in his tone didn't quite mask the aggression. 'Christ, I'm sorry,' she said. 'It wasn't meant—'

'No, no.' He cut her off. 'You're not the first. There's a theory afoot that policemen are largely brutal and stupid. Few have season tickets to the ballet. Even fewer litter their conversation with quotations from the Greek philosophers. As it happens – give or take a degree of stupidity – it's a theory I tend to agree with. Like all generalizations, it's true in a general sense. Depressing, isn't it? If you really want a laugh – I met Maggie at a lecture on Jung and the West Country. Cornish myths and customs, tribal myths and customs. God moves in mysterious ways. I was there because I'd been afflicted by a wholly errant idea that to know something about analytical theory might provide some insight into the mental processes of people who nail each other to garage doors for fun. Maggie was there because she was in analysis.'

'You picked her up.' Laura sounded amused by the notion, though not in any patronizing way.

'I suppose I did. There was a bit more to it than that. I think I fell in love with her in the first moment that I saw her. I've puzzled over it since. Was it really like that . . . as immediate? I sometimes wonder whether I mightn't have forgotten the bits and pieces of life that came between knowing her and loving her, but when I reconstruct the time I simply can't recall any period of indifference or mere liking. I met her; I loved her. I can't make it any other way.'

'Maggie felt the same way?' Laura asked. He nodded. 'It sounds remarkable.'

'You mean unlikely.'

'Not at all. I mean rare. Lucky.'

'Lucky,' he said slowly. 'Yes. That hadn't occurred to me.' Then: 'The luck didn't hold, though, did it?'

The bleakness in his voice left Laura helpless. There was something that Deacon wanted from her – a version of Maggie he didn't own – but she wasn't at all sure that she could offer him that. Maggie had come to Oxford after taking her BA at Vassar; she'd elected to spend another year at Oxford where she'd begun her PhD. Laura remembered a quiet self-possessed young woman, a little secretive about her life, a little secretive about her men. Her money – or, rather, her father's money – was evident in Maggie's lifestyle: unlike most students who shared flats and, at best, ran a jalopy, she had bought a small house in north Oxford and drove a throaty sports-convertible. She and Laura had certainly been more than passing acquaintances, but less than close friends. More than anything, perhaps, Laura had found Maggie intriguing, and she had discovered, during their more recent friendship, that her odd curiosity about Maggie was still there. There had been little enough time, though, for any deeper relationship to grow.

What do I tell him? she thought. Then: Nothing. At the moment, nothing. She felt the weight of responsibility involved in having her version of Maggie. She didn't know what he wanted to hear, or what he ought to hear, or even what she wanted to tell him. It was corrupting.

'What are you thinking?' he asked. Laura detected an eagerness in his voice.

'About the programs. I can't sit there half the night at Kate's VDU. I'll have to print them out and bring them away with me. I wonder' – it was something she had wanted to ask without being sure whether she would – 'would you mind if I had a bath? At my place it's . . . I know I'll have to try to stop thinking about Kate. But it makes my skin crawl.' Immediately, she thought: A mistake. A mistake. I don't know him that well. But he answered her in a casual enough way.

'Sure, of course,' he said, and smiled at her as if he were half-thinking of something else.

9

What happened next?

The woman read and smoked a cigarette and ate some fruit and drank some gin. She must have been a little drunk. He shared those moments with her – common, domestic, strangely intimate moments. After a while, she took her packages into her bedroom and took her clothes off. But she didn't try any of the new dresses on right away. She looked at herself in the mirrors – a full wall of mirrors that had reflected her and him and everything in the room – and she had danced, watching herself, and he had danced with her.

Danced?

Not that she jigged or hopped about, or held her arms as if encircling some imaginary partner. Just these slow graceful movements, slow and graceful because of the gin perhaps; and it was touching, at first, to watch her fantasy. Herself as prima ballerina, her body taller, more slender, more muscular; younger. And he danced with her, moving with her sometimes, sometimes in opposition, their gestures marrying or crossing one another to make a fleeting pattern in air. But then her isolation began to madden him. He wanted to break in on it. He wanted her. He wanted to let her feel his power. It was different; not the same as with Kate Lorimer.

How different? Say how.

What he felt was stronger. What he wanted was more. More time. More sensation. More of her. There were things he wanted to do.

What happened next?

Things he wanted to do. . . .

Never mind that now. What happened next?

While the bath was running – yes, she went to start the bath – she walked naked about the living-room and the kitchen. She took a peach from a big wooden bowl and peeled it over the sink, then bit into it, letting the juice run down her forearm. The peach was very ripe, and when she took a second bite she raised her chin as if she were drinking, and drops fell on to her throat and breasts. It didn't matter. Tracks of the sticky sweetness that could stay there until she got into the bath. She made a call on the kitchen phone, but whoever she wanted to speak to wasn't home. There was an answering machine. He eavesdropped on her message. It was odd. Exciting.

What?

That she should be in the kitchen; naked in the kitchen. By the sink, by the stove. While she was on the phone, she leaned against the door-jamb. He suspected she liked the coolness of the tiles on the soles of her feet. There was a rack of kitchen implements on the wall. While she listened to the answering machine voice, she toyed with them, idly moving a ladle from one hook and exchanging it for a can-opener, rearranging the pattern. When she spoke, she stopped doing that and began to stroll to and fro, taking the telephone lead to its limit. Because it was all but dark outside, her reflection went to and fro in the kitchen window.

What happened next?

She got into the bath.

But first she hung up the phone.

She hung up the phone and walked along the hallway to the bathroom. Her timing was perfect – the bath-water was just at the depth she wanted. She unstoppered a glass bottle and scattered some lilac-coloured crystals into the water, moving her arm in a graceful arc – an echo of her dance-movement. She tested the water with one foot, then got in and lay back. She sighed.

What happened next?

It was probably the gin. Probably the fact that she must have been a little drunk. But she was light under his grip, compliant, following his lead like a dancing-partner. Her face seemed to go beneath the sheet of the water so smoothly, so quietly, the surface rising beside her cheekbones then breaking across her lips and her eyes, a thin skin of it, a rind of water, until he took her deeper and her body bowed a little, just flexed, her hips lifting as if stirred by a lover's touch. The movement was languorous, making a small wave flow on the water, a perfect match for the motion that had produced it. He held her for a while in what seemed complete stillness, her eyes looking at the underside of the water and the blurred world beyond. There came another sinuous undulation of her torso, this time stronger and slower so that she almost brought her belly above the water, but he settled her with his hand, fingers splayed on her throat just by the jawline. Two enormous silver sacs, big pouches of air, started from her open mouth and hung motionless for a moment, then wobbled up, making a turbulence that distorted her features. Then she was still. He took his hand out of the water very slowly, not wanting to disturb the silence. He was fizzing with energy and excitement.

What happened next?

He towelled his arm. He went back to the bedroom. Five minutes later, he was ready to leave. He looked around the flat for traces of himself, but knew there wouldn't be any. He took a peach from the wooden bowl to eat in the street.

It wasn't enough, was it?

It was dark when he left. The night was very warm. There were plenty of people about. He walked along-side the park, eating the peach.

It wasn't enough.

He thought of her naked beside the stove, that strange juxtaposition. He thought of her pirouette in front of the mirrors. He thought most of the way she had stood with arms raised as the rich silk cascaded down her body.

It wasn't enough, was it?

No, it wasn't enough. There were things he wanted to do. . . .

It was cool in the basement room, cool and quiet.

Over there, close to the window, the shadow that looked like a knight. Higher, up by the ceiling, the shadow that looked like a bird. The flute-player. The sheela-na-gig. The lights were dim, two cockleshell shades on the wall, one fringed lamp; the same lamp that Mother had leaned towards as she sewed. He felt slightly feverish, though it wasn't an unpleasant sensation. It resembled the small illnesses of childhood that seemed to put the world at one remove and render everything dream-like, making colours brighter, making sound more mysterious, making sensations leak into one another.

Elaine would come to his room in the early evening, bringing him gifts – chocolate, books, jigsaw puzzles. Downstairs, their parents would be sitting in the usual places. Elaine would smile her smile, her hand cool on his forehead and cheek. He'd shake with excitement, but didn't dare to move or encourage her. All the power was hers. Sometimes she'd smooth his hair and whisper something, then leave, closing the door quietly but firmly, not looking back, as if she had found him asleep. But sometimes she would sit on the bed and smile again. He would close his eyes and sink back on the pillows. Her hand cool on his forehead. Her hand lifting the sheet.

Tell me again. Tell me how it looked when she put on the dress.

10

Rupert Lawson was a waste of time.

He made the assumption that Deacon was a policeman, and Deacon didn't bother to set him straight
about that. His Chelsea flat was very expensive,
impeccably furnished and over-equipped. The mix
said everything: a Le Corbusier lounger, a Tizot
desk-lamp, a Hockney lithograph, a Blaupunkt sound-
system, a cordless phone, a six-face clock unit that
gave the time of day in London, Tokyo, Sydney, New
York, Johannesburg and Brussels. There was little
doubt about the ownership of the white Porsche that
stood outside. If Lawson had been carrying a Filofax
in a shoulder-holster, Deacon would not have been
surprised.

For the first couple of minutes, Lawson was jumpy;
a little too expansive, a little too insistent in offering a
drink. His eyes flickered round the room as he offered
Deacon a chair. He was eager to please, but his mind
was elsewhere. It took Deacon a second or two, then
he guessed. A little stash somewhere: good Moroccan
stuff, or a couple of ounces of coke tucked away in a
desk-drawer. The style of the new market-gamblers:
fast cars, fast money, sweet dreams.

Lawson was a tall man and well built, if a little on
the meaty side. He had sandy hair and pale eyelashes
that made him slightly resemble a bullock. He lodged
on the edge of a large refectory table that ran half the
length of one wall and twisted the crested ring on the
little finger of his right hand. When Deacon told him

that Kate Lorimer was dead, there was a moment in which a look of relief preceded his concern.

'How terrible,' Lawson said. He moved from the table and sank into an armchair, his apprehensiveness gone. 'How did it happen?'

'An accident,' Deacon told him. 'She drowned in her bath. It seems she must have slipped . . . banged her head.'

'How terrible.' Lawson got to his feet and went to a drinks-trolley on the far side of the room. 'Are you sure?' he asked.

Deacon shook his head. 'Not for me.'

Lawson gave himself a brandy and took it back to his chair. He didn't seem to need the drink; in fact he set it down on the floor without bothering to take a sip. 'What do you want of me?'

'We just want to know a little about her. It's usual to check with friends.' Deacon allowed a tiny pause before adding: 'Close friends – you know.'

'Is it?' Lawson looked puzzled. Then he said: 'Oh, you can't think – I don't believe Kate was the suicidal type.'

Deacon shrugged. 'No, I'm sure. But there are always a few questions to be asked.'

'Routine,' Lawson suggested.

Deacon smothered a smile. It always amused him when people like Lawson decided they could afford to be patronizing. 'Yes,' was all he said.

'OK.' Lawson slid down in the chair and lazily crossed his legs, ankle to knee; he was settling down to be helpful.

'Can you remember when you last saw Kate?' Deacon began the questions already knowing that if someone had killed Laura's flatmate it wasn't Rupert Lawson.

'It must have been a month ago. I could check.'

'Not more recently than that?'

'We had dinner. Near here. Mario and Franco's, I

think. No – a month ago at least. We weren't that close, you know.'

'No?'

'No, not really.'

'I'd heard you were lovers.'

Lawson didn't look at all foxed. He waved a hand airily and said: 'Oh, that – yes.' He paused, smiling. 'Lovers. . . .'

'What?' asked Deacon.

'No.' The pale eyelashes dropped as if the other man were generously closing his eyes to some small social gaffe. 'It's a strange word. Romantic.'

'What would your choice of word be?'

Lawson appeared not to notice the edge in Deacon's tone. 'We saw each other from time to time. From time to time we went to bed together. No one was asking for the world – or expecting to get it. All pretty harmless, really.'

Is that right? Deacon thought. He said: 'Was that usual – a month between meetings?'

'I don't have much of a social life.' The remark was made with a hint of pride. 'Long hours, irregular working-times.' As if on cue, the phone rang. Lawson unwound from his chair to answer it. Someone wanted to discuss a deal. Lawson took the phone to the window and stared out, talking in rapid bursts, weighing one factor against another, interrupting, firing questions. It was almost possible to see cold cash hanging in the balance. His back was to the room and, although he continued to look out of the window, it was obvious that he saw nothing. His mind was focused, his eyes blank.

After ten minutes, Deacon got up and touched the other man lightly on the arm. Lawson jumped, as if he had forgotten Deacon was there. He said, 'Just a moment,' then again, louder, when the excited voice on the phone didn't stop. To Deacon, he said: 'I'll be through in a minute.'

'It doesn't matter. If you hadn't seen Kate in a month. . . .'

'At least that.' The phone squawked. He put it back to his ear and said, 'Wait. Hold on for a moment.' Then: 'It really is tragic. Poor Kate.' He gestured with the phone. 'I did wonder why she hadn't called.' Deacon backed off. 'Can you . . . ?' He left the rest unsaid: *see yourself out?*

Deacon walked out of the room and made for the front door. He could hear Lawson picking up where he'd left off, his voice interrogative, eager and engrossed.

Don't Forget Me had won the 2,000 Guineas. It wasn't that. Unite had won the Oaks. It wasn't that. Miesque had won the 1,000 Guineas. It wasn't that.

Still trying races for that year, Laura had tapped in the winner of the Grand National: GOOD MORNING. KATE LORIMER. Hunched over a green screen all day, programmers like to pretend that they're not talking to themselves. Tiny pointless conversations, cheery greetings make a relationship of a monologue. If psychiatrists don't have a theory about it, they should.

GOOD MORNING KATE. PASSWORD.

Laura had typed MAORI VENTURE. She'd got the brush-off straight away. NOT RECOGNIZABLE, the computer had told her. She'd glanced again at the list Deacon had given her.

SHAHRASTANI. The Derby winner for the previous year. NOT RECOGNIZABLE.

MOON MADNESS. The winner of the St Leger. NOT RECOGNIZABLE.

MIDWAY LADY, she'd typed. And the computer had smiled and asked her what she wanted to know.

'It won both the Thousand Guineas and the Oaks in eighty-six,' Deacon said. 'If Kate backed it, she'd certainly have had a soft spot for the horse.'

Laura was sitting on the floor of Deacon's flat, surrounded by reams of computer printout. 'Well;' – she flicked one of the sheets – 'these are our winnings. Maybe. I'm beginning to think we backed the wrong runner.'

'Nothing there?'

'Not so far. Programs galore; no sign of any trace, though.'

'Wouldn't it have been simpler . . .' Deacon hesitated.

Laura looked up at him, a sardonic smile answering his half-formed question. 'To look at the stuff on the VDU – is that what you were going to say?' Deacon shrugged apologetically. 'Sure. You think I'm enjoying this? I simply couldn't spend that much time at Kate's desk. So I sent everything she had in personal and public to the printer.'

'What if someone had seen it being printed?'

She shook her head. 'No. Little risk of that. Sheets are coming off the thing all the time. People are only interested in their own stuff.' She was leafing through as she spoke. 'The last time I saw him', she said inconsequentially, 'was in the kind of restaurant where they bring you hot bread rolls wrapped in Irish linen and the bill in a calfskin folder with an embossed escutcheon.' Before she had unloaded the printout on to the floor, Deacon had told her about his meeting with Lawson. 'At one point, a waiter had brought a telephone to the table. The phone conversation was the most he said all night. There were four of us. Rupert wrote a cheque for one quarter of the bill.'

'It's how the rich get rich.'

'It's how the rich *stay* rich. God knows what Kate saw in him.'

'Just that, perhaps.'

'What?'

'Money.'

Laura looked up, opening her mouth to protest,

then paused. 'Yes,' she said slowly. 'Well, I'd never actually thought of that.' She went back to turning the pages of the printout. 'I suppose that might have been it.' She sounded disappointed.

'How well *did* you know Kate?' Deacon asked.

'I've had people share the flat before. Mostly they came and they went. There was one person I liked a lot – a man; we're still friends. Mostly, I just tried to pick people who would pay the rent on time and be tolerable to live with. It was different with Katie. We really liked one another. I'd worried about the fact that we worked together – thought that spending so much time in one another's company might chafe. But it was fine. How well did I know her?' She stopped turning the computer sheets, and her gaze unfocused for a moment. 'I'm not sure. We think we know our friends, don't we? Friends and brothers and sisters and lovers and parents. We think so.' Her voice had grown quiet, as if she were recollecting something. 'We base a way of life on that belief. We do some of the things we do, think some of the things we think, plan what we plan, give what we give, all because of how we see some other person.'

She's been hurt, Deacon thought. He waited, prepared to hear more, but Laura became brisk with the folded pages before her on the floor.

'Whatever it was,' she said, 'even if it was money, he wouldn't have been worth it. I told you he was a prick; also a waste of time.'

'Right on both counts,' Deacon agreed.

It took her the rest of the evening. Deacon read, looking up from his book now and then to watch her as she sat cross-legged on the carpet, flipping through the concertina'd pages. He opened some wine for her and made coffee for himself. When he handed her the glass, she looked up and smiled without speaking. There was something comforting about her concentration, something companionable. It had to do with the fact that she felt sufficiently safe to be in his company in this easy way. She was engrossed, bent over her work, the blonde hair falling past her cheek and masking her face, all but her chin and the tip of her nose. The casualness of the way they were spending the evening was likeable, and it frightened him.

She threw the last wad of paper aside and lifted her glass. 'Well,' she said, and drank her wine.

'Nothing?'

'If it was there, it's not there now.'

'Which means?'

'That it's been wiped.'

'Not necessarily sinister, right?'

'Not at all. Once a trace has served its purpose, that's what you do – erase it. Except that Kate didn't. We know that. The computer clogged.'

'And she wrote "query trace" in her diary.'

'Right. But she also cleared the computer.'

'And, in doing that, wiped the trace.'

'Not necessarily. She cleared the trace *files* – the records that were plugging the pigeon-holes. She could have left the trace itself in personal. But she didn't.'

'So, if it exists, where is it?'

Laura sighed. 'She'd have printed it out; that's my theory. A few sheets of this somewhere' – she gestured at the pile in front of her – 'or it's on the back-up tape.'

'The what?'

'There's a back-up tape that records each week's work.'

'Where?'

'At the bank. In the basement rooms.' She got up and stretched. 'The only way of looking at that is to run it *in situ*.'

'Risky?'

She nodded. 'Risky. Possible, though.'

'We've gone this far,' he said. 'What do you think?'

'I think I'm confused,' Laura said. She smiled wryly. 'I think that, if I were you, I'd have told myself to give up on all this. I think that maybe Kate slipped and drowned accidentally. I think I might have been having a flight of fancy.'

'No, you don't.'

Her smile broadened, acknowledging that he was right. 'I think I'd like to have a bath,' she said. 'You know —.'

He nodded – *Of course* – and she slipped her shoes off and padded out of the room, yawning.

Deacon collected her glass and took it, together with his coffee-cup, into the kitchen and rinsed them under the tap. When he came back, he looked at once towards the discarded shoes, as if they had been on his mind all the time. They lay at an angle to one another, the left canted up slightly on the instep of the right. Shoes without their owner. A woman's shoes carelessly kicked off and left in the middle of his living-room.

A feeling struck him of such intensity that he almost reeled from it. It was as if the days of the past year had fallen away, days of booze and dread, and at any minute she would emerge from the bathroom wrapped in the dark-blue ankle-length robe he'd bought her, and step over her shoes and curl up on the couch with her usual brandy nightcap.

He could hear the bath-taps running. A faint scent of warm pine reached him. He stared at the shoes as if their particular position, the angle they made, offered some particular memory of some particular night.

The phone rang. It was Phil Mayhew suggesting a walk in Green Park next morning. Deacon went to the window and unlatched it to watch the swallows, black shapes on a near-black backdrop. He seemed only to have been there a minute or two before Laura's reflection appeared, a shaky image, blurred by lamp-light in the half-opened pane.

'I found this – OK?' She tightened the belt on the blue robe.

11

'We're not doing this properly,' Deacon observed.
'You're supposed to make an entrance from the west
side of the park, carrying a crumpled paper bag
containing some bread and a piece of fruit-cake. You
stand on that little wooden bridge over there, feeding
bread to the ducks. Then I wander along from the
opposite direction and lean on the bridge, but not too
close. After a while you walk off and I'm holding the
bag. I feed the rest of the bread to the ducks, but not
the cake, because one of the raisins is a microdot.'

Mayhew regarded him wordlessly for a moment,
then looked away. 'Up yours,' he offered.

Deacon laughed. 'No,' he said, 'I love it. Skul-
duggery.'

'Not really. You know what it's like. Most of the day
I sit at a plywood desk inhaling body-odour and
side-stream smoke. That, or I'm in a pool car with
carbon monoxide hissing through the air-vents. This
weather's bound to break. I thought I'd get close to
nature.'

'Not in this park. The pigeons get detox treatment.
What about over there?' Deacon nodded towards a
patch of grass that was largely free of sunbathers.
Mayhew was wearing a gym T-shirt. He stripped it off
and lay on the grass, his biceps bunching impressively as he clasped his hands behind his head.

'And so?' Deacon queried.

Mayhew closed his eyes against the glare of the sun.
'And so you might be right.'

A fizz along the nerve-endings; the little rush of adrenalin that occurs when something suspected becomes something true. Something real. Deacon asked: 'What? Forensic? What?'

'Not forensic. No, I don't think anything was missed at Lorimer's flat.' Mayhew hoisted himself on one elbow. 'There was a shout in Knightsbridge, day before yesterday. Montpelier Square. The cleaner let herself in, as she almost always does. She cleaned the kitchen; she cleaned the bedrooms.' Mayhew paused invitingly.

'Then she cleaned the bathroom.'

'Yes.'

'Or, rather, she didn't.'

'Yes.'

'Go on,' said Deacon.

'Olivia Cochlan. Actually, *Lady* Olivia Cochlan. She'd been dead about twelve hours.'

'Is there a theory?'

'She'd done about half a bottle of gin, so if anyone *wants* a theory it could well be that she passed out in the bath having drunk more than she intended. In fact it's just that theory that her husband – the noble Sir Bernard – is asking us to hush up.'

'Where was he?'

'Paris.'

'Confirmed?'

'Oh, yes. By two air-hostesses, five businessmen, a hotel manager, a head waiter and an unbelievably expensive hooker.'

'You're obliging him, I expect.'

'Not in person. Someone will, I've no doubt. Although I gather that Lady Olivia's liking of the bottle was no great secret. I suppose there's a difference between being a bit of a piss-artist and a skeleton in the cupboard for generations to come.'

'What have you got?' Deacon asked.

'The cleaner was off the wall to start with, but she

calmed down after a while. Her opinion was that Lady Olivia could drink the Brigade of Guards to a standstill. Half a bottle would have been a knock-off.'

It is, Deacon thought. Half a bottle. Just starters. He said: 'This time might have been an exception.'

'Possibly.'

'Or she could have been taking pills. Tranks. Mogodon.'

'Or that, yes.' Mayhew lay back again, shielding his eyes with one hand in order to look at Deacon.

'Except that what we have here is a coincidence.' Mayhew nodded, still squinting up under his raised hand. 'And the first law of coincidence. . . .'

Mayhew finished the thought for him. 'Is that there are no coincidences.'

'So there's an alternative theory.'

'But not a public one.'

'Why not?'

'To begin with, the flat was as clean as a whistle. No forced entry, no sign of a struggle, no sign of anyone having been in the place but the waterlogged Lady Olivia.'

Deacon wasn't surprised by the asperity in Mayhew's tone. 'You're letting your class-prejudice show, Phil,' he said.

'Fuck 'em,' Mayhew retorted, 'sodding parasites. Second, no one's likely to want to tell Sir Bernard that there's a possibility his old woman was topped and follow that by saying that there's not a shred of evidence to prove it. He's worried enough by the thought of rumours spreading about her drinking.'

'Third,' Deacon guessed, 'the case of Kate Lorimer is closed and filed neatly under Accidental Death.'

'Fourth, we're not sure there's a connection.' Deacon remained silent. 'OK,' sighed Mayhew, 'we'd sooner there wasn't.'

'Who?'

There was no answer at first. Mayhew dropped his

hand and turned his face towards the sun, his eyes closed once more. Eventually, he said, 'I don't know for sure. I got it from D'Arblay.'

'And he got it from?'

A shrug. 'Who knows?'

'Would you have let it drop,' Deacon asked 'if you'd had the choice?'

'Come on, John; you know how it is. There are fit-ups and deals. Trade-offs. Everyone fiddles the clear-up rate. They just don't want to know about this one. It's too difficult. One closed case – a definite death by misadventure. Some toff with a lot of clout who's made it plain that he expects no aggravation.'

'Why are you telling me?'

'You wanted to know.'

'And?'

'And, to tell you the truth, I'm curious myself.'

A squirrel popped across the grass in a series of little weightless bounds and sat quivering, close to Mayhew's outstretched foot. Mayhew opened an eye, as if he'd sensed the creature, then sat up and clapped his hands, plosively, once, sending it on its way. 'Little bastards have got a bite like a rat,' he observed.

Deacon laughed. 'The nature-lover.'

'I said I wanted to be close to it, not mix with it.' Mayhew was south London, born and bred. Parks were as much as he wanted to know of wide open spaces. Parks were ordered and tonsured and shorn, flowers in neat ranks, tarmac walkways, a nip of exhaust fumes in the air. He'd been to the country a couple of times, it gave him the heebie jeebies; it was empty.

'You know none of this. If you're spotted on the inside track, I'll have to disown you.'

Deacon held up both hands, acknowledging the risk. 'Lady Olivia isn't going to make the press,' he concluded.

'Just the obits.'

'No inquest?'

'The family doctor also has a knighthood.'

'Well, well. The English establishment knows how to close ranks, doesn't it?'

'The spirit of Rourke's Drift,' said Mayhew. 'The thin red line. The flag that saw no setting sun.' Looking away, he added: 'Bunch of shitbags.'

The sky blue from horizon to horizon, the heat like a canopy bearing down, everything breathless as if vast steel doors had slammed shut all over the park. Deacon and Mayhew walked back towards the wooden bridge, stepping between inert girls in bikinis.

'It doesn't suit us,' Mayhew asserted. 'It's not our climate. We got our sexuality from Victorian furtiveness – you know, everything covered up because it's dirty; everything enjoyable against God's law. It's impossible to pretend indifference.' One of the girls turned on to her back as they passed, holding her unfastened top loosely in place. 'We're a nation of voyeurs, keyhole artists, peeping Toms. It's a shock to the system, all this' – he gestured, searching for a word – 'visibility. I ought to arrest myself for what I'm thinking.'

'It can't last,' Deacon told him. 'We're moving into drought conditions. It's bound to break soon.'

'The sheer choice makes me dizzy,' said Mayhew. 'It's dangerous to walk down the street.'

They reached the point at which they would part. Deacon held up a hand and walked a couple of steps backwards. 'If there's more. . . .'

'You'll get more,' Mayhew assured him. 'John.' He took a step forward in order to be able to lower his voice. 'John – do you know what's going on?'

'No.'

'There's a connection, though – the Lorimer girl and Lady Olivia.' He was asserting it.

'I know as much as you do. As little.'

Mayhew sighed. 'It could be – what? – something and nothing.'

'I doubt that. So do you.'

'Yes.' Mayhew patted Deacon on the shoulder. 'Yes.' He turned away and started back across the park. Deacon waited a moment to watch him walking a mazy investigative line through the splayed bodies, like a scavenger on a battlefield.

What do we retain of the dead? How much do we keep of what they leave us?

Kate's father had looked about him in a sheepish puzzled manner, as if uncertain of how to behave. Her mother had wept softly, neither poker-faced behind her tears nor howling; there was a certain decorum in the way she acted which made no concessions, nor asked for comfort. She'd worn white gloves and had been to the hairdresser. A pair of curtains had parted like a marionette-show, and the coffin had whispered away between banked flowers. Everyone had seemed to sing a little louder, but there was no rumble and roar to be drowned out. It was possible to think of what was happening behind the wall where the coffin had gone, but not possible to think of it for long.

Afterwards, Kate's parents had gone back to Laura's flat. They had never been there before and they'd felt obliged to make polite noises as if they were looking at a prospective home for their daughter, rather than visiting the place where she'd died. Eventually, Mr Lorimer had to ask where the bathroom was; he was an elderly man and had reached the age where pissing isn't something you can wait to do. He didn't come back for a long time, and his wife, while she talked, had kept shifting her eyes plaintively towards the hall door.

Laura had shown them into Kate's room and left them there. They'd taken a few pieces of jewellery and a photograph-album. It was all they wanted.

* * *

101

Sifting through the wardrobe meant starting memories up, little tableaux that suddenly whirred into motion. A dress, a matching pair of shoes, a flea-market blouse frothing with lace, a hat bought for its outlandishness – a shopping expedition that cocked a snook at overdrafts, a lunchtime barbecue, a party they had thrown once at the flat. Laura rifled pockets. She sorted through the sweaters and T-shirts, under-clothes and handkerchiefs in the drawers of the tall-boy. She took everything out of Kate's desk, gradually moving the papers and letters and documents and notebooks from a pile on her left to form a scrutinized pile on her right. Old diaries, loose photographs, hotel brochures, cheque-book stubs, bank statements, some greetings cards she'd received on her last birthday, two smooth riverbed pebbles and a lump of coral, a paper-knife, a calculator. . . . Much more, much more; but nothing that even resembled the green-lined sheets of a computer printout.

Kate's suitcases were empty, save one which held two cards written but never mailed and a whodunnit stained with suntan-oil. One of the postcards was addressed to Laura.

Samos not what it was. Yuppies windsurf, Americans doing Europe play folk guitar on the quay. Germans lie naked on rocks like beached seals. Retreating inland. Love, Kate.

Her spare handbags were empty. Her sports-bag was empty. There was nothing folded into any of her books or into her boxed sets of records.

It was the first time that Laura had cried for Kate. She had cried about her, but not *for* her. Now she held the postcard from Samos in her hand and read again the message she'd never received and wept for the loss of her friend.

There was a patina of dust on the pavements, and in the gutters compacted wads of dust and felt and fibrous bits and pieces, so that the streets began to take on the look of deserted attics where dry detritus gathers.

Posters had begun to appear exhorting people to save water. Tired jokes had begun to appear, too – graffitists adding the legend 'shower with a friend'. The trees in Laura's street looked as if they had just returned from a long wearying trek.

Deacon pressed Laura's bell. The voice on the entryphone was hoarse and small.

He found her in Kate's room, still surrounded by the sad remnants she'd been sieving for the past three hours. There was a postcard in her hand, and she was crying.

'It's not here,' she said. 'It must be somewhere, but it's not here.'

Deacon stood off from her; he didn't reply.

Laura's gaze was fixed on the card. 'I know I'm right. I'm sure of it. On Monday I'll try the back-up file. Somewhere. . . .' Her voice faded.

Deacon knelt down, took the postcard from her hand and read it. His seeing it made her distress all the greater; she looked at him, tears a gleaming sheen across her cheeks. He recalled how he'd assembled Maggie's things, item by item, and why it had taken so long to do. He remembered how the nails had sounded as he'd driven them into the packing-case lids.

'Don't,' she told him. 'You don't have to. Don't.' But he put the card on top of the pile and held her while she cried, because that was what she wanted. Because anyone would have done that for her. Because that was what he wanted to do.

Elaine was dressing to go out. Wooden blinds, partly closed, kept the room's coolness and gloom. Clothes were spread on the bed, on the sofa, on the big armchair. She moved among them dreamily, selecting this, rejecting that. Most of the garments were simple, elegant and obviously expensive. She never dressed sloppily. Even in this weather, jeans and a T-shirt weren't her style. A Cacherel blouse in pale apricot caught her eye, and she draped it under her chin, turning to the cheval-glass that held dim reflections of objects half-lit. The material glowed in the false dusk.

'What do we know about her?'

The man also liked the blouse and nodded approval. He said: 'A lot. Quite a lot really.'

'And what does she know about us?'

'Nothing. Nothing that matters.'

'You're sure?'

'Oh, yes.'

'Will she find what she's looking for?'

'I don't know. I shouldn't think so.'

'We'll wait. Wait and see.'

'She could be next. . . .'

'No. No, that wouldn't be wise.'

A skirt from Jap, calf-length, quite full, a bold, random design of black and white strokes.

'Because of the man?'

'Yes. He's dangerous. A wild card.'

'We couldn't have known. . . .'

'Of course not. It isn't our fault. Don't worry.'

'We're safe, aren't we?'

'Yes, safe. Don't worry.'

Simple white sling-back shoes with a low heel to make less of her height.

'I didn't know. . . .'

'What?'

'How it would feel. How good it would be. Not until it was happening, actually happening, and I felt my power like something I'd always possessed, but never used before. I could see things so clearly – everything seemed so bright and hard-edged. The bathroom walls were yellow; there were green tiles on the side of the bath and underneath the window-sill. They

104

glowed. The walls and the tiles and the bottles of blue bath-crystals . . . vibrant; the colours sang like they do in mountain-light or sea-light.'

A plain gold chain, with Greek key-pattern links, around her neck. On her wrist, a bracelet of gold and turquoise. A reef-knot ring of dull gold on the middle finger of her left hand.

'You make it sound beautiful.'

'It was, it was. The mirrors, and the colours hurting the eye. It was a brilliant grotto. When I held her under, my power drummed around the room.'

'Tell me her name again.'

'Kate—'

'The other one.'

'Laura. Laura Scott.'

Now she was dressed, he stood behind her to see the effect.

The mirror was smoky, like a twilit pool; its uppermost corner held the images of the flute-player and the barbaric contortion of the sheela-na-gig. He adjusted the blouse for her, making it a little fuller at the waist. Their dark heads were close, pale features, blue eyes almost luminous. Their breath fogged the glass.

He whispered something to her and she smiled a slow smile.

12

Charles Thwaite lived an orderly life. One indication of its orderliness was the fact that no one called him Charlie and no one ever had. In fact most often people automatically referred to him as Mr Thwaite. He was in his late forties, and that seemed to be the age he'd been born to achieve. Just as some aspire to wealth, or fame, or happiness, Charles Thwaite had aspired to middle age. The middle of things was where Charles most liked to be. Indelibly middle-class, he lived in a suburban house midway between the city and the green belt. If you asked him how he was, he'd like as not reply: 'Oh, middling, you know.' He liked to describe his political position as middle-of-the-road. It hadn't occurred to him at any point in his average life that the middle of the road is where you get run over.

A conversation with Charles would lead you into a welter of clichés, most of which had to do with notions of tidiness and order. He often asserted that, as cataloguer at the bank, he ran a tight ship. It was true; he did. 'A place for everything, and everything in its place.' He was a joke, and a bore.

Laura knew that she would have to get past Mr Thwaite's tiresome punctiliousness if she was to gain access to the back-up tape for the week before Kate's death, so she'd concocted a convincing reason for needing the tape, and chosen a time when the manager would be closeted with a couple of heavy-duty auditors from the Paris office. Some details from the tape would be needed for that very meeting. Among other characteristics, Charles possessed attitudes typical of the NCO; he would want to check the instruction with his superior, but wouldn't dare interrupt the meeting. Nor would he dare withhold material that Paris office had asked for. The danger was that he'd make some reference to it later. Laura had decided that she'd worry about that if it happened.

All in all, it was a pretty good ruse. It would almost certainly have worked. Charles Thwaite twitched his moustache. He wrestled a moment with conflicting responsibilities. He muttered something about 'irregularity'. Then he got up from his desk and went to the wall of tape-racks.

There was no question about where the tape should have been. Mr Thwaite could have located it blindfold in the unlikely event of that being required of him. In his suburban villa, plates were arranged in descending order of size; unpaid bills lay in one file, receipts from paid bills in another. The surface of his office desk was a geometric perfection of memos, correspondence and outgoing mail. His 'things to do' pad was invariably blank.

It was unthinkable, but chaos had erupted in Charles Thwaite's little domain. The tight ship had sprung a leak. There was a fly in the ointment, and there'd be the devil to pay. The tape was missing. It was one of the worst days of Charles Thwaite's life.

'Which means what?' Deacon asked.

Laura looked at him in surprise. 'That it's been stolen.'

'Yes,' he smiled. 'I think I'd got that far on my own.'

'Oh, I see. . . .' The faint breeze from the open window was thick and damp. One of Deacon's neighbours had trained a bougainvillaea vine up a west-facing wall that abutted the back of Deacon's flat, and its hot sweet scent lapped the sill. Laura jabbed the plunger on her inhaler and gasped, pulling the Ventolin into her lungs. 'Which means that Buxton will get to hear of it.'

'Buxton?'

'The manager.'

'And then?'

'I'm not sure. Nothing like it has happened before. I don't really know what Kate was working on, but I'd be surprised if there was anything on the tape that could seriously compromise the bank. I suppose a few of our programs might be slightly more efficient than those of some other organization, but beyond that. . . . It *is* confidential material, though, strictly speaking. There's bound to be some kind of rumpus – not least because Thwaite was damn-near apoplectic. He looked like a chef who'd found a turd in the soup.'

Deacon nodded. He said: 'What's in the bag?' Laura had arrived clutching some purchases she'd made at a neighbourhood supermarket.

'Pasta, pesto, salad, cheese, fruit.'

It made sense: of course it did. They had to talk to one another; they had to eat. Laura was finding it increasingly difficult to be at her flat – she'd put the place on the market and had begun to look at estate agents' sheets on other properties. She would take a bath at Deacon's place when she was there, and he could understand why she wanted to do that. It all made sense; but, looked at from the outside, their meetings would have appeared to be adding up to something other than just business. They knew that and, in their different ways, it made them wary.

'I'll do it,' he said, and took the bag through to the kitchen. One aspect of his wariness was not to let her cook in his flat.

Laura watched him while he began to prepare the food. After a while she said: 'It's different now, isn't it?' Deacon had told her about his meeting with Mayhew.

'It's the same – we see it differently. At one point it was just your theory. Now we know it's a fact.' He stopped what he was doing and looked at her. 'We could stop.'

She didn't answer at once. Then: 'No. You're thinking that I might be frightened of it. I suppose I am, a bit. At first, it was a matter of asking someone to believe me. Well, you did; or at least you took me seriously. But nothing might have come of that. Then you started to look for some sort of proof. We could've drawn a blank. Maybe it would have been possible for me to pull out at that stage. Not now.'

Deacon took a salad-bowl from a shelf and began to shred lettuce. 'Lady Olivia Cochlan,' he said.

'Never heard of her. Before you arrived, I phoned Kate's parents – they'd never heard of her, either. I looked through Kate's address-book – nothing.' He grunted, as if what she'd said confirmed his own suspicions. 'So what next? What happens now?'

'We know you were right,' he said. 'We still don't know why. Your instinct was working for you when you decided that Kate's death wasn't an accident. Which tends to make me believe that you're right about the trace – about the importance of that. The fact that the back-up tape has gone missing underlines it. Somehow—'

She cut him off. 'It's not on the printouts. I've searched the flat. I've been through Kate's clothes, her desk . . . I can't think of anything else to do.'

'Then we'll simply have to wait.' He filled a saucepan with water.

'For what?' He didn't reply. His back was towards her as he lit a burner on the stove. 'Wait for what?' she asked again.

Without turning, he said: 'For another death.'

When the streets grew a little cooler, when the deep striated red of the sunset began to fade and the sky took on a blue bloom, dull like plum skin, you could walk in the deepening shadow and hear voices and music nearby, but not be seen. You could pass restaurants and the tables set outside, each with its candle-flame, and look at the faces half-lit by the yellow glow, but not be seen. You could stroll past the drinkers and talkers who lolled in pub gardens or sat on the low walls; you could be just one of the passers-by, part of the promenade in the blue light. It was the best time.

Elaine knew the street and she knew the house. She had taken a roundabout route to get there, as if she were savouring the moment of arrival. Off the main road and along the side of a leafy square. It was quiet: just the faintest sound of music – a piano concerto – though it wasn't possible to know which house the sound came from. A slight breeze, like a drawn thread, touched a silver birch in the square's private garden bringing, for a moment, a sound like running water.

She looked up at the window, open wide, the light seeming to spill from it and douse the wall. Three people were coming towards her: a couple arm in arm, a man walking his dog. She slowed her pace; then, when they were past and out of sight, went back and stood close to the trees that bordered the square and looked again at the window. Excitement ran through her like a charge of electricity, almost painful, as if her nerve-endings lay above the skin.

Up there, up there, up there.

The window seemed to grow in her vision. She could almost believe that sheer energy and delight had buoyed her up, bringing her close, the window a proscenium arch, the room a stage, the people inside acting the script that she had written for them. If she could see them and not be seen, watch them from cover, the way of the predator, just a glimpse, perhaps . . . a glimpse would be enough for now.

Deacon came into the room carrying two bowls, one

with pasta, one with salad, and set them on the table. He went away, then returned a moment later with a block of Parmesan and a cheese-grater.

Laura smiled. He looked absorbed and confident when he cooked, and she liked that.

He said: 'Almost set.'

Just before sitting down to eat, Laura went to the window to take the feather of breeze on her face.

13

The building was grey and black and very tall. On a dull day its smoked glass and girders made it a basalt monolith, the penthouse suite sometimes above the weather, sometimes battered by snow or rain that scarcely dampened the streets below. On a bright day, like this one, it gave back fragmented images of other parts of the city and the sun sidled round the dark glass as if trapped there.

You could look east over Hell's Kitchen to the Hudson, or west towards the Empire State. A little further north, the skyline was broken by the Chrysler Building and Citicorp. South was the World Trade Center. Towers and pinnacles.

Circumnavigating the penthouse, Austin Chadwick could believe that only they existed, the lofty rooms of the elect. Had he paused and rested his forehead on the sheet-glass and looked directly downwards, he would have seen dwarfs and tiny cars on Sixth Avenue, but he almost never did that. Those lives, that circus, didn't matter much to him. He could control it without damn well having to look at it.

He liked to imagine the gridlines of power that went from one tall building to another: to tall buildings in Dallas and Los Angeles, in Tokyo and Frankfurt, London and Paris. The world over – he knew it was true – men like himself in offices that dominated skylines issued orders and made decisions while the people in the streets performed their pointless antics.

112

When Harold Steiner entered, Chadwick was standing in the middle of the room, facing the door, like a man who had been kept waiting. Before Steiner had taken more than a couple of paces, Chadwick said: 'Well?'

'We don't know. I mean, it's not clear.' Because Chadwick held his ground, Steiner was obliged to stay just inside the door; he couldn't advance on the other man, or walk round him to one of the leather chairs in front of Chadwick's desk.

'Something's gone wrong? What?'

'It looks that way.' Steiner lifted a hand in reassurance. 'Nothing that can't be fixed.'

Chadwick stared until Steiner dropped his gaze. 'Really, Austin.' His voice had weakened. 'Local trouble.'

Chadwick maintained the stare for a further ten seconds. A silence grew that only one man could break. Finally, Chadwick strode to his desk, sat down, and began to read through a sheaf of handwritten notes. He was a big man, over six feet, fifty-ish but still trim. The desk was a solid strip of mahogany; other men might have looked silly or pompous behind it. After a moment, he said, 'For Christ's sake,' waving his hand at the nearest chair. Steiner advanced and sat. He looked like a man waiting while a doctor scrutinized his ECG tape.

Chadwick said, 'Fuck,' softly. Without taking his eyes from the page, he added: 'You've read this.' It wasn't a question, but it begged one.

'No one really knows—'

'What's going on.'

Steiner wasn't sure whether Chadwick had finished his remark for him or was waiting for an answer. He opted for a positive remark: 'We dealt with the woman – Lorimer.' No response. Chadwick continued to read, though it was evident that he must have known what the notes contained. Steiner tried again. 'That all went smoothly enough.'

113

'Did it?'

Steiner shrugged. 'Sure.'

Chadwick didn't offer a direct contradiction, but without looking up he asked: 'Who's this guy Deacon?'

'No,' Steiner said, 'I mean when Lorimer was. . . .' He seemed to cast about for the appropriate word.

'Killed,' offered Chadwick.

'Killed,' Steiner nodded, happy to use the word after Chadwick had sanctioned it. 'That was fine. That went off well.'

'Is that a fact, Harold?'

'Sure.' Steiner's response came out as something between a laugh and a cough. He'd said the wrong thing. Chadwick's soft, almost prim use of his given name let him know that.

Gently, as if he didn't want to disturb the cool controlled air, Chadwick laid the papers down on his desk, then directed his gaze to the left, just a little above the other man's shoulder, taking in the skyline where it cut crenellations out of a bold blue background. He sighed briefly; there was a dreamy look in his eyes.

'Harold,' he said again, 'Harold, let me tell you something. I put in a lot of hours. This office sees a good deal of me. Deals – you know, Harold – deals going down here and there, decisions to be made. There are problems. You think this is a problem-free job, Harold? Let me tell you something. It's not. World currencies going ducks and drakes across the choppier waters of major markets, supply and demand failing to get themselves in the right order, competitors leading you on to the sucker punch, governments. . . .' He paused; Steiner wasn't enjoying any of this. 'Governments behaving like kids let loose in the candy store. Do you know what I mean, Harold, when I say "the candy store"?'

No answer came; none was expected.

'The world, Harold. The world is the candy store.' Chadwick shifted his position slightly, and his eyes fell on Steiner. Behind the soft-focus gaze lay something unyielding, like coral a fathom below the surface of a calm sea.

'It's all very taxing, Harold. I'm second-guessing, I'm predicting the future. I'm a soothsayer. I'm balancing the likely profit against the likely loss, I'm judging the effect of this action or that. I'm a diplomat. I'm spending a lot of time being very nice to assholes. I'm a proctologist, Harold. And what comes of all this hard work, this expertise, this carpetbagging and kowtowing? Listen and I'll tell you. The company stays healthy. The flame of free enterprise burns more strongly. The voice of democracy echoes round the globe. And creeps like you, Harold, dickless wonders like yourself, drive Volvo station-wagons to your houses in the Hamptons each weekend accompanied by wives whose greatest fear in life is cellulite and by children who will grow up to disappoint you. I want you to know, Harold, that in my opinion the better part of you ran down your father's leg. I also want you to know that when I issue an instruction that something be done I *expect* it to go off well.' He carefully separated the words Steiner himself had chosen. 'I require it. By and large, Harold, it's not negotiable. I wonder whether I might be getting through to you.' The voice was still quiet, apparently unruffled by anger.

Steiner kept silent, as he was required to do; in his mind though, he was repeating a litany of '*Shit shit shit shit shit. . . .*'

As if he were asking for the first time, Chadwick said: 'Who's this guy Deacon?'

'He used to be a cop. Next he had an investigation agency. He's a lush. The girl who shared an apartment with Lorimer – she retained him.' All as businesslike as he could make it. These details were in the papers Chadwick had been reading.

'Why did she do that?'

'It appears that she thought Lorimer's death suspicious.' It was like a classroom comprehension exercise.

'So perhaps it didn't go off that well, Harold. What do you think?'

Steiner struggled, looking for the right formula. 'There's reason to believe that he might prove useful.'

'Because he's looking for the person who killed Lorimer.'

'Yes.'

'As are we.'

'Yes.'

'It's a theory.' The way it was said made it sound more like a congenital defect. 'Only if he can be controlled.'

'We don't anticipate problems in that area.'

'That's good to hear, Harold. That's terrific news.' Chadwick steepled his hands and rested his chin on his thumbs. 'Let me tell you what worries me. If he concludes that Lorimer's death wasn't misadventure, then he's going to be looking for a motive, wouldn't you say? I mean, I might have got this wrong but, as I recall, motive plays a pretty big part in that sort of an investigation.'

'There's no possibility. . . .'

'And Laura Scott works in that bank, doesn't she? In fact she's a programmer, isn't she?'

He knew the names and what they meant. Steiner wasn't surprised by that. 'Deacon might make suppositions, but we've sanitized those aspects.'

'Have we . . . ?' Chadwick lowered his head as if speaking to himself. 'Have we?' For a moment he seemed lost in thought. Then: 'Now, tell me about Lady Cochlan.'

'Well, we're having trouble quantifying that factor. There are—'

Chadwick cut in. 'Do you have a secret yearning for a career in politics, Harold?'

116

'No.' Steiner looked nonplussed.

'Then, why do you talk like a fucking robot?'

'There are three—'

'Why do you do that, Harold?'

A pause. Chadwick smiled at his subordinate in a manner anyone would have taken for polite inquisitiveness.

'There are three possibilities. A connection between Lorimer and Lady Cochlan.'

Chadwick asked: 'We don't think that, do we, Harold?'

'No.'

'Because our man would have told us, wouldn't he? Before killing Cochlan.'

'If he killed Cochlan. That's the second possibility – that he didn't.'

'Do the people in London have an opinion about that?'

'Yes. They think he did.'

'That's what I was led to believe. That's what it says in these notes, Harold.' Steiner wanted Chadwick to stop using his given name that way. Every second male in his family had borne the name – a tradition – and his stepfather had used it against him just as Chadwick was now; each childish misdemeanour had provoked the same sneering emphasis. 'Why did you do that, Har*old*? Don't think much of these grades, Har*old*.'

'So', Chadwick continued, 'what's the third possibility?'

Steiner was obliged to continue the game. He did his best not to sound like a little boy being encouraged to discover the correct answer to some mathematical calculation. 'That he did kill her and that there's no connection with Lorimer.'

'And why would he have done such a thing, Harold? What do you think?'

Steiner shrugged. The conclusion lay before him,

but he shrugged anyway. He'd made too many wrong moves in this session already.

'You know the answer,' Chadwick coaxed, 'and so do I. He did it because he damn well wanted to, Harold. I think this is very dangerous. I think we're in trouble with this one. I think we might have a nut on our hands.'

'It's possible.'

'That's right. It is. You just said so. And the idea doesn't make me at all happy.'

Chadwick got up from his desk and began to circumnavigate his office. Steiner didn't like it that Chadwick was behind him. He felt that, if he turned round, that would be the precise moment in which Chadwick would return to his desk, leaving Steiner facing the wrong way. He sat still, waiting, facing front. He looked at the empty chair. Chadwick seemed to be away for a long time. Finally, he spoke. Steiner turned to find the other man looking directly at him, his back to the vast sheet of plate glass on the south side of the office; he gave the impression of a man who had been impatiently waiting for someone to pay attention.

He said: 'This is a very delicate operation.'

'I know that—' Steiner began. Chadwick talked over him.

'Big stakes, big risks.' Now he paused, seeming to expect some contribution. Steiner was outboxed; he said nothing. 'I don't want it fucked up, Harold. I'm counting on you.'

'They're keeping tabs on Deacon: in case he's going to be useful to us. Give us a lead. Otherwise, he's harmless.'

'A lush.'

'Right.'

'He started to hit the bottle when his wife died. Well, you know that, Harold. His wife's name was Henderson. Margaret Henderson.'

118

'Yes.'

'Well-connected people, Harold. Old money. Rich liberals, do-gooders. You know the type. It makes me edgy. Show them Plymouth Rock, they'll show you the footsteps of their ancestors. Kneejerk Democrats. They make me sick. Edgy and sick. A couple of days' drive from here, some people whose wages I pay are doing dangerous things. They're a long way from home. More important than that, the company has a lot of money riding on this thing. A lot.'

Steiner opened his mouth to reply, but Chadwick waved a hand at him, vaguely gesturing towards the door. 'OK, Harold,' he said and turned his back.

Steiner made no sound as he left. Chadwick looked out on the elegant towers. What he saw was more to him than the skyline of New York. He saw energy, like a live network of golden lines, strung between the buildings. He saw, as an emperor might see it, a shining city, charged by the power of an élite, fuelled by money. Whole walls gleamed brilliantly where the sun struck back off the glass. White and gold. The spires of Byzantium.

14

Carole Blane was tall and pretty and blonde. She had good legs and a slender waist, and she helped the blondeness, just a little, with streaks that gave her long hair a tawny look. Just to make everything copybook, she also had large breasts.

Men stopped to stare when Carole passed by in the street. Some even stopped and turned round to stare, though few did that when they were walking with their wives because Carole was the kind of girl who made them feel automatically guilty. For some reason, because she looked the way she did, they assumed that she would go to bed with them. Another assumption men tended to make about Carole was that she might not be too bright – the hair, the figure, the pretty face seemed to add up to that.

In fact Carole was happily married to a nice guy who fixed central heating systems, and she wouldn't have entertained the notion of being unfaithful to him. She'd got used to being stared at, she'd got used to fending off free-floating hands at the office Christmas party, she'd got used to hearing all sorts of offers and suggestions that she had no intention of taking up.

Unfortunately Carole didn't escape the stereotype in all respects. She was very attractive and very faithful, but she wasn't too bright.

Laura was standing by the printer waiting for some material to show when Carole walked over to her. Like every secretary in the place, Carole saw no distinction

120

between a programmer and a computer engineer. It was enough that someone used the machine to make Carole believe that the same person could fix it: like expecting every driver to be able to repair and tune a car. She was holding a printout, which she thrust at Laura.

'There's something wrong with the computer,' she said. 'Look.'

Laura took the paper and read the memo that had come off Carole's word-processor. She recognized the prissy phraseology; it was that of Tom Buxton, the manager. The memo had something to do with stationery. She looked at Carole. 'I can't see—'

'No. Here.' Carole turned the paper over. 'There's other stuff on the back.'

There were five sheets in all, each of them overprinted. Laura had spread them out on the floor.

'How?' Deacon had asked.

'I should have thought of it. People use anything to print on. It's often the case that someone will send something to the printer as back-up, then decide it's not needed. The sheets are used like scrap paper, especially when the material isn't going to be stored or referred to again. Kate ran a few copies of her trace and simply left them at the printer. If she kept one, it's gone now – stolen . . . whatever. But these were simply waiting there in a pile of other data. Somebody shoved them in. They came up on the back of a secretary's memo. She thought the computer had gone haywire.'

'You've looked at it – the trace.'

'Yes.'

'And?'

'It's an exchange program: one currency to another. The sort of thing that's completely standard in a bank like ours; from time to time, an updated or more efficient program is devised. Kate wrote this one about three months ago. It would have taken that long for the repeated trace to gum up the works.'

'So it's been in use?'

'Oh, yes. It went to public as soon as Kate was happy with it.'

'And?'

'As I say: it's standard; a means for converting currencies. This isn't a lending bank we're talking about. You need better than fifty grand to get in the door. We don't clear cheques: they go to one of the high-street banks. Suppose a client wants to change some of his cash holdings into another currency – he's heard that the exchange rate is going to benefit him; or he needs a hundred thousand pounds in Swiss francs or kruggerrands for some reason. He calls and asks for the exchange to be made. The program does the work. I've written similar stuff myself. This is a particularly efficient version – Kate was good at her job. It's got everything it needs. Only trouble is, it's got that and a little more.' Deacon peered at the sheets, trying to find the wild card. 'Just here,' Laura pointed.

'You'll have to tell me.'

'The computer is programmed with the exchange rate for the day. What Kate asked it to do was to find that rate for a given currency and make the conversion. But there's a command here that modifies that instruction. The rate is being adjusted to favour the bank. Only by a very small amount, but adjusted none the less. Between the rate the customer *should* have got and the rate he's being given, money is being shaved. In effect, the program says: "Find the exchange rate, adjust it slightly and keep the change."'

'Keep it where?'

'That's the most interesting part. It's being paid into another account.'

'An account in your bank?'

'Yes.'

'Whose?'

'Twin Wake. It's a company name. Off the shelf, most like. Quite meaningless: it might as well be John Doe.'

'Someone must know.'

'Not necessarily. You walk into a bank with a few grand to deposit and say your name's Judas Iscariot: they'll take it and print your cheque-books for you. If anyone knows, it'll be Buxton. No reason why he should, though.'

Deacon moved the sheets around, as if a different angle might bring enlightenment. 'Trace,' he murmured. 'So this is what puzzled Kate.'

'This, yes. . . .' Laura had been sitting cross-legged on the floor. Now she got up and started across the room. 'Can I have a drink?'

'You don't have to ask.'

'It's not that. . . .' She paused near the drinks-table.

He smiled. 'You wonder whether it mightn't be tactless.' She waited. 'Look,' he said, 'it's there all the time. No point in having a booze-free house unless you live in a town with booze-free pubs, booze-free off-licences. I look at it every day. I confess that I started my trip on the wagon by pouring a couple of bottles of Scotch down the sink. Even while I was doing it, it seemed a pointless gesture. A bit like making a promise that you know you don't have to keep.'

Laura poured herself two fingers of Scotch and added a squirt of soda, then went back to sit with him on the floor. 'This' – she picked up her previous remark – 'but something would have puzzled her more.'

'How it happened.'

'More accurately, who did it. And, before you ask, the answer's "No". There are two other programmers. It's out of the question. This isn't just a matter of someone with a hand in the till. Apart from which, I know them both; I've worked with them—'

'The Yorkshire Ripper had a wife,' Deacon said.

'No, John. I'm positive.'

'OK. You tell me.'

Laura thought for a moment. She put her head in her hands so that only her eyes and the tip of her nose were visible and her hair hung over her wrists. A curiously childish gesture; it was fetching. 'Someone with access. Someone who can program. Someone who has been given specific instructions. Someone who's been told about the exchange-rate program.'

'Someone with access.' Deacon selected the qualification that really mattered.

Laura followed his line of reasoning. 'I'm sure that what you're thinking is logical. But I spend all day with those people. Have done for some time. To someone who doesn't know them – in this case, you – it seems the most likely conclusion. But no. I'm not suggesting that either of them is above putting his private mail in the out-tray or using the office phone to make a theatre booking. . . . You've trusted my instinct before. Believe me.'

'Who knew enough to interpret the word "trace" in Kate's diary?' Deacon asked. 'And possessed the knowledge necessary to gain access to her personal file, then obtain the programs and interpret them? Who was able to be at a VDU after banking hours – apparently working late – and come home with a ream of printouts? Who spotted the aberration in this' – he gestured at the sheets on the floor – 'and knew what it meant?'

'Yes,' she said. 'It *ought* to be one of the other programmers. It's not.'

'But someone with access.'

'OK.' Laura pushed her hair behind her ears, then put her palms flat to her cheeks once more. 'It can't be that difficult. Not during working hours. No opportunity. Someone who can program, though I don't know he can. She can. No one knows. So someone who's employed in some other capacity.'

'And someone, what's more, who's there spec-
ifically to doctor this program. A secretary,' Deacon
offered, 'a cashier—'
'We don't have cashiers. I've told you: it's not that
kind of—'
'An accountant, a – what else is there? I don't—'
'Clerks, assistant managers, Buxton. . . .'
'Buxton.'
'He can't program.'
'Says who?'
'I know he can't. I've watched his eyes glaze over.
He's a manager. This is the point, John. We're talking
about someone who *can* do what I did when I jem-
mied Kate's file, who *can* understand what the program does and has the skills to change it. You can't
muddle along; you have to learn it, practise it, be
involved with it. That's why the logical culprit would
be one of the other programmers.'
'But then you're positive—'
'Yes, I am; but the problem is that no one else has daytime access to the computer. A clerk, a secretary couldn't
simply sit down at a VDU and start to tinker with it, or be
there after hours without arousing suspicion; especially
if they were in the programmers' department. To begin
with, the security guards—' She stopped.
'The security guards,' Deacon repeated. 'Or the
office cleaners. You have office cleaners?'
'Yes.'
'Who are they?'
'I don't know.'
'Who supplies them? What agency?'
'I don't know.'
'What does any of them look like?'
Laura shook her head.
'How do you recognize them?'
She swallowed the last of her whisky. 'They have
vacuum cleaners.'

* * *

A woman's eight was sculling close to the towpath, their singlets dark with sweat. A man in an inflatable dinghy was calling the rhythm through a loud-hailer. Eight pairs of bare thighs jacked back to glistening shoulders, then straightened as the women leaned into the stroke. Noonday sun swamped the surface of the Thames and silvered the drops that shook from the broad blades.

'You're off your patch down here,' Deacon observed. The women were going for technique rather than for speed, and the two men could easily keep pace with the scull.

'It has its compensations.' Mayhew watched the rowers. 'Anyway, I'm on my lunch-break.' He was clutching a paper bag blotched with grease marks. 'You'd think there might be a bit of a breeze off the river.'

'Lady Olivia made *The Times*. A regretful paragraph.'

'Regrettable would be more accurate. So far as the noble lord is concerned. The funeral was discreet to the point of being surreptitious. I think he would have preferred it if she'd had a hunting accident. Wholly traditional: no whiff of scandal in that.'

'Will there be a scandal?'

'Nah. Lady Olivia's fondness for the bottle was no secret in Fleet Street; a couple of over-keen hacks were doorstepping at the country mansion for a couple of days, but. . . .' Mayhew shrugged.

'They were seen off,' Deacon guessed.

'Paid off, more like. Or someone had a quiet word with the paper's proprietor in one of the better Pall Mall clubs. That's how the fucking country's organized. A nod and a wink in the Athenaeum; a string pulled in White's. A share-price confirmed here, a seat on the board conceded there. Your security people are white as the driven snow, by the way.'

126

'Are you sure?'

'Yeah – ex-coppers to a man.'

'So what?'

'No,' Mayhew laughed, 'it just made running a check that bit easier.'

'A nod and a wink in the local boozer,' Deacon suggested.

'A string pulled in a nearby bookie's. Yes. I'm not too clear about what it is you need to know about them.' He was looking away to his right, where the women sweated and pulled. A slow gathering, knees to chin, as the blades feathered the water, then the legs snapping out, torsos flexed, everything synchronized, even the grunt of effort as the oars dug in. 'What are you looking for?'

'I wondered whether one of them might have been more than he seems.'

'Yes . . . well, that tells me a lot.'

'It's just an idea. . . .'

'Are you frightened of looking stupid, or are we both groping in the dark?'

Deacon paused, then said: 'A computer programmer.'

'A what?' Mayhew stopped walking. He began to laugh. 'As ex-coppers go, these are the common or garden variety, John. Computing a four-horse accumulator would probably make their brains hurt.'

'That's what I wanted to know.'

'This'll do.' They had reached a wooden bench that overlooked the river. Mayhew flopped down and opened his bag. A sausage sandwich on white bread. Holding the soggy sides together, he bit into the middle. 'What is it? Industrial espionage? Someone diddling the bank?'

'I'm not sure; it looks a bit that way.'

'Laura Scott figured this out?'

'Happened across it,' Deacon lied.

'So it might not have anything to do with Kate

Lorimer's death.' Mayhew's words came indistinctly through a mouthful of sandwich.

'It's all very vague.'

'Especially the way you tell it.'

A jogger went past on the path behind them, pitter-patter, tiny clouds of white dust rising from each heel like a cartoonist's effect to indicate speed. Mayhew snorted. 'He'll melt.' Then turned back to the river and went on with his lunch. The women had shipped oars and were taking a break, bent over their hands, heads low, their bowed backs heaving.

Deacon looked for a way of keeping Mayhew's trust without involving him too far. He said: 'Look, I've got sod all that's positive. You're right – even if there has been a bit of villainy at the bank, there's nothing that connects it to Kate Lorimer. And certainly not to the Cochlan woman. It seems as if there might have been some sort of fiddle going on. If I discover that there has, I'll give it to you if you want it. It's yours to do what you like with – trade with some cop on another patch, trade with the villain for something juicier. I don't mind. If there *is* a link with Lorimer, then I'll tell you that, too, and we can decide what to do about it at the time. As things stand, I pretty much *am* groping in the dark.' He meant some of what he said. There might well come a point when he'd need more help from Mayhew than he had a right to expect and, if that were the case, he'd have to give more in return.

Mayhew nodded, thumbing in the remnant of his sandwich. He chewed for a while, still looking out over the water. 'OK.' As if to demonstrate that a deal had been struck, he said: 'It's clear that the Cochlan business is going to be a conspiracy of silence, though maybe that's too grand a term. Those who know can see the connection all right – with Lorimer – but the message is to ignore it.'

'An unspoken message?' Deacon asked.

'More or less. D'Arblay wagged a finger and tried to

128

leave the impression that the whole business was being taken care of elsewhere.'

'Is it?'

Mayhew shook his head. 'Why should it be? What for? Even her husband thinks she got pissed and blacked out in the bath. What we have here is a three-monkey event: see no evil. . . . You know. And ask no questions.'

As if by common consent, they got up and began to walk on down the towpath. 'Not even of yourself?' Deacon wanted to know.

There were smears of grease on Mayhew's cheeks, close to his mouth. He walked with a coronet of flies just above his head. 'Of course. There's something there.' Mayhew paused. 'I guess I'm thinking what you're thinking. Maybe there is a connection between Cochlan and Lorimer, though Christ alone knows what it might be. That's what you're looking for, I imagine. If you find it, I'll be glad to share it with you. After that – like you said – I'll decide what to do with it; if anything. Maybe there's no link, apart from the fact that they died in just the same way.'

'Were killed by the same—'

'Yeah. I mean, the link could be something as simple as they were getting screwed by the same guy. He conned them, or whatever. Was Lorimer rich?'

'No.'

'Well – I don't know – but it's often something like that, isn't it? Especially in Cochlan's world. Some toffee-nosed cow starts putting out for a piece of rough trade. Money changes hands – he claims to know of a nifty investment or two, or else he's giving her so much of what she likes that she's prepared to dip into her bank account sooner than lose him. Then there's a cash-flow problem that hubby gets to hear about, or the stud puts the bite on a bit too hard, so the lady crosses her legs and threatens to yell copper. Fucking the help is frowned on, but it's a misdemeanour compared to selling the family silver. The only way out for lover-boy is to try to arrange an accident. I've seen it before. Some broker's wife, a year or so ago' – he searched for the name – 'Beattie, got nudged off a cliff in Scotland. Turned out she'd been having the boots put to her by some little toe-rag who'd bought himself a suit and a new accent – had a string of women from Beauchamp Place to Belgrave Square. He managed to convince her that he knew just the man to perform a quick in-and-out deal with a spare ten thousand quid she happened to have lying around. He knew that she'd be a trifle unhappy when the money didn't come back, but guessed that she'd keep her mouth shut and put it down to experience. He guessed wrong. She decided to have him done, and bugger the consequences. So he stiff-armed her off a high place.' Mayhew flapped a hand above his head as if he were waving to someone. The flies buzzed and rose, then descended and continued to weave their little black halo.

'It's difficult to put Lorimer in that kind of a daisy-chain,' Deacon said.

'Sure. I don't know. I'm rehearsing ideas. Cochlan doesn't bank at—?'

'No.'

'No . . . well, you'd have thought of that first off.'

'So would you.'

Mayhew looked sideways at him, scarcely turning his head. 'Yeah. OK. Just testing.'

'But if nothing puts Cochlan and Lorimer together?' Deacon decided to let the other man's deception pass. Noted it, though. He wasn't annoyed or surprised. Mayhew was bound to be curious.

'Ah. Well, if that's the case, then something very nasty is going on. It's impossible to keep quiet about that sort of thing. Do you remember that string of deaths – started in Bristol?'

Deacon nodded. Four scientists, each working for an electronics company, each involved in some way with confidential government contracts, had died violently within a couple of months of each other. Two were put down as suicides. In one case, a guy had apparently tied his own hands and hanged himself from a bridge. The official statement claimed that he'd been manifesting signs of serious depression; unfortunately his family maintained that he'd been living a life of uninterrupted contentment. Anyone could make a significant and sinister connection between the men. Even so, the police investigation bogged down in a month and the whole business was forgotten within two.

'Even something like that can be choked off,' Mayhew observed, 'but there's no ignoring a psycho. If it's that, then I'll give you a penny to a pinch of dog-shit that Lorimer wasn't the first.'

'And Cochlan won't be the last.'

'Damn right. So, sooner or later, D'Arblay will be pulling two files out of his drawer; and there'll be some red faces in the Athenaeum.'

The scull came up alongside them as they walked. The man with the loud-hailer was putting the women through their paces, calling a brisk stroke-rate. The bow-wave glittered and fell; there was an audible hiss.

A pleasure-craft stiff with tourists went by, chopping out broad troughs of backwash that raced towards the bank. The women ignored them, hauling on the oars and arrowing the toothpick of a boat through the rough water before it had time to yaw.

'Do you think it's that?' Mayhew asked.

'I wonder.'

'Because there's something you'd need to think about. Something crucial. Something basic. A piece of knowledge that anyone faced with a series of random killings must have.'

'How the victims are selected,' Deacon said. 'I know.'

Mayhew turned on the path, an abrupt about-face. 'Time to get back.' They walked in silence for a while. 'How far do you plan to go with this, John?'

'It depends what I find, I suppose.'

'Does it?' asked Mayhew. 'Maybe it depends rather more on what finds you.'

You go through a door, and it shuts behind you. Then another door, which shuts. Along corridors, down flights of stairs. A third door. A fourth. Soon you're lost in the house. Rooms beyond rooms, each one more difficult to get back from.

They crossed Hammersmith Bridge. On the north side, crowds of people sat at trestle tables or lounged on the walkway; the riverside pubs had never been busier.

'Spruce,' Mayhew said as he unlocked his car. 'They're in Soho; Dean Street, I think. They're in the book.'

The office cleaning agency. Deacon said: 'Thanks, Phil.'

'OK.' Mayhew got in and gunned the engine. Without looking back, he swung the wheel and pulled straight out into a line of cars. A girl driving a red VW yelled inaudibly and stood on her brake; the long blast on the horn was an afterthought.

Rooms beyond rooms, Deacon thought. On an impulse, he returned to the bridge and walked halfway across, stopping there to watch the river traffic.

A shadowy house, ill-lit, the air inside motionless and heavy and bearing a sour smell. He pictured it. He saw himself going towards the door, stepping into the dim hallway. The rankness flared his nostrils. And the place had an unearthly stillness about it.

He knew that deadness in the air. Laura had described it when she told him how she'd discovered

Kate's body. Deacon's imaginings took him to the end of the hallway and up to another door.

He suspected that whatever he was looking for lay further back in the house than he wanted to go.

15

The phone rang, but when she picked it up no one spoke. There was just a faint wash of static, like the sound that turns in the convolution of a conch when you put it to your ear and imagine you can hear the sea. She said, 'Hello,' and waited, then said it again. Nothing. After a moment she hung up.

Crossing the room had taken her close to the cupboard where the drinks were kept, so she gave herself a small whisky and added a splash of water from the kitchen tap. When she came back into the living-room, the phone rang again. A distant beach, slow surf; but no voice. As she put the receiver down, she smiled ruefully. Someone was being defeated by technology.

She sat down, took her book from the arm of the chair and read a paragraph. The phone rang. She said, 'Damn,' softly, setting the book aside.

'Hello? Hello . . .?' There was a note of resignation in her voice. She spoke louder, as if she might overcome the fault on the line by making a greater effort, and waited a little longer to give the countless miles of wire and junction boxes a better chance. Eventually, she gave up.

She took two more silent calls before it occurred to her to worry.

On the sixth occasion she said nothing. It was different. The idea that someone on another phone somewhere was deliberately staying quiet made the susurration of static sinister; it seemed laden by the weight of things that were not being said. She waited until the dialling tone came and put the phone down, but didn't move away from it. She knew it would ring again, and it did.

It was at once eerie and ridiculous, two people with an open line between them and neither making a sound. Like two blind people suddenly and deliberately turning to face one another.

After a while the violence in that repression defeated her. She said: 'Who is it?' A pause, then: 'Who's there? What do you want?' Another pause. 'What's going on?'

She imagined for a moment that she had heard something, the hiss of muted laughter, but it was nothing more than the electronic voice of the circuit. 'What do you want?' she asked. 'OK, I'm putting the phone down, then I'm going to take it off the hook, so don't bother calling this number again.'

There was no right thing to say. The threat punched energy into the circuit. The threat of banishment that separates the lover from the object of desire.

The voice was a whisper, coaxing and mellifluous; impossible to guess whether a man's or a woman's. 'Laura . . . Laura. Do you know who I am? No, of course' – the voice gave her no time to answer – 'of course you don't. But I know you, Laura. I know many things about you. I know – '

'Who is this?'

' – where you live and what you look like and what you wear. I like – '

'What do you—'

' – the yellow dress, the sleeveless one. Is it a favourite of yours? You often have it on, Laura, it's pretty, you look so pretty, with your hair tied back that way behind your scarf, I saw you at the window, Laura, just a day or two ago, you looked out, it was evening, the lamp-light was on your hair, making it glow, it was very quiet in the street outside your

135

house, I almost thought, almost imagined you might lean out and speak to me, we seemed so close, if you had spoken I would have heard you, there would have been no need to shout, and if I'd answered you'd have heard me, too, everything was so still, as if we had been standing next to one another, you leaned a moment on the window-sill, do you remember? Your arms straight, your body curved between them, your head raised, looking away from me, looking upwards, like someone . . . like a swimmer turning underwater and striking for the surface, I looked at you – '

'Who – what do you want?'

The voice held her, what the voice was saying held her, as if she were listening to a story, like a child wanting the end, but wanting the telling, too. The hushed, almost monotonal whisper was perfectly pitched for the tale it was telling; its gentleness, its even measure promised malevolence.

' – framed in the light from the window, like Rapunzel, like the prisoner in the uppermost room, are you wearing the dress, Laura, the yellow dress? I'd like to think that you're wearing it now, I followed you, you didn't know I was there, in the street and I stood close to you, just behind you when you stopped to buy a paper and then on the Tube, you didn't know, among the crush of people – I was there, it was so hot, wasn't it hot? – and I could see tiny droplets of moisture caught in the fine hairs at the corner of your mouth, Laura, that close, that close . . . are you wearing it, the yellow dress? If I came to you now, if I stood outside and you went across to the window, would I see you in the yellow dress? If I were outside your door, if I rang the bell – '

That was the story. Of course it was. *And the Prince came to the dark tower where the maiden was imprisoned. . . .*

' – would you be there, wearing the yellow dress? Isn't it strange? You don't know me at all and I know you so well, I think about you, Laura, I think about you often, and I dream such dreams of you, I dreamed, oh – not long ago this dream, that you were ill, you came to me, I was the surgeon, and I changed you, you changed under my hand, it only took a touch, I touched you, that was all I had to do, I could feel my own power and I touched you on the place where you were ill – '

She put the phone down. She was trembling. She felt empty – scooped out – as if she were terribly hungry or terribly tired. Her face was wet, so she must have been crying, though she hadn't known it. There was a dull ache in her wrist and forearm, and the fingers of the hand that had gripped the phone felt numb and cramped. Movement was beyond her. She stood still, registering a tension that bound the room like a membrane lining the walls, taut as a drumskin, where the whisper still circled and echoed.

When the phone rang, her hand went out to it.

' – I do think of you, Laura, I think of you often, I imagine you in your flat, going from room to room, the night when I stood outside I knew I would see you, I knew that just by being there I could draw you to the window, I knew you wouldn't disappoint me, Laura, and there you were, leaning on the sill, the light catching your hair – '

The Prince to the Dark Tower came. . . .

' – and afterwards I could still see you, after I'd left I could still see you, going from room to room, in the bedroom, in the bathroom, oh – I thought of you that day, going into the bathroom, when you got back, when Kate was there – '

One moment she was listening; the next the phone was back on its cradle; between was a black gap.

She was swaying, both hands on the phone, her arms stiff and bearing down, as if she had caught some lethal creature and couldn't let go of the lid of the trap. Oddly, her mind was clear. She knew what to do

137

next. For a short while, she stayed still as if time had to elapse during which the creature would suffocate. Then she lifted the phone and reached out to dial a number.

' – I've wondered, Laura, I've wondered what she looked like. Can you tell me? – I've wondered whether she looked as she did when I left her, I've wondered what you did and what you thought, I've watched you, in my mind's eye, opening the bathroom door and going in—'

'Who are you?' Her voice was hoarse; she gagged on her own fear. 'What do you want of me?'

And, because she had asked, the voice gave her an answer. What the voice wanted, what it wanted to do, how badly it wanted to do it. The voice mentioned the yellow dress, it mentioned her hair; it mentioned her face and her body and what would happen and how it would feel, inch by inch, moment by moment, it dazed her with imaginings and she listened, rapt, a child lost in the story, and the voice continued, a low chant, now and then saying her name – *Laura . . . Laura . . . Laura* – like a blessing.

When her doorbell rang, she simply pressed the button to release the lock. It didn't matter. Whoever arrived would be the person she needed now. The moment wasn't hers to control.

When Deacon came into the room, she looked at him blankly at first, then her mouth opened and she half-lifted a hand, as if he were beginning to grow in her view – a figure advancing and coming into focus.

She made a noise, far back in her throat, then more sharply. She looked like someone who wakes to find that she has walked, in her sleep, to the edge of a very high cliff. Deacon kept his distance; he didn't speak.

One step, stumbling, towards the brink, then another, arms outstretched, in the hope that he would see how high the drop was, how far she had to fall. Then she walked into air, seeming to turn as she floated off the cliff, her limbs loose with shock, before he caught her, his arms hauling her in.

the light from the open door beyond her; she had to pull
two sheets, working free and swimming to him, as one
wants to the child to pass herself with shock before
he could tell his parting smile.

16

Laura cried for a long while.

If he moved, she moved with him, terrified of losing touch. He went to make coffee, and she followed him, standing close while he collected cups and filled the kettle. Later, after she had begun to find her voice, he went to the window to look out into the street, and she followed him there, putting herself behind him and just to one side so that she stood out of the light.

As time passed, she told him more and more, starting and stopping, piecing together fragments of the story that she'd listened to on the phone. And, as she told it, she came to see that it wasn't a story. A story is the past and has an ending. What she had heard was a promise.

Deacon held her while she told him what the voice had promised. After that, she slept for half an hour, propped against him, exhausted by the recollection. When she woke, she started and grabbed his arm as if he had moved a crucial inch or two away. He could feel the fear stringing her muscles tight, and since there was no other solution, since there was nothing left to be said or done, she followed him again into the bedroom, and stood while he undressed her, keeping close while he undressed himself, and held him tightly while he entered her, winding her legs around to press him closer still.

She cried out and bucked her hips, wanting him as deep as he could go. Her legs were scissored on his back. Their arms circled and gripped. They were baled up together but, even so, she banged up at him and swayed from side to side, passion and fear all one thing, as if she were someone possessed. As if he were her exorcist.

The sun was high and hot and shining on the green bedroom curtains to fill the room with an underwater glow. Deacon was dreaming about the house.

It stood in the middle of a forest and was surrounded by thick briar. In one moment he was outside, looking at stone gable-ends and mullioned windows; in the next he was inside, where it was perpetual dusk, and dusty so that his lips felt caked. There was a faint repetitive noise. When he attended to it, he knew it to be the percussion of doors closing, one after the other, as if the sound of his passage through the house had been delayed and was only now becoming audible. A playback; a reminder. Before him was another door. Before he could reach it, he sensed something and stopped. At first, all he registered was a presentiment of danger, reacting as an animal does when instinct precedes knowledge. It was a smell, harsh and hot, that lodged in his throat and rasped his sinuses. He turned towards it and, though he could see no evidence, knew at once what it was. The house was on fire.

Fear sprang him from the dream. He woke with a great leap, as if someone had laid electrodes to his chest, and looked round frantically for an instant before the green glow reassured him. His first rational thought was: What now?

The pick-ups, the random girls he'd had since Maggie's death, had entered and gone from his life without leaving a trace. He didn't know their names; he couldn't remember their faces or voices. There wouldn't have been time, even if he'd been looking for them, to discover those characteristics by which we come to identify people. The fact was that he'd worked hard to avoid such things.

141

What had happened with Laura the previous evening worried him. He knew that it would be possible to isolate the incident, to make it depend on the phone calls and Laura's terror – an evening that had been nudged sideways from reality, when neither of them had acted as they'd intended to and so couldn't be held accountable. Leave at once. Make no reference to it now or later. Be unavailable for a couple of days and then – not frostiness, but something casual, chummy, but clearly at arm's length. None of this, of course, would have anything to do with what Laura might feel or need, but the technique could only operate out of that sort of callousness – other people's pain is other people's pain. The rejected have their own methods: hibernation, guilt, self-hatred.

What worried Deacon was not whether he could starve the moment and let it die, but whether he wanted to. He thought back to Laura sitting on the floor in Kate's bedroom, clutching the picture postcard of Greece, and weeping. Deacon had held her while she cried, but not because he had to. He knew that their lovemaking had been an extension of that gesture, and knew that he didn't regret it. His difficulty was in separating pity from desire. He'd spent so long pitying himself.

There was no sound of Laura, though he assumed she must be somewhere in the flat. The muffled thrum of traffic wound upwards from the street; otherwise there was silence. He remembered the dream and in the moment of remembering caught a trace of the stench that had woken him. A smell of burning.

He went along the hallway, moving fast, and into the living-room. Laura was naked, crouching before the open grate. Great ropes of yellow flame were being hauled up the chimney by the draught; she'd helped the fire along with something – turpentine, perhaps, or methylated spirit. She prodded at the seat of the

142

flames with a kitchen knife. She was either too intent on her task to notice Deacon or too intent to acknowledge him. He went closer and peered over her shoulder, but still she didn't look round.

She was burning a dress in the grate, though it was difficult, at first, to be sure of that because the material was the same colour as the flames.

17

On one side was the best delicatessen in London. On the other was a peepshow.

Men with bad memories thumbed in coins and peered through a letter-box as the light came on: rows and rows of bodiless unblinking eyes. There was music. A tired girl appeared in a cubicle and waved her crotch, then turned round, bent forward and waved her arse. She made her tits bounce. She pushed a finger up herself. She looked away to where another light had come on in another cubicle. The men built fantasies in which they were brutal and tireless and the girl really wanted them. Their memories were as bad as that.

Between the deli and the meat-market was a narrow door that let on to five flights of stairs. Spruce was at the top. There was a small. outer office. On a desk was a typewriter, a phone, a Rolodex, tissues, nail varnish, and a copy of *Cosmopolitan*. Deacon went through and opened a further door. A man was sitting behind a somewhat larger desk eating one of the deli's salt beef sandwiches. He peered round Deacon at the empty room beyond and sighed, then put the sandwich aside and stood, hand extended. 'Cotterell,' he said. A tall man, though his bulk made it less evident. His blond hair was thin, and his smile revealed wide gaps between his teeth. He gestured towards the outer office. 'She comes and goes. Her habits are a mystery to me.' Deacon sat down in an upright black leather chair opposite the desk. 'People usually phone,' Cotterell went on. 'Our operatives go straight to the contract from their homes. How many square metres do you have?'

'No metres, no contract,' Deacon told him. 'I'm not here to give you a job.'

Cotterell sighed again. 'You're the filth, are you?'

Deacon had a card. Underneath his name was the word *Enquiries*.

Cotterell glanced at it and passed it back. 'I don't have to talk to you.'

'That's right. I don't have to talk to the police.'

'Shit.' Cotterell picked up the sandwich and took a bite, then waved it, backhanded, a gesture that meant *So get on with it*. He didn't seem to doubt that Deacon might have something to talk to the police about.

'Where do you get your people?'

'Advertise.'

'You interview them?' Cotterell nodded. 'You have files on them?'

'Files. A phone number, maybe; an address, a National Insurance number.'

'Yes?' Deacon cocked an eyebrow.

'OK – *sometimes* a National Insurance number. What's the problem here?'

'They come and go, I imagine.'

Cotterell shrugged. 'Some new faces, some old. I've got a few people who've been with me for better than five years.'

'But not many.'

'It's casual labour, not a lifetime's work. I get moon-lighters and people who just happen to need extra cash for some reason. They pay off the talleyman or the bookie; they don't come back. Would you make a career out of cleaning other people's lavatories?'

'Where do you get your contracts?'

'Advertise.'

'Who interviews you?'

'No one. I supply impeccable references on very classy headed notepaper. The guys go in, they hoover, they dust, they empty wastepaper-bins, they put bleach down the lav. For this they don't need qualifications. What – a PhD in disinfecting? Look, I'm asking you, what is this?'

'You see some villains.'

'Sure.'

'Some opportunists.'

'Of course.' Deacon left the question unspoken. 'No.' Cotterell assured him, shaking his head to add emphasis. 'It's a mug's game. I'm clean; the business is clean. A little black-economy labour, maybe. What do I care if a guy's drawing unemployment benefit?'

'You care because you make more of a profit: lower pay, no employer's contributions, less paperwork.'

Cotterell waved that away. 'Whatever . . . I spot a villain, I show him the door.'

'Do you always spot them?'

'I've never had any complaints.' Cotterell swallowed the last of the salt beef, then unwound a paper-clip and began to pick at the gap between his front teeth. 'That's it, pal. Tell me what you want or fuck off.'

Deacon named the bank and found that he suddenly had the other man's complete attention. 'Oh, Christ,' Cotterell groaned. 'A fucking bank.' The improvised toothpick jutted from beneath his upper lip. He appeared to have forgotten it was there. 'I thought you were going to tell me that someone had been nicking office stationery or had it away with a word-processor.'

Deacon shook his head: *No*.

'No.' Cotterell paused for thought; after a moment he looked less worried. 'No, because if that was it I *would* be talking to the filth, wouldn't I?' He looked at Deacon and continued to worry the fragment of food in his teeth. He was sizing up the issue and sizing up the man. He said: 'Go on, then.'

'You don't want to know,' said Deacon. 'If I told you what it was, you'd piss on the floor. You're talking to me because I *do* know about it. The police don't; neither does the bank. As far as I'm concerned, things can stay that way. In fact you'd better pray that it does or your little business is likely to have the long-term prospects of a snowball in hell; that's to say nothing of what the Inland Revenue would turn up. You forget that you've seen me, and I'll be more than happy to do the same for you. How many regulars at the bank?'

'All of them; all the guys are regulars. A job like that?'

'You service many contracts of that sort?'

'A few, yes.'

'Always using regulars.'

'Always. I wouldn't put casual labour into a bank. Casuals go to magazines, small stores – like that. I never put together a workforce of new employees anyway. There have to be a couple of guys who know the ropes.'

'If someone goes sick—'

Cotterell worked the paper-clip up and down until it came free. He said, 'Shit,' this time speaking softly. A concession; a realization. He took a ring-backed folder from his desk-drawer and began to leaf through a wad of work-sheets. He stopped briefly at one of them, before continuing to the end. Then he began at the beginning again. As before, he paused only once. 'We're talking about this year?'

'This year,' Deacon agreed.

Cotterell had kept a finger in the page. He glanced down once more, then pulled a narrow wooden file-box towards him and turned the cards over until he found what he wanted. He extracted a card and handed it to Deacon.

Ambrose Jackson. An address. No phone number.

'Just a week,' Cotterell told him. 'I don't remember the guy, but I remember what happened. One of the regulars was a friend of this Jackson. They went drinking together. The other guy got drunk, fell over,

147

cracked his head on the kerbside. Jackson turned up with the news late the next afternoon.' His mouth turned down. 'Too late for me to start switching people from other jobs, now that I come to think of it. He said he was looking for a bit of moonlighting: HP to pay on a car – something like that. When he quit, I figured he must have had a win on the dogs or something. Anyway, nothing unusual. Some stick, many don't.'

Deacon had memorized the details on the card. He handed it back. 'Keep it, for Christ's sake,' said Cotterell. 'I never met the son of a bitch.'

The secretary was still missing from the outer office. As Deacon made for the far door, Cotterell called after him: 'Good luck, pal.' No response was needed – the remark had been entirely sardonic, and Deacon knew why.

Ambrose Jackson's address was in the ghetto.

The BMW had been a write-off. Fast lane, a container-truck; there hadn't been much left. Deacon could have had any car he'd wanted, so, perversely, he'd chosen a basic Suzuki jeep. When he came to analyse the choice, he realized that it was the vehicle least like a luxury saloon. In the city, though, it was a lot more noticeable. He parked in the dreary streets of no man's land, close to the pub where he'd met Mayhew, and began to walk in from there.

There wasn't a wall round the ghetto, but there might as well have been.

First, there was a narrow belt of buffer streets that the police called the front line. It was the place for raids and skirmishes. It was where the deals went down: coke, smack, hash. It was usual that at any one time, night or day, there'd be as many as fifty pushers in the space of three or four streets. Mostly, the police would bust the buyers, following them clear of the area before making an arrest. Any action that directly involved the pushers could easily wind up looking like a race riot, and no one wanted that; it dragged in people that neither the ghetto nor the police wanted: newspapermen, television reporters, sociologists, politicians – the outside world. The war on the front line was a private one. Both sides preferred to lick their wounds and bury their dead in secret, though now and then some zealous new boy with more pips on his shoulder than brains in his head would get religion and order in the troops. The last time, it had started out with a paddy-wagon, a dozen arrests and a broken head or two and wound up full riot-gear, petrol-bombs, baton charges and four dead.

After the buffer-zone came the first streets of the ghetto, run-down redbrick houses that had once been part of a respectable Victorian suburb, though the only evidence left of that was in the street-names, the work of some long-dead poetry-lover: Milton, Spenser, Dryden, Cowper. These were the outskirts, but from there you could see the centre, the keep – a complex of high-rise blocks connected by a labyrinth of walkways that went from ground-level to upwards of a hundred feet.

The blocks were constructed on concrete stilts. Some days the wind-tunnel effect was enough to blow people over. At night, the spaces beneath the buildings were useful for revenge killings, gang rapes, and dog fights that usually had at least a grand riding on the outcome.

The flats had started to come to pieces within five years of being built. Plaster cracked and sagged, window-frames bled gouts of rust down outside walls, ceiling-paper grew mushy with damp. The lifts never worked. The stairs were as bleak as factory catwalks. When your neighbour played his radio you shared every note.

The blocks had been designed by architects who

lived in five-bedroom houses surrounded by a few acres of garden. The architects were white. If there were white people in the ghetto, no one had ever seen them.

The ghetto had its laws, but they didn't apply outside. By the same token, outside laws were meaningless in the ghetto. Deacon knew he was in a foreign country. His only advantage was that he was behaving irrationally. If he'd been a tourist – curious or strayed – he'd have looked like one. A buyer wouldn't have ventured further than no man's land. A dealer from another district, looking for wholesale supplies, would have sent word. A poacher would have come mob-handed. And if Deacon had been a copper there would have been two of him or more. His chance of getting through lay in the likelihood that they wouldn't know what to make of him.

Ambrose Jackson's address was close to the high-rise sanctum. The top flats in most of the blocks had been letting rainwater for years, and the city authorities had moved the people out. The empty rooms made perfect sniper-galleries in times of siege. When things were quieter, kids would go there with crossbows. It wasn't just one army in the ghetto; there were several. Often the warfare was internecine, and the empty flats were important vantage-points at all times. Deacon worked hard at not looking up. He walked neither too slowly nor too fast, and tried to leave the impression of someone who knew exactly where he was going.

The house was two streets away from the centre. A scabrous three-storey terrace of flaking brick and boarded windows, enlivened only by a chain of graffiti that ran the length of the ground-floor flats: black warriors coming at you head-on, bristling with weaponry, silhouettes delivering roundhouse kicks, slogans, tag-names. A slim bottle, cleverly copied, tapered away to become a syringe, underneath the carefully scripted legend *Things go better with coke*.

To have looked for a bell-push would have been

pointless: like waiting at the edge of a jungle for someone to come and collect your calling-card. Deacon opened the door and walked straight in. He knew that he hadn't gone unseen. Groups of youths were hanging out on most corners – the ghetto's security patrols. They didn't go to school, and there wasn't a school in the city that missed them or had anything to teach them. By the time they were ten, they knew all they needed to know.

Inside, the jungle closed in: steam-heat, a rank stench of mildew and rot and cooking odours like layers of fog. There was a dark corridor and two doors, one with fractured panels. As Deacon advanced, the door opened and a man came to the threshold and leaned against the jamb. He was wearing cutaway jeans; a thin gold chain undulated over his pectorals. He raised a beer-can to his mouth, and his biceps popped.

'Ambrose Jackson,' Deacon said.

'Say what?'

'Do you know Ambrose Jackson?'

'Sure. 'e ain't 'ere.'

'Is that right?' said Deacon.

The man took another slug of beer. 'That's what I'm sayin'.'

'How do I find him?'

'You know where you are, man?' He laughed. 'What you doin' up 'ere?'

'Looking for your friend Ambrose.'

'What you wantin' 'im for?'

'How do I find him?' Deacon persisted.

''E don't live 'ere now. I live 'ere now.'

'Who are you?'

The man looked at Deacon closely, puzzlement on his face plain to see. 'What you wantin', man?' There was a silence, then he seemed to have made up his mind. 'You alone?'

'Yes.'

151

'We 'ad some like you up 'ere. What you want to trade?'

Deacon didn't reply. The man continued to sip his beer, not taking his eyes from Deacon's face for a second. From somewhere upstairs came the continual sound of running water: a tap that wouldn't shut off. The heat and the odours weighed on Deacon's chest, making him conscious of every indrawn breath. The man turned and went inside, leaving the door open.

The room was neat and crowded. A television, a sound system, a bed that was covered with blankets to make a sofa, a chair, one wall draped with clothes that hung from the picture-rail. A set of training-weights occupied one corner. The bar looked to have close to two hundred pounds loaded on.

'I'm Viv.' A half-constructed joint lay on a low table close to the bed, pale grass on a jigsaw of papers; he picked it up and began to furl it. 'I ain't the man to see.'

'Who is?' Playing it by ear, a stranger in a strange land.

'That depends on what you got, man. What you want. . . .'

So, Deacon thought, there's still enough of the copper about me to show. Not a tourist with a poor sense of direction, not a messenger from some out-of-town syndicate – a bent policeman, a greedy policeman with information for sale. He said: 'A new Commissioner, new attitudes, new opinions. This one believes in God and family life. For hard work – reward. For loyalty – praise. For sin – punishment.'

'What colour that God?' Viv laughed. The rich smell of dope eddied through the room.

'This one thinks it's a war.'

'' 'E fuckin' right.'

'It's good to have someone in the enemy camp.'

'Yeah. . . .' The slow note of contempt drifted out on a plume of smoke. He spoke softly, as if confirming to

152

himself something he already knew. 'White police-*man*. . . .' He smoked for a little longer, enjoying himself, making Deacon wait. 'I ain't the man to see.'

'Who is?'

'Nah, man. It's not that easy.' Everyone – everyone bought and sold.

Deacon took some money from his wallet and tossed it on to the table. 'It's all I have.'

Viv let it lie. 'You say.'

'It's all I have right now.'

'Where I find you, man?' He scooped the money up. 'Don't make it far.'

Deacon named the pub in no man's land, but got no reaction. He glanced at the weights. 'Northmore,' he said. It was a sports complex, close enough but on neutral ground. Viv nodded. They fixed a day. They fixed a price. Viv took another beer from the fridge – a door half-hidden by the hanging clothes opened on to a cupboard-sized kitchen. He didn't bring one for Deacon.

'You'll talk to him?'

'Yeah, I'll talk to 'im.' But not about the money; this was Viv's private score. And Deacon's only advantage. Viv yanked the ring-pull one-handed and ducked his head to catch the spurt of foam, then alternated with a toke on the joint. 'So', he said, 'white police*man*. . . .'

No such thing as a truce; not in this war.

The streets were hotter. A thin tart stink of petrol fumes replaced the damp cooking smell. The light dazzled him.

As he walked down the steps from the front door, Deacon had a decision to make and no time to falter. He turned to the right – away from the tower-blocks – and walked about thirty metres before going into a small shop to buy cigarettes. The man behind the counter looked startled. Deacon went to a wall-rack by the door and leafed through a magazine, taking risks.

The man sat down on a stool, his head turned, and waited for Deacon to go away. Two minutes, three, then Viv went past the window. He'd pulled on a blue singlet.

Deacon emerged in time to see his quarry turn the corner. He guessed at getting the pace right and judged it well. When he came in sight of the next street, Viv was just leaving it, taking a route that led towards the fringe of the ghetto. Deacon hoped he wasn't going far. The technique was bound to break down quite soon – a street too short or too long.

Twice more he had a glimpse of the blue singlet, then he came into a longer, broader street and the man had gone. There was a launderette, a post office, a betting-shop. And about fifty house-doors to choose from. Deacon kept walking because there was nothing else to do. The streets looked empty, but they weren't; to pause, to look around, would be lousy tactics.

As he came up to the bookie's, someone came out, shoving the door wide, stepping round Deacon and with a sharp sideways look. There was a blast of noise from the race-relay, and a tidal wave of smoke and sweat that caught Deacon in its undertow. Viv was standing by the wire mesh at the cashier's window, placing a bet with Deacon's money.

18

The notes from the flute were breathy and quick. The knight galloped on the pale backdrop of the wall but held position as if the room revolved to fix it there – arched neck plunging and tossing, mouth hard against the bit. The bird glided close to the moulded ceiling.

He had brought them with him, camouflaged by the city's other shadows, or invisible in the shade from buildings or trees. His power had released them; and in the hard bright outdoor light it had been possible to see them more clearly. The flute-player walked on crooked legs, a pelt of fur smothering his loins and flanks. The bird was built for speed and silence. The horse was skinny and wild-eyed.

No one had seen them. The woman couldn't see them now. They had walked to her house, a procession of shadows, sharp-edged in the sun, led by the shadow of a man. Against one wall was a small roll-top desk where the woman sat writing a letter. Just above her and slightly to one side the sheela-na-gig clutched at her own fullness, wrenching herself open, her belly swollen with richness. A cornucopia. A harvest.

It hadn't been possible to bring them out before. They had lived in the room, in Elaine's room, like familiars confined to a place of power. Now it was different. Kate Lorimer had made it different. Her death had nourished him, and he in turn gave strength to the others. Even Elaine had gone, under cover of darkness, to the house where Laura Scott lived.

He had always known that he possessed power.

Others sensed it, too, and would submit to it: weak people, people who were ill and wanted to borrow strength. He had learned from his father how important it was to be strong. The strong controlled the world. *And the Son of Man,* he heard his father's voice, *shall come into His glory.*

The memory staggered him. He flooded with joy; muscles cranked in the small of his back, and he felt the heat and stiffness in his groin. The bird swooped and checked over the woman's head.

She had laid out fresh clothes. He had already watched her do that and had watched her put on a kimono before going to the desk to write her letter. She had just got out of the bath, her hair still wet and smelling slightly of perfumed shampoo. The knight reared, its eyes stoked with fury.

A magnetic strip fixed to a wooden support held six knives. He took the fifth, feeling a tug as the broad heavy blade gripped for an instant before coming free; then he went back to the woman. Before he entered the room, he caught her reflection in the cloudy glass of a gilt-framed antique mirror fixed to the far wall. It was taller than it was broad, so he saw her entire, bare feet to damp hair, as she stood by the desk to reread the letter. The flute music was a choppy staccato, high-pitched.

It wasn't enough. . . .

She put the letter in an envelope and sealed it, then took a half-step, as if she would move away and take her reflection out of the glass. He put a hand on her shoulder, and she stopped, her face frozen; the expression someone wears who is conscious of having forgotten something, but not what it is.

. . . things I wanted to do. . . .

He slipped the bow on the belt that held her kimono. The robe parted, and he gripped it beneath her neck then pulled it down from her shoulders, down her arms, and let it drop at her feet. A slight

156

movement of her head towards him made it seem as though she were peering through a mist. Her mouth opened. Her eyes narrowed, like the eyes of someone bringing an object into focus.

He looked sideways to where they stood in the mirror, and watched himself showing her the knife. His left hand was on her throat, restraining her. He noticed the slight droop of her breasts, the curve of her belly. Muscles jumped in his extended arm. Power coursed through him like a charge, between his legs almost a pain, and the woman said, 'My—' but he brought his mouth down onto hers, keeping his eyes on the mirror, bending slightly to be able to see the knife as he lowered it, holding it tightly, cutting-edge up.

Their reflections almost blended, a taut curve, her spine arched and her hair, now, drawn back in his grip.

The blade disappeared between them as he pouched it. She went up on her toes like a dancer, locked, her body rigid. She looked straight into his face.

'My—'

He harvested her, all her richness, all her ripeness.

The shadows danced on the wall till the reaping was done.

19

The weather had grown hotter. In the extreme west, in
the north, and on the east coast, a drought had been
declared. Official pronouncements had forbidden the
use of garden hoses, and car-washes had been closed
down. In some areas, domestic supplies of water were
cut off for part of the day and stand-pipes erected at
street-corners. Householders went to and fro with
buckets, collecting their supplies at certain hours. Ice
and mineral water were at a premium. Pubs ran dry of
beer.

Phil Mayhew arrived with a frosted six-pack and a
carrier-bag of Spa Reine as if he were bringing a
house-gift. Labouring up the last few steps to Deacon's flat, he said: 'This is beyond a fucking joke.'

Mayhew cracked one of the cans before Deacon
stowed the rest in the fridge. When he came back,
Mayhew was sprawled in an armchair. He said: 'You'll
have read about it – seen the news on TV.'

'Of course,' Deacon told him. 'Until you called, I
hadn't really been sure whether—'

'No . . . well, I'm not surprised.'

'There's no doubt?'

Mayhew shook his head. 'I wish to Christ there
were. And I'm not alone in that. D'Arblay's back and
forth like a fart in a colander.' He took several swallows from his can. 'Jesus, what do you think's happened? Is the sun going supernova?'

Deacon fetched him a replacement. 'Tell me about
it,' he said.

'Well, they're in a hell of a fucking bind. As things stand, the MO lets them off the hook. No one's going to put this one together with Lorimer and Cochlan. Shit, no one really *knows* about the other two – accidents, nothing. . . . Right now, they're not intending to come clean. It's too late. The file on Lorimer is closed and forgotten, and Cochlan's a hornet's nest. Can you imagine someone having to confront the noble lord with the information that not only was his old lady unlawfully done to death, but also we knew about it at the time but chose not to tell him? I mean, forget it. The problem is that the three incidents ought to be bagged up and looked at together if they're going to conduct a proper inquiry. You know – one piece of information sheds light on the next.'

'What makes them sure?'

Mayhew sighed. 'Well, to be honest, John, there was a bit more to the Cochlan thing than I bothered to mention.'

'Thanks.'

'No, it made no difference. We could both see that it wasn't a coincidence.' He paused. 'They picked up a print in Lorimer's flat that didn't tally with the elimination prints from either Laura Scott or the victim. Well, the flat was thick with prints, of course, like hoof-marks on a race-track. No point in bothering – all the people that come and go in a place – but this one was on the mirror-tiles. It was the only one. People almost never touch a mirror.'

Deacon nodded. 'And they lifted the same print at Cochlan's flat – where?'

'It wasn't worth mentioning because the print isn't on record. It took them nowhere.' Mayhew started on the second can. 'Also, it raised an issue that no one wanted to think about.'

'Where?' Deacon insisted.

'She'd been shopping up west – expensive places; bought some new clothes. Specifically, a dress;

159

light-coloured silk, pearl buttons all down the front. Very slinky.'

'One of the buttons.'

Mayhew had the can to his mouth. He looked at Deacon across the rim. 'Several of the buttons.'

'He undressed her.'

'It looks that way, doesn't it? Whether she wanted him to or not is another matter, but you'd have to allow that she might not have objected. After all, there were no signs of violence.'

'What's going to happen?'

'The air's thick with shit over this one, as you'd imagine. They'll simply treat it as an unlawful killing without making mention of the other two and hope to get away with it. The problems will arrive if some unignorable connection crops up. The trouble with a full-scale inquiry is that you can't really stop one thing leading to another.'

Deacon went to fetch another beer for Mayhew. He said: 'Tell me about it.'

'OK.' Mayhew sat forward slightly, ordering his thoughts. 'Meredith, first name Jessica, wife of a prominent and noisy back-bench MP, Christopher Meredith, who, at the time, was in his constituency: North Yorkshire. Murdered in their Chelsea mews house. That much you already know.'

'"Died of stab wounds."' Deacon was quoting.

'Well, that's one way of putting it. He filleted her. Then he decorated the mirror.'

'Dec—'

'Using her blood.'

'Are you on this one?'

'I took the shout. She was expected for dinner at her sister's house. When she didn't arrive they phoned and got no reply. Gave up and had the dinner-party without her. Phoned again later and got no reply, phoned the MP in Yorkshire, who said she hadn't changed her mind and gone with him, phoned the next morning quite early, still no reply. I gather they were more curious than worried. Probably suspected her of having a naughty secret that had taken her mind off dinner. Anyway, the sister had a key, so she went round there after a morning's shopping.' Mayhew grimaced. 'They poleaxed her with something – "under heavy sedation" was the term used. No one's going to get much sense out of her for a long time – though I doubt whether there's much that she could tell us. She went in, fainted into a lake of blood, managed to make a largely incoherent phone call, and remained largely incoherent until someone slipped the needle in.'

'Where was the print?' Deacon wanted to know.

'Where wasn't there a print? Doors, walls, the knife-handle. The best ones were on the mirror.'

'You've got the knife.'

'Oh, sure; he took it from the kitchen.'

'Where was she killed?'

'In the drawing-room.'

'So he was in the place before her. Unless she waited patiently while he rummaged through the knife-drawer.'

'Possibly. He might have dragged her into the kitchen with him.'

'Then why not kill her there?'

'Come on, John, you know how it goes. He probably spent some time enjoying the sight of his victim being scared shitless – waving the knife around, listening to her plead or try to bargain, playing with her.'

'Maybe. No sign of a break-in?'

'No.' Mayhew shook his head. 'And there the similarities end. If it wasn't for the print, I wouldn't have put this down to the same guy in a million years.'

'When you arrived—'

'The sister was there, along with her husband – she phoned him, he phoned us. He'd managed to get her into the bedroom – not that he wasn't in shock, you understand, but she was gibbering. No surprise – one of my PCs threw up. The Meredith woman was in the middle of the drawing-room floor. Well, most of her was. Opposite the mirror. Blood on the walls, high up near the ceiling, on the furniture, the curtains, puddles on the floor. Like an abbatoir. She'd been dead about sixteen hours. You could smell it as you went into the place.'

'Why?' Deacon wondered.

'I said, she'd been—'

'No, why drown the other two quietly and then suddenly be afflicted by this – what? – frenzy?'

'A good word; that's just what it looked like: frenzy. I'd never seen anything like it. One odd thing: she had just taken a bath, or that's how it seemed. Bath-mat still on the floor, uncapped shampoo by the taps, her hair was anyhow – uncombed – and she'd been wearing just a robe, a kimono.'

'Had been?'

'It was on the floor under her; crumpled.'

'Maybe he arrived a little late.'

'Yes. That raises an issue, doesn't it?'

'The timing?'

'Sure. I'd sort of assumed that Lorimer and Cochlan were *put into* the baths where they died. That they were threatened, perhaps with a gun, taken into the bathroom, made to fill the bath and climb into it, then the guy held them under. It hadn't occurred to me that they were taking baths because they wanted to – that the killer arrived while they were in the tub. After all, how would he gain access?'

'They got out of the bath to answer the door.'

'OK. That would explain one thing: when I checked, I discovered that both women had added something to the water – crystals, bubble-foam or whatever. I don't see them doing that with a gun in the ear. What it wouldn't explain is the coincidence involved in both of them being in the bath when the killer arrived.

162

Particularly since that was the method he chose. Why not ignore the bath and kill them some other way?'

'He wanted it to look like an accident – we sort of assumed that. It's even possible that he put bath-salts in the water to add credibility.'

'All right. Then you can lose the coincidence; take it that he forced them into the bath. But it still doesn't answer your question. Why be so careful to make things look accidental in two instances, then hack the Meredith woman about with a six-inch blade? And, in any case, you don't quite lose the coincidence. Meredith had just got out of a bath.'

'OK, he had the opportunity to kill her in the same way as the other two—'

'Somehow provided himself with the opportunity—'

'Yes, all right, and chose not to take it.'

'Why?'

'That's what I just asked you.' Neither man spoke for a moment. Deacon fetched another beer and wiped its cool wetness across his brow before handing it to Mayhew. 'There's something wrong about all this, Phil. Look, forget Lorimer and Cochlan for a minute. You've just walked into Meredith's apartment. You see what you see. What do you think?'

'Either a crazy or someone who wants to make it look like a crazy.'

'Which?'

Mayhew pondered briefly. 'A crazy.'

'Why?'

'What had' – he looked for a way of saying it – 'happened to her. You couldn't invent that by trying to guess what someone else might do. John, he'd festooned the place with her. Put her on display.' Mayhew's mouth twisted. 'We've kept all that from the press so far, but it won't be long before you see a "Chelsea Ripper" headline.'

'Right. Well, that's what doesn't make sense. It looks like a different guy.'

'It's not. There's no mistake about the print.'

'Had he raped her?'

'They're not sure. Not yet.'

'What about Kate Lorimer?'

'So far as I know, it wasn't raised as a possibility. I could look at the post-mortem.'

'And Lord Cochlan managed to avoid an inquest.'

'That's right.'

It started out differently, thought Deacon. It started out with a purpose – a rational purpose. Now it's just about killing. Like an infection that spreads, as if the first death had got under the skin, then a mild fever, and now this rage, this rabid heat.

Out loud, he said: 'It's hopeless. How in God's name does D'Arblay think he's going to get into this one without reopening the cases on Lorimer and Cochlan? If the guy is a nut, the selection of victims is the only hope, unless you get amazingly lucky, you know that. Look at Sutcliffe – he'd been interviewed Christ knows how many times; got stopped for a driving offence and had the murder weapon on him. Look at Nilsen – he could have gone on for ever if he hadn't blocked the drains with what was left of the people he'd killed. And that was with full-scale police work. There's no other method – you have to find out what puts Lorimer, Cochlan and Meredith together in this man's life, how he picked them, and that involves questioning friends, relatives, parents, neighbours.' He watched Mayhew's expression. 'That's not going to happen, is it?'

'I'm not sure. I don't think so. Face it: D'Arblay – someone – would have to supply a reason. They've dug themselves a hole. Lorimer is happily put down as misadventure: case closed. A possible connection is visible between her and Cochlan, but since Lorimer's history no one wants to admit that. It's given the benefit of the doubt.'

'Not by you. Not by me.'

'In truth, not by D'Arblay.'

'Or whoever pulled his string.'

'Sure. If someone had put the prints together sooner, things might have been different. But too late; the damage was done.'

'They must have seen the likelihood of another death.'

'I suppose so. Now they've got one.'

'But not a look-alike.'

'Exactly. Less embarrassing than a third body in a bath. We might as well clear these up.' Mayhew went for another beer. 'You can keep the water. Look, if you want to know what they're thinking, I'll tell you. They think the killer's a psycho. So do I. How he chose the women he killed is crucial, of course, but they hope they can get ahead on that without winding Lorimer and Cochlan into it. They're worried about the flak they'll catch if they reveal that they knew of a connection and said nothing. They also figure that since it's a psycho. . . .' He left the rest unsaid.

'There'll be more killings, and therefore other opportunities to make a chain of circumstances from a series of links.' Deacon laughed. 'No prizes for compassion. I expect everyone's looking forward to the next one; it'll provide something to work with.'

There was a short silence. Mayhew said: 'This was my shout, John.'

Deacon looked unrepentant. 'Then, why do you keep saying "they"?'

'I might as well', Mayhew said, giving him a level stare, 'say "you".'

It was in Deacon's mind to tell Mayhew about the phone calls, but if Kate's death was to remain a closed book Mayhew and D'Arblay couldn't go back to her unless Laura became part of their conspiracy. He didn't want to deliver her up to that. In any case, what could she offer? A voice on the telephone. But the words *selection of victims* and *chain of circumstance* had hollowed his stomach when he'd spoken them.

He said: 'I'm not a police force. I don't have a forensic department. I started out with Lorimer as a favour to a friend. Maggie's friend. . . . If this guy's mad, if the killings are motiveless, then I might as well call it quits.'

'Will you?'

Deacon shrugged. 'I'm not sure. In the mean time, I'll let you have anything that comes my way.' He wondered whether the lie sounded convincing.

Mayhew had arrived carrying a small document-case. He stood up and made for the door, unzipping the case on the way. 'This turned up.' He handed over a thin blue book. Before Deacon could examine it, he added: 'Lorimer's diary.'

Deacon took it, but didn't speak.

'In a drawer – someone's out-tray. . . .' Mayhew fastened the case. 'Who knows.'

'Of course.' Deacon smiled wryly. 'Thanks.' They went to the door together. 'You said he'd decorated the mirror.'

Mayhew was still holding his beer. He took a last swallow as he stood at the top of the stairs and gave the can to Deacon. 'Yes.'

'What was it?'

'He'd used her blood to write a word on the glass. *Glory*.'

Deacon lodged himself on a stool close to the window and watched the swallows performing their circus acts. They screamed with delight at their own virtuosity.

The logical time to turn back. Curiosity about Laura; deeper curiosity about Maggie; and, if he were honest, a desire to know whether Kate Lorimer's death was more than a sad accident. Old habits die hard. He could read his own motives well enough. Wanting the

166

link with Laura – with Maggie – had been an indulgence. He hadn't known where it might lead, and he hadn't much cared. Now there were all sorts of things at stake, and all sorts of things that he couldn't quantify. He felt like a man walking into a narrow tunnel and wondered why he didn't seem to possess the wit to retreat. Was Laura the reason for that? He thought she might be, but the notion worried him. She had told him why she'd burned the yellow dress, and he hadn't been able to shake the sense of responsibility the knowledge gave him. He'd watched her poke at the embers and had felt afraid.

He looked at what he had. The killings, the computer-theft, Ambrose Jackson. They ought to be separate things, but they weren't. To make Kate's discovery of the aberration on the trace nothing to do with her death was to trade off coincidence, and coincidence had already offered itself too readily. The phone calls: a madman getting his kicks from threatening the flatmate of a girl he'd killed? Just that? No; there were too many puzzles. *I thought of you that day, going into the bathroom, when you got back, when Kate was there*. . . . How had the voice known that?

Deacon thought of Laura's face as she'd looked up from the fire. He thought again of the word *victim*.

It was almost six-thirty. He got up and switched on the answering machine, then collected a few things he would need. He'd promised Laura that he wouldn't leave her alone.

She hadn't asked him for that, but he'd promised anyway.

20

Three blocks away a tower took the sun. A slender rectangle of dark blue glass, a globe of molten gold in the top left-hand section, bleeding hot light across the pane. The colours fused – intensity at the centre fading to a pale glow, then aquamarine, falling through a dozen shades before reverting to a deep opaque gentian.

Austin Chadwick stared out, letting the colours flood his retina. When he turned, the room he stood in ran with blue and gold; Ionian grandeur.

He spoke quietly while Steiner listened, at times almost having to struggle to catch what was being said. Chadwick seemed to be soothing himself with his own words.

'It's a big concept. A campaign. It depends on strategies, on tactics – flanking movements, feints, frontal assaults. For ten years we've been progressing towards this. Ten years ago, it started. A small group of like-minded people. Things have gone well: at one time a purchase of arms, at another a purchase of minds; a currency put under pressure, a corporation swallowed. We've helped out where we could. None of it cost us a cent, and no one knew we were there.

'This is different. Maybe we'd send aid, or advice; sometimes a representative or two. Now we are generals standing on a hill dispatching battle-plans and watching the ebb and flow. Counting the cost.

'We've reached a delicate moment. You remember the Russian.' For the first time, he appeared to address

Steiner directly, though the remark required no response. 'The Russian has been bought. I was sure that would prove possible, and it has. Almost everything is going very well.' Steiner was there to hear about the *almost*.

'Generals on a hill,' Chadwick mused. 'Do you know this – "For want of a nail, the shoe was lost; for want of a shoe, the horse was lost; for want of a horse, the rider was lost; for want of a rider, the battle was lost; for want of a battle, the war was lost"?' The haze of colour was clearing from before his eyes, dissolving at the edges, so that the room began to swim into focus and Steiner was a dark shape standing motionless by the broad rectangle of the desk.

'A tiny setback; a small problem, easy enough to solve. At least, you'd think so. And what do we have? A madman. Someone whose passion has run away with him. It's very dangerous, that kind of fervour. It serves its own purpose; it doesn't obey rules. It runs amok.' He turned his head towards Steiner as if seeing him there for the first time. 'Speak to London. I want him taken out. I don't care how it's done as long as it's done efficiently and very soon. Use this man Deacon; use the girl as bait; it doesn't matter. I want him destroyed.'

Laura's body still tingled where Deacon's hands had been on her. After that first night together, there had been nothing between them that had to be explained or supported. No loyalties, no debts. His eventual choice had surprised her. But she could sense, too, his own puzzlement.

After the phone calls there had been fear, and the deliverance from fear through passion. No system of checks and balances governed that; it didn't grow from a past or depend on a future. But this time they had gone to bed as if being together gave them the right.

Whether he understands it or not, Laura thought, my role has changed. He wanted something of Maggie that he believed I could supply. I suppose I could have done that; in a small way, I'd already started to. What harm? I didn't owe him anything that mattered. I owed Maggie even less. That's changing. He's already begun to earn things from me. Dependence and open-handedness. Honesty.

Deacon was awake, too, but his eyes were closed. He could see a room, but couldn't adequately describe it to himself. The woman didn't matter much. He set her in the middle of the room opposite to the mirror and, for no particular reason, made the kimono white with blue flowers.

A man came into the room. He had no face: not masked, but featureless from brow to chin, a white alabaster surface. He stood before the woman. He didn't speak, though had he done so the voice would have been the low androgynous whisper that Laura had endured.

Thinking of it, and thinking of her, seemed to disturb her, and she stirred at his side, drawing her leg up to make contact with his. He remembered something Mayhew had said: *You really can't stop one thing leading to another.*

There was the woman, reflected in the mirror. Here came the man, his face wiped clean. He was carrying the knife. He couldn't be seen from windows across the street, because the curtains were drawn. . . .

Were they?

He came into the room, the knife in his hand. The woman screamed. She started to run. . . .

Had she?

There were the man and the woman, across from the mirror, in a large room papered in pale green, covered with cream carpeting, and close to one wall an oak table with barley-sugar legs.

No. The green was drawn from the morning light through the curtains in Laura's bedroom, the cream carpeting was in her living-room, the table was Deacon's own.

The man came through a door, gripping the knife. The woman stood in the centre of the room, her back towards him. . . .

Could that be right?

The woman glanced in the mirror. She saw the reflected image of the man advancing on her, holding up the knife. . . .

Was that possible?

He reached the woman; he turned her round. . . .

Perhaps.

She watched him coming; she couldn't move. . . .

Perhaps.

Their images came together as he struck, blood gouting on the cream carpet, the pale green. . . .

No.

The room altered shape and colour; its furnishings changed. The mirror gave nothing back of the place – only the likeness of the woman in the blue kimono. Red kimono. Yellow. . . . The man came into view. All Deacon could see was a face like a peeled egg. All he could hear was a lipless whisper.

He got out of bed and went to the living-room. Laura felt him go but didn't stir.

Mayhew's voice was foggy with sleep. 'John?'

'Phil. I'm sorry. I know it's late.'

'Late.' A pause. 'Jesus, it's almost four.'

'Can you get me into that house?'

'What?'

'In Chelsea – the Merediths' house. Can you get me in?'

'Sure, if we choose our time. Everything's been picked over by now, you know that. Forensic have been and gone.'

'No – just for a feel of the place.'

Mayhew understood. 'It shouldn't be a problem. I'll get back to you.'

The birds had started up. He got back into bed and closed his eyes.

The faceless man stood in the room, the knife held out before him. The sudden realization made Deacon twitch with shock. *Naked.* He was naked. Of course he was. So much blood – on his hands and arms, on his body. He couldn't have done what he did and then gone out in the street.

Deacon couldn't understand the narrative he'd invented, but neither could he make it happen any other way.

The woman stood in the room wearing a kimono, fresh from her bath. Somewhere in the house the man stripped off. He came in with the knife. He butchered her. He washed himself. He put his clothes back on and left.

21

You could see into the workout room through a circular window in the door. A slightly overweight man with freckled arms was treading an exercise-bike and chatting to his friend who was turning a light poundage on the curl-bar. On the far side of the gym, a black guy with a heavy mane of dreadlocks hauled lat weights; his head dropped forward as he brought the bar down across his shoulders, his forearms and torso a web of muscle. Twelve reps, a short rest, then twelve more. He looked to be pulling more than two-thirds of the stack.

'You think 'e's good?' Viv had come up behind Deacon. His voice was low and chiding. Deacon didn't reply; he continued to peer through the porthole window. 'Four circuits with me, 'e'd be praying to stop. Six, 'e'd forget 'ow to breathe.'

'Is that right?' Deacon strolled off, making for the flight of stairs that led to the sports-hall and squash-courts. From the elevated corridor they could see serious swimmers putting in length after length like mice on a treadmill. A double set of doors led to a viewing-gallery. Only one of the courts was in use. The squash-ball made a sound like axe-blows on the trunks of trees.

Deacon went to the back of the gallery and sat down on a moulded plastic chair in the middle of the row. Viv hesitated by the aisle seat, as if Deacon had chosen ground that was difficult to retreat from, then threaded his way along the row and sat three seats

173

away. A tiny *cordon sanitaire*. He took a sealed envelope from his jeans pocket and set it down on the intervening seat closest to him, then trapped it with a finger.

'Who's that from?' Deacon saw it in the corner of his eye; he was watching the game.

'The man you want to see.'

'Ambrose Jackson.'

'Nah. You can't see 'im, man.'

'Who, then?'

Viv gave the envelope a little push. 'Jackson work for this guy.'

'Do you work for him, too?'

'Sometimes.'

'Like now.'

The angle foreshortened the players' bodies. Between the crowns of their heads and their oddly enlarged feet, the telescoped torsos swivelled to the doglegged flight of the ball, their rackets appearing and disappearing as they went for the stroke. It was even-handed: the score had stayed at six–five through a number of hand-outs.

Viv picked the envelope up as if threatening to take it back. Deacon was unimpressed. 'We made arrangements, man.' The voice was still low, but had taken on some urgency.

'You went to see someone,' Deacon mused, 'and you told him about me – not Ambrose, but someone else; and this someone has said he'd like to meet me. We had an arrangement, it's true. You wanted money; I wanted Jackson. Now, you tell me whether I've got it right. This man has sent you on an errand. You're the errand-boy, Viv. I don't think you can deliver Jackson, and I don't think you can leave here without giving me that envelope. Am I close? You see, I came here with some money for you, but if I don't give it to you will you take the envelope back to the man who gave it to you? The money was for Jackson. Do I want to meet

174

the man you work for? I'm not sure. Maybe. Maybe not. Why don't you just hand me the envelope since that's what you've been told to do?'

'I could break your arm, man. I could break your fuckin' back.'

Deacon laughed. 'You know, Viv, you scare the shit out of me.'

'What you want?'

'Ambrose.'

'You can't 'ave 'im.'

'What does your boss want?'

''E want a bent white police*man*.' Viv separated out the syllables, filling the spaces between with contempt.

Down on the court, someone took the match ten–eight. They went straight into another.

'Give me the envelope, Viv.' A pause. 'And I'll give you this.' Deacon took a roll of money from his shirt pocket. Viv put the envelope back on the seat, then took his hand away. Deacon extended his arm. 'Take it.' He turned to face the other man and smiled. 'You're in a box here, aren't you? I think you need this money. You're wondering whether I'll tell this man – your boss – that I paid you off. Because I'd be surprised to learn, Viv, that you mentioned our agreement to him. What happens if you do take it? You're putting yourself at risk. What happens if you don't? I'll tell you. He's going to hear about it anyway, because I'll tell him. Take it, and I won't. Just remember something: you haven't finished earning it yet.'

'Motherfucker.'

'It's your cage. You climbed into it.' Deacon guessed that before the afternoon was over a horse somewhere would be chasing whatever Viv thought he needed to buy the key of the cage. He'd been in the cage for a long time, always looking for the price of the key, and that was sad because it wasn't for sale. Viv hadn't guessed this yet; he probably never would.

'I need a number.' Deacon watched the other man stow the cash in his jeans. 'If I call, it'll be between seven and eight. I wouldn't want to break up your evening.' He knew the number already; it was in the book under "Jackson". Viv got it right.

Deacon smiled appreciatively. White police*man*, he thought. I guess I look the part. Good acting, or a hidden inclination? Everyone has a price; everyone has someone who's guessed what it might be. You can't stop one thing leading to another.

Viv went through the gallery doors without a backward look. Deacon gave him five minutes to get clear. The envelope lay on the seat next to him. It was sealed and seemed thin enough to be empty.

It should have been a fifteen-minute drive to Chelsea, but this was Friday afternoon – the beginning of the weekend – and traffic was backed up on the main routes out of the city, jamming the minor roads. They would drive in lines to the coast or the countryside where no one wanted them.

Walls of petrol vapour rose like forcefields, hot and noxious. Not a breath of wind. Sunlight hammered down on the roofs of the cars.

When Deacon parked, the door of a white Escort XR3i opened right in front of him and Mayhew stepped out. He opened his mouth to speak, but Deacon forestalled him. 'The place is emptying out,' he said. 'Within three hours, the south coast will be under siege. It took me forty minutes.'

'It's OK,' Mayhew said. 'We've got half an hour.'

'Someone's coming here?'

'I have to get back. Some kid walked into a corner shop in Queensway and emptied the till.'

'Doesn't sound too serious.'

'No . . . well, the owner wasn't too anxious to part with the money, so the kid gave him a seeing-to with a Stanley knife. Wiped it around the guy's face and hit the carotid. Don't expect he meant to. I'll pop by and get him after this.'

'You know who it was?'

'Oh, yes. Three eye-witnesses. Kid called Norman Blackett. Low IQ and a severely damaged septum. By the time I get there he'll have a nose full of coke. Doubt he'll even remember.' Mayhew inserted a Banham key in the natural-wood door of the Merediths' Victorian terrace.

The house was fashionably – eccentrically – arranged. On the ground floor, a kitchen, a dining-room, a second bathroom, and a music-room domi-nated by a baby grand.

'Who played?' They went from room to room.

Mayhew shrugged. 'Don't know.' He opened the door of the drawing-room. 'In here. The bathroom's off to the left.'

Not green wallpaper, but soft deep pink Regency stripes. Not cream carpeting, but beige. No table – a roll-top desk with a maroon leather writing-surface and a dozen tiny drawers fronted with brass handles. Three tall sash windows hung with full-length cur-tains that offset the wallpaper with a slightly darker pink. A sofa. Two armchairs. A sewing-chair. The mirror.

Deacon placed himself opposite the mirror, facing the windows. He was just off centre in the room. 'Here.'

It wasn't a question. The carpet bore a large, dark, irregular stain.

'Nothing's been moved,' Mayhew said. 'The chairs, the sofa, the desk. He spread her around. She was feet to the window, lying just where you're standing. Her guts were hither and yon. Not a pretty sight.'

Someone had cleaned the mirror.

'Christopher Meredith, MP,' Mayhew told him. 'After we were through he sent Gentle Ghost in. Don't suppose they'd had a job quite like it before. Must have strong stomachs. They steam-cleaned the carpet. The coroner had already removed the offal.'

Deacon nodded and went through to the bathroom. It was predictable, like the rest of the house. Victorian chic – an old-fashioned lavatory with a pull-chain, a marble-topped and panelled washbasin, a claw-foot bath, brass taps. In one corner, a shower unit with heavily decorated glass panels.

She got out of the bath and towelled off, then slipped into the kimono. Somewhere in the house, downstairs in one of the bedrooms perhaps, he was getting out of his clothes. Before that, he had gone to the kitchen and selected the knife.

He came upstairs, naked, holding the knife. He waited in the drawing-room. Waited there. Deacon looked round. A small circular shaving-glass on a swivel support stood on the marble top of the handbasin. Other than that, the room had no mirrors.

She took a brush from a shelf in the bathroom and went.... The brush was on the middle of three shelves above the basin. Two baggy spider plants, toothpaste, a jar with several toothbrushes, a conch and a piece of coral, shampoo, face-cream, a razor – the usual litter; and a brush. *Went into the drawing-room, not bothering to attend to her hair just yet, and....*

He came into the room, carrying the knife.

Deacon left the bathroom. Mayhew was leaning against the far wall. He said: 'I can't sit down in this place.'

'What did you get?' Deacon asked him.

'Sod all. The prints, of course. It seems she hadn't been raped, though there were traces of semen, which gives us one elimination point: A-positive. Finger-prints and semen would be terrific if the guy had ever been picked up for a drunk-in-charge. As it is, he's Joe Public.'

'Semen traces where?'

Mayhew said it in a matter of fact tone. 'On her face.'

178

'Before or after?'

'After, for sure.'

'Jesus.'

'Yes.'

Deacon went downstairs to the kitchen. Mayhew knew better than to go with him.

The rack of knives was there, blades in ascending order of size, a gap at the further end between a vegetable-parer and a cleaver. He took the vegetable-knife from the rack, feeling the resistance as the magne-tized surface yielded it, and stroked the ball of his thumb along the edge, very softly. It stung. A bead of blood hopped up. He began to climb the stairs to the drawing-room, still carrying the knife.

Into the house. How? It doesn't matter. Don't worry about that for now. *Up these stairs. The woman is in the bath, or just emerging, . . .* Is she? And how does he know that? How in hell does he know that she's there at all?

Mayhew watched Deacon into the room.

'Nothing else?' asked Deacon.

'Not really. She'd been writing a letter; or we think she had. It was on the floor, as if she'd finished writing it and had – I don't know – walked about with it, reading it through or something, then put it in the envelope. There was a stamp on the desk.'

'What was it?'

'Nothing. A chatty note to a friend somewhere in Leicester. Nothing.'

'That's all?'

'What in hell do you want? "I've been receiving death-threats from a certified crazy and his name is dot dot dot"? The guy is not one of the Norman Blacketts of this world. I wish the fuck he was. This is someone who kills women, likes to do it, quite definitely hasn't got both oars in the water, comes and goes like the Scarlet fucking Pimpernel and we don't know the first thing about him. Why are you holding that knife?'

179

Deacon went back downstairs, stopping at the first floor. He went into all the bedrooms. *In here perhaps. Unlacing his shoes, having put the knife down on the bed. His socks, his pants. . . .*

The woman was signing her letter. She took an envelope from one of the small drawers and laid a stamp, in readiness, on the maroon leather, then got up and began to wander about the room, to read through what she'd written. He came into the room holding the knife. The woman was standing opposite the mirror.

Yes, that would be important, wouldn't it? Wouldn't it, you *bastard*? Deacon entered the drawing-room again. He'd forgotten Mayhew was there.

Yes. He came into the room. He was holding the knife. The woman was standing there, her reflection clouded by the dull glass. And you wanted. . . . Yes. . . . There were things you wanted to do. Crossing the room towards her, naked, the knife ready. Yourself in the mirror, she in the mirror.

He occupied the stained patch of carpet and turned slowly, watching his reflection come and go, holding the knife up and outwards, like someone defending territory.

Mayhew said: 'I ought to go soon.'

Just here. You stood just here, like this. If the woman saw you coming, she didn't move; or, if she moved, you brought her back, to this spot, where you could see everything, the knife, your hard-on, you miserable bastard, and you wanted everything, everything she'd got to give. She shrank when you cut her, like someone who's camera-shy, but you brought her back into the frame. Right here. . . .

Deacon put out a hand, almost as if he might find the outline, still in place, the shape they had made, a silhouette of two people as they merged, then fell away, then merged again. As if shadows had substance. He sniffed the air as an animal does, and it seemed that a raw tang of fear hit the membrane in his nose, scorching. It was the woman's fear.

First, a bath. Then there would just be time to write that letter. The cool cotton of the kimono, walking round the room to go through what you'd written, then looking up and seeing him. And everything changed. That was what it was – a smell of things gone bad, of virtues corrupted, illness in the blood.

Like words when they stifle you. Like a look when it's rooting inside you. Like laughter when it siphons off your breath.

His words, summoning you; his look drawing you on; his laughter that came with the first cut.

'OK? I ought to go.' Mayhew stood up.

Deacon put out a hand, beckoning him, not wanting to speak. Mayhew stood close to him, but at an angle, not knowing what was wanted. Deacon held him by the shoulders, the knife-blade close to the other man's ear, and arranged him eye to eye, in profile to the mirror. Mayhew laughed, then fell silent. He looked sideways, as Deacon looked, at their reflection; he could smell the foxy odour of sweat. Toe to toe, almost lip to lip as Deacon moved his head. Mayhew flinched. There was a hand hard in the small of his back and the knife dropped out of sight. He felt light-headed. He was breathing shallowly and swaying a little on his feet, like someone whose body-space has been invaded by a garrulous bore at some party. In the middle of the room, he felt as if he'd been backed into a corner.

'OK?' An embarrassed laugh that wouldn't quite take hold.

Deacon didn't answer; he didn't move. *Like this. Like this, you bastard.* He stared at the two images, at the dark antique glass, and the images stared back. His eyes unfocused. His arm, trapping Mayhew, began to quiver with effort.

Mayhew said: 'John?'

Toe to toe, lip to lip. They could have been lovers. They could have been anyone.

* * *

Deacon replaced the knife. The air in the kitchen seemed light and breathable. Mayhew looked in from the hallway, already rehearsing the arrest of Norman Blackett.

As they walked to the front door, Deacon asked: 'At Cochlan's place – were there any mirrors, in the bathroom or wherever?'

'The bedroom. A whole wall.'

'Not in the bathroom?'

'No.'

'She was going out to dinner – Meredith.'

'At her sister's.'

'What time?'

'Seven-thirty for eight.' Mayhew made a joke of it, twisting the vowels into Sloane-accented English. He shrugged: 'I don't really know.'

'She died—'

'Around seven. Difficult to tell apparently. Hot weather . . . and the method of killing.'

'And there was just the kimono.' Deacon remembered the neat pile of clothes in Kate Lorimer's bedroom, the fingerprints on the pearl buttons of Lady Olivia's new dress.

'That's all. What are you thinking?'

'The kimono was under her – crumpled up, a mess.'

'That's right.'

'Where did you find the dress that Cochlan had been wearing?'

They had reached Mayhew's car. He paused to think, fishing for his keys. 'There were two others, still in their bags. . . .' He frowned. 'On a chair, I think.'

'Just thrown there—'

'Christ, I can't remember. Does it matter?'

'No. I'm trying to make something out of nothing.'

'Let me know if the trick works.'

'I will.'

Deacon got into his own car and watched as Mayhew split a line of traffic just as he always did, not even bothering to look towards the driver he'd balked.

Something . . . something. . . a pattern.

With the windows up and standing in the sun, the car was like a furnace. He started to sweat from the temples, beads that ran down his cheeks and found the line of his jaw.

What did you want, you bastard? What did you want from her?

Glory.

22

'You're not telling me much.' Laura put the mouth-piece of the Ventolin inhaler between her lips and jabbed the plunger.

Deacon smiled at her. 'I'm going to. Is it bad?' He'd begun to understand the rhythms of her discomfort.

'Not bad; not good. I wish flowers could find some other way to reproduce.' She leaned her head on the chair-back a moment, eyes closed, her face tilted up. She appeared tired. In repose, Deacon thought, she looked particularly lovely; not pretty, as he'd thought at first; she lacked the pert quality that goes with prettiness. Her mouth had a slight natural downturn at the edges that made her look as if she were thinking stern thoughts. She read his mind and said: 'Smoking doesn't affect me much, really. I haven't been showing deference.'

As if prompted, he lit a cigarette, though he suspected she was lying. Not deference, but generosity perhaps. 'No way of knowing where the money goes?' he asked.

Laura shook her head without opening her eyes. 'When W. C. Fields was at the height of his career – and because he was paranoid about people laying hands on his money – he opened John Doe accounts all over America, salted cash away, then died – as we all do – without meaning to. The loot is known to be there – somewhere – but it might as well not be. Spiteful old sod, if you want my opinion. No, it's all confidential.'

'Would what's-his-name know – the manager?'

'Buxton.'

'Right.'

'It's possible. He doesn't have to. He would if the client confided in him, but it's not a prerequisite to opening an account.'

'What is?'

'Lots of money.'

'OK.' Deacon exhaled a plume of smoke, aiming for the open window. 'What happened about the missing back-up tape?'

'Yes,' Laura said. She sat up slightly and opened her eyes. 'I've been thinking about that, too. Nothing happened.'

'How sure are you of that?'

'Pretty sure. After all, it was my request for it that brought the loss to light. No one's asked me a single question. A weasel called Thwaite – he's the records man – was in paroxysms about it. I thought he was going to wet himself. So far, though, I've heard nothing from Security and nothing from Buxton.'

'Is it – would they think it serious?'

'Difficult to say. I don't suppose it's ever happened before. In itself, *not* serious I should think. I can see it would be a big issue for an anal type like Thwaite. He's the kind who'd make his wife press his underpants. Still, the mere fact that the tape's missing would be bound to excite *someone's* curiosity. The actual material it contained wouldn't be of any real importance. Except', she added, 'that in this case—'

'It probably contained the trace.'

'Yes.'

'Which, if you think about it, makes the lack of any inquiry more sinister than less.'

'Yes.'

He stubbed out his cigarette and immediately wanted another. Trying not to smoke – wanting not to, for her sake – made the desire almost constant. 'There are two things,' he said, stating out loud the thoughts that had been plaguing him. 'But, in some way I don't comprehend, they're the same thing.' Laura tucked her feet up under her and turned to face him more squarely, one forearm resting on the arm of her chair.

He'd told her about Meredith. He'd told her about his visit to Spruce and what had happened in the ghetto, then later at the sports centre. It hadn't been his intention to tell her everything he knew about Meredith's death, but she had been able to sense from the words he'd chosen and from the way he'd constructed the story that he was holding back, and she'd pushed at him to get it all, pushing a little harder each time he'd tried to stop, refusing to be content with the partial additions and modifications he offered, until he'd looked slightly away from her, his voice flat and hard, to tell her what she'd insisted on hearing. When he turned back, there had been a dead look in his eyes and she'd known that there was nothing left to tell.

'A madman has killed three women. Two he drowned in the bath. No signs of violence, no sign of a struggle in either case. Why a madman? He sounds like a pro. Well, a madman because when he kills the third he loops her round the room like carnival bunting.' Laura didn't blink. 'Now, why these three? You'd look for a connection that had to do with the killer – that's what I'd do anyway. How did he find them, and why did he pick them? What made them special to *him*? It's bloody difficult. In fact it's a nightmare; quite simply the most difficult kind of killing to solve, since in order to know what the motive is you have to know that man. Most murders are either domestic – at least, committed by someone close to the victim – or they occur in the process of a crime. A wages robbery, say, when someone decides to be heroic. What a copper wants least is a homicidal nut. There aren't any discernible patterns to what happens. To understand a crazy you have to be able to think like a crazy, and who can do that? More: you have to be able to think like that *particular* crazy. The only hope is that you'll get lucky or he'll get careless. Or he'll reach a stage where reality is so far removed that the cunning will go out of what he's doing – the deception – and he'll start to behave as if he's got nothing to hide – as if killing people wasn't really that remarkable a pastime. Mostly, the police get lucky; that's when someone gets caught, I mean. The clear-up figures on that sort of thing are small. Just because it's random.

'That's one thing – three random killings offering all the difficulties I've just mentioned. The other factor is the trace. Kate was murdered the day after she discovered that her program had been tampered with. And it was made to seem like an accident. It's inconceivable that the three are coincidental: her discovery, her death, the way it was rigged. Even if we stretched our imagination beyond breaking-point and tried to make it happenstance, the fingerprints bring us back to one man and an unignorable link.' And the phone calls. Neither of them needed to say it.

'Someone killed Kate, trying to make it seem a piece of domestic clumsiness. Then killed Cochlan the same way. Then he killed Meredith, and something changed.'

'What?' asked Laura. 'What was it that changed?'

'The man himself; that would be my guess.'

'I don't understand.'

'I think that Kate was the first person he'd ever killed. I think he did it for a purpose.'

'The trace.'

'Yes. But I think he found he liked doing it; and he wanted to do it again. The next time he killed as he had before. Perhaps he didn't imagine the death – the act – beyond that same method. With Meredith. . . . Something had happened to him.'

'He'd grown madder. More mad. . . .' Laura couldn't find a term to match the concept.

'Madder? What's that? It's like a hill becoming hillier, or a stone stonier. What he *did* might seem madder, but the impulse was there. He's always been that way.'

'Always?'

'No, I don't—' Deacon waved a hand at the irrelevance. 'I'm not this guy's fucking analyst. I mean, it was there when he killed Kate.'

'Oh. Yes.' Laura's voice was small, as if she were suddenly picturing for the first time what she might have found when she returned to the flat that day.

'I don't know.' Deacon hesitated. 'It's as if he'd slipped the leash.'

'Will he . . .?' Laura turned away, fiddling in her bag at the side of the chair. Another puff on the inhaler, interrupting herself while she allowed the thought to form. 'Will he do it again?' She brought them back to the phone calls.

'Almost certainly, yes. He'll go on until he's stopped, although it's often the case that there's a long gap between incidents. A trigger, a need – it's there, but this isn't someone completely out of control. Jessica Meredith's death has become very public: wife of a Member of Parliament, ex-model, pretty, rich, fashionable; and a Ripper-style killing. It won't be long before all the details are out. I expect the inquest will be standing-room only. Newspapers have an inexhaustible appetite for that kind of thing. My suspicion is that whoever did it will lie low for a while.'

'When he. . . .' She lowered her head so that her hair fell past her face and masked it from him.

' . . . *are you wearing the dress, Laura, the yellow dress . . .?*'

She was the closest; she had been in touch with that voice, that unstoppable whisper. When she thought about it, and she had thought about it often, it was like being touched by a dirty finger. He knew what she looked like and where she lived. He'd followed her, noticing what she'd been wearing. It was a kind of theft; she'd been rummaged through, like a cupboard. He knew her name. That was the worst thing of all.

'When he what?' Deacon asked.

She altered what she'd been going to say. 'Why do you suppose he did that – followed me, called me?'

'A sense of power, maybe. It's vicious, but it doesn't necessarily mean anything. If you consider it, both of the other women were married. It happened that you shared your flat with Kate. He doesn't kill men, he kills women; that's how it seems so far, at any rate. Because he'd been inside your place, he had access to you. I mean,' he said hurriedly, 'he knew the phone number, the address. He also had an opportunity to go through your things. I know that's not a pleasant thought, but it is possible that he was able to describe you – the dress and so forth – simply by being there. Is there a photo of you in the flat?' Laura nodded. 'He might not have followed you at all. It's like the con-trick techniques. Someone says he followed you and that you were wearing a yellow dress. If you *have* a yellow dress and you've worn it recently, you tend to believe him. I doubt he'd get a thrill out of phoning Cochlan's husband, or Meredith's. . . .' Deacon stopped short. 'Though, if he did, there'd be the hell of a mess: Cochlan's I mean.'

'Aren't the police being a bit mulish about that?' Laura was glad to be offered a change of direction.

'Maybe,' said Deacon. Then: 'Yes, you're right; they are.' He noticed the way her voice became chipper – like someone ignoring a symptom. He went over and took her head in his hands, gently, and he was right to do only that because an embrace would have overwhelmed her.

'What do you think?' Her meaning was clear.

He said: 'I'll look after you.' It wasn't what he'd

intended to say, but it was what he felt. The words were as strong as any embrace, and she started to cry.

It was odd that he should have reassured her in that way on that particular evening. A little later, he had to say: 'Is there someone you can be with? I have to go out.' She looked up, questioning. 'The man who runs Viv.'

'I'll be OK. If I get edgy, there are friends I can go to. Where are you meeting him?'

He expected she would laugh, and she did – just as he had when he'd opened the apparently empty envelope and found the ticket inside. Life was full of surprises.

'The Royal Opera House,' he said.

Sunset. The walls of the city were decked with decapitated heads, eyes staring, lips drawn back in a death-snarl. Soon, another man would be executed: the Prince of Persia. Like the others, he had failed to solve Turandot's three riddles. Because of that, she had escaped marriage and each of the suitors in turn had been put to the sword.

A new suitor, a mysterious prince whose name no one knew, looked on Turandot's face and fell in love with her. He accepted the challenge of the riddles.

It was one of the best seats in the house: front row of the dress circle. Before the lights went down, Deacon had looked round covertly, but had seen no one who looked likely. Left and right of him, and in the rows behind, were bored executives and their equally bored wives, block-booked by companies who wanted their business, their loyalty or their money. Maybe all three.

When the curtain descended on Act One, and the lights came up, Deacon glanced round again, concentrating on the boxes either side of the stage. Nothing. Some of the boxes appeared to be empty; that, or their occupants were sitting back in the shadows.

Deacon went to the Crush Bar and fought through the throng for a glass of Perrier which he took on to the balcony overlooking Bow Street. Why make it easy? He waited, but no one joined him.

*   *   *

The Prince, whose name was Calaf, solved all three riddles. Turandot wailed in anguish. She had sworn vengeance on men for the dishonour of her ancestress at the hands of barbarian invaders. It was difficult, perhaps, to accept this as the real reason for her hatred of men, since the incident had taken place a very long time ago, but the opera's plot depended on it. Something a bit closer to home would have been more credible – a father whose affection for his daughter went beyond what was strictly proper, perhaps – but the story was insistent about the ancient grudge.

Turandot was the daughter of the Emperor of China and obliged by honour to fulfil her promise now that the Prince had guessed the riddles. She must marry him. The Prince, though, was in love with the Emperor's daughter and anxious not to press his advantage. Maybe he was a born gambler. In any event, he told Turandot that if she could discover his name before morning he would release her from the marriage contract. Now *she* was stuck with a riddle. Life is circular. A grey-haired man in a dinner-jacket, sitting across the aisle from Deacon, snored gently, his chin resting on a second, larger chin, which in turn rested on his chest.

This time, as the dutiful execs and their wives trooped out to the bar, Deacon kept his seat. The sleeper snuffled and came awake, disturbed by the house-lights.

A man in a dark suit was standing up in one of the boxes, a hand resting lightly on the back of his chair and looking directly at Deacon. The auditorium continued to empty. The air-conditioning left a good deal to be desired, and people were hot and thirsty. Deacon returned the stare. In his other hand the man was holding a programme. He lifted it slightly, something between a wave and a summons, then stepped back out of sight.

Deacon counted the boxes, then counted them again a few minutes later as he walked along the row of doors. The man was alone, but only one of the remaining chairs was empty. The other two were spread with food, champagne-glasses, a bottle of Dom Perignon in an ice-bucket.

'The sandwiches are smoked salmon. Would you like a glass of champagne?'

'I don't drink.' Deacon sat in the vacant chair.

The man paused, bottle in hand, and glanced at Deacon with raised eyebrows. 'Really? It hadn't occurred to me.' He seemed chastened, a host who has made some small social gaffe.

'Don't worry.' Deacon selected a sandwich and bit into it. 'Good,' he said.

The man got up and left the box. Ten seconds later he was back. He poured champagne for himself and sat down. 'Puccini never finished the opera, did you know that?'

Deacon shook his head. He was both amused and irritated.

'No, he died of cancer of the throat – died, in fact, with the uncompleted score in his hands. Toscanini conducted the first posthumous performance and stopped at the point where Puccini had stopped. The piece was completed by Franco Alfano from the composer's sketches.' He wasn't looking at Deacon, but down towards the stage and the heavy safety-curtain, as if anxious for the next act to begin.

'Typical and untypical,' he said. 'As with much of Puccini, the psychology of the heroine is all-important. Calaf's real purpose is to draw us on to Turandot's bitterness and isolation, don't you agree? But it ends happily, unlike *Bohème* or *Tosca* or *Butterfly*. Oh,' he broke off, 'perhaps I am spoiling it for you by telling you that.' When Deacon didn't respond, he went on. 'Many don't care for Puccini – the *fin de siècle* and so forth. He'd heard Stravinsky of course, but his

193

sensibility was fixed in the past; his music was always passionate, radiant . . . morbid. Always the same.' There was a knock at the door; the man ignored it. 'You might think that this is a place where I'd be particularly conspicuous. A black man at the opera – particularly in London. Not so in America, perhaps, where the cultures are sometimes less obviously divided.' He pondered the notion. 'I wonder. . . .'

He went to the door, as if someone outside might offer an enlightening opinion. Another ice-bucket, containing a bottle of mineral water, was just to the right of the door when he opened it. He brought it in. 'The fact is that this is a very *safe* place for me to be. A shebeen, a pie and likker shop, one of Brixton's half-and-half restaurants?' He shook his head. 'Nah good, mahn.' The West Indian accent was mockingly thick; then he reverted to the neutral classless tone he'd been using before. 'A room full of white liberals makes me uneasy. Not all niggers wear hats; not all policemen have big feet and narrow foreheads. Besides' – he gestured towards the stage – 'I like this music. I didn't grow up in Port of Spain; I grew up in Cheltenham.' He laughed as if he were hearing the fact for the first time; then he said, 'Deacon,' softly, thoughtfully – a chairman raising a new topic on the agenda. 'You took a risk, didn't you? Your business with Ambrose must have been very important to you.' He poured mineral water into one of the champagne-glasses and handed it over.

The amusement had gone; the irritation had turned to edginess. Deacon knew what the man was up to, but since he was the petitioner he had to sit still for it. 'You know my name. I don't know yours.'

'Marcus Archangel.'

'Is it?'

'A sobriquet. As close as you're going to get. The people who brought me up were called Ffitch. That's not going to help you very much, either. Why did you want to see Ambrose?'

'Do you speak for him?'

'Yes.' The playfulness went out of Archangel's voice.

'I'd sooner talk to him.'

'Not possible. You talk to me.'

Deacon mentally flipped a coin that came up heads. He suspected it might have been a double-headed coin. 'Ambrose Jackson worked for a short time – very short – at a company called Spruce.' He paused and said: 'It's a sort of pun.' Not a particularly effective riposte, but better than nothing. 'They clean business premises when the people who work there have gone home. Among the sorts of places where they hoover, dust and swab are banks. I wanted to ask Ambrose about one bank in particular. I also wanted to ask him whether he had any job-qualifications that extend beyond mopping the men's toilet.'

'I see, yes. Deacon' – Archangel poured himself more champagne; the sandwiches didn't seem to be to his liking – 'the place you went to – the ghetto – what do you know about it? What goes on there?' Deacon waited to be told. The two men's eyes met for a second as Archangel took a sip of his drink, then he looked outwards towards the stage once more.

'The country we live in, Deacon, is an entrepreneur's paradise. Had you noticed? The poor grow daily poorer, the rich are becoming very rich indeed. In all things, division is more noticeable. The new Brutalism. We've become rather warlike in a way. This sort of thing' – he waved a hand towards the lip of the box – 'culture, the arts, what have you. . . . Who cares much about it? It doesn't turn a profit, does it? No. Our leaders care nothing for it. Look at us. We bristle with weapons, we send task forces, we impoverish education and the medical services, we tap telephones, we censor the press, we despise the disadvantaged among us. Commerce, Deacon. Business. Revenue. A free-market economy. We live in strange times and we worship strange gods. If there is a tiny humanist enclave somewhere, it can't hold out for long. The barbarians are at the gates. What are the great intellectual concepts of our time, Deacon? What are the masterpieces? I'll tell you. They are deals: takeovers, mergers, insider trading, the intuitively conceived, carefully sculpted investment opportunity.

'Now, how to deal with this? How to survive amid philistines and the disciples of Mammon?' He paused a moment and smiled. 'Do you know what blacks call white society? Babylon. How to survive in Babylon?' A bell rang, and people began to drift back into the auditorium. 'The ghetto still looks the way it did, I imagine. It's more difficult for someone who has watched something grow judge its rate of expansion. It's more than it seems, Deacon, let me tell you that. It's more than it seems.

'Everyone depends on resources, you understand that? Money, oil, people, skill – whatever. Such things are the source of power. The ghetto is a vast dynamo – yes, one can think of it that way. People and skills were certainly there, but also energy and ambition and anger. Certainly anger; an enormous subterranean sea of it. But it was misdirected. All those resources were misdirected. That, or they weren't made use of at all. It needed its entrepreneur.'

'You,' Deacon suggested.

Archangel smiled. 'What did I have to work with? What was there to overcome? Well, a few local warlords had to go. Divisiveness, you see. Wholly unproductive. After that, it was a matter of marshalling the resources, reviewing them. Stockholdings. Capital value – that had to be calculated. Some of it was pretty obvious: drugs, prostitution, a wealth of talent in violence and theft. . . .'

The house-lights went down, and Archangel stopped immediately. The curtain rose.

*   *   *

196

The slave-girl Liu was dragged before Turandot. The Emperor's torturers stood over her. Turandot demanded to know the name of the mysterious Prince, but Liu was in love with Calaf and refused to speak. They put the thumbscrews in place. A last chance: Turandot asked again for the name of the Prince.

Frightened that she might give the name under torture, Liu took a knife from the folds of her robe and killed herself. With her dying breath, she prophesied that Turandot, too, would fall under the spell of so powerful a love.

It was true. Confronted by the Prince, Turandot revealed that she had, indeed, fallen hopelessly in love with him. The precise moment at which this fierce emotion takes hold is difficult to spot, but the drama would be nothing without it.

The time arrived for Turandot either to reveal the Prince's name and send him to his fate, or to confess that she didn't know it and accept the contract of marriage. 'His name is. . . .' She paused. 'His name is *love*!' They fell into each other's arms. The people of Peking rejoiced.

'Drugs, prostitution, violence, theft. . . .' Archangel picked up as if he'd never been interrupted. They were occupying a table for two at L'Opéra – plain grilled Dover sole, more champagne, more Perrier. Deacon had given in to what was happening. He had begun to think of Archangel as an actor from a play no one had yet seen, dramatizing himself in order to stay in character. Arriviste. Black grandee. A Don.

'The world has need of these things, Deacon, it always has, but nowadays other kinds of talent are just as valuable to people who are determined to dominate. Such people might need accountants or engineers, printers, explosives experts, futures analysts, journalists, skilled people from all fields.'

'Computer programmers,' Deacon suggested.

Archangel ran the flat of his knife along his fish and plucked out the backbone. 'The ghetto is a going concern, you see. We'll do business with anyone and supply what's required if we have it. Most often, we have it. All this takes central organization, of course; that's what I have to offer. Life goes on much as it always has in the ghetto, except that now there's a core, a nexus, of people who aren't content to play the role life meted out to them. The place is an enclave, you see, a walled city. What better premises to operate from? Drugs and prostitution are not just local business. Violence and theft are valuable exports. Knowledge and ability no longer go to waste. People hear of us: word of mouth, you know. Our fees are reasonable. Most important of all, we don't mind who we work for or what we do.

'Now, I'm not suggesting that we're a city state; far from it. We're still embattled; we're still black. In a sense that works for us. But we're becoming . . . well, an economic factor. We're becoming powerful: for what we do and for what we know. Yes, not least for what we know.' Archangel smiled urbanely. 'Why am I telling you all this, Deacon?'

'I expect I'm about to find out.'

'To begin with, it's not entirely a secret. If you advertise, however discreetly, word gets round. The problem faced by the forces of law and order is that we're not any longer a bunch of riff-raff Rastas selling smack in the front line – though, as a sideline, I'm not prepared to knock it. We work close to the people who pull their strings.' He chuckled. 'You can't imagine what pleasure it gives me to witness their discomfort. The second reason is that you are about to become a customer. Or have I got that wrong?'

'I saw a man called Viv. He seemed to think you might want to make a trade.'

'A trade. . . .' Archangel went through a charade of seeming to be puzzled: a slight frown, a shake of the head, then a sudden raising of the eyebrows as he mimed comprehension. 'Ah, yes. Of course. Because he believed you were a policeman.' He leaned over and spoke in a stagey confidential whisper. 'Viv isn't terribly intelligent, I'm afraid. So. . . .' A precise alignment of knife and fork on the plate indicated that Archangel had eaten as much as he wanted: two, perhaps three mouthfuls. He lifted his glass but didn't drink from it at once. 'There is a trade, I suspect, though not the one you were hoping to make. I confess that one more corrupt and greedy law officer on the payroll would be no disadvantage, and I'm sure that in the fullness of time just such a man will present himself; but you are not he, Deacon. Are you? No. . . .' His eyes were on Deacon as he sipped from his glass. 'So we must determine what you have to offer me.'

'That cuts both ways, wouldn't you say?'

Archangel smiled broadly, as if Deacon's reservation were too silly to be taken seriously. 'Oh, I know what you want to know, Deacon. The question is can you afford it?'

'Try me.'

'Ten k.' Archangel named the sum rapidly as if the necessity for mentioning money at all offended him.

'Yes, OK,' Deacon said. The response gave him his first score of the evening. Archangel stalled over his drink, but recovered quickly, taking his time to swallow some champagne and set the glass back on the table.

'You'll be contacted and told where to meet me.'

'No. Contact me if that's what you want to do. I'll name the meeting-place.'

'You don't trust me?' Archangel's smile had returned. 'I'll make you an offer, Deacon. Tell me *why* you want to know what I know and we might make a deal that costs you a little less.'

Deacon stood up. 'No,' he said, 'ten grand's fine.'

'I should have asked for twenty.'

It was Deacon's turn to smile. 'Don't spoil a good act,' he said.

After Deacon had left, Archangel called for the bill and sipped more champagne while he waited for it to arrive. He felt as though he'd made a small but important error somewhere, though he couldn't decide quite what it was. Fifteen grand, perhaps? Surely not – such an in-between sort of sum. 'Ah, well,' he reflected, 'let's wait and see. The opera's not over until the fat lady sings.'

24

'And Jesus said, "He who is not with me, is against me". No room for manoeuvre there. He didn't say, "Ignore me except on Sundays," or "Only turn to me in time of trouble". He didn't say, "Keep some of the Commandments; only sin occasionally; observe God's law when it suits you". No, he made it clear that salvation won't come through part-time love of the Lord. "He who is not with me. . . ." And that's the question each of us has to ask of ourselves: "Am I with the Lord Jesus? Am I a disciple of Christ? Have I let Him into my heart . . .?"'

The preacher was young and filled with fire. A hank of blond hair flopped over his brow as he moved from one side of the long pulpit to the other, unwittingly dividing his congregation into 'with me' and 'against me' with wide sweeps of his hand. Above his ears, his hair was dark with sweat; from time to time, droplets would gather on his chin and he'd cuff them away harshly, as if expelling doubt.

It was a long time since Bob Gower had been to church, and in any case his few memories were of the polite orderliness of Anglican services which seemed to promote the notion that God was a tolerant Englishman who could become stern if he noticed a lapse in good manners. This Baptist fervour made Gower uncomfortable. It was faintly embarrassing – a lapse in good manners in fact. The preacher gripped the rail of the pulpit and glared unblinkingly at those in the crammed pews. He wanted their love for Christ. He also wanted it for himself.

It hadn't taken long. The man Gower was looking for had been missing for something more than a week. A number of people who had expected to see him had been told that he was unwell. His secretary had made the calls: a few cancellations and apologies. Gower hadn't expected to find the man at his home or at his office; other people had looked in both places without success.

It's easy to hide in a city. In cities no one cares much who you are, or cares what you do as long as your behaviour causes them no grief. The old principles of camouflage apply: hide a book in a library, money in a bank and yourself among people. It's possible to make mistakes, though – allowing a pursuer to trade off what he knows about you, for example.

Gower knew a number of things about the man he was seeking, and one of them had brought him to the chapel. It was close to where the man lived and, for that reason alone, Gower hadn't really expected to find him there; other seekers had gone farther afield. Still and all, Gower reasoned, the guy wasn't acting rationally in other matters. Compulsion had led him to kill two women; and compulsion of some sort had brought him to this place. Gower didn't need to understand it, just trade off it. He peered over the gallery and down into the body of the chapel. The man was sitting in a pew close to the altar, his eyes fixed on the preacher.

' . . . from those close to you,' warned the preacher, 'and you can hide sins from yourself if you try hard enough, but you can't hide sins from God.' He raised a hand, the fingers slightly cupped, as if he held a soothsayer's crystal. 'He will look into our hearts and see what we have concealed there; He will look into our souls. . . .'

From his car, Gower had watched the man arrive.

He'd given him five minutes, then followed him into the chapel. He was an unexceptional type, Gower thought, apart from the jet-black hair that made his skin seem waxy and pale. Average height, average build; but, then, there's no reason to suppose that killers look any different from the rest of us. Gower had killed some people in his time; he looked like a suburban householder. In fact that's exactly what he was.

There was a difference between the two of them, though, and Gower had looked for evidence of it. Gower had killed men – and two women – under instruction and in an efficient and businesslike way. This man had killed for the – what? – pleasure of it. *The pleasure.* Gower pondered the notion, trying to gain some sense of what it might mean, but he couldn't make a connection. He looked down at the man again, at his black hair swept back across the crown of his head, the white collar, narrow shoulders under a pale-blue cotton jacket. Nothing. Nothing to distinguish him. Victims, he thought, victims are easier to spot.

' . . . be called to account.' The preacher's arm was extended, his finger pointing randomly at members of the congregation. There was a curious blankness in his eyes, as if he had been staring into the sun. His shirt was patched and fissured by sweat. 'You and you and you and you. The sheep shall be separated from the goats, the tares from the wheat and cast into the fire, no one shall escape the reckoning when Christ comes into His glory.'

There was a prayer, a final hymn, the benediction.

He thought he'd got the timing right, but as he came down the flight of wooden stairs from the gallery, Gower almost collided with his quarry who had been delayed by the people pausing to shake the preacher's hand at the chapel door. The man stood patiently behind the jam of worshippers, his head bowed, a half-smile on his lips. He looked like someone tolerating a joke he'd heard before. Once past the crowd and clear of the chapel gate, he began to walk at an even pace, his head still slightly lowered, paying no attention at all to passers-by, looking up only briefly when he crossed a road.

At first, Gower thought he was going home, but before they reached the street where the man lived, he turned off, heading away from the main thoroughfare. The houses were big, but slightly shabby, some of the fronts peeling and lacking chunks of plaster from sills and pediments. There were fewer people in the street, and Gower hung back, trying to maintain a distance that would be safe but still enable him to keep the man in view. Six entrances, seven, eight – the man pushed open a gate set in cast-iron railings and descended the steps into a basement area. By the time Gower got there, the flat door had closed.

He walked past, briskly, and took refuge in a porch in the next house but one. He could see the steps into the basement, a little of the tiny forecourt and, if he leaned outwards slightly, the windows masked by blinds. He brought his upper arm into his side to feel the hard outline of the gun beneath his linen coat: a 92F 9 mm Beretta. He'd been told that it was unlikely that the man would be armed, but he decided to shift the weapon to a side-pocket and keep a hand on it just before he rang the bell.

A couple of people passed by, but neither paid him any attention. He waited for a short while longer. The man wasn't going to reappear. The heat seemed to sing off the pavement. It had blistered the tarmac coating on the step beneath the porch, and Gower shifted his feet, feeling the tackiness.

He went down the steps to the basement door. He transferred the gun to his coat pocket. He rang the bell; and then he turned his back. It was the only sure way to make the man open the door wide enough for

204

the rush that would take Gower into the place before caution could turn to suspicion and suspicion to certainty.

As it happened, the door didn't open. Gower turned to a rapping noise. The curtain had been drawn back, and a face was looking out at him, eyebrows raised, eyes wide with apprehension. A question was being mouthed: *Yes?*

It was a woman's face, pale, framed by long black hair, fashionably bright lipstick on the mouth that was asking the soundless question. *Yes?*

A flight of eider wheeled against the piercing blue and arrowed in on the lake. The birds broke formation to land, fanning out as they made their gliding approach, all energy and grace, each raising a tiny bowsprit-wave, before settling, inert and placid, on the still surface. A string of riders went by half-hidden by the bracken. Once clear of the lake area, they broke into a canter, heading for woodland half a mile distant. Richmond Park looked sere and brittle under the drought.

Viv looked at the scene with suspicion and ill-concealed edginess. 'Why ya bring me 'ere, man?'

'The biggest of London's green lungs,' Deacon told him. 'Henry the Eighth used to hunt here. I thought you might enjoy a chance to look at the wildlife: red deer, hooper swans, nuclear families each with its Filipino nanny. . . . Aren't you a nature-lover?'

'You full o' shit, man, y'know?'

Deacon smiled and got up. He and Viv had been sitting on a bench close to a lake. 'Let's go for a walk.' He led off, turning almost at once from the path on to a track that passed between tall ferns. 'I met a man called Marcus Archangel.'

'Who?'

'Marcus Archangel. You know him?'

'Nah.'

'He seems to know you pretty well.' There was no response. Deacon could hear the *swish-swish* of Viv's feet through the ferns; the track was narrow, and they were forced to keep single-file. 'He knows Ambrose Jackson, too.' He waited, but got no reply. 'He asked me for money – just like you did. Only difference is, he wants quite a *lot* of money. And, to tell you the truth, Viv, I got the impression that wasn't all he wanted. I've been hoping that you might be able to tell me about that – about what Marcus Archangel wants.' Deacon quickened his pace, leaving Viv to make up ground, and deliberately lowered his voice.

'I din' hear ya.'

It was Deacon's turn to remain silent. He walked on for another two or three hundred metres, maintaining a brisk pace, letting Viv putter along in his wake until he reached a clearing with a small stand of young chestnut trees at one side.

'I said, "I wonder whether you've made any good bets recently".' Deacon sat, putting his back to the bole of a tree. Viv stood in front of him, his height and broad torso blocking the sun. He looked uncertain. There were grass seeds on his trousers.

'Let me tell you what I think.' Deacon spoke without looking up. 'I think you have a habit. Now, I know about habits. You don't just wake up with one some morning; they have to be cultivated. Before you can become addicted, you have to find . . . not a habit you like, but one that likes *you*. You court it, Viv – understand what I'm saying? You flirt with it. For a while, you're not too sure whether you'll get along together, but you hope you've made a good impression. You ask it out, and it agrees to go. You're walking down the street, and there, on your arm, is your brand-new habit. You like the way it feels. You get to know it a little better. You find out things about it, and they're exciting – you know? – they're something to get up in the morning for. Then, as time goes on, you begin to believe that the habit really *does* like you – it's noticeable. The habit comes up with terrific ideas about how you should spend time together. You don't see your friends as much as you used to because you're seeing so much of the habit. You begin to wonder: Could this be the real thing? Then comes the big moment, Viv. You take the habit to bed. And when you wake up in the morning there it is; it didn't get up and leave in the night. And you have breakfast together, and you think – you both think – what shall we do next? And the habit knows what. Sit down, Viv.' The shadow disappeared from in front of the sun. 'After that, you really begin to spend a lot of time together. You don't remember getting married, but you must have because the habit goes everywhere with you and, frankly, it's begun to nag a little, it's become a trifle insistent, and there are times when you'd like to tell it to go straight to hell, but that isn't possible and the habit is very strong, very tenacious; you can't pay it off, and there's no possibility of a divorce. Why? Because by this stage the habit likes *you* better than you like *it*. There won't be any children as a result of this union, Viv; it won't brook any liberal ideas like separate holidays, time spent apart, any of that; it's a very jealous habit and it wants you all to itself. You're the breadwinner in the relationship and you know that each day you have to feed it and each day its appetite seems to grow. Now, do you know what I'm talking about, Viv?'

'You wastin' me patience, man.'

'Is that right?' Deacon plucked a feathery grass-stem and twirled it in his fingers. 'Marcus Archangel asked me for ten grand. How far would that go to cover your debt at the bookie's?' Deacon took some money from his shirt pocket and tossed it on to the grass. 'How far would this go?'

Viv let the money lie for a few seconds, then picked it up and counted it. 'Wha' ya think ya buy for this?'

'I'm not paying for anything – you know that, don't you? This is a gift. You're already bought and paid for.' An amount too small to cover any real debts, but big enough to bet with. To keep him coming back.

'Some day, man. . . .' Viv was squinting, as if he were looking at a target.

'Sure,' Deacon nodded. 'How powerful is Archangel?'

'He run some things. People go to him for things.'

'What do you do for him?'

'Be a minder. Drive he car some time.'

'I shall be seeing Archangel soon. The idea is that I'll give him ten grand and he'll tell me something I want to know. A straightforward trade. Or it should be. The problem – my problem – is that I don't entirely trust the man. You might think that unreasonable of me, Viv, but there we are; put it down to an innately suspicious nature. It's occurred to me that Archangel knows what I want to know, but he doesn't know why I want to know it. He doesn't know what it's for. But he'd like to; he suspects he might be able to make use of it. There's another thing: whatever Ambrose was doing, he was doing for one of Archangel's customers. Archangel's in business; it's not good business practice to make your customers unhappy. So I see it this way: Archangel certainly wants my ten grand, and he wants to find out what makes the information he's got for me so important. Now, you're a gambling man. What odds would you give me on Archangel making an honest trade, then letting me walk away?'

Viv shrugged. 'You doin' the talkin'.'

'Long odds, that's my feeling. Here's what I do in his position. I'd hope to persuade the other man to tell me what makes the information I'd sold so important. If he didn't want to tell me, I'd try even more persuasion. In fact I'd persuade away for as long as it took. I'd keep the money he'd brought with him; and because the man would probably feel cheated and aggrieved

I'd make quite certain that there was no chance of his ever coming back to complain.'

Deacon stopped, as if inviting comment. Viv sighed. 'Wha' you wan' for your money?'

'To know whether I'm right. And, if I am, I want to know how he'll try to take me. All the details: the method, where I'll be held, everything.'

'Too much.'

Deacon stood up. 'You talk as if you had a choice. You haven't. Don't forget that.' He pointed. 'Walk a mile in that direction, you'll come to Roehampton Gate. I don't have much time on this. I'll give you three days. After that, Archangel gets to hear about where you've been scoring your stake-money.' He walked away without looking back.

Viv continued to sit on the ground. A foot or so away, a horsefly was hovering before a stalk of clover blossom, its wings invisible with speed. He watched as it made a sharp backward dart, then forward, then back again: little hysterical twitches to and fro like a nervous predator. For a long time he thought the problem through, looking for a way out, but there wasn't one. He hoped that the day would come when he'd have the chance to kill Deacon. He hoped it would be soon.

The shadows were silent and attentive. The man loaded the bowl of the spoon with heroin and lemon juice, then thumbed the wheel of his cigarette-lighter. A smell bitter as aloe filled the room.

Such a long while. . . . Such a long while since they'd done this. Then, after the second time, the time when he'd danced with the woman, watching her image sway in the mirror, watching himself as he moved behind her, he'd been so full of power, so full of strength, that he thought he wouldn't be able to contain it. And Elaine had reminded him of this – a way to stay level, a way to remember everything, to relive it, all the details. Light swimming on a bathroom window. The scent of peach juice. The startled softness of her mouth as he kissed her.

He tore the end from a cigarette-filter and dropped it into the spoon, then drew the solution up into a syringe through the spongy fibres. Using one of Elaine's stockings, he made a tourniquet for his upper arm and tied it off tightly, one end in his teeth, then pumped his arm like a weight-lifter, opening and closing his fist at the same time. A vein began to bulge in the crook of his elbow.

He was naked, sitting on the edge of Elaine's narrow bed. Her childhood bed. He leaned forward to steady his free hand by resting his forearm across his thigh. The needle slid into the distended vein. He eased the plunger back a little, drawing off some blood, pressed it, then moved it back again to gel the blood with the smack. The shadows moved a little, as if a carousel were starting up. He lay back on the bed.

Sweet notes from the flute; a slow percussion of hooves. He shot the smack into his arm and loosened the tie. A pulse-beat, another, then the rush, fast and brilliant, a rip-tide of light, a rogue wave that took him on its crest. His eyes were closed; the needle still hung from his arm. He felt Elaine straddle him, felt his erection like a pole as she knelt and impaled herself, then squatted to get him deep.

She slid the needle out.

She took the stocking from beneath his arm and looped it round her own.

She put lemon juice and smack into the spoon.

Bob Gower's eyes were fixed on the bed. He sat in one corner of the room, his mouth open, jaw drawn to one side so that his lips made a crooked oval. He might have been in the act of laughing, or uttering a cry. His arms lay almost at shoulder height along the upholstered sides of an easy chair. He appeared startled by what was happening in the room, but also

210

engrossed by it. He sat, wide-eyed, a Caesar enjoying some new form of spectator-event.

Except that if you'd looked closely you'd have seen that his arms lay on the sides of the chair heavily, like the arms of a sleeping man. That his body was roped to stay upright. That his eyes never blinked. That he looked at the bed only because his head was fixed in that position by a long knife, the haft supporting his chin.

The man on the bed was flooded by sensation. Even though his eyelids were closed, he could see, more vividly than normal sight would allow, the silent rapt onlooker in the corner of the room. He could see the women, each of them, as they yielded to him; faces beneath the water, faces in the mirror. And, without opening his eyes, the imagining better than any reality, he could see Elaine, her hair curtaining her face as she pressed the plunger.

She yanked the tourniquet loose. She left the needle to hang.

The shadows flickered and whirled.

25

Father in Father's chair and Mother sewing; a wall-mounted pendulum clock making a slow deep-throated *tock . . . tock . . . tock*, the only other decoration a picture of a golden-haired man, his beard fragrant and curled, his robe spotless, descending through shafts of brilliant light and trailing clouds of glory. Christ come to judge the world.

Myles Allardyce was ten years old. He had no doubt that the day would dawn when sinners would find judgement; he only hoped that it would be a day when he had been cleansed. Each Sunday he would sit in a pew close to the chapel's unadorned altar-table and hear his father affirm the Terrible Day.

I saw the dead, small and great, stand before God. The fearful and unbelieving . . . idolators and all liars shall have their part in the lake which burneth with fire. I am Alpha and Omega . . . the bright and morning star. . . .

It was clear to Myles that his father knew about the awful temptations offered by the world, its snares and pitfalls. They were to be avoided at all costs; and it was for that reason that the family sat in silence in the vast high-ceilinged room, Mother diligently sewing, Father reading reports of the iniquities of men.

Myles would have liked to listen to the radio that sat on a small table close to the fireplace and near Father's controlling hand, but it was put on only for the news. Other programmes – stories, plays, music, variety shows – were trivial frippery and fraught with danger. He knew that sometimes, when his father was visiting

212

parishioners who were ill or in need of the comfort that only Father could provide, his mother would switch on a concert, turning the radio off again long before the expected moment of Father's return.

On one occasion, Myles had been sent home from school with a temperature and a sore throat, and had come into the room to find his mother turning and circling on the large worn carpet, one arm out-stretched, the other hooped round an imaginary part-ner's body. The radio was playing softly, and he could hear her voice above it, a sweet contralto, as she hummed to the tune. Back and round she went, taking her invisible partner's lead, dipping and gliding in waltz-time, her eyes closed to help the imagining. When she opened them, Myles was standing in the doorway. Neither of them spoke. His mother's arms fell to her sides, as if she were suddenly weary, and after a moment or two she went to the radio and switched it off. They never spoke of it; and Myles kept the secret from his father. It wasn't his sin, so he saw no need to confess it, and he thought that one day it might be useful to him to know his mother's weak-ness. Myles's own sins he confessed to God and, on the days of cleansing, to his father.

Joseph Allardyce hadn't always been a minister. He had taught, for a while, in a private school for boys where he'd been known to the pupils as 'Holy Joe'. In truth, he was ill-qualified to teach, but he'd taken up the post during the war when standards were understandably lax. Holy Joe had one leg marginally shorter than the other; he wore a built-up boot to compensate for the deformity and walked with an odd swinging gait, his left side a little in advance of the right and bending slightly as he hauled the weighted foot after him. He was never called on to explain to anyone why he wasn't in the armed forces.

It didn't much bother Joseph that the boys in the

school made cruel use of his disability with wildly exaggerated parodies of his swaying walk. That sort of thing had been happening to him all his life; he'd come to expect it. He knew the world was a place of evil, of weakness and indulgence and filth. He knew that the time would come when it would be purged in fire. It had seemed, for a while, that the purging might be at hand, that a new order might arrive to sweep vileness and corruption from the world, but as the war progressed it grew increasingly apparent that the time was not yet ripe. These feelings he kept to himself, though he never lost an opportunity to help the boys in his charge to come closer to God. He helped, principally, by beating sin out of them as often as possible, thereby leaving room for the Saviour.

As soon as the war ended, reports began to filter through of ghettos and atrocities, of places like Auschwitz and Bergen-Belsen and six million dead. The accounts made Joseph tremble with fury. He knew them to be lies spread by liberals and communists and other representatives of the Antichrist. Brave hopes for a world cleansed by fire were lost. In his efforts to expel the Devil, Joseph grew sterner with the boys in his charge, his punishments harsher, until his zealotry led, one day, to a boy being taken to the local hospital. During the flogging that Joseph had administered, the pupil had bitten through his own lip. Joseph was asked to leave the school. It was done discreetly: the school wasn't anxious for publicity. Joseph resigned, and his resignation was accepted with formal regret. He didn't mind; for some time, he'd believed that his true calling was to the ministry.

He became a stalwart of his local chapel: lay preacher and Sunday School teacher. He was eloquent, uncompromising, fervent and much admired. It was evident to him, though, that he lacked one qualification; before he could be considered as a minister, he would need a wife. Helen Dean was a teacher in the Sunday School, devout, shy and unmarried at thirty. He chose her because she was available to him and for no other reason.

A year later, he was given a ministry. A year after that, Myles Allardyce was born. Despite her age, Helen's delivery was swift and unexpected. When the pains started, she didn't mention them to her husband. From the time that her belly began to be noticeably swollen, Joseph had taken to sleeping in another room. The whole process angered and disgusted him. The pains grew unignorable, and Helen told Joseph what was happening. He told her to do whatever she had to do and retreated to his study, saying he had a sermon to write.

When the midwife arrived, she found Helen, still half-dressed, lying on her bed. She was screaming with terror. The bed's coverlet was swamped with blood, and the child's head was about to be born. Downstairs, Joseph was pacing his study reading aloud from the Bible in a booming frenetic voice that effectively obliterated his wife's hysterical cries. Later – much later – the midwife went downstairs to tell Joseph that he had a son. He nodded politely. She informed him that it would be fine, now, for him to go up and see his child and his wife. He replied that he would certainly do that eventually, but that he was writing a sermon.

A woman from Joseph's congregation was detailed to look after Helen over the following few days. She assumed that Joseph was keeping out of the way while women's work was done. In fact it was nine days before he went near his wife and newborn son. He slept in his own room at the far end of the hallway. The child's thin unappealing cries would wake him in the night, and he would get out of bed and kneel on the room's threadbare carpet to pray for his own soul. The birth had seemed to him as disgusting a business as the conception. Back in bed, the covers pulled above his ears, he shuddered for his guilt and shame.

For the first few years of his life, Myles Allardyce stayed in the company of women: his mother, his maternal grandmother, Helen's few friends from the congregation. His father was like a remote, almost invisible figure who took little or no interest in Myles. Like her husband, Helen took solace in prayer, though she knew that what she prayed for could not be granted. She also took solace in her child. The room that she now occupied alone became their refuge: a place of laughter and games, even a place of song, since nursery-rhymes and cradle-songs – like hymns – couldn't be called the Devil's music. To Myles, Joseph was a presence somewhere in the house, or in the room at the end of the hall. Even when he grew a little older, the distance was maintained. People called his father 'Minister' or 'Mr Allardyce'; his mother called him 'Father'. Myles was twelve before he discovered his father's given name.

It wasn't until Myles began school that Joseph began to take an interest in the boy's welfare. His son had gone into the world, and the world was a Devil-ridden place. It would be necessary to watch him for signs of wilfulness and corruption.

Myles was seven when he received his first real beating. He had forgotten to take his cap off when going into chapel. From that moment on, he began to understand about sin – how it had to be beaten out. He began to understand that the opposite to sin was cleanness. He began to understand the connection between cleanness and pain. The world of womanly virtues seemed lost to him, then. Soft hands, scents of lavender and violet, laughter, song, the smooth texture and bright colours of their clothes. As he grew older, he began to understand a little more of his father's sermons; he identified those lost things with a time

216

before the Fall, a time before sin and the perpetual need for cleansing. He looked back on them as Adam would have looked back on the delights of Paradise. He saw that he lived, as everyone must live, in a place that echoed to the harsh words of his father's sermons and obeyed rules that issued from the uncompromising hand of God. A place of hard, masculine angularity. The stiff, starched white shirts and dead black suits his father wore attested to the colours of that place, and to its nature. There was black and white; there was sin and cleanness.

A pattern became established. Each Saturday evening, Myles would go to his father's study. He understood that in order to be able to attend chapel the next day he had to be rid of whatever sins he had committed during the week. He would kneel with his father and pray, following Joseph's lead, taking care not to stumble over the ritualized phrases. When the prayers were ended, Joseph would sit in the wooden armchair at the desk where he composed his Sunday addresses and Myles would stand before him. He had no knowledge of any other religion save Joseph's, so the words he'd been instructed to use didn't seem odd to him, or blasphemous. 'Father, I have sinned . . .' he would begin. And then would offer his list of wickedness. He was anxious to include everything, and because sometimes he feared he might have left out some moment of envy or sloth, some forgotten weakness, he would admit to sins he hadn't committed at all. When he'd finished, his father would allow a short silence, then he would point to a corner of the room. Two malacca canes leaned against the wall, one thick and stout, one whippy and curved along its length. Myles would walk to the corner and return to his father, bearing the cane he had chosen to be beaten with. The choice was always his. And, of course, in truth there was no choice at all.

217

He would take the cane to his father. And then the cleansing would begin.

Myles understood that his tasks in life were to please his father and to please God; it was clear to him that, by and large, they were the same thing. He read the Bible daily and believed, as he'd been taught, that every word in it was true. He pitied and despised those who denied the Word: this group seemed to consist of almost everyone from his classmates to people called 'heathens' who lived on the other side of the world and were visited by the chapel's missionaries. At one time Myles wanted nothing more than to be a missionary himself and made a start by trying to convert his friends. He took them aside, one by one, and urged them to give their lives to God. Before long, he discovered himself to be friendless. He was angry rather than hurt, and consoled himself with the certainty that those who jeered at him and avoided his company would suffer the torments of Hell. He checked the Bible to remind himself just how hideous those torments were and felt both calm and glad. The days of cleansing came and went. As each approached he would feel fear, as he knew he should, but more and more the fear became mixed with a hot excitement. Walking down the long uncarpeted corridor to his father's study, he would tremble and his face would flush as if he had a mild fever.

After it was over, he would lie in bed, still feeling the pain as it welled and ebbed in his loins and thighs, and think of the ecstasy of the saints.

26

In his thirteenth year, Myles Allardyce underwent three revelations. They changed his life.

One winter's night, he opened his eyes after four hours of sleep, not knowing what time it was or what had woken him. He listened, thinking there must have been some sound or another that would probably come again, but the house was utterly quiet. As he lay there, it began to occur to him that he had been disturbed by the very silence itself – a silence beyond silence, an exaggerated stillness, as if the air had become numb. And then he knew what it was.

He climbed out of bed, shivering in the unheated room, and went to the window. Before he drew back the curtain, he was aware of the new pale light beyond the glass – unmistakable – a sense of hush like the sky holding its breath.

It must have been snowing for some while. The lawn and the trees by the far garden wall were laden with white so pure, so wholly untouched, that it made the world outside the window appear limitless. The fall had dwindled to a thin dust that eddied and dragged across the crust. As Myles looked, he became aware that the gleam from the crust – from its own luminosity – was aided by another light yellower and softer; it was the oblong glow cast by the lamp in his father's bedroom. He opened his window and leaned out. The sharp coldness struck him at once; granules of snow drifted into his hair and clung to his eyelashes. The blur of droplets smudged what he saw; the light broke up into yellow and white spangles when he blinked; but there in the lamplit frame was his father's shadow, distorted for being cast so far – a vast black representation of the man. It was stock-still at first, then the arms moved. It seemed to be binding itself. When that was over the arms moved again, raising something and settling it on the shadow's head.

Myles opened his door and went down the passageway, tiptoeing past the room where his mother lay sleeping. He had a vague plan – to say that a nightmare had brought him awake, or the snowfall; or perhaps to confess some sin he'd omitted before. He listened a moment, but heard nothing. He couldn't tell what drove him to this. He had never been inside his father's bedroom. Oddly, he felt no fear. He opened the door.

On the far side of the room was a cheval mirror. His father stood before it, in profile to Myles, and apparently oblivious to the boy. He had put on leather riding-boots, black breeches tucked into their tops, and was wearing a black shirt crossed by a heavy black Sam Browne belt. On his head was a peaked cap, also black with a silver braid. A swastika arm-band circled his right bicep.

Myles stood in the doorway. His father must have known he was there, but he neither turned nor spoke. On a low table, just in front of the mirror, stood a crucifix, a wine goblet, a silver milk-jug and what looked to Myles like a thin wafer biscuit. A makeshift altar. Joseph stepped forward and knelt. He broke the biscuit and put a fragment of it in his mouth. Then he poured something from the jug into the goblet. Myles had never seen wine before; he thought it might be the blackcurrant drink they sometimes took on picnics. Joseph raised the goblet with both hands and drank from it. He continued to kneel for a short while, head bowed as if in prayer. Miles was dizzy from holding his breath. He watched as his father rose and stepped back, getting himself full-length in the mirror again. He raised his arm, fingers rigid and palm down, in a Nazi salute. He turned to face Myles then, but said nothing.

The boy wilted in his father's gaze. Joseph seemed taller and broader than usual. His face was grave, but he didn't seem to be angry. He beckoned to Myles; then, when the boy moved to join him, held up a hand to stop him and pointed to the door. Myles closed it, then went to stand next to his father. He noticed that Joseph was compensating for his lameness by standing with his shorter leg on a book. To some, that might have been laughable, but not to Myles. Without the lumpish built-up shoe, his father seemed leaner and more powerful.

As Myles reached him, Joseph put an arm round the boy's shoulders and pulled him in alongside. They stood, father and son, regarding their reflections in the long glass. Myles's whole being burned with gratitude. He wanted to cry. He wanted to hug his father, but it was clear that this wasn't possible. He remained still, fizzing with happiness, feeling for the first time the companionable weight of his father's hand on his shoulder and glorying at the sight of the two of them: himself embraced, under the protection of his big, black-clad father. When Joseph released him, Myles simply turned and went back to his own room as if he'd known that was what he should do next.

That was the first revelation. Afterwards, the cleansings became sterner and more exacting. Myles could see that it was necessary.

In the summer of the same year, Myles was sent to Bible camp. There were morning and evening services and Bible-readings. The rest of the time was given over to bathing in the ocean, rambles along the cliffs and foreshore, coach trips to places of interest. Most afternoons, the boys were allowed to do as they pleased.

More often than not, Myles would spend his free time studying for the evening Bible class. He was always anxious to read if he could. He'd arrive early, sometimes, to have a word with the teacher about his text. Since he was the Minister's son, the teachers didn't like to refuse him, though they would sooner have avoided Myles's readings. He seemed to concentrate too much on passages from the Old Testament – accounts of bloodshed and divine retribution, of fratricide and betrayal; but, more than that, he would read with embarrassing fervour, his voice intense, his tone sometimes low and threatening, sometimes shrill with passion. It might have seemed bad acting – an adolescent tendency to over-dramatize life – had it not been for the almost sinister similarity to Joseph's style of preaching. Myles would stand in the big bell-tent where meetings were held, Bible in hand, though he scarcely ever needed to consult it, and read as if Pentecostal fire burned above his head. His free arm would be extended, fingers half-curled. Flecks of white spittle would cram the corners of his mouth. His eyes would be wide like those of someone who looked upon a holy light. A few of the other boys shared Myles's zeal and were pretty impressed by this. The others thought him a creep.

Myles usually spent free time alone. He would walk on the cliff-tops and ponder the sea, using its vastness to summon images of God's love and wrath; or he would lie in the dunes listening to the rustle of sand drifting through the marram grass. It reminded him of the sound of the spindrift along the snowcrust on the lawn. Eyes closed, he'd construct fantasies of Joseph and himself as soldiers of the Cross putting down heathen hordes. His father carried an enormous blazing crucifix that burned with a low roaring sound like slow explosions of surf. The flames flickered round his hands and forearms, but he didn't flinch. Myles carried a sword. The heathen fled before them; they were herded into a compound with watchtowers and high wire fences.

It was in the dunes that Myles came across two of the boys. They were in a sheltered declivity quite close to the beach, half-lying opposite one another, their backs to the sand-wall. They were naked from the waist down and gripping themselves. They appeared to be concentrating hard on their own groins, because their heads were bent over in scrutiny as their hands moved.

Myles watched until first one of them looked up, then the other. There was a moment's silence. Myles had led a sheltered life. He asked them what they were doing. The taller of the two boys snorted with laughter and took his hand away so that Myles could see. Even so, he didn't know what they meant. He went down into the dip between the dunes, and the boys helped him to understand.

He was frightened at first, but soon the feeling overtook fear. The boys watched until he had finished. Then they jumped him, laughing. One of them wrestled him to the ground, face down, his knees trapping Myles's shoulders; the other kneeled behind him. There was a hard pain, then an awful hollow ache like a sudden flux. Myles yelled, but his mouth was against the sand. He could feel its grittiness on his teeth. It seemed to go on for a long time. The boys were silent, concentrating as they had before. Eventually, they changed positions. Knees on his shoulders, hands gripping his hips.

When they had gone, Myles lay in the sand, dry-eyed, for half an hour. Then he inched his way up the dune until he could see the ocean. He stared. It seemed to swell and boil like an enormous abscess.

He knew he couldn't report what had happened, and he knew the boys knew that, too. It was the second revelation and the first thing he ever kept from his father on the day of cleansing.

His life had changed. He started noticing young women in the street and among the congregation on Sundays. He began to have thoughts about them. Although he knew that the thoughts were unclean, there was no way to stop them. It tore at him that he would sit in God's house, and under God's scrutiny, thinking such things. Each time he bowed his head in prayer and closed his eyes, the imaginings would pile up like filth behind a dammed stream.

The young women were an endless procession, a limitless supply. They would stroll down the street in their summer dresses, breasts moving softly under gathered bodices, hips swivelling as they walked. They were narrow-waisted; their arms were brown and slender. A breeze would stir their long hair, blowing wisps across their lips. Their very demureness in chapel was a provocation. Myles noticed that, before sitting down, they would smooth their dresses under them, hands stroking their own rumps. He yearned for the young women and he hated them. They were deliciousness and damnation. At night, in bed, he would conjure them up. In his fantasies, he possessed only in order to destroy.

On a day when his parents were out Myles wandered from room to room, pretending that he didn't already know where he was going. There would be time. His father was hospital-visiting – a day-long task; his mother had gone to visit a friend and would return only in time to cook the evening meal.

Her room seemed warmer than Joseph's: not just because of the flower-patterned bedspread and the chintz curtains; the walls had kept in the heat generated by her body as she slept, as she sat at her dressing-table glowing after her bath. Myles had been to his mother's room before on days he'd spent alone in the house. He'd opened drawers and cupboards and discovered things about his mother that no one else knew. Each time there had been something he'd wanted to do, but he'd always held back; the very thought of it made him dizzy with excitement. Now he could wait no longer.

He stood by the bed and stripped, laying his clothes carefully on the coverlet. That neatness, that deliberation, was part of the ritual. The second drawer down on the left in his mother's dressing-table contained the secrets. Myles guessed that she wore them often – delighted, probably, by his father's ignorance of what she was doing; to sit at dinner with him, to be in the same room quietly sewing, and to go undetected. Silk French knickers with a lace trim on the legs; one red pair, one black. Myles drew on the black pair, catching his breath as the material fluttered over his thighs. He took out a matching brassiere and looped the straps over his arms; after fastening it, he found some stockings to stuff the cups. In the wardrobe was a pale lemon dress, sleeveless, slightly flared from the waist: the most frivolous thing his mother dared to be seen in. He put it on.

Sitting before the dressing-table mirror, he combed his black hair forward and parted it in the middle, letting it hang at the sides so that it just covered his ears, then unscrewed the tops of the jars of cream and rouge that his mother used for special occasions. He decorated his face, leaning forward, mouth pouting, to apply a coating of lipstick.

When he'd finished, he opened the wardrobe again and stood in front of the long glass that was fixed to the inside of the door. He felt faint and slightly feverish. Trembling, he passed his hands over his profile. He was looking at a new person.

It was the third revelation. He called the person Elaine. He knew who she was because he had read about her. *Mystery, Babylon the Great, the Mother of Harlots and Abomination of the Earth.*

His sister. His lover.

Myles adored her and he hated her, too.

27

Joseph Allardyce died when Myles was twenty-three. Cancer had eaten him to the bone. He lay in his room with the shutters half-drawn to make a false dusk, the outline of his wasted body scarcely detectable under the covers. His head on the pillow was skeletal, nose lofted like the prow of a ship.

Each day after the crisis arrived, Myles sat with his father, watching him slip from coma into death. People said that his mother had taken refuge in being busy – she took on her husband's visiting duties, she attended to paperwork, she cleaned the house with a new vigour – but Myles thought he could detect a lightness of mood where others saw only muted hysteria.

He suspected that he was witnessing some crucial event – crucial to himself. The doctors had agreed that nothing could be done, and so Myles had brought his father home to die – a place where Myles could keep vigil as he felt he should. It took twelve days.

His mother was in the kitchen, preparing lunch. Myles sat by the bedside listening to the slow difficult sound of Joseph's breathing. He could have played the radio or read a book but he sat, almost at attention, staring at the wall, seeing nothing and feeling nothing.

The rhythm of breathing changed: little gasps that were held for an impossibly long time before being exhaled, then a long, harsh, rasping sound that was the death-rattle. For some reason, Myles looked at his watch: it was twelve-thirty. It struck him as a ridiculous time to die. He looked at his father and wondered what it was that had, just a second before, gone from him. The room seemed to grow still. A calmness accumulated that Myles found soothing, and he sat on, while his mother clattered and banged below, trying to identify the emotion that was settling on him. He couldn't be sure, but he thought it might be happiness. When he went downstairs to tell his mother that Joseph was dead she stared at him, frozen, a frying-pan in one hand, a rasher of bacon hanging incongruously from the other. He thought it was shock at the news that had fixed her there, but it wasn't.

Her son stood in the kitchen doorway. He had just said: 'Father is dead.' He had lipstick on his mouth. His eyes were empty. And he was smiling.

The journey from the Manse to the cemetery was a short one. Helen Allardyce leaned on her son's arm as they walked behind the coffin to the open grave. People remarked, afterwards, that she had 'borne up well'. What they read as stoicism in suffering was, in fact, resolve; she had already made plans to go away. She wanted a cottage close to the sea, a flower-garden, rooms filled with music and light. The clods of earth that rattled down on the coffin-lid seemed to her to resemble the sound of chains being cast off.

Three days after the burial, when the wreaths and bouquets had become brown and wilted, a young woman visited the grave. She was tall and shapely; long jet-black hair hung to her shoulders. It was late in the evening and no one else was around. She stood at the graveside for some time, her head bowed in thought, or perhaps in prayer, then put her tribute close to the top of the mounded earth and walked away.

Next morning, the handyman who kept the grave-yard tidy came to clear away the dead flowers. He

228

found the fresh offering, and realized at once that someone had made a mistake. It wasn't possible to know who the tribute was meant for, though, so he left the new flowers on the Minister's grave. An odd choice, he thought: black tulips. Since the card was inappropriate, he took it away with him. It read: 'From your loving daughter, Elaine.' It was her first appearance in the world.

After that, Elaine made regular outings, She never sought out others who were like her. It was enough to walk after dark in the streets or to stay in the basement room that was hers and no one else's, where she would dream extravagant dreams that were helped by the occasional drugs that Myles was able to supply. It was a mutual trade – Myles had become a professional man and was enjoying some success. He didn't bother much with a social life; Elaine fulfilled most of his emotional needs.

Only once did he become involved with another woman. She was young and pretty and married to a man of some prominence. Her husband was away often on important business, and she was bored and lonely. She made it obvious that if Myles were to invite her to dinner she wouldn't refuse.

They dined, they drank – she a lot, Myles sparingly – and they wound up in bed as she had hoped they might. He was a pretty average lover, she thought; half the time his mind seemed to be elsewhere. They lay side by side on his bed, the woman wondering how soon she could leave without appearing crass, when he got up and crossed to a wardrobe, then returned carrying two ties. She was puzzled for a moment; then, when he turned her on to her face and began to bind her wrists to the bed-rail, she smiled to herself. Maybe there was more about him than she'd thought. He went away again and she turned her head, lifting it from the pillow, to see what he was doing.

Myles had taken a small mirror from the top of a chest of drawers; he was holding it close to his face; in his other hand was a tube of lipstick. As the woman watched, he smeared red on to his lips, taking care to follow the outline of his mouth. He didn't once glance towards the bed; he was completely self-absorbed. He took a long black wig from a drawer and settled it on his head, peering at the mirror as he fluffed and arranged it.

The woman was frightened. When he went back to the wardrobe and removed the cane she felt panic. Shortly after that, as the cleansing began, she started to scream.

It was only the fact that the woman was married – and to a public figure – that saved Myles. She could tell no one – not even her doctor – Myles knew that; but he was angry with Elaine for having put him at risk. They talked it over and agreed that he should go to prostitutes in future. If he paid enough, he and Elaine could do pretty much what they liked.

Myles prospered in his career. He came to know some wealthy and famous people; some of them could be counted friends. He dined out a good deal and frequently spent his weekends in grand homes.

At a house-party, on a warm evening in June, Myles was standing among a group of guests to watch a firework display laid on by the host to celebrate his wife's birthday. The host was an earl. Among those watching were three Members of Parliament, two film stars, some popular broadcasters, a cook who rarely went near a kitchen but now owned a string of restaurants, and a golfer who had recently won an international tournament. Myles fell into conversation with a man he'd seen often at such gatherings: Major York. People called him 'Major', as if he had no first name. The Major knew a lot about Myles and showed a keen interest in his profession.

After a while, they went to the library where they could talk in private.

The Major spoke of threats to freedom and of world-wide tension. He spoke of an enemy within and of need for constant vigilance. Myles was flattered and intrigued. When the time seemed ripe, the Major revealed that he belonged to an organization that didn't officially exist, though it operated with the Government's knowledge and with government funds. He named a few of Myles's clients: important people, or the wives of important people, and suggested that it would be possible for Myles to pass on odd snippets of information he might glean. 'It's a war, really,' the Major said. 'We have to be on our toes.'

Myles recollected the term for what appeared to be happening. He asked if he were being 'recruited'. The Major smiled and said he supposed that, yes, that summed it up. An image came to Myles of a man marching, holding before him a burning cross. In some ways, the major reminded him of his father.

Some arrangements were made – for giving information and receiving instruction – then the Major led the way back to the lawn and the extravagant finale to the firework display. Myles felt powerful and pleased with his new secret.

The shadows came to rest; the music faded, Elaine's presence began to dwindle. He could summon her, just as he had summoned her as a boy, putting her in the chair between his parents, his eyes closed, making her touch herself, making her smile; but she always left of her own accord. She left when his need of her had abated.

He got up and went to the armchair in the corner of the room. Gower sat there looking attentive, the death-spasm still locked into his frame. Myles squatted down and peered at the man's face.

231

'Now, who sent you?' he asked. Then 'Well, you
don't have to tell me; I think I know.' He patted
Gower's hand reassuringly, then went through to the
kitchenette and began to grind some coffee beans.
Coming down from the heroin, he felt calm and a little
removed from things. Pleasantly hollow. As he sipped
his coffee, he thought it might be best to stay out of
circulation for a while. There was one commitment,
though, that he felt he should keep, even though it
involved some risk.

He had an appointment with Laura Scott.

28

'He could be calling your bluff,' Laura said.

Deacon shook his head, still listening to the shrill of the ringing tone. He waited for a few more seconds, then hung up. 'I don't think so.' Deacon had been trying to phone Viv for a couple of days. 'He needs money and he needs my silence. If he'd come after me – OK, I could understand that. Going to ground doesn't make any sense. He couldn't hope to hide for long. From me, perhaps; not from Archangel.'

'What will you do?'

'Look for him.'

'Now?' She knew the answer, but didn't want to see him go.

'It's the best time.'

Laura went with him to the back door, then walked back to the window and watched him down the street and out of sight. I can't take much more of this, she thought. Her mind was on Maggie.

Deacon was thinking only of his route through the ghetto. In some ways it would be easier; in others, more dangerous. Each year there was a carnival: two days when the ghetto lowered its drawbridge and the streets filled with bands, dancers, people in costume, onlookers, policemen, pickpockets, drunks, liberals, social workers and community leaders. Some years there had been deaths during the carnival. Once or twice, there had been a full-scale riot. It was good cover, Deacon knew that. On the other hand, an attack would probably go unnoticed. There were better than half a million people in the area, a lot of noise, a lot of distractions.

He was a mile from the ghetto when he hit the fringe of the carnival: police lines cordoning off the route of one of the processions, roads closed to traffic, noisy street-parties. He'd chosen his time with care: three in the afternoon; too early for serious street-violence if there was going to be any, but late enough for the carnival to be in full swing. He walked a mazy course towards the centre, sometimes taking side-roads, sometimes main thoroughfares, trying not to look as if he had any particular destination in mind.

Further in there were long slow processions of dancers and players, gaudy costumes, floats, pavements thick with people, children hoisted on shoulders, colossal music, a low miasma of charcoal-smoke, laughter, beer-fumes, the thick smell of ganja. Groups of kids cruised through it all like sharks.

Near Viv's address, things were quieter, as if the row and activity were contained in concentric rings that narrowed to a silent epicentre. Deacon slowed as he neared the place, taking time to look around unobtrusively. People went by packing big sound systems on one shoulder, like soldiers hefting kitbags, but there wasn't the blare that you could hear in areas where the carnival snaked through heaving and bumping. The music came and went. Dope deals were going down in plain view.

Deacon walked past the doorway and out of the street, then tagged on to a crowd that would soon turn the corner and take him back again. The stairs had been empty the first time, the door part-open. When he came level the second time, nothing had changed. Getting what cover he could from the people he was following, he turned and walked unhurriedly up the steps, then through the door, trying to look as though he were lost in thought. The hallway was deserted. Viv's door carried a hasp-and-ring clasp that would have been secured by a padlock when the man was out. It wasn't fastened.

Deacon went through fast, opening and closing the door rapidly then stepping at once to the side. The room was in half-darkness as before. As soon as Deacon's eyes grew accustomed to the dim light, he saw Viv; and as soon as he saw Viv, he knew the man was dead.

He was lying back on his exercise-bench, face-up. It seemed as if he was about to go for a bench-press – a big one. The huge muscles in his thighs were set to brace for the lift, and his torso reared slightly as though the grunt and heft were about to come. But his arms weren't bent to jack the weight upwards. They were trailing on either side of the bench. The bar was across his throat.

Deacon stepped forward. Viv's eyes were wide, his tongue out of his mouth to the root. A depression across his throat, under the bar but wider, meant that the thorax was crushed. Deacon put a hand to Viv's cheek. Feeling the warmth, he turned at once for the door, guessing already that he'd be too late.

Something came in from the kitchen, moving low and startlingly fast. Deacon side-stepped, but it wasn't enough. He went back against the wall, hard, his attacker driving at him with a braced shoulder; the breath banged out of him and he began to fall; all he could do was wrap his arms round the other man and lock his fingers. It was effective for a short while. They went down in a heap, anchored by Deacon's weight. He could feel back and biceps muscles tensing, trying to throw him off. He hung on, feeling his grip unfastening. The other man reared, getting to his knees, then hauled himself into a squat before straightening his legs, coming upright and taking Deacon with him. The movement required a lot of strength. There was an ache in Deacon's shoulders; his arms were opening. He sensed the man readying himself for the outburst of energy that would free him and let him get his hands up.

When it came Deacon let go instantly and took a step forward. His attacker was caught in the violent momentum of his own energy. Flinging his arms out and his body backwards to shake Deacon off, he suddenly found the motion too great, the explosion of strength too extravagant. As he went off balance, Deacon's forward motion emphasized his unsteadiness and, for an instant, the man looked like someone who has stepped backwards off a high place, arms wide, belly up, the moment just past when his foot had been on firm land. Instead of using the moment to gain the door, Deacon took another half-pace forward and kicked, stiff legged, using every ounce of his weight. The follow-through line would have bisected the man's head. As it was, he landed it on the upper ribs, just below the armpit. The man sat down, still for a fraction of a second, and Deacon kicked again, aiming straight into the face, but an arm came up and collected the blow. The speed of that reaction was frightening; it was enough. As the man shuffled rapidly backwards to take himself out of range, Deacon went sideways to the door. Back in the street, he walked half a block, weaving through the crowds, then turned to look. The man was following, staring directly at him. His left arm was hanging straight down: probably useless.

Six streets, seven streets back. The tides of music and people were cover for both of them; too risky, though, to try getting lost in the throng. Losing himself would mean losing sight of his pursuer, who was certainly a better man for the terrain. Just ahead was a column of people spread across the centre of the road. Deacon got among them, walking a little faster to bring himself up to the tail of a procession – men and women in traditional costume around a small float that carried a steel band. The crowd was turning and

236

weaving like a slow snake; joints and bottles of wine going from hand to hand. They were approaching a small square: trees, shrubbery, a groomed lawn. Deacon knew that the iron-bar gate would be locked. The railings were close to seven feet high.

Someone passed him a bottle of wine. He took a slug and turned as if to pass it on, but turned again, dancing with the dancers, holding the bottle by its neck and lengthening his step until he grew level with the float. He hadn't looked back since that first time; even so, he could feel the man behind him as if the street were empty save the two of them. He would be waiting for Deacon's move. There was no question of getting clear.

Deacon got in front of the float as it came up to the square. He had a few seconds to pick a place – a screen of shrubbery just to the left of the gate. The float masked him. He tossed the bottle over onto the grass, took a run at the railings and jumped to grab the top horizontal bar, then straightened his arms to bring his torso up. A toehold on the bar for leverage and he was over. A dozen or so people nearby watched him. A voice said, 'Hey, man,' then he was gone, and the float had moved on and the spectators with it. He collected the bottle and left the shrubbery in a crouching run, heading for the small wooden pagoda that stood in the centre of the square. He thought he might have a couple of minutes.

Three, in fact. The man was ambling across the lawn, certain that Deacon had made a mistake. He was looking round, trying to decide between the pagoda, some clumps of shrub and a stand of small plane trees in the far corner of the square. Deacon wedged the base of the bottle into the waistband of his jeans at the back so that it pointed straight up from the base of his spine. The pagoda had six walls that radiated little spokes from the centre and were connected by slatted seats. Three of the wedge-shaped spaces were visible

237

to the man as he approached. His eyes flicked off to the side continually: shrubbery, trees, then back to the pagoda again. He looked big and capable and unhurried.

You could dance with your eyes closed, and the music would slam through you and buffet you and buoy you up. Reggae and rock and the plangent clang of steel-band drummers, everyone moving and laughing and yelling; booze and good Moroccan spliff and, in quieter corners, fast lines of coke. Flawless skies and the sun like a brass cauldron.

Now and then, someone keeled over: drunk, drug-ged or wiped out by the heat. Ambulancemen fought to get through. Steamers went through the crowd: thirty or more kids carrying knives, rice-flails, the butt-ends of pool-cues. They would section off an area fifteen feet square, saturate it, take wallets and purses, necklaces and wristwatches; no one moved against them. They piled into an off-licence and took what they wanted from the shelves while the owner stood mute. The police were ten minutes behind them wherever they went. If things got close, the gang split – thirty unconnected guys having a good time, watch-ing the processions, dancing in the street. Close to the main parade a sixty-year-old woman had a heart-attack. Dozens of tearful children looked for lost parents while their parents looked elsewhere. A policeman danced with the crowd, embraced by a fat laughing lady: tomorrow's front pages. With every minute the scene changed: an endless array of brilliant costumes, bands, throngs, faces. No one gave anyone a second glance.

Perfect, thought Elaine. She had walked there and was carrying nothing – nothing to steal. An envelope was lodged in her bra, between styrofoam breasts and beneath the demure short-sleeved blouse; the sheet of paper it contained was blank. Her scalp itched slightly under the wig, but she scarcely noticed that; it was great to be out, to be anonymous. From time to time, she lingered to watch the parade.

No hurry, she thought, no hurry. But the excitement was in her, lifting her, making her light.

The street where Laura lived was comparatively quiet – a few people, distant music: the fringe of things. The door of the phone-box closed, stopping the noise. Four rings, five, then Laura's *Hello?*

Elaine laughed. 'Laura' she said, 'Laura. . . . It's so long since we spoke. . . .'

Clockwise or anticlockwise? the man was coming straight at the pagoda, leaving the choice to the last minute. Deacon put himself in the man's place and decided he'd want his right arm active. Anticlockwise, then. With only a second to spare, he moved in that direction, occupying one of the spaces that had been in view as the man approached. The best technique for his pursuer would be to walk around the pagoda, giving himself ten or twelve feet of clear space; that way he'd see what was there without running the risk of being jumped. He allowed two seconds for each V-shaped section.

One and two and. . . . He moved into the next space back. *One and two and. . . .* Back again. *One and two and. . . .* Too late to change; too late if the man back-tracked; too late if he changed his pace. Deacon came round to the space he'd originally occupied and stayed put. Too late if he walked round a second time.

One and two and. . . .

He appeard to Deacon's right, having made a complete circuit. His eyes were fixed on the plane trees. The arm that Deacon had kicked appeared to be back in use: he was flexing it slowly. The other hung by his side, an open switchblade jutting, like a silver tooth-pick, from his clenched fist. He was ten feet away, maybe twelve; three strides.

As Deacon came within arm's length, the man turned. There hadn't been a sound, but his nerve-endings were up to the skin and he felt Deacon's approach like a sudden cold draught on the back of his neck. Knife in the right hand, so he swung to the right by instinct, arm lifted, the blade describing an arc across his body.

Deacon stepped sideways and stepped in, the bottle already travelling upwards from his side; his whole torso swivelled left like a discus-thrower's, putting everything into that single swing, yelling with effort in the moment of contact.

The bottle exploded. For the briefest instant it was as if nothing had happened. Deacon staggered slightly, following the inward direction of the blow. Then the man's face dissolved in a welter of blood and glass. His legs went from under him so fast that he hit the ground like something dropped from a height. Deacon wrestled the dead weight back into the pagoda, then went to the railings on the far side of the square. He paused for a moment, hidden by shrub, and stripped off his T-shirt, using the tail-end to wipe his forearms, then wadded it into his hip pocket. It was nothing unusual, this summer, to go shirtless.

The parade was still going by. A few people watched incuriously as he clambered over. No one showed surprise. He'd gone to take a leak, maybe – or a snort. Later, perhaps the next day, some of them might remember enough to know that they'd seen something important. It might even be that there was a public-minded citizen or two among them. Deacon wasn't too worried. He'd heard a lot of descriptions in his time, and seen a lot of photofits. They all added up to the Invisible Man.

He followed the crowd. The crowd followed the parade.

Laura slammed the street-door and set off at a near-run. If the pavements had been emptier, it wouldn't have been possible to follow without being obvious. She went blindly through the press of people, not caring much where she was going: enough to be among the onlookers; enough to be out. She walked into the thick of it, wanting the throng, the safety in numbers. After ten minutes, having no destination, she stopped.

A tall man wearing a peacock-tail cloak was leading a troupe of dancers. He was very black and smoothly bald, the dome of his head glossed by sunlight. A hundred people stood still to watch. Laura was one of them. The cloak undulated and wafted as he spun, weaving fugitive patterns of rich blue and brilliant green. She was breathing hard, and there was a tight pain in her chest. The man came abreast of her, the cloak fanning out, colours merging to iridescence.

Like some small creature transfixed by a stoat-dance, she had listened. Like that: like prey. *Laura* . . . *Laura. . . . Laura. . . . And then I'd like to. . . . And then. . . . And then. . . .* She was shivering, but her mouth was baked, no spit to moisten her lips. Her eyes burned as if she had been up for nights.

Elaine stood directly behind her in the crush. Her wrists ached with the effort of not touching. The way that Laura's back hollowed at the base of the spine was vulnerability itself. Her arms bare in the summer dress, the slope of her neck where it curved into her shoulders. . . . Elaine leaned forward a fraction and pursed her lips. The outward breath disturbed a strand or two of blonde hair. Enough. Enough for now.

Deacon got back first and found the letter just inside the door. He took it upstairs and propped it on the mantelpiece, then went directly to the bathroom. The mirror showed him a smudge of blood over his eyebrow; his jaw, on the right side, was freckled with it: a hundred pinhead dots, dry now like a razor-rash. He washed, scrubbing at his face with the towel. Although Laura had given him keys to her flat, he didn't know it well; he hunted for a bucket to put the T-shirt in but couldn't find one. In the end he tossed it into the kitchen sink with half a packet of washing-powder and ran hot water in.

He felt jumpy and restless, unable to settle any-where. He went from room to room, finally perching on a stool in the kitchen; even then, his foot hopped like someone working a treadle. Years ago, he and Mayhew and two others had answered a call to a pub in the northern part of the patch. Two men had been refused service because they were drunk. They were systematically wrecking the bar. No point in trying to calm the situation – as Deacon walked into the place a flung bar-stool clouted him on the shoulder. One of the men had torn off a table-leg and was handling it like a flail; the other had just finished with the barman and was looking for something else to do.

Deacon wound up with a busted hand and slight double vision that lasted for three days. Mayhew was cut behind the ear; he'd broken his stick on one of the men. One of the other coppers had taken a long gash just under the hairline; it wasn't bad, though rivulets of blood ran from its length across his eyes, down past his nose, his cheeks, his ears, making his face seem fissured with red. The two brawlers had gone by ambulance to the closest hospital. On the way back to the station-house, the copper with the bloody face had started to laugh. Energy and vio-lence, fear and a sinister delight were banging about in the car like escaped electricity. They all began to laugh: shouting laughter, their mouths stretched, their shoulders heaving. Mayhew could scarcely con-trol the wheel.

Deacon sat on the stool and jiggled his foot. He drummed his fingers on the wooden work-surface under the window: the Devil's tattoo. It occurred to him to wonder where in hell Laura might be.

Ten minutes later, the phone rang. When he answered he could hear the collapse of relief in her voice and knew what had happened. He waited at the street-door for her. She was running.

That wasn't all.

He took her in like a refugee, her face pale and serious, and she told him about the phone call. He held her while she spoke, and even though his arms contained the shake in her body it was there in her voice also: a tremulousness that made her speech a rapid staccato. After she had finished speaking she stayed in the caul of his arms as if she were taking his warmth; when she freed herself and poured a drink, he realized for the first time how much he would have liked one. She went to the sink to add some water to her Scotch and saw the T-shirt floating in a froth of bloodied suds. He told her about Viv and the man who followed him.

'I'll have to phone Archangel,' he said. 'Arrange the meet.'

'But that— It must be even more dangerous now.'

'But there's no alternative. At one time there might have been a way of backing out. I've thought of doing that often enough. Old habits die hard; I could see how there might be more to Kate's death than the official version allowed, and I wanted to find out about that. I wanted to know you, I wanted to be close to someone who had been close to Maggie, it was a bond and I needed it, but also I was curious. It might have led nowhere: suspicion is chaff in the wind. But then you found out that something odd was going on at the bank – the trace. Well, that might have unravelled quickly – a simple fraud that I could have handed over to Phil Mayhew. That didn't happen; it led to Archangel, and I don't know what that means. The person

243

who phoned you – this time and the last – could have been one of those poisonous ghouls who seem to swarm round a death like flies; a lot of people get sick phone calls. But it's not like that. There have been other deaths; and whoever it is that phones knows things that shouldn't be known. On top of all that, I'm getting clear signals from Phil that officialdom is refusing to put two and two together for fear of coming up with something suspiciously like four.' He watched the level of her drink fall and felt the itch.

'Understand? It's too late to go back. We can go on or go away, though I'm not sure even that's possible. What do we know? Someone is killing women. One of them was a friend of yours who uncovered a fraud. Someone is threatening you, possibly the same person. A ghetto godfather says he knows something about the computer-trace. An informant was killed by someone who would probably have killed me. It's not enough. It's too much.'

She nodded. 'I wish—'

'Don't say it,' he asked, 'because I wish it, too.'

She walked away from him, angry to have to listen to things that she would have sooner not have heard. The letter fell on to her eyeline: hand-delivered since it bore no stamp, though her address was written in full.

'What's this?'

Deacon came out of the kitchen. 'It was on the mat.'

Laura opened it and read. Deacon had half-turned away, but was suddenly conscious of a rigidity growing in her as if her joints had begun to seize.

He took a half-step towards her. He said: 'What—?'

Laura swivelled, stiff-legged, her arm held out, not offering the letter but reaching; someone in a morass, sinking, reaching for firm ground. A cawing sound came from her throat. Her eyes rolled up. Deacon

244

made a grab as she fell, only half-catching her, and they went to the floor together, her limbs unbolted by the shock, her body across his like a sack of rags.

The peacock cloak had glittered, seeming to throw back beams of sunlight. The bald man crouched, and it fell around him, a glossy carapace; he whirled, and it spread like a fan.

Elaine had left Laura standing at the roadside; she'd walked for a few hundred yards, then found a bench where she could sit and write, taking a small gold pen from the pocket in her dress that also held her door key. Then she had gone back to Laura's flat and delivered the letter.

Dearest Laura . . . watched you leave and walk to . . . and followed you there, so close I could have . . . your pretty white dress, the touch of lace on the neckline . . . arms and their golden tan . . . fine hairs glistened in the sun. I stood so close, right behind you . . . watched the dancer with the peacock eyes sewn on his cloak . . . your shoulders rising and falling because you'd hurried there . . . pulse-beat in your neck, I could have kissed . . . Laura, I could have . . . could have . . . could have. . . .

29

Austin Chadwick appeared to be asleep, but he was not. He sat behind his broad desk in the office that was sometimes above the clouds. His eyes were closed, his hands clasped, his elbows resting on the polished wood. His thumbs supported his chin; his forefingers lay atop his nose. He was breathing evenly. The room was very quiet, but there was something menacing etched on to the silence.

Chadwick had just conducted a telephone conversation that had begun and ended with a question.

'What has happened?'

'We're not sure, Austin.'

'Not sure?'

'We don't know.'

'Do you feel able to make a guess?'

'Gower's very experienced. He was in Ireland for two years; a senior field-operative. He'd been checking in regularly – reporting back. It's as if the earth had swallowed him.'

'You're assuming he's dead.'

'Yes.'

'Jesus Christ on a rubber fucking crutch.'

'He wasn't the only operative on this.'

'Married?'

'No.'

'No one to miss him.'

'No one.'

'But there's no trace of Allardyce.'

'None.'

'Others are still looking.'

'Yes. So far – nothing.'

'You know how delicate things are? There are two reports on my desk, the most recent dated three days ago. They're both telling me about a war that could soon be won. Everything's going smoothly. We can't disrupt that, and we can't delay.'

There was a pause on the other end of the line.'Austin, I've been asked to tell you. . . .'

'What?' The single syllable crackled off the walls.

'I've been told to ask you to consider the possibility of holding things back. At least until we've tidied—'

'Do you realize,' Chadwick interrupted, 'how much money is invested in this? Have you any idea of the long-term economic and political implications of failure?'

'Of course.'

'It's a colossal gamble, and the rewards are colossal, too. We've made all the right moves. There's been risk, but we haven't suffered from it yet. But not everything down there is under our control. You do know that, don't you. We can't assume that matters will always go our way. When the moment comes, we have to seize it. It looks like coming soon.'

'It's not a matter of—'

'Do you know what we stand to lose?'

'Austin—'

'*Do you?*'

'Yes.' Another pause. 'Austin, you're a corporation. We're a government agency.'

'Are you apologizing or threatening?'

'I'm saying that we have to be listened to.'

'Why?' Chadwick didn't wait for an answer. 'Let me tell you something: there is no Santa Claus, no one lives happily ever after, and it's not love that makes the world go round. It's power. Let me give you a quote: "Power grows out of the barrel of a gun." Mao Tse-tung. He was right. That's what we've been investing in: guns and the people who carry them. And what we stand to gain – our return on that investment – is power. A hell of a fucking lot of power. Now, let me tell you what will happen when we get that power: we'll make a fuck of a lot of money. And here's what we'll do with that money: become more powerful, And that way we'll make even more money. Got the picture? The other thing that could happen is that we could fall on our ass. Now, listen carefully: that's not going to happen. So don't ask me to hold anything up, OK? Don't ask.'

'I know all this, Austin. Even so. We might have to insist.'

'Really? Don't joke. You're in up to your armpits here, mister. You're not thinking straight. You imagine you can hurt me? Well, maybe; it's possible. But I can raise a shit-storm over there that'll make Irangate look nickel-and-dime. I can bring the Government down. Had you thought of that? I can make a whole bunch of people over there wish they were fucking *dead*.' Chadwick laughed. 'Insist. How the fuck do you think you're going to do that?' He hung up the phone. After a moment, he pressed a button on his intercom. 'Send him in,' he said.

Sonny Moreno felt uncomfortable in the suit. It wasn't the heat; the place he'd flown in from was hotter, and few of the buildings could boast air-conditioning. The suit was camouflage, but it restricted and chafed in a way that the battle-fatigues he'd worn until yesterday never did. He eased his collar as a secretary opened the door to Chadwick's office. She was pretty, and Sonny had been sizing her up for the last ten minutes. Maybe he'd get himself a piece of ass before making the return trip. Not this girl, though. He didn't want any more contact with Chadwick and Chadwick's organization than was strictly necessary. That was another thing that made him uncomfortable – coming to the Am-Daw building was a risk Sonny didn't like to take. But, as with all risk, it had to be set against gain. Sonny was operating in a country where Chadwick had a lot invested. The occasional report – what harm could it do? Hell, they were both on the same side after all. Chadwick simply wanted to know what was happening down there. Now and then, Sonny would tell him. The pay-offs made a government salary look sick.

Chadwick read the unease on Moreno's face and said: 'Don't worry.' He glanced at the dark unexceptional suit. 'You look exactly like a junior exec.'

Sonny thought he detected a hint of mockery in Chadwick's tone. 'You don't say so.' He took the chair directly in front of the vast desk.

'OK.' Chadwick straightened his blotter – the kind of gesture he habitually used to call a meeting to order. 'So – who's winning the war?'

They talked for a little longer than fifteen minutes, no more. Chadwick found out, during that time, what he wanted to know. There were problems, Moreno told him: difficult terrain, a tough enemy, a local population that would do whatever it could to make life difficult. Often it wasn't easy to identify enemy troops; one minute they were fighting-men, the next apparently harmless villagers. And they knew the terrain – used it well. Even so, they couldn't win. 'They got balls,' Sonny said. 'They ain't got firepower.' And he nodded, as if agreeing with himself.

Chadwick appeared not to have heard. He was playing with a silver propelling pencil, releasing the lead, then catching it with the little jaw at the pencil's tip. Then he said, 'Fine,' absently, and paused a moment before looking up and brightening, and saying the word again, more briskly. 'Fine.'

Moreno got up and made for the door. 'I don't know when I'll be up here again. I can only come when I'm reporting to the Department, and that only happens when I'm due a furlough.'

'Just let us know,' Chadwick told him.

'Listen.' Moreno stopped before he reached the door. 'There's gotta be some other way. Coming here – it's heavy, y'know?'

Chadwick smiled and clapped him on the shoulder. Moreno would have worried if he'd known how untypical a gesture that was. 'It's OK,' Chadwick said. 'The private elevator . . . and the street-exit's covered. It's better this way. No phones – you understand?' He patted Moreno's shoulder again, as if soothing a dog. 'You're not in any danger.' He gave Moreno an envelope, 'Small bills,' he said, and opened the door.

After the door had closed, Chadwick walked to the window. Somewhere below, Moreno was mingling with the crowds. Another face, another dark suit. In truth, a phone call would probably have done it, but Chadwick didn't want it that way. Moreno was photographed when he entered the building and again when he left. Chadwick liked to have that kind of insurance: just in case he ever needed to put the bite on Sonny. A man working for a government agency who'd taken a little extra work on the side could be useful if a time came to issue threats or call in dues. It probably wouldn't be necessary, though. Sonny was just a way of keeping tabs. He didn't know about the money and what it was for; he didn't know about the Russian, or about the other people Chadwick was paying off; he didn't know about Chadwick's real purpose. Hell, Sonny Moreno didn't know what fucking time of day it was.

30

At regular intervals on the motorway there were
hoardings exhorting people to be frugal with water.
Laura tilted the passenger seat back and slept for a
couple of hours, her hands folded under her cheek, a
child's pose, her blonde hair fluttering like a pennant
in the breeze from the open window. Two asthma
attacks in as many days had drained her strength.

On the day of the carnival they had gone to Deacon's flat – a respite until Archangel had phoned.
Nowhere was secure from phone calls; Deacon
watched Laura watching the instrument, and by the
end of the evening her edginess was like a constant
pluck at his sleeve. He had taken her head in his
hands and said: 'We'll get you away. I know a place
where you'll be safe.'

'Tomorrow,' she'd said. As it happened, they'd left
two days later.

When she woke they were driving along narrow lanes.
High hedges spoiled the view, but she could smell the
ocean. They had set off early, and the sun was now
almost overhead, clanging off the car roof; a twister of
white dust followed them. Deacon parked on a patch
of grass above the beach and opened his door, but
Laura made no move to get out. The engine ticked as it
cooled. There were country sounds – a bull's bellow
from several acres away, magpies like rock-drills in
the hedgerow – and the slow rasp of the sea beyond
the house.

'This was your place with Maggie.'

'It doesn't matter.' He unloaded her bag and waited.

'Doesn't it?'

'I don't think so.'

The house was still bright from the coat of paint Deacon had put on a month before. White clapboard, a green shingle roof, and inside white walls that bore posters in snap-frames: Bonnard, Cézanne, Modigliani. Over a reading-lamp hung a framed map of the county. A sofa and two battered easy chairs were covered by soft grey and maroon patterned rugs.

On one side, a blue and white kitchen; on the other, a small bedroom: sheepskins on the floor, an oak dresser, a pitcher and bowl. A brass bed. The place had been shut up, and the rooms held weeks of heat.

Deacon switched on the fridge and loaded it with the food they'd brought. 'I've got an hour,' he said. 'I'll be back in the morning. Maybe we can spend a few days here – decide what to do next. I might know more by tomorrow.' He and Archangel had arranged to meet that evening; it meant three four-hour drives in two days, but Laura's need to be away had been unignorable.

She said: 'For God's sake be careful.'

'I'll be back before midday.' Because it seemed the kind of reassurance only a child would believe, he added: 'If not, contact Phil Mayhew.'

He showed her how the house functioned. After that they went for a walk, Deacon hanging back to let Laura dictate the pace and direction. Instinct took her along the beach and up on to the cliff-path, and she paused at the place where Maggie had always paused. Deacon had been prepared for the moment, expecting to be shaken by it, but the anticipation left him nothing to feel.

'What did people say about you?' Laura asked. 'Friends and so on. Were you the perfect couple?'

'I don't know if people said that. We said it.'

'And were you?'

'Not those words; we didn't express it that way. We liked our life; liked the same things, the same places. We didn't have to search around for happiness: in one way or another it was always there. No one pushed, no one grabbed; our ways of being ourselves meshed without any real effort. It worked because we trusted each other to get it right.'

'Did you?'

'Get it right?'

'Trust each other.'

He shrugged. 'Sure. I just said so.'

The path levelled out from the point where they had stopped. Looking at it rationally, Deacon could see that anyone would have taken a break at this point: it had the best and highest view over the ocean. It was a place to catch your breath, especially if you could feel the lingering tightness of asthma.

Laura walked on, her words floating back over her shoulder. 'I didn't know Maggie as well as you might imagine. We met when I was in my second year; she had already put some time in – first Vassar, then St Hilda's. She had a car and a small house near Port Meadow: all rather grown-up. It was clear she was well off – you know, supplied from inexhaustible family funds – and I was having a pretty heavy flirtation with the Communist Party at the time, so it wasn't really on the cards that we'd become friends. Oddly, we did. It wasn't the kind of friendship that was built to grow and deepen – a lasting acquaintanceship more like – but we saw quite a lot of one another. I think that what I liked about her was her independence. You got the feeling that she was happy to be included in other people's plans, but wouldn't have cared much either way. She used to take off for three or four days: no one would know where she was or what she was doing, then she'd be back. I don't mean there was anything peculiar about it – just that she seemed to have a life of her own that she was somehow at ease with. Grown-up, you see. She was the same with men. You did want to hear this, didn't you? What do we do here?'

'Keep going,' Deacon said. 'The path picks up beyond that outcrop of rock.' Then: 'Yes, I did.'

'She appeared to have a way with men that permitted her to be serious but not intense. I mean, I could be wrong about all of this, because it's my impression and I was young and people change and I was stoned quite a lot of the time – OK?' He didn't reply. 'It was how it seemed to me, in any case. Her relationships weren't trivial, but they weren't hysterical, either. There always seemed to be someone crushed between love and the desire for a double first; I lost count of the times that I stayed up all night with a vat of coffee and a suicide threat. I can recall times when someone did the same for me. Not Maggie. She was committed to it while it lasted and let it go when it was over. I remember wondering where she'd learned the knack. I make her sound so composed, don't I? I suppose it's what I recall best. I don't know . . . there were mad parties, drunken outings in punts, that sort of thing; and sometimes we went to lectures, if you see what I mean. She never used to eat much – did that change?'

'No.'

'I think I've run out of things to tell you.'

He quickened his pace briefly and touched her on the elbow. 'We ought to get back.'

'You go.' She continued to face up the track. 'I'll walk a bit further.'

'The path goes down into a bay about half a mile from here.' She would find it anyway.

'OK.'

He touched her arm again, more firmly, but she

wouldn't turn. 'Don't,' she said. And then: 'It's not your fault.'

He returned to the car wondering what it might have cost her to tell him those things. A lot, he suspected, but that didn't stop his need to know them. He couldn't begin to sort his feelings into place. Laura had been with him almost constantly since the first phone call, the time when she'd burned her dress. They had made love. She had been so frightened over the past two days that it was difficult to guess how far she depended on him. Or he didn't want to guess.

After Deacon had taken Archangel's phone call, they'd moved to her flat because she had to pack. Neither place seemed safe. She had taken the phone off the hook while Deacon walked a couple of streets away to meet Phil Mayhew. Deacon had heard the locks falling as he went downstairs. Mayhew imagined that he and Deacon were keeping secrets and wouldn't talk in front of Laura. Deacon didn't want him there in any case.

The pool car had been parked illegally, close to an intersection. As soon as Deacon got in, Mayhew had handed him a package.

'You're bloody dangerous to know. What do you want that stuff for?'

'I thought you might have some knocking about the place.'

'Under lock and key, in theory.'

'Not while the barter system works. Do you know a guy called Marcus Archangel?'

Mayhew had looked both startled and curious. 'You're keeping odd company.'

'How well do you know him?'

'Well enough to know that he's fireproof.'

'He's about to get singed.'

'With that?' Mayhew had stared at the package in Deacon's hand. 'You're crazy. It isn't possible, John;

255

don't think it. Look, we'd love Archangel behind bars, but it's common knowledge that he's more dangerous in than out.' He'd looked panicky. 'John, it's been *decided*. We've walked a razor's edge with this guy for months; you can't expect me to fit him up and march him down to the nick like some penny-ante dealer. Apart from the fact that we're all under instruction to stay off his case, the ghetto would go to war. Jesus. I'm prepared to believe that you don't know what's at stake here, but you're well out of your league. Go home. Forget it.' Mayhew had made a pass at the package, but Deacon had kept it out of reach.

'Calm down. You haven't listened to what I want.'

'If it involves taking Archangel, I don't want to.'

'He knows something we want to know.'

'I don't want to know it that badly. You're the one on a crusade.'

'I just want you to be there – in plain view. He knows you?'

'He's seen me, yes. You don't expect to frighten him?'

'I do.'

'No chance.'

'We'll see,' said Deacon. 'Will you do that? Just be visible?'

'No arrest?'

'No arrest.'

'He walks away unharmed?'

'I'll take an umbrella for him in case of rain.'

'Don't joke. This guy's got his finger on the fucking button.' Mayhew paused for thought. 'I don't know, John.'

'I'll do it anyway. If you're there, it's a good bet; if not . . . .' He shrugged.

'Jesus Christ.'

Deacon had got out of the car, holding the package away and out of reach, then leaned in through the open window. 'Seven-thirty,' he'd said, and given the day and place.

Mayhew had started the engine. 'Expect me if you see me.' He'd been looking straight ahead.

Back in Laura's flat, Deacon had gone straight to the bedroom and shoved the package under the bed. Later, when they set off, he'd transfer it to the car. They had planned to leave the next morning, but asthma had immobilized Laura until mid-morning and left her washed out. Deacon had opened all the windows, trying to find a breeze, and she'd slept on and off, propped in an armchair. When the phone rang, she'd woken with a start and picked it up without thinking before Deacon could reach it.

It wasn't what she feared. Rather, there had been relief in her tone. Deacon had gone back to the kitchen where he'd been making a sandwich.

'That would be good,' he'd heard her say. 'I'd tried to reach you.' She'd confirmed an appointment. 'At five o'clock. All right, Myles. See you then.'

They'd eaten and played some music. Deacon had gone to stand by the window each time he smoked a cigarette. Laura had left in a taxi and returned at six-thirty. Next morning, they'd left for Cornwall. Deacon hadn't been happy about the delay, but when Laura explained, he saw that it had been necessary.

The bay was a crescent of sand that lay beneath a sheltering curve of cliff sixty feet high. Gulls were riding the thermals, sometimes just above, sometimes just below the grassy lip. They spread their wings and hung there or twitched to seaward and slid down the wind. Pure white on fierce blue; the cries of dead sailors.

She lay on the sand, spreadeagled, and looked straight up, dizzied by the lack of landmarks and horizon. Her mind's eye put Deacon on the motorway, then on the London approach road, then at the place he'd chosen for his meeting with Archangel. She wanted it to be over and she wanted him back. I love him, she thought. I don't know what to do.

The tide had ebbed, leaving sentinels of granite in the narrow outlet of the bay. The heat was beginning to go out of the sun. Laura went over the hard wet undulations of sand to the thin line of foam, took her shoes off, walked in until the water just covered her ankles and paddled across to the far curve of the cliff. The sea was utterly calm, a blinding sheen thrown over it where it carried the sun's reflection. She came to the path and walked it barefoot for a while. Another stretch of sand took her back to the beach-house.

Inside, she circled the rooms unable to settle. Finally, she opened the front door and sat on the step to watch the sun redden and the sky darken shade by imperceptible shade. The attacks had wrung her out; she could still feel the tight heaviness in her lungs, as if they'd been stretched. She dozed, came to, dozed again.

A noise brought her alert: a rapid whickering sound that came from somewhere in the house, Laura froze to listen. A frenzied fluttering – wind in a loose sail, or someone drumming on parchment. It was intermittent, distantly violent, panicky.

Slowly she got up, her back braced to the door-jamb, and looked in among the shadows that were accumulating on walls and along the floor. The sound had stopped. There was nothing to see. Then it was back, fast and brittle, eerily sudden in the evening silence. Laura felt her chest constrict. The noise stopped again. Walking carefully, as if quietness could be an ally, she went into the room, stood at the centre and waited. Everything was still. At the very edges of her hearing she could detect the faintest whisper of pebbles in the ocean's undertow. And then again: abruptly, making her leap with shock, the scrabble and batter of something trapped.

The fireplace had been boarded up, thick plywood

258

fixed across the hearth, screws countersunk into firm battens. Laura went outside and looked up at the roof. The chimney was broad and uncowled. She went back in and heard it plainly for what it was: the flap and clatter of wings in the grate, claws and beak rattling haphazardly on the board and fire-blackened brick. It seemed to fill the room.

Laura started opening drawers and cupboards, looking for a screwdriver or a claw hammer: there were saucepans, plates, cups and saucers, knives and forks, a torch, rolls of paper towel. She took one of the knives and knelt down in front of the fireplace. As if it sensed her presence, the bird began to crash and flap in the dark. The board was flush to the battens; no purchase for the knife, which did no more than raise a few splinters. With Laura so close, the bird was half-crazed with fear; and Laura felt it, too, cramping her chest, as she hacked at the unyielding wood. She began to gasp, holding the knife two-handed and chopping sideways with it to try to get into the join, but it was a hopeless task. She held the curved blunt end of the blade against the crack and hammered it with her hand, ignoring the pain that shot to her elbow. It sank a fraction and she levered sideways. The tip of the blade snapped off.

Sobbing for breath, Laura leaned her forehead against the plywood blockage. The bird was suddenly still. Laura's face was just an inch or so from the creature. She imagined its eyes wide and bright and terrified in the blackness. There was nothing to do. She got up and backed off to the middle of the room, still looking at the fireplace as if some solution might strike her. How long would it take to die? Outside the light was leaking out of the western sky, the line of the horizon growing blurred. Laura took the inhaler from her bag and held it to her mouth. One blast, then another, loosening her lungs. The bird's wings sawed briefly.

259

The telephone rang.

Outside the Royal Albert Hall there were posters advertising some forthcoming concerts. Tchaikovsky, Brahms, Mahler, Gounod, Strauss. Inside, Deacon watched a support-bill middleweight slip a punch and throw a loose right-hand counter. He was a stocky dark guy: Greek maybe, or Spanish. His opponent was taller but didn't look ring-fit. The Greek was fast over the canvas, picking his man off with lazy hooks that didn't have too much sting. He could have finished the fight two rounds before, but looked too bored for the required work-rate. The hall was two-thirds full and noisy: middle-aged men with a lot more money than taste who had made the trip too fast from grimy streets to gravel drives and lawns. They wore Rolexes and chunky gold wrist-chains, Savile Row suits and Italian shoes. They smoked Havana-Havanas and howled for blood.

Deacon had reserved two seats in the middle of a row and close to the ring. He sensed rather than saw Archangel arrive – the way that you can hear the passage of a breeze in a cornfield running under all the other sounds. The spectators seemed to sway a little: astonishment and curiosity. One very rich dude with three very big minders. A lot of people in the hall had walked along the narrow borders of legality in their business dealings. Those who didn't know Archangel watched him and felt edgy; those who knew him felt edgier still. He shouldn't have been there.

The ringside row was full apart from the vacant seat next to Deacon; he had chosen carefully. The minders sat where they could. Archangel shuffled along and took his place. He spoke softly, his words under the din.

'Well, Deacon, you have a wry sense of humour.'

'I thought it might amuse you.'

'Yes. The Royal Albert Hall,' Archangel smiled. 'I

thought perhaps an orchestral concert – Haydn, maybe, or one of those winsome English composers. It didn't occur to me to check. But, then, you had expected that. I confess I was prepared to be patronizing about your choice. Now I find you've been unforgivably witty. You've also put me at risk: there are some people here I would sooner not see. I'm rather angry – not least with myself.' There was a shake in his voice.

The bell went for the seventh round. The Greek's opponent was cut over the left eye, and his corner had told him to slow things down and stay out of trouble. He leaned on the Greek, trapping the man's forearms, and wrestled him round the ring to a hurricane of booing. The Greek turned to be blind-side of the referee and head-butted the cut eye; the tall guy released him and immediately took a right hook to the injury. A spray of blood and sweat flew off the glove, and the boos became yells of delight.

Deacon took a document-case from beneath his seat and placed it in Archangel's lap before the other man had time to prevent him. 'Your money,' he said.

Archangel's lips tightened for a moment, then he sighed. 'How do you expect . . . ?' He broke off, shaking his head. The Greek had worked his man into a corner and was firing some heavy-duty punches around the ribs; when the tall man tried to find ring-space, he found himself being hooked back into position. The bellowing grew louder, and some of the ringsiders got to their feet. Archangel lifted the upper flap of the document-case and half-removed the package. It was Sellotaped at both ends. He turned it over, then slipped it back, looking at Deacon with a quick frown. 'You don't expect me to count it here?'

'No.'

The frown deepened. 'Well, it's your game. What are the rules?' Archangel had begun to sound uneasy, sensing that something was wrong.

'There's nothing to count.' Archangel's hands leaped as if he'd touched a hot wire, then clasped and came to rest above his lap. 'Inside the package is a lot of wrapping. Inside the wrapping is a box. Inside the box there's two ounces of pharmaceutical-grade heroin.' Deacon paused a moment and put a hand on Archangel's arm as the other man made a move to rise. 'In some ways, the outside of the package is even more interesting, though. It's coated with nin-hydrin. Mean anything?' Archangel's face was like stone. 'In case you're not sure, I'll explain. It's a dye. You can't see it, but it's all over your hands. Under a UV light, they'll be a deep shade of mauve. It's standard technique, but effective. You can't rinse it off and, in any case, you won't get the chance.'

The tall boxer's cheek was glistening with blood; it had splashed onto his shoulder near the neck and down onto his chest. He was up on his toes and dancing, laying what were supposed to seem light-hearted jabs, but no one was fooled. The Greek went after him flat-footed, cutting down the ring, weaving from the waist and biding his time. He caught up with the man in his own corner and feinted a left to draw him on. The right hook that followed took the sap out of his opponent's knees; his hands dropped, and the Greek was all over him, but he'd left it too late and got caught by the bell. The tall man's seconds swarmed round, pasting adrenaline cream on to the lesion.

Archangel still couldn't see where the trap lay, but he knew there was one. He sat still and waited to be told. 'There's something I need to know,' Deacon said. 'Tell me and you walk out of here and back to your car safely.' He could sense Archangel's puzzle-ment and anger. 'One row back,' Deacon offered, 'three seats in.' Archangel turned and saw Phil Mayhew. His head snapped front again.

'You're crazy. He's crazy. There's nothing to gain.'

'For me there is. Tell me who hired Ambrose Jackson; tell me how he was used.'

'Fuck you, man.' The pose slipped, Archangel half-looked sideways, trying to locate his minders.

'Don't look at them. My friend didn't come alone.' Archangel couldn't judge the truth of that. 'Get helpful or get busted. Your choice.'

'No.' Archangel shook his head, 'You wouldn't dare. *He* wouldn't dare. Stick with this and you're looking at a forest fire. He knows it.'

'Maybe he doesn't care.'

'No,' Archangel said again. 'Good try, but I don't believe you.'

'Make a move and find out.'

There was something in Deacon's tone. Archangel looked like a man with one foot in the boat and the other on the shore. 'They've been told to walk softly round me – you think I don't know that? I can put troops on the streets, you fool.' He glanced round again, meeting Mayhew's gaze. A smile came back to his lips, and the throatiness that had come into his tone softened. 'You've fucked this up. You're bluffing.' He moved his feet, making ready to get up.

'No,' Deacon said, 'he'll do it.'

Archangel grinned. 'Maybe I'll take the smack – if that's what it is.'

'He'll do it,' Deacon said, 'because he's got your ten grand.'

Impossible. Impossible. 'I know a place where you'll be safe.' Laura could hear him saying it. How could it not be true? But she could also hear the voice on the telephone, monotonal and mad, as if she still had the instrument to her ear.

Laura . . . Laura . . . I know where you are. I'm close by, Laura, I'll be there soon.

She had looked at the open door and the dark

263

beyond it – a country dark, each a step in blackness. The voice seemed to hear her thoughts.

Why don't you come to meet me, Laura? I'm out there. I'll find you. I'll know just where to look. Yes . . . come and meet me. Or else I'll come to the house. Whichever you like. I'm very close. I want to be closer still. Soon you'll see me. Close enough to touch, Laura, close enough to—

She sat in the centre of the room, below the level of the windows, crouching and hugging herself like someone sheltering from a storm. The silence sang around her ears. Then the bird leaped in its prison, clouting the board with its wings, and she screamed.

It was all over in thirty seconds. The tall man defended the cut but not well enough. He was bone-tired and hurt, but he kept going forward as if he had a point to prove, something bovine and submissive about the way he advanced on his punishment. The Greek found the place and opened it up like a surgeon: two rapid jabs, a pause, then two more. When the gloves went up to cover, he sapped his man under the heart with a sound like a flail hitting dead meat. The man staggered, his hands drifting; the Greek opened his shoulders and took his full body-weight on to the next blow. The tall guy came apart. His knees buckled, and his body sagged, so that he seemed about to sit, then he started to run backwards on his heels, taken by the momentum of his fall. The Greek went after him, swinging at the lowered head. The referee stepped in to confirm a technical knockout.

Archangel sat still and said nothing. Deacon was content to let him think it through.

The phone rang, and she went to it as if in a dream.

Laura . . . I'm close to you now . . . so close. I can be there soon. Laura . . . .

Afraid to be in the house, afraid to go out.

Laura, I want to—

264

A wind had picked up, coming off the sea. It whinnied under the eaves. She went to the door and put her hand on the catch, then stopped. There was nowhere to go.

The phone rang, and the bird's wings erupted with it, the sounds tangling and amplifying each other. There were iron hoops round her chest; she wheezed with every indrawn breath, a high hysterical discord.

Laura, I'll be there soon . . . .

Phil Mayhew watched as the next two fighters climbed into the ring, then switched his gaze to Deacon and Archangel, their heads close together like conspirators. There was a strong urge in him to laugh, which he knew was nervousness. From where he sat, nothing looked good. He had got to the hall early and watched Deacon arrive, then Archangel. He'd noticed a stillness about Deacon – minimal movement, even in the moment when Archangel had sat down next to him. The tense concentration of someone dismantling a bomb. Mayhew was acutely conscious of being close to the blast area.

Archangel was figuring the odds. He said: 'It's occurred to you that, whatever happens here, I'll have you killed?'

'It's occurred to me that you'll try,' Deacon said. 'Who hired Jackson?'

She opened the door and went outside. Beyond the light from the windows, the darkness was thick and almost palpable. It seemed to choke her, like gobbets of flock. She went towards the sound of the surf, stumbling on tussocks of marram grass, her hands held out like a sleepwalker's for fear of what she couldn't see. The tide was rising, and the breakers were brisk with the wind behind them. She could hear the slow suck of the waves drawing back, followed by a dead silence, a vacuum; then a whisper that became an extended hiss; then a low, extended roar as the water heaved over and broke across the shore. At first, she intended to find the path. Now she was out there, she didn't know how finding it might help. Ten steps this way, twelve steps that. No notion of where she was going or why. Although her eyes were open, she was as good as blind, the wind flapping in her face like a black flag.

Without knowing it, she came to the sea's edge and stepped in as a breaker hit the sand. It knocked her down and swamped her. She struggled back, the breath whining in her throat, and crawled out of the foam. The house-lights were her only refuge, and she started back towards them like a traveller taking the last steps of a long journey.

The bird in the chimney, mad for freedom. The ringing of the phone. The voice. *Laura.* . . .

Archangel pushed the document-case onto the floor. 'A man called Buxton,' he said.

Deacon released a silent breath. 'The manager at the bank.'

'Yes.'

'And Jackson's a programmer?'

'Yes.'

'Why did they want him?'

'I didn't ask.'

'Try again.'

'He altered a program. Added something.'

'OK. How?'

'I'm not a —'

'Not how did he do it – how did he alter it? In what way?'

'He eased the exchange rate on certain currencies in the bank's favour.'

So that much was established: Deacon was getting the truth. 'Who profits?'

'I told you – the bank.'

266

'Give me a break. Where does the money wind up?'

'I don't know.'

'I hope you packed your toothbrush; you won't be sleeping at home tonight.'

'I can't tell you, because I don't know. Jackson didn't know. They didn't tell him, so he couldn't tell me. Why would they? He's a mechanic. They paid me. I paid him. Be sensible.'

'I might choose not to believe you.'

'Whatever. It's all I've got.'

Deacon believed him. 'You can go now, Marcus,' he said.

The new bout was between two heavyweights who had started fast and didn't look inclined to go the distance. The roars of the crowd rendered Deacon's dismissal almost inaudible.

'Why did you give it to him?' Archangel paused for the afterthought. 'Why not give it to me and make the trade?'

'I trust him,' Deacon said. 'I don't trust you.'

Archangel nodded. 'You can trust me now. Look over your shoulder – I'll be there.' Before getting up, he added: 'Hold that thought.'

Throughout the night the bird grew weaker. Throughout the night the telephone rang. Nowhere to go.

Laura had over-used the Ventolin. Tachycardia reproduced the symptoms of her fear – a vicious circle. She crouched on the floor, feeling her heart galloping under her ribs, and listened to the bird as it died.

The wingbeats became less frequent and less violent, a ragged diminuendo, though sometimes the bird would find a burst of strength and smash wildly for a few seconds. After such surges of energy, there would be a long pause before its next, feebler, attempt.

Throughout the night, the terrible scamperings echoed her pulse, strong then weak. Once or twice she fell asleep against her will, exhaustion carrying her

over the edge. Each time the phone brought her back
again.

*Laura . . . I'm very close . . . almost outside . . . almost
there. I can see the lights of the house . . . I can see the
door . . . Laura, I want to . . . want to—*

Nowhere to go. The wingbeats, the dying bird, the
telephone – a circle of terror that tightened with each
passing hour, as her lungs tightened. She felt as
though a block of wood had been jammed in her
throat with a pinhole aperture for breath. Madness to
be inside, madness to be out; madness to keep the
lights on, madness to be in the dark. Madness to
move, and madness to stay still.

At the dead hour just before dawn the wingbeats
stopped. The bird had begun to wait out its death.
Laura waited, too, watching the door. It would almost
be a relief to see it open, to own the moment, to be
under his hand.

Laura, I want to . . . want to—

She waited like a child, wide-eyed and breathless.
She waited like a bride.

268

31

Deacon parked, pipped the horn a couple of times, and started towards the house. It was just before eight o'clock, and the sun was still low, keeping the beach in shadow but spreading a buttery light on the sea. He'd grabbed a few hours' sleep and started out early. He came down on to the grass where it shelved away from the road and began to approach the house, walking into the long shadows where there was still a touch of dew; he'd half-expected Laura to come out to meet him, but supposed she must still be asleep.

The house was empty. Deacon wasn't alarmed at first – she'd have gone out for an early walk – until he realized that the bed hadn't been slept in. Then he saw the broken knife and the scarring on the plywood board.

Outside there was just the shriek of sea-birds and the mild susurration of the waves. He called her name and waited. Nothing. He called twice more, circling the house, then started across the fringe of sand that would take him to the path. When he gained the rise, he looked back and saw her – or saw someone – a figure seated close to the ebbing lip of surf, back turned and utterly still. He went down, crossing the warm loose sand, starting to run when she didn't respond to his call. His feet smacked the sheen of water on the foreshore. Her legs were in the tiny tuck of foam, and she was bending slightly forward, her body folded over her arm. Deacon stood behind her. He said: 'Laura?'

*　　*　　*

She told him everything there was to tell, not moving, not looking at him, not responding when he sat beside her and looped an arm, protectively, round her back. She looked directly out to sea. Her voice was expressionless. Sometimes she would break a sentence because she couldn't get it all in one breath; it made her sound eerily childlike.

When she had finished he said. 'I'm sorry.' And then: 'I won't let you be alone again, I promise.' Much later, he said: 'Laura, we have to go.' She had barely moved.

The sun was hot, and the tide had begun to turn. He lifted her, and she leaned on him, feet unsteady like the victim of a road accident. He could feel her shaking, but she was still too weak to sob or rave. She went with him to the car while he fetched a tyre-lever, then followed him to the house. He found a rock to use as a hammer, and the board took five minutes or less.

It was a blackbird, ragged as an old glove, one wing still extended as if in flight, the other collapsed and broken. Death had drawn a white glaucoma over its eyes. Deacon took the corpse out and tossed it beyond some bushes, then he locked the house and went with Laura to the car. As they drove slowly through the single-track lanes that led from the house her head began to sag. Within a mile of the place she fell asleep.

Deacon drove for a couple of hours before coming off the motorway. There was something he wanted to say, and he thought it better to get it said before they returned to London – to his flat or her flat. She woke as he filtered off an A-road and found the countryside again: flatter than in Cornwall, trees and pastureland and gentle valleys.

'What are we doing?' she looked round, half-smiling. There was still a deadness in her voice.

'Looking for a pub. A drink, something to eat.' He sketched in the details of what Archangel had told him the previous night.

'Buxton,' she said.

'Yes.'

She was silent for a while. Eventually, she sighed and said: 'I suppose it had to be something like that.'

'Yes.'

'I'd like to stop it all. I know we can't. That time when I came to your flat to tell you about Katie . . . I knew I was right, but I didn't know what it meant. I feel as if I'd started a game and other people have joined in – big people, frightening people – and changed the rules and raised the stakes; I want to stop, but I can't because I invented the game. I invited them in.' She looked at him. 'It's too late, isn't it?'

He nodded. 'In any case—'

'What?'

'Whoever killed Kate – the person who's been phoning you – he's the wild card in all this. I don't have many answers, but it's clear that there's a bank fraud going on with the collusion of the manager. Kate found something crucial that made her dangerous and she was killed. It was supposed to seem like an accident. OK. But the killer hasn't stopped with Kate. He's slipped his leash. What started as a commission has become a hobby. Clearly he knows about you – he's been in your flat, he's followed you. . . . What I'm saying is: it could have been impossible to avoid all this whether you'd come to me or not.'

'He might have. . . .' She tried to think of a way of saying it. 'He might have wanted me anyway.'

'Yes.'

Laura knew he was right. She had known it all along. 'What are you going to do?' she asked.

'Talk to Buxton. You have his home address?'

'Yes. Is that the right thing to—?'

'God knows,' he said. 'It's all I can think of.'

'Then?'

'Talk to Phil Mayhew, perhaps. It depends what I get.'

'Buxton.' Laura smiled bleakly. 'Of course. It would be. Banks, brokers, companies; bonds, surpluses, loans. . . . Hot money slipping over frontiers. The world makes money go round.'

They found a country pub with seats in the garden. She insisted on going with him to the bar. He carried their drinks and some sandwiches out into the sunlight and found a place some way from the door of the pub. There was a question he didn't want to ask; something he didn't want to tell.

'When the phone calls came, last night. . . .' She nodded. 'I want to hear about that.'

'I already—'

'I want to hear it again.'

She dropped her eyes and folded her hands round her beer-mug. She could hear the voice deep in her inner ear. 'I don't know how many times. Eight, maybe a dozen. Each time. . . . Each time, he said. . . . ' And she repeated to Deacon the lines that he knew she had by heart.

When she'd finished, her voice had grown so faint he could hardly hear her. 'Why didn't you take the phone off the hook?' he asked.

She looked at him, stricken, as if he were offering crucial advice but much too late. 'I don't know.' Her eyes were wide. 'God, I don't know.'

'OK,' was all he said. A silence grew between them that she couldn't interpret. It frightened her, and she allowed her mind to drift to other things.

He was about to speak when she said: 'I can't go back – to the bank. Not immediately anyway.'

'No. I agree.'

'I told them about my asthma attacks. They won't be surprised. I've taken time off because of that before. But it's been two days; I ought to let them know.' She rummaged in her bag, looking for change. 'I could call from here.' She was speaking more briskly than before, glad to have something to do, some ordinary task.

272

'There isn't one,' Deacon told her.

'Yes.' She selected coins. 'In the corner of the bar.'

Deacon shook his head. 'There isn't one,' he repeated.

His tone was level and hard. Laura lifted her head, saying: 'Wha—?' then was quiet. He was looking straight at her. She felt suddenly cold, as if someone had clapped an ice-pack to the base of her spine. He couldn't mean that. Couldn't mean. . . .

'At the beach-house,' Deacon said. 'There is no phone. There never has been.'

32

Laura woke in the dark at 4 a.m. Coming out of sleep, she felt as though her entire body had convulsed and reared up, though in truth it had been the merest twitch. She had dreamed that she was standing on the beach, getting ready to go in for a swim; but instead of removing her clothes, it was her skin she was stripping off – peeling it back over her shoulders and thighs like latex – and the cold water was a scalding agony on her nerve endings as it rose along her shins. She had got so far, then plunged forward in a dive, howling as a wave engulfed her. She was still completing the dive when her eyes opened. Deacon woke in the same moment and laid a hand on her shoulder.

'I don't understand,' she said.

'Neither do I.'

She had been sleeping with her legs drawn up, and turned now to stretch them, bringing the whole length of her body against his. 'I was dreaming.'

He wasn't sure what she meant – dreaming then or now. Cautiously, he asked: 'Was I in the dream?'

'No. I was swimming; I'd shed my skin like a snake.' She meant now. He hadn't dared to suggest that what happened at the beach-house had been a dream – a long waking dream. It would have made her sound like a hysteric. Something had happened ... and nothing had happened. He wondered whether it was her own fear that pursued her. Shapes in the darkness, voices in the wind.

As if half-reading his thoughts, she said: 'The bird was real.'

'Yes,' he said, 'the bird was real.'

They were speaking in whispers as if frightened of being overheard. He stroked her back to soothe her, long sweeps with the palm of his hand that rose on her hip and tapered away. After a moment she took up the rhythm, her body flexing slightly, her fingers trailing the long muscle from his shoulder to his waist. She felt him stir and harden against her flank.

Is this important to us? she thought. Is this the best of our sex – consoling and protecting, a refuge from fear?

Their hands shifted, jostling gently against one another. She raised a knee, opening up for him, then cupped him at the root before drawing her circled forefinger and thumb along the hard line of his cock; then again, then again. He brought his hand up to her breast and lowered his head to browse her nipple; she shifted her hips, the better to crook her legs, and his touch travelled back across her belly.

'What will you do?' she asked: still a whisper; her hand still moving.

'Buxton?'

'Yes.'

'Find something to threaten him with.'

'What?'

'I don't know. Something he loves. Something he fears.'

'What?'

'You're the most likely person to tell me that.'

Their voices were so low that the rustling of the bedclothes all but drowned them. She put her palms on his shoulders and slid across his body, her lips brushing his lips, his eyes, and stalled above him. 'You asked me for his address. Why there? Why not at the bank?'

He held her breasts as they drooped towards him,

then extended the gesture to sculpt the curve of her ribs, the swell of her buttocks, the undersides of her thighs. She shifted in order to straddle wider, and reached between their bodies to make his cock glide between her legs, not letting him enter but moving him back and forth to take a jolt of pleasure with each forward motion.

'He's not so vulnerable at the bank,' Deacon said. Then, as if he'd forgotten having made the remark: 'He's more vulnerable at home.'

'I can't go with you,' she said. 'I can't stay here alone.'

'No, of course not. No. Don't worry. Some friends, maybe. . . .'

'Maybe.' The word was breathy, her mouth close to his ear.

'You'd still be uneasy?'

'I think so. I'm not sure.'

Talking was part of it now – part of the rhythm. The dislocation between what they said and what they did was exciting. It made the sex seem covert. In the dark room they were mostly texture, taste and smell to each other – voices jumbled with sighs and the murmur of rumpling sheets. She positioned him then sat back, slowly, taking him in.

'I can't live at my flat. Do you mind that?'

'No.'

'It doesn't have to mean anything – my being here.'

'Perhaps it does.'

'Do you think so?'

'I don't know.'

'I like this place. I like the high ceilings, I like the swallows each evening.'

'I remember you said that he works late. Buxton. On Thursdays?'

'Yes.'

'Every Thursday?'

'More or less, I think.'

276

Riding him, not swiftly, the muscles in her thighs bunching as she swung forward and back, his arms looped round her. Each time she rocked towards him, his fingertips ran down between her parted legs, touching her, touching himself.

'In my dream the water burned me, like dry ice.'

'Where were you?'

'On the beach, in front of the house.'

'It was just a dream.'

She worked at him harder, bearing down, sawing to and fro. Her back hollowed beneath his grip. He quickened his hips to her pace. Now and then he glimpsed the outline of her head and one shoulder against the curtained window a darker black on black.

'It's never that. It's never *just* a dream.'

'I know.'

Their whispers circled the walls. She sat up, head up, spine straight, her hips and belly undulating, taking him as deep as she could.

'Safe with you. . . .' It was what he thought she said – her breathing muffled the words.

'Don't worry. Don't worry. I won't let you be alone.'

She cried out, moving faster, and cried out again. He arched his torso, bearing her weight on his hips, and still she circled and swerved, leaning away and clutching behind his thighs. Her voice swooped up in an arc, holding the note at the top – a quiet sustained scream – then her body toppled forward, her voice toppled down the scale; she sank on to him and he could feel her hair washing across his face.

She stirred when her heartbeat slowed, moving her head on his shoulder to fit the hollow close to his neck. 'I don't understand what happened. I thought it would be safe.'

'So did I,' Deacon told her.

'It seemed that way. I went down to the bay – you know.'

'Yes.'

'The sea and the gulls over the cliff.' Her mouth close to his ear, the whisper drumming in her throat. 'I felt away from everything. I felt secure.'

'No one goes there. It's miles from the nearest village.'

'Even when I heard the noise in the fireplace—'

'Walkers sometimes, but they stay up on the cliff—'

'I wasn't afraid. . . . And then. . . .' She didn't say what happened then, because she was no longer sure. Deacon cradled her head; his free hand travelled the length of her spine.

'What will you tell Phil Mayhew?' she asked.

'About Archangel?'

'Yes.'

'I haven't quite decided.'

'Don't you—?' She changed it to: 'You don't trust him.'

'Not that so much. He's an old friend. We've had to look out for one another in the past – rely on one another.' His hand rotated in the dip of her waist. 'I don't trust the people he's reporting to.'

'D'Arblay.'

'Yes.'

She shifted position slightly, and he gasped, so she kept the motion going, the merest drift this way and that of her body like the tick and tap of a mild backwash.

'It might be time,' Deacon said, 'to find out how much Phil *wants* to know.'

'He came through for you with the heroin.'

'He didn't want to.'

'But he did.'

'Yes. And it makes me wonder what he'll want in return.'

'Any guesses?'

'Most likely, he'll want me to stop. At the beginning, he was helping a friend. He was curious, too. He's probably gone too far already.'

278

'Will you?'

'It isn't possible. You know that: you said it yourself.'

'I know.'

She reached behind her body and stroked him between the legs. He gave a little buck. She could feel a faint breeze from the open window, but the heat of the day was still in the room and their bodies were slick with moisture. She lowered her face and licked jewels of sweat from his temple.

'Will you tell him about Buxton?'

'I shouldn't think so. Not yet anyway.'

'When are you going to do that?'

'Buxton?'

'Yes.'

'Tomorrow night. I'll think of something by then.'

'Put me on my back.'

He turned her over, keeping himself inside. She forked her legs wider and lofted her knees. He withdrew, then stroked into her slowly, then withdrew again, all at one pace, keeping the rhythm unbroken like someone bowing a cello. She slipped a hand under his chest, then down, letting the underside of his cock ride on her fingertips.

'It used to be just myself,' Laura said. 'Now I'm frightened for both of us.' When he quickened slightly she shifted her hand to let him have her, open and generous. He moved in the blackness above her, oiled by sweat, easing the sensation along. 'I could hear the sea,' she said, 'and the bird's wings. The bird was real.'

'Yes, it was. A blackbird.'

'Trapped there, behind the fireplace.'

'Yes it was there, I found it. Don't worry, Laura.'

'I thought I must have gone mad – when you told me that there wasn't. . . .'

'I know.' He dipped his head and kissed her.

'What was it? What happened?'

279

'I don't know.'

He cradled her, one arm round her shoulders, the other about her waist, and hauled her up, driving fiercely as if to rid her of fear. The darkness seemed to thicken – his body pressing so close – and he groaned on an outgoing breath, a long unbroken monotone.

She felt him come and loosened in every limb.

They lay still, touching at hip and shoulder, not sleeping. A steely light edged the curtain, seeping into the room and giving them sight of each other. There was birdsong from the garden. Someone shouted in the street, then laughed. A car went by.

'He has daughters,' Laura said.

'Buxton?'

'Two daughters, a wife and a dog. There are photographs on his desk.' Deacon waited. 'He talks about them a lot – the girls. He's a family man.'

After a while Deacon began to doze. Laura watched as the light grew harder, until the sun was fully up and the curtain glowed. She felt strange, having told him of Buxton's daughters. As if she herself were threatened.

If points of no return really existed, then people would have the advantage of retreating from them. The truth is less dramatic: one event overtakes another, one step follows another, and there's no way, really, of mapping the gradual progression to disaster or success. You can't second-guess the unknown.

Deacon knew that seeing Buxton would change things. To begin with, Deacon would be in the open; also, he'd be closer to the heart of whatever was happening. If he got what he wanted from Buxton, then he'd know more – and knowledge is dangerous. But he and Laura had already taken plenty of steps on the journey that had begun with her first phone call to him; this was another – risky and inevitable.

He was driving through the suburbs and felt a familiar dislike – part oppressiveness, part hostility. People lived in suburbs because they feared the wildness of city and countryside alike. In between was safer: everyman's land, a place of order and regularity.

He found the road; it contained big houses, widely spaced, with expansive gardens at front and back, all of them sheltered and partially masked by trees. The whole area said money and comfort. Expensive cars, private schools, second homes. It didn't say *want*, but it did say *I want*. Deacon parked directly outside Buxton's house and went through a formal flower-garden to the door. A woman answered the bell. She was elegantly dressed, forty-ish, and had a natural tan. The clothes were that season's and just a shade too young for her.

'Are you Mrs Buxton?' Deacon asked.

'Yes.' She held the door open as if she knew she had nothing to fear.

'I'd like a word with your husband.'

'We're having dinner.'

'I'm sorry.'

She hesitated, then motioned him in, 'Does he know you?'

'My name's John Deacon.'

She left him in the hall and went away. A couple of minutes later, Tom Buxton appeared. He was a short man, dapper almost – the kind of appearance that used to be referred to as 'well-groomed'. Dark hair combed straight back, a papery skin that was the result of too much close shaving, small hands. He wore blue lightweight trousers and a Lacoste shirt – off-duty clothing. There was a little cobweb of broken veins high on each cheekbone. He was half-smiling – politeness leavened with puzzlement.

Deacon said: 'A girl called Kate Lorimer used to work for you. She found out that someone was massaging the exchange-rate factor on one of her programs. Later she died.' He had spoken rapidly, his voice low. The smile

281

went from Buxton's face. He took a step backwards, then another. Deacon said: 'Don't.' Buxton paused as if reckoning the odds. 'Don't,' Deacon repeated. 'I'd have to stop you. Think of the consequences.'

Buxton nodded, but still didn't move. Finally, he said, 'In there,' and pointed to a door on Deacon's right. It was a study, workmanlike rather than comfortable. There was a desk with a word-processor on it; the walls were shelved for files. Buxton sat at the desk, which left Deacon to stand. His face was stiff, and his gaze rested nowhere. He looked like someone who has just found himself in a railway compartment with a drunk.

Deacon spoke as if he hadn't been interrupted. 'Kate Lorimer discovered that the program had been tampered with. It juggled the exchange rate to give preference to the bank. Spare cash. She was murdered. The program was modified by a man called Ambrose Jackson. He was hired through Marcus Archangel. He was hired by you. I want to know who killed Kate Lorimer and I want to know where the money goes.'

Buxton looked up at Deacon, then away again. 'Who are you?'

'Let's start with who killed the girl.' Buxton glanced at the phone, then at the door. He shook his head. He had no idea of how this had happened or what he should do. 'All right,' said Deacon, 'let's start with the money. But start.'

'Kate's death was an accident. The rest of what you're saying is gibberish.'

Deacon laughed. 'I'm tired of this already. I mean, I'm not going to have one of those circular conversations where you say things like "I've no idea what you're talking about". My sense of humour doesn't extend that far. I've told you what I know; I've told you what I want to know. Now it's your turn.'

'You're not the police.'

'Obviously.'

'Then, who *are* you?'

'You asked that before. It's boring. I'm someone who's dangerous to you, and growing more dangerous by the minute.'

Buxton had recovered slightly; he was looking for ways out. 'I've nothing to say to you.'

'Is that right?' Deacon sat down on the floor with his back to the door. 'I'm told you work late each Thursday evening.'

'Work late.' Buxton spoke as if he were trying to identify what the words meant.

'At the bank. After hours. When everyone has gone home.'

'I don't see—'

'Listen carefully. There are two girls – Sue and Beverley. They have a large flat in an expensive part of town. Each Thursday evening, when you're thought to be working late, you pay them a visit. You've been doing it for quite a while. They're careful girls; they make little notes about their clients just in case they might be useful some time. You arrive at about eight and leave before ten. While you're there, they do all sorts of things to you – the sort of stuff your wife wouldn't want to do. It costs a lot of money. I don't want to go into details about your sexual preferences, because it makes me sick just to think about them, but the girls won't mind talking about it. After all, they have to think about it all the time. They have to *do* it. They told me a little, and it made my skin crawl. I imagine most people who heard about it would feel the same.'

Buxton's hands lay on the desk close to the word-processor. They were shaking visibly. It looked as though he'd been using the keyboard and had forgotten to stop his fingers working. He said: 'It isn't true.'

'No. What is true is that there are two girls called Sue and Beverley and they're happy to talk about your hidden sex-life for as long as anyone will listen.

283

They're happy to do that because they've been very well paid. And since they *are* hookers and do spend their nights fooling around with rubber underwear and chains and whips for freaks, they won't have to delve too far into their imaginations when they're talking to your wife. Or your daughters. Now, if you're doubtful about any of this, here's a phone number you can ring.' Deacon tossed a folded piece of paper on to the floor. 'One of the girls will answer. She'll probably tell you that she's looking forward to seeing you on Thursday.'

Buxton stared at the paper that lay on the floor between them. He said: 'I don't know what to do.'

'Well, that's honest. I can see how you must feel. One minute you're eating dinner with your family, the next I'm offering you a choice you don't want to take. Sadly, it's in the nature of choices that you have to do something. Did you think you would simply be able to carry on living as you had before – back and forth to the bank, evenings at the theatre, holidays with the family? Someone *died*.'

'Of course,' Buxton said.

'What?'

'Of course I thought that. Why not? It's the usual thing.' Deacon looked at him and waited. 'I didn't know that Kate would be killed. I simply reported that she had noticed the program change on the trace. She told me about it; I said I'd deal with it. I liked her. I didn't have any control over what would happen.'

'Who do you report to?'

'It's a phone number. It won't help you, but you can have it if you like. I don't suppose it matters much since I'm telling you all this. The number stays the same, but the person on the other end of the line moves around. Just a voice on a telephone; it won't get you anything.'

'Who are they?'

'I don't know.'

'Who do you think they are?'

'I *think* they're MI5.'

'Official?'

Buxton laughed. 'Official? What does that mean?'

'And the money?'

'I don't know.'

'Bullshit.'

'Jesus Christ.' Buxton shook his head and passed a hand over his eyes. 'Look, I don't know who in hell you are or where you're from or who you're working for or what the fuck you expect to gain. I know two things. The first is that you are threatening something I want to protect, and that makes you powerful – at present anyway. I've said that I don't know what to do about this, but what I appear to be doing is telling you things you want to know. After that, I can't tell what'll happen. The second thing is you don't have the first idea what's at stake here. You're talking as if I'd been caught with my hand in the till. It isn't like that. Listen: I don't know where the money goes. What's more, I don't know where it comes from. Do you think banks are there to keep a friendly eye on your salary and make you a loan for your new car? Wrong. They're transit-camps for international finance. They don't care where the money comes from as long as they have it to loan or invest. And the money's on the run all the time looking for a better deal or a safer place to be. Who knows where it's been before it comes to us? Who knows where it goes when it leaves?'

'But you know if it smells,' Deacon said.

'Not necessarily. Good money, bad money – it's like a shuffled deck. Money doesn't have a conscience so it doesn't hang its head.' He shrugged. 'There are some accounts we know about. If we're being used as a laundry – arms money, drugs money, something like that – we take a one per cent handling charge. It's normal. Profit from insider dealing – one per cent also. Government money goes through banks and shell companies before it winds up in Hong Kong or Florida to fund MI6 operations abroad. This is baby-talk. The money you want to know about isn't trackable. Forget it.'

'Let's talk about it anyway.'

'Can I get a drink?'

'No,' Deacon told him.

'Christ—'

'No.'

Buxton leaned his head on his hand for a moment and closed his eyes. When he opened them he said: 'It's originated money. It doesn't exist before we create it. We only use minor currencies where the exchange rate fluctuates a good deal: a little here, a little there. It's a new thing; that's why some programs had to be changed.'

'How many?'

'A lot.'

'On whose orders?'

'The bank's owners.' Deacon waited. 'Am-Daw. Dawlish-American. It's a multinational company.' Buxton waved a hand. 'They're in the book.'

'How did you find Archangel?'

'How does a pig find shit?'

'And you knew Kate's password.'

'They're on file – locked away. What would happen if a programmer walked under a bus?' Buxton laughed. 'You know, the truth is that it's all a pretty small deal. Computers are a lot more dangerous than this petty fiddle might make them seem. I'm not a programmer. If I were, I'd be looking at ways of getting seriously rich. British banks transfer about thirty billion pounds a day through an automated clearing system. World-wide it's about a hundred and fifty billion. Someone who found a way of hacking into the system around the world could drain this country of sterling in a few minutes. OK? *Minutes*. Everyone lies about computer theft, all the banks, because everyone's scared shitless.'

286

'You said you don't know where the money goes.'

'Yes.'

'It goes to Am-Daw.'

Buxton looked weary. 'Yes, yes. We're manufacturing the surplus; after we've done that, it takes off. Flight capital – have you heard of that? It's the term given to gigantic sums of money circling the globe looking for things to do. Sometimes seeking a place to get washed, too. It puts down here and there: this bank or that. Fake shell companies. A Liechtenstein *anstalt* account. The Cayman Islands, the Bahamas, Switzerland, offshore deposit facilities. Where does it originate? Your guess. Governments, the Mob, arms dealers, pension funds, Marcos, the Moonies. . . . Petrodollars, cocadollars, pussydollars.' Buxton grimaced. 'Then it takes off again. Where does it go? Poland sells arms to South Africa. Russia buys foreign goods with it. America sells arms to Iran via Israel and funds the Contras. It's loaned back to the countries it first came from to top up the foreign-exchange reserves, and the debt grows. It goes to the Vatican's favourite charities. It breeds. It buys banks. It changes shape – sometimes heroin, sometimes diamonds or oil or guns. I've told you where the money's *made*; I've told you who makes it – Am Daw. Where it winds up and for what purpose – you tell me. I'd like a drink now.'

'No,' Deacon told him, 'not if you have to leave the room to get it. Who runs Am-Daw?'

'A man called Austin Chadwick.'

'What does Am-Daw trade in?'

'Money, of course.' Buxton was sweating. He drew a forefinger across his forehead to take off the drops. 'There are interests in Latin America: timber, mining – coca, I expect. It owns some banks apart from ours. It's big.'

'Why would it want the money from shaving exchange rates? Isn't it rich enough?'

'There's no such thing as rich enough. Exchange

287

rates are just one method of many. I guess it has the advantage of being clean, since it starts up in the bank – doesn't have a history.'

'Clean until now.'

'Yes.'

'Who killed Kate Lorimer?'

'I told you – I made a phone call, reported that she'd found the irregularity on the trace.'

'No, *who* killed her?'

'A name?'

'Yes.' Buxton shook his head. 'How old are your daughters?' Deacon asked. 'I imagine they're going to be pretty puzzled by some of the things the girls dreamed up for you.'

'You're a bastard,' Buxton said evenly, 'and I wish you dead. I don't doubt that you'd do what you've threatened to do, and somehow you managed to find the lever that couldn't fail with me; I'd like to know how you managed to do that. Everything I've done, I've done for the girls' future, and if you think that sounds maudlin I couldn't care less. What do you know about my family – how we are together, what things mean to us? How can you sit in judgement? You're blackmailing me by threatening to make me a pervert in the eyes of my daughters. Do you think I *deserve* that? For Christ's sake, I'm just a businessman. What I've done isn't remarkable; the world runs that way. It's how the world works, don't you understand that? I've told you these things and now I have to work out what the hell happens next. I don't know what you'll do. If I knew exactly who killed Kate, who actually went there and did it, I'd tell you. I don't know. I can't tell you. That doesn't make any difference to what's going to happen to me, but it makes a difference to what you'll do – to what my family might suffer. So you have to believe me.' Buxton's lips had whitened round the edge; he was shaking with effort.

Deacon got up and went out of the room, then let

himself out of the front door and walked to his car. Laura had gone to stay with some friends in the northern part of the city. Deacon had left her helping with the kids' bathtime. As he drove to collect her, his mind was on families. He thought of Maggie. The children they had never had.

Sally Buxton stacked the dishwasher. The girls had gone upstairs to play records. She went to her husband's study and tapped on the door before going in. Her husband was sitting at his desk, not moving, staring at the floor.

'He's gone,' she remarked. Buxton looked up; he nodded. 'Is everything all right?'

'Sure. . . .' A smile came and went. He forced it back. 'Sure. A bit of a problem. . . . Nothing.'

'I've put your dinner in the oven to keep warm.'

'OK,' he said. 'In a minute.'

'Tom—?'

'In a minute.' He turned away, opening a drawer in his desk as a distraction. The door closed. Buxton looked at the piece of paper with the number on it. Everything he wanted was inside the house; everything he valued. He could almost feel the seismic tremble in the foundations as if an earthquake were brewing.

He dialled the number. A recorded voice told him that the zoo opened at 9 a.m. and shut at 6 p.m. The last admission, he heard, was half an hour before the gates closed. He put down the phone and started to cry.

33

A young man went into a drugstore on the corner of Sixth Avenue and Fifty-fourth street. He had a headache and needed something to cure it. Ignoring the assistants, he took some aspirin from a display-counter and started to walk out. When someone tried to stop him, he took out a gun and fired a shot which smashed some bottles on a back shelf. Then he left.

Outside the Hilton, a cab that had been trying to beat the lights ran into a limousine pulling away from the hotel and mashed its rear fender. Traffic piled up while the cabbie and the chauffeur argued. Horns blew non-stop. The cabbie didn't speak much English and had a short temper. He took a swing at the chauffeur, catching the man on the shoulder. They started to wrestle.

A couple of blocks downtown a small crowd had stopped to watch a row between a man and his wife. They acted as if they had done this before; at any rate, they were word-perfect. He said he wasn't taking any more shit from her and she said that was just fine. Eventually, he snatched some packages from her hands and threw them into the street where they were knocked back and forth by cars travelling uptown; then he walked away, leaving her to shriek at him. She didn't try to follow.

Sirens bore down on the area like noise in a funnel.

Austin Chadwick saw none of it, heard none of it. The street, the sidewalks, were places of silent patterns warped by the shimmer of rising air and the thin noxious mist of exhaust fumes. Mostly, he looked straight out at the sunlit pinnacles of corporate power. If he looked up, he saw the sky, hard and blue and blank like a surface to write your thoughts on.

He said: 'Who took the call?'

'I did,' Steiner told him. He couldn't think why it should, but the admission made him feel guilty.

'What did you tell him to do?'

'Wait for instructions.'

'And what do you think he *will* do?'

'I don't know, Austin. Wait, I guess.'

'Buxton,' Chadwick said. 'Buxton.' As if he were tossing the name from hand to hand, testing its weight and texture. 'You're sure he told you every-thing – everything that he gave Deacon.'

'Absolutely sure.'

'How?'

'What he told him – that's everything he knows. He could have said less, but not more.'

Chadwick walked to his desk and drummed his fingers softly on one edge. 'Wonderful,' he said. 'This is just terrific. One pissant money-source from one pissant bank, and what have I got? A hit-man who's gone off the rails, a bank manager with a loose mouth, and an ex-cop who turns out to be the son-in-law of the saintly Peter Henderson, lifting up rocks. I don't need this shit, Harold.'

No one needs it, Steiner thought. I don't need co-ordinating this business and catching the fucking crap. Things happen. The trouble with you, Chad-wick, is that you expect to be able to make the fucking world snap to attention. His face was expressionless; he stayed quiet and waited to be told what to do.

'I'm looking at a blackboard, Harold. I see all sorts of things written there. Names, places, events, informa-tion, I don't like what I see. I want it wiped clean. You understand?' Chadwick walked round his desk, but didn't sit down. He picked up a paperweight, a glass

291

globe, fist-sized, with the countries of the world engraved on it, and peered at it like a soothsayer looking for shapes in a crystal. 'Clean,' he said

You asshole, thought Steiner. He said: 'Yes, Austin.'

Chadwick hurled the globe at the plate glass opposite his desk. It bounced off. Steiner ducked and threw up an arm. Chadwick bellowed. '*Clean!*'

'Where are you going?'

'For a walk. Not too far.'

'Will it be safe?'

'Oh, yes.' Elaine was wearing one of her prettiest dresses – cream with light-green polka-dots, a slight flare from the waist.

'To Laura's flat?'

'Perhaps.'

'I'm not sure you should.'

'No one knows me. No one's looking for me.'

'You're right, I suppose you're right.' Allardyce selected a lipstick for her: more pink than red.

'You want her. You want Laura, don't you?' It wasn't clear which one of them had spoken.

Allardyce replied. 'You know I do.'

'We have to be careful.'

'Yes.'

'I don't want to kill her yet.'

'The man – Deacon; you're frightened of him.'

'No, not that. He'll have to die as well.'

They selected some shoes that matched the dress. Allardyce handed them over, and Elaine put them on. She sat before the mirror and arranged her hair. 'Do you think it went well – at the beach-house? Do you think she was frightened?'

'Oh, yes.'

'I wish I could have been there – to watch, to see it all.'

'If I'd been there—'

'You'd have killed her.'

292

'Yes.'

'Afterwards. . . .'

'Yes. Afterwards. After a while.'

'I don't want to kill her yet.' Allardyce chose some earrings, and Elaine leaned forward to clip them on.

'Soon, though.'

'Yes, soon.'

'What will you do to her?'

Elaine leaned forward, coming so close to the mirror that her breath misted the glass; bringing her face close to his. She whispered excitedly; as he listened, he smiled. Elaine smiled back.

Gower sat in the chair like an eavesdroper. He hadn't changed position, but he looked different. His face was grey wax loosely thumbed. It was puffy, as if he were holding a breath between his cheeks. Some flies had got into the room. They clustered on his lips like a black sore. They walked on his eyeballs, but he didn't blink.

34

Laura had woken at three and got up at five. During those two hours, she had argued with herself. It was an argument she'd been having for some time. It was no easier to resolve now than it had ever been. She knew the case for both sides because she represented both sides. She put the claim and counter-claim, plea and rebuttal. She switched points of view so fast that she found herself advocating one outcome before she had really finished insisting on the other. She had made up her mind, but it had nothing to do with logical deliberation. It had to do with the fact that she had fallen in love with John Deacon and now she was living with him and she seemed to come across Maggie at every turn. She knew the 'living with' had to do with her fear and with what was happening, but the knowledge didn't make much of a difference. She knew that loving him wasn't wise, but she didn't really care. And she knew that her decision was lousy tactics, but she couldn't help it. Other people might have waited; other people might have waited for *ever*. She couldn't do that. The thought was almost always in her mind; it went from room to room with them; it shared the bed. It banged at her brain, and she had to let it out.

Deacon had cleared out a lot of stuff. Even so, there were pieces of Maggie all over the place: her choices, her taste. The curtains and the cushion covers. The pictures and the rugs. That antique wooden roller-calendar. That earthenware pot. A gilt mirror, a lamp, a wicker trunk. The silver frame that carried Deacon's photograph.

She sat in the kitchen and drank coffee until he woke. He came in and kissed her, then went to take a shower. She allowed herself the respite. When he returned, she poured coffee for him. There was no easy way, but she didn't say it straight out.

'Maggie and I . . . saw each other from time to time.'

'I know.' He nodded. 'Quite often. After you turned up at the party that day.'

'We went to a Turkish bath once: ladies' night, you know – a massage, a steam, plunge-pool, all that.'

'She told me. You made it a regular date.'

'Maggie went in the plunge-pool; I didn't. I've never been good at doing uncomfortable things that are good for me.' She was simply remembering the time; it wasn't important. Some smallness in her voice made him look up.

'What?' he asked and put down his coffee-cup.

'That was the only time.'

'The only—' For what? he thought. He couldn't quite follow what was being said.

'We did meet sometimes – for lunch perhaps, or for a quick drink. The Turkish bath was just once. Lunch – I don't know – once a fortnight. If we met for a drink, Maggie was usually going on somewhere else.' He didn't understand, not yet, not entirely, but he heard the shake in her voice and saw the tears on her face. She said, 'John . . .' and put out a hand to cover his. And then he did understand, but he didn't believe it.

'Say it.' He didn't recognize his own voice.

'It isn't something I. . . . She didn't ask me to lie to you; it wasn't that, I mean, only if you should ask, or it might get mentioned, perhaps you might mention it if we were all together, so she had to tell me in case I should say the wrong thing or, you know, look blank. She just asked me to . . . cover for her. I didn't like it. I mean, I didn't even know what I would do if you asked. I didn't expect. . . . She said it wouldn't come up: you were both independent and often went. . . . Just that if we were all together that you might make some reference to our evenings at the baths and I wouldn't know. . . . ' She was going in circles and couldn't get to 'sorry.'

'Who?' Deacon asked her. 'Who was Maggie seeing?'

Laura shook her head. 'I didn't ask her. She didn't tell me.'

It was clear to him that she was telling the truth – about that, about everything. He sat very still, not speaking, for five minutes. Laura watched his face; it was like looking at a fast-forward film of a flower closing, the bloom folding tight like paper crumpling to a fist.

'John—'

'Was it . . . did it matter to her? Was it important?' His voice was level, as a taut wire is level.

Laura had thought he would ask that. It was the question she would have asked. She didn't want to give the answer, but there was no room for man-oeuvre. 'No,' she said. 'I don't think it was.' Then: 'It wasn't; she told me. It had been going on for a while, I think – six or eight months. It was an affair; there wasn't much at stake.' It was the worst thing – Laura knew that. Maggie hadn't been obsessed or driven; not wildly in love and tortured by her deception. She hadn't betrayed Deacon out of ungovernable passion; it had been an exciting diversion, a whim.

He got up and went back to the bedroom and put his clothes on. His pace was measured, his actions careful, like a man walking a parapet. Laura followed him, watching helplessly. At one point, she put her arms out and he looked at them, the extended hands, like someone being asked to identify an object he'd never seen before. Then he left, closing the door softly.

Laura went to the living room and sat down. The

morning heat bred an awful silence. She was at the
dead epicentre of an unearthly stillness. The explosion
had occurred, but she could neither hear nor feel it,
though she knew that somewhere just beyond her
vision, just beyond the range of her senses, there was
violence and chaos and fragments hurtling outwards
in a vast percussive roar.

Deacon walked for several hours. It didn't matter
much to him where he went because, although he had
no real destination, none the less he knew where he
would wind up. It took time for him to get there; not
that the place was far or difficult to find – he passed it
several times in several guises. One bar is pretty much
like another. He wasn't wrestling with himself while
he walked. He was reconstructing in his mind things
that were too painful to be borne – not fighting, but
surrendering entirely. Maggie joining him a couple of
days late at the beach-house, or returning to London
now and then while he stayed down there: things to
do, money matters to be resolved, a visiting aunt –
impossible, now, to separate the lies from the truth.
Best to assume that it had always been a lie. A health
farm for three days, an early-evening movie, the
Turkish bath. He thought of her returning to him in
Cornwall – her apparent delight at seeing him again,
the walk they would take to the bay. He thought of her
coming back to the flat after an evening out. He
thought of her in bed. He thought of her driving back
on the motorway after their last time together, and
wondered what she had really been returning for.

The place was dim and cooled by big brass fans
set horizontally above head height; there was a
tape playing softly: a jazz vibraharp. He ordered a
Scotch and then he ordered another. This was a
different journey – to a place that didn't appear on
any map.

The swallows were silhouettes on a cobalt backdrop;

297

their shrill screams hung in the line of flight like a ribbon of sound.

Laura sat with the window open. Before her was an untouched cup of coffee that she had poured more than two hours earlier Her breathing was laboured and from time to time she used her inhaler. She was frightened to be in the place on her own but she was even more frightened of what she had done. She stayed at the window for another hour knowing that it was a formality. He wasn't coming back. She went through the flat, switching on lights, looking for Deacon's address-book. When she found it, she went to the phone and dialled a number. She waited, her eyes flicking round the room. The curtains, the wooden calendar, the silver photograph-frame. You can rearrange the past, she thought, but you can't control what happens after that. One thing leads to another.

'Mayhew.'

She told him only that something important had happened and Deacon had disappeared. It wasn't necessary to say that she was worried and frightened: the timbre of her voice did that.

'I can't be there for an hour or so.' He was asking a question.

'I'll wait. I'll be OK.'

Mayhew said: 'Call me if he gets back. I'll be as quick as I can.' He hung up.

Laura took some eggs from the fridge and a bowl and a pan from the kitchen cupboard, then assembled them by the stove. She stood over them for a moment, then went away as if the necessary technique had deserted her. She put on the television and watched for ten minutes without seeing. The light had gone. The swallows had gone. There was just the orange-yellow glow of the city's perpetual neon dusk.

The streets were like tunnels where baking air had

been trapped. Although it was late, there were crowds of people everywhere – leaving theatres, leaving cinemas, leaving restaurants. Leicester Square and Piccadilly were busier than they would have been at noon. Groups of young men tattooed like willow-pattern plates muscled through with beer-cans. Fifty or so people sat silently on benches and in doorways around Piccadilly Circus waiting for midnight when they could take their methodone prescriptions to the all-night chemist's.

Deacon walked an unsteady line, looking for the next bar. Engines gunning, voices yelling and laughing, music, a kaleidoscope of coloured lights blurring in his eye. He went through it like a tired swimmer clouted by a rising sea. He found the place he was looking for by instinct: one he'd thought he no longer owned. A side-street, a door, a flight of stairs, a room where the smoke and the smells seemed several days old. In a corner, over the bar, a television was playing with the sound turned off. Actors gesticulated and went in and out of close-up, mouths working to no effect. Their mute energy suited the place; all the noise was outside, all the tension inside. Behind the bar was a tall skinny guy who moved with a strange awkward grace like a long-legged bird; only his hands were quick – nimble among the bottles.

The people in the room drank silently, their eyes fixed on nothing in particular: nothing any of them would remember. It wasn't possible, but each felt as though his back was turned on the others. Up on the television screen an audience applauded wildly from a vacuum.

Deacon ordered whiskies until his money ran out. He was in his stride now – through the first drunkenness and out the other side – and his need was strong. He toured the room, trying to bum a drink. His speech wasn't too bad, but the motor responses in his legs showed a delayed reaction and, although he got from one table to another, he couldn't recall the little journeys involved. Someone bought him a Scotch, and he took it back to his table. Within a minute or two he was circling the room again. One of two men sitting by the wall opposite the door glanced at Deacon, then at the barman; he raised an eyebrow. The barman shrugged and watched as Deacon made a second circuit. He fetched up at the bar and asked for another Scotch. The barman poured it, then looked over Deacon's shoulder and nodded. By the time Deacon had downed the drink, the men were standing behind him.

'Time to go home, pal.'

They walked him to the door and out on to the landing at the top of the stairs. He turned round to go back in, and they turned him again, full circle. He pulled free and tried to get between them, stiff-arming one of them in the chest with the heel of his hand. The man gave a weary half-smile, stood off a pace, dropped his shoulder and whacked Deacon once, hard under the ribs. Deacon went on to one knee; he was showing his teeth, and his breath came in a series of tiny indrawn grunts, like someone quietly enjoying a joke. When he had recovered a little, they took him downstairs and put him into the street.

The crowds had thinned. It seemed that the couples and the groups of people had gone, leaving the solitaries. No one was speaking except those who spoke to themselves. He had lost his ability for distances, focusing on something relatively close and making for it, then sighting the next object and homing in on that: a car, a doorway, a street-lamp – walking a mazy track. He crossed a road, not bothering to look, and a motorcycle-rider leaned his bike left and right like a skier round a slalom-pole. Deacon felt the tug and wham of the slipstream but didn't know what it was. The violent pitch of the engine bowled through him, filling his head with a whirlpool roar. When he reached the far side, he walked a few paces, then sat down without knowing he was going to. He got up and continued to walk, his feet moving under him, the paving-stones moving under his feet.

'Why did you tell him?' Mayhew was sitting across the room from Laura; she had taken up a position close to the phone.

'I tried not to. For a long time I didn't.'

'For a long time you did the right thing.'

'I'm sorry.'

'Laura, I'm not blaming you.'

He rested his chin on his hands. The way his biceps compressed made him seem restless.

'What do you think?'

Mayhew shrugged. 'His car's outside.'

'I know.'

'Did you tell him who it was – the man Maggie was seeing?'

'She never told me.'

'I don't suppose it matters much anyway.'

'I don't know.' She had caught the note of disbelief in his voice. 'I really don't know. I can't imagine the name would have meant anything if Maggie had chosen to tell me and, in any case, I wouldn't have wanted her to. I didn't want to be part of it; I never really said that I would be. I wasn't being asked to construct elaborate lies. Maggie was simply telling me that I'd become a part of *her* lies. I didn't care for the idea much, but—' She broke off.

'But you went along with it.'

'Not really. Yes.' She shrugged. 'I didn't *know* him. We'd met a couple of times. It was just in case he ever mentioned. . . . So that I wouldn't . . . .' Her voice trailed off. 'I didn't know him then.'

'And now you do.' The tone of his voice showed that he understood. She nodded, and his image blurred. He ignored her tears; there was nothing he could say to console or reassure her.

'Can you find him?'

'I'll try. There are places to look.'

'He's in danger out there.'

'You know about Archangel.'

'Yes.' So far it was all the hard information they'd traded.

Mayhew made to get up. 'I'll look for an hour. It's late. He'll likely have gone to ground. Do you want me to phone?'

'If you find him. Otherwise, no.'

'Don't worry,' he said reflexively, and felt for his car keys.

'I remember a time,' she said, 'when Maggie and I were having a drink – not far from here. She was on her way to . . . well, whoever it was. I asked her why. I hadn't before, and I wasn't really that curious, but' – Laura shook her head – 'I hadn't ever done what she was doing and I suddenly wondered what it was for. What it meant. She said: "It started out as a screw; now I keep it on as a secret. It's good to have a secret." She was wearing one of those things in olive green that resemble battle-fatigues until someone like Maggie puts it on. She said. "I don't love him," as if in some way I would be gladdened by that. I sort of felt that she was waiting for me to add something – something that would let her off the hook, or demonstrate my complicity in her deception. I asked her if she loved John.' Laura paused, remembering the moment. 'She said: "Now and then." It had never ocurred to me that such a thing was possible.'

Mayhew got up. He said: 'Stay by the phone.' He didn't understand what that might cost her.

A scream woke him; either that or he woke in the same moment as the scream was uttered. He listened and heard it again – a high, fluting, almost musical screech. Then there were more, overlapping, each extending the previous one until they became a cacophony. Deacon was occupying that brief moment of clarity and well-being that precedes the express-train arrival of a hangover. He lay on grass close to the line of a carefully tended hedge. Just beyond, a double row of beeches marked a pathway. His clothing was wet with dew. The sky was bright but fragile; it had a liquid paleness about it that meant that the sun had barely risen. The trees cast long shadows, and between their sharp dark edges the grass was spangled with white – a sheen like a sugar frosting – where light struck the moisture.

It took him only a few seconds of dazed disconnection to work it out. The park was not far from where he lived. The screams were peacocks in a small fenced-off wildlife area just past the beeches and the footpath.

He struggled on to his hands and knees, head low, arse up. An iron bolt rattled down the chain-link of his spine and smashed against the top of his cranium. His eyeballs felt hot. His stomach flooded with bile. He scrambled back to the hedge, ducked his head under the lowest sprays of green and threw up: great racking convulsions that went on long after he was emptied out. He was shivering, his face pale as pork fat. He crawled into the nearest patch of sunlight and lay there, his back to the cool dampness, his face lifted to the sun so that its colours ran beneath his eyelids – pink and yellow and flashes of crimson, like fluorescent cells separating on a microscope-slide. It was the best distraction he could find.

The same low sun lofted above the humps of the Sussex Downs, making shadows run from hilltop to valley. The first sweetness was still in the air, and the woodland on either side of the road was shrill with birdsong. A wispy ground-mist hung over the low acres, collecting like smoke in dips and hollows.

Tom Buxton stood beside his car and looked around. There had been three phone calls, two of them from Harold Steiner, one from Steiner's assistant. Each had told him to do nothing: to stay at home so that they would be sure of where to find him. Buxton thought that he knew what was going to happen next and didn't want it to happen anywhere near his house, his wife, his daughters; he didn't want it to happen at all, but that was a different consideration. Most of all, he didn't want it to happen *to* him: didn't want to wait for a moment he hadn't chosen and an event over which he had no control.

The back seat of the car was stacked with cans of petrol that he'd collected from various filling-stations. He had parked on a hill to watch the sun come up and now he looked down the long, straight, empty road to where it made a sharp left turn by a clump of trees bordering a field. Cattle were grazing close to a brook about twenty feet from the turn. He looked at his watch. Sally and the girls would still be sleeping. He'd told them he had to attend an out-of-town meeting and would be making a very early start. Sally had stirred and murmured something as he'd begun to get out of bed, trailing a sleepy hand to catch his thigh and draw him back for a brief hug. To support his story, he'd had to shower and shave, then dress in a formal suit and put on a tie. Before going downstairs, he had paused on the landing, wanting to go into his daughters' rooms, but in the end he hadn't the forti-tude for it. He had driven to this place – a spot where, sometimes, the family had taken a picnic – stopped the car on the rise and transferred the petrol-cans from the boot.

When he got behind the wheel again and switched on, he was making tiny weeping noises: faint, like the cries of a kitten. The car travelled slowly to begin with, then picked up speed. Some sixty metres from the turn, the brake-light flashed on and the car checked heavily; almost at once it took on speed again, roaring as Buxton went through the gears. By the time it reached the bend he was at top revs. The car bisected the curve and became airborne when it met the roadside ditch, slamming into the stand of limes, ripping away bark and low branches. The herd of cattle wheeled in panic, galloping for the far side of the pasture.

For a moment there was complete silence. It seemed that the countryside had absorbed the violence of the impact like an air-duct plucking smoke. One second, two seconds of total stillness were followed by a renewal of birdsong, the faint hissing of leaves in a breeze, the distant sound of a ewe bleating for her lamb. Then there was a low seismic thud that ricocheted up the hillside like a battering-ram of compressed air and the car put out sudden brilliant petals of flame that pulled back and caught the bodywork in a fist of fire, red and orange and flowing like the sun.

Deacon had fallen in and out of sleep. He could hear voices laughing and squabbling: children walking through the park to school. He sat up. The moisture had burned off the grass, so he turned over to present his soaked back to the heat. He felt hollow and light-headed, but when he stood up he found that walking wasn't as difficult as he'd thought it would be. He set off towards the main gates of the park, in search of a drink.

PART
TWO

PART
TWO

35

The bird had a massive wingspan, twelve feet or more, and it drifted on the wind as if it weighed less than a flake of ash. If you had calculated the centre of its circle of flight and dropped a line straight down to earth, you would have found the dead llama foal. The mare had stood spraddle-legged and shucked the newborn creature out, rupturing the birth-caul; but the foal was weak and despite the mare's urgings hadn't been able to fasten on to the teat. It had failed to feed before nightfall – a sure indication that it would die.

The mare had kept vigil over her young for three days. She had guarded and protected the small lifeless form as if the fierceness of her instinct might restore life. Predators and scavengers had tried to approach, and each time she had clattered at them, angrily, until they had given up. Sometimes there had been three or four of them circling the corpse, and she had run this way and that, pursuing one, returning to the foal's body, pursuing another that had closed in from the opposite direction. Now she was weak also, her instinct thinned, and it was time to abandon the dead. She sniffed a last time at the little inert sack of skin and tangled limb, licked it, then trotted off between tall boulders.

Sonny Moreno watched the bird as it lost height and planed in alongside the carrion. 'Jesus,' he muttered to himself, 'they're big mothers, that's for sure.' Using its hooked beak, the bird opened the foal up with swift sure rips like someone tearing fabric, then stabbed its head to get among the guts. It came up with a twist of pipes and rending tissue, its bald dome dappled with gore.

It was a routine patrol, and they were taking a break: Sonny, the Dutchman and the Garbage. There were three other patrols out, spread over an area of about ten square kilometres. Base-camp was thirty K's to the south; the main task-force was there. This was Sonny's home ground; he'd worked it for a long while – apart from taking time out in Vietnam – and sometimes, when he thought just how long, it made him weary; but that was the problem with a career – you beavered away at it for years and then it was too late to do anything else.

'I was in Bolivia when them li'l injuns run down Guevara,' he said to Dutch. 'Now here I am still chasing commie ass.' He hadn't taken his eyes from the bird as it yanked at the rag-doll carcass.

'We do what we can,' Dutch said. He was a heavy man, but not more than ten pounds overweight: blond, thick-necked. The machine-pistol that swung from a shoulder-strap and tapped his right hip looked too delicate for his big fists. His name was Piet Knopper, but no one called him that. He and Sonny had met before: a small war here, a revolution there. The difference between them was nominal: Sonny was an adviser, Dutch a mercenary. The terms didn't matter when it came to killing people, which was what they were there to do.

Lounging on the rocks nearby were some twenty men: soldiers of the Republican Army. The Garbage – Sonny's name for them. There were two officers he'd named Snaggle-tooth and Shit-for-brains; he knew their real names and used them when he had to. He spoke the language pretty well, but used it sparingly. He didn't like the sons of bitches and didn't give a fuck whether they knew it or not.

Sonny had stopped thinking about the politics way

310

back in his twenties. None of it meant shit. One man's terrorist was another man's freedom fighter; liberation for some was oppression for others. The pattern here was nothing new – a government hated by the people but liked by politicians back home; assassination and bombings in the cities; guerrillas in the boondocks: an Army of Liberation – 'Los Libertadores' – nourished and supported by villagers. Hell, a lot of the bastards *were* villagers. Just like Nam.

To begin with, it hadn't looked to Sonny like much of a war. The enemy was badly equipped. Their lines of supply ran from village to village, that much was sure, and it made them difficult to hurt; but their weaponry was crap. Two things kept the conflict alive: the fervour of the guerrillas and the quality of the men who fought them, the Garbage.

Snaggle-tooth was passing a canteen round. From the eager looks on the faces of the other men, it contained something more interesting than water. Sonny sighed. 'Whaddya say?'

Dutch nodded. 'OK.'

Sonny levered himself up and spoke to Snaggle-tooth in his own language. The man shrugged and collected his canteen for a final slug. Sonny led off, heading south. There were three villages in the area, any one of which might contain the arms-dump the patrol was looking for.

The foal was just offal now. More of the birds had arrived and were grouped round, looking for their share. They waddled and hopped round the corpse like participants in some ungainly drunken dance of death, snatching at the wet remnants and half-spreading their wings to mantle the food. Their beaks and heads were red; the ground was red under the spread tangle of pelt, legs and intestines. The foal's eyeless head pointed the way Sonny was taking.

They hit the village after a two-hour march and fanned

311

out just back of the tree-line to watch for a while. Nothing was happening: women cooking, men lying in hammocks, children grouped near one of the larger huts. The kids were quiet, and this told Sonny that the village knew he was there. Dutch had taken some of the men and circled to the far side of the clearing, opposite to where Sonny stood. They walked in at almost the same moment – Sonny's appearance acting as a signal to Dutch.

The women left their cooking-fires. The men swung down off their hammocks. More villagers appeared from huts. As the patrol advanced, the soldiers at either end of the two lines spread out, describing arcs of a circle so that the villagers were enclosed.

Sonny's M-16 was on rapid fire. He motioned with the barrel, and men went left and right in twos to search the huts – one backing up alongside the doorway before going in low, the other establishing a line of fire above the first man's head. Shit-for-brains had set up an LM-6 at one side to make a potential killing-ground. Sonny grimaced with contempt. The LM-6 is the squad-weapon version of the M-16; used inexpertly, it would at best ship dirt into its system and at worst find targets indiscriminately. Some of the Garbage were directly opposite the weapon, but they didn't seem to notice.

Snaggle-tooth told him the huts were clean. Sonny nodded, then motioned to Dutch. Together, they walked up to the silent group of men and women who had gathered, as if for protection, close to the largest of the huts. One man stood slightly ahead of the others, looking as if he expected to be spoken to – short, light-skinned, creases on his face that, when you came closer, were tribal markings. Dutch couldn't understand much of what Sonny was saying, but he knew the routine.

'We know you harbour guerrillas.'

'What guerrillas?'

'We know you give them food and shelter.'

'We are peaceable. No one comes here.'

'We know you store guns for them. Grenades. Ammunition.'

'What guns?'

'We know the weapons are hidden in this village.'

'There is nothing hidden here.'

'We know that some of your men are terrorists.'

'We are peaceable. No one leaves the village.'

'We know the guns are here.'

'What guns?'

'We will see.'

Sonny grasped the man's arm and turned him, then raised his boot and nudged the small of his back, shoving him forward. They toured the village twice, but there was nothing to find. Behind one of the huts, out of sight, Sonny said: 'Tell us where they are hidden and we'll destroy them, then go away. It's better you do. No one will be hurt.' To Dutch he said: 'He ain't seen no soldiers; he ain't seen no guns.'

Dutch smiled. 'I ain't seen none, either.'

Sonny laughed. He swung his weapon up from the waist, taking the man on the side of the head and smashing his cheekbone; the man sat down but made no sound. Sonny circled him, picking his spot; he kicked hard at the base of the spine, grunting with effort. The man howled and rolled on to his side.

'Where are the weapons hidden?'

'Truly, there are no weapons.' The words leaked out in little gouts of pain.

'Whaddya think?' Sonny asked.

Dutch turned down the corners of his mouth. 'Who knows? We could look for ever.'

'Yeah.' Sometimes it was easy – they'd find a pit or a cavity wall, the weapons stacked there, some of them new, greased and wrapped in wax paper – but mostly junk or captured Armalites.

'Listen,' Dutch said, 'let's forget it.'

There was a yell, some laughter, some angry shouting. Sonny and Dutch went back to the village clearing, leaving the man Sonny had kicked lying on the ground where he was trying to become invisible. The Garbage had pulled a girl out of the pack and were running her this way and that, pouncing at her when she wheeled or dodged to escape so that she had to turn towards another of the soldiers. They had stripped her. One of them held her skirt and snapped at her with it as if he were flicking a wet towel in the locker-room. Finally she collided with Snaggle-tooth and fell. The soldiers closed in. Two of them held her while Snaggle-tooth kicked out of his pants and clambered onto her like someone swarming belly-down over a tree-trunk bridge. She was looking to one side, eyes wide with shock and fixed on Sonny; her small breasts quaked with the violence of Snaggle-tooth's attack. While he was on her, the others stood round, clapping their hands in time: rednecks at a hoe-down.

When Snaggle-tooth was through it was the next man's turn. The villagers were wailing and shouting. One of them, a man, stepped forward, three steps, four, then ran towards the soldiers. Shit-for-brains looked up and grinned. He hefted his gun from the hip and fired a short burst that tracked across the villager's approach. A woman in the group went down with a bullet in the thigh; the next three slugs, rising, took the man in the ribs, chest and shoulder; the rest clipped twigs from the trees.

Sonny retreated to the edge of the clearing and sank down with his back to a tree. Dutch squatted nearby, forearms loosely across his knees. The soldiers had the girl up on her hands and knees. She looked to be about fourteen. A tall man had mounted her, one arm forward to grip the rein of her hair, the other aloft, still clutching his AK-47. His hips pulsed: a rodeo cowboy.

He yelled and loosed off two clattering streams of bullets that went just left of the villagers.

Dutch back-pedalled a short way and sat down next to Sonny. He watched the crazy excitement, flame-like, licking from man to man. Those who no longer wanted the girl were darting mad glances at the people bunched in front of the large hut and cackling with half-hysterical laughter. The noise children make to imitate gunfire.

'They're going to trash the village.'

'I know.' Sonny took a joint from the map-pocket of his shirt. Good stuff, locally grown. He lit it, long habit causing him to cup his hand round the match. He shook his head. 'Shit!'

Dutch reached out and took the joint. He pulled off three big lungfuls then got up and crossed the tree-line, walking out of sight.

It was a different war in the capital. The occasional mortar-attack, or a skirmish close to the outskirts followed by a running battle on one of the major highways to the interior – but mostly assassinations, sabotage, bombings. You could see evidence of it in bullet-scabs on a wall or the boarded-up window-space of a bank. These things happened in the centre of the capital where, otherwise, life went on as normal. The city fringe was shanty-town where the bombs were made, where the urban guerrillas sometimes lived, coming and going, indistinguishable from the half-starved Indians who had drifted in from the rural areas and built the tar-paper and petrol-drum build-ings. Now and then, the Army would roust shanty-town, the young soldiers going in among their own people, their own kin, to look for arms, detonators or grenades. They rarely found anything, but people still got killed: it was a time for showing class and settling scores.

Oleg Volkov walked out of the embassy and made

for the waiting limousine. During the brief journey from air-conditioning to air-conditioning, he could feel his shirt crumpling as the humidity soaked in. This country, he thought, snow and thin cold air in the mountains; down here, fungus in the closets and mould in the creases of your laundry. Further north it was not like this. Lounging on the lush leather behind smoked glass, he closed his eyes and summoned up images of places he hadn't yet seen. New England in the fall – trees like furnaces; the dry Arizona desert; the savannahs of the South. He thought New England, maybe, but he hadn't fully decided yet.

The limo cruised through the city like a long black shark. The driver had done this before and knew the routine. Just before they reached the northern slipway to the main highway, he eased over, barely stopping, and collected a passenger. They would drive for twenty miles, during which time Volkov and the Indian would talk in a language the driver had never bothered to learn; then he would drop the man at a bridge close to route 18 and take Volkov back to the embassy. Even if the driver had mastered the language, he wouldn't have been able to hear: soundproof glass cut him off from the limo's back seats. And, even if he'd been able to hear and understand, he wouldn't have known that Volkov was telling the Indian lies.

'I have had reports. From what I hear, things are going well.'

The Indian nodded cautiously. 'Better. Much better. Before we had the men, but only poor weapons. Now. . . .'

Volkov's grasp of the language was formal and limited. The Indian spoke carefully, making short sentences, so that the Russian would understand – spoke slowly, avoiding the dialect of his region and the slang of shanty-town. As a result, their exchanges were clipped and starchy – a parody of Noble Savage

316

meets White Father. The Indian saw this and was amused by it. Volkov thought their conversation sounded impressively fluent.

'Are your people ready?'

'Ready. . . .' The Indian shrugged. 'Yes, we are ready. A short while. Some more weapons. We will have more weapons?'

'Oh, yes.'

'They are beginning to lose the war out there.' A nod towards the thick tree-cover beyond the highway. 'They have no allies among the villagers of course. Patrols go out – hired killers. The rabble they call an army. At one time we could not match them – their firepower. Now it is different.'

'The army officers?' Volkov asked.

'We have some, not all. But when we bring the war to the city the others will turn. Some perhaps will run, but most will turn. They argue among themselves. They have no beliefs. Those we cannot frighten, we can surely buy.'

'Good.' Volkov nodded to indicate his pleasure. 'Good.'

'As long as your government's promise to us holds,' the Indian said. 'We will be cut off, after the victory. We will be in great need of all that you have offered. The country is poor, the people are poor. There will be no one else to help.'

'Don't worry. The West will turn its back, but we will not.'

They talked more: time-scales, delivery-dates, programmes for civil rule. The Indian sat on the edge of the rich upholstery, an uneasy visitor in the cool air of the luxurious car. When the driver pulled over and set him down by the bridge, he walked away without looking back. The road was empty. There was a muted squeal and a plume of white dust as a U-turn brought Volkov round for the return trip. He glanced over his shoulder at the short dark figure crossing the bridge,

317

then relaxed into the leather, closing his eyes as before. Scenes from a dream. New England, he thought. He'd be there in time for the first reddening of the leaves.

The limo slipped back through the city. Volkov's eyes were open now, but he saw nothing. He was still deep in his imaginings. They drove two sides of the main square – a mixture of new chrome and glass buildings and some fading remnants of colonial grandeur. Soldiers, businessmen, street-vendors, beggars. Cafés and shops. A boy going through the tall, ornate, curved doorway of a church. Volkov shook himself out of his reverie as they neared the embassy. He was looking forward to a drink: Jim Beam, his favourite.

The boy's eyes adjusted quickly to the half-light in the church, though he wasn't at all confused about where to go and what to do. He put a dab of water to his forehead and genuflected with practised rapidity, then walked down the broad central aisle towards the altar. To one side of the altar table was a small shrine to Our Lady. A tall plaster figure under a neon halo stood with arms outstretched, assuring sinners of her readiness to intercede. The blues and whites of her robe were bright as if freshly painted, and her placid face was smooth as eggshell.

The boy reached into his satchel and took out a few coins. The church bore a frozen silence, and the rattle of the money into the wooden box sounded hollow and loud. He took a candle, lit it from one of fifty or so others racked up before the Madonna, then went to a pew just in front of the altar and knelt there in silent prayer, hands clasped, head on hands, eyes lowered. He was listening. No one was moving around. The only sound was the whispered litany of three old women who had been at their devotions when he entered. Their hoarse hissing chant floated up and swilled the cupola.

318

After a short while, the boy lowered one hand and took something from his satchel. He reached back beneath the pew, pressing upwards. When he withdrew his hand it was empty. He laced his fingers once more and finished his prayer, then crossed himself and started back towards the door.

His bare feet made no noise. The women whispered their circular pleas. The Madonna's arms beseeched, her face rigid with tolerance.

The patrol had circled for more than twelve hours without finding trace of either of the other two villages. It wasn't easy going: the terrain tough and wild, the maps little more than crude approximations. Sonny had managed to establish an intermittent radio contact with one of the other patrols and discovered that they'd had no better luck. Now they were marching due south. No one had said that they were heading for the pick-up point – and from there to base-camp – but that's what they were doing.

A couple of the soldiers were drunk. A personal stereo was being rented by its owner, who kept a zealous account of the time-to-money factor. Whoever was using it leaked a tinny unrecognizable bass-line.

Shit-for-brains had slung his weapon behind his back as if he knew he wouldn't need it; he laughed when one of the drunks snagged his foot and stumbled on to his knees. Sonny turned to Dutch. It was in his mind to say: 'Isn't one of these dumb fucks knows what's going on.'

He said, 'Isn't one—' and a thin hot rope of gunfire went down the line of the patrol, taking out the first three men as if they had been lassoed and snatched away.

A rapid burst from an M-16 climbs right to two o'clock. When Sonny turned towards the source of the incoming fire, he started his weapon to the left and close to the ground, allowing for the traverse; he was

319

moving backwards as he fired, hoping to find cover. It was impossible to tell how close the ambush was. Dutch emptied two clips on the run and bellied down by a clump of trees at the same time as Sonny.

'Where are those suckers?' Sonny was unlimbering a field-radio.

'I d'know. Somewhere high.' Dutch was trying to take a fix on the incoming. The three dead men lay out near the track, the rest had gone to ground twenty metres away, loosing off at random. They were under fire from grenade-launchers.

'What the fuck's that?' Sonny was throwing up the aerial, bending it backwards to keep it out of sight.

'Over-and-unders. They're getting the range.'

'Three hunnerd metres?'

'Four maybe.'

'Shit.' Sonny came up for a look. 'They got snipers closer in.' His head came down, and he started to talk on the radio.

The firefight was non-stop, a blanket roar of automatic weapons that made rip-tides in the air. It was like building a wall that the enemy would have to walk into. Sonny could hear the hammer of the LM-6.

'What the fuck do those mothers think they're killing?'

Dutch shook his head. 'They can't see shit.'

'I know.' Sonny went back to the radio. He couldn't give any co-ordinates but his own, so when the F-4F came over fifteen minutes later it was just for appearance's sake. The pilot overflew the area, then banked fast and came back for a second look. A figure on the far hillside stood up, a shoulder-hefted launcher in place. He stood fast, pirouetting with the plane's track until it was going away from him and the jets were exposed; then a missile started up in pursuit.

Dutch got up and moved forward, letting a clip go at the man. A shower of twigs dropped from nearby trees. He stepped back, then back again, and sat down. Three damp patches, each the size of a fist, had appeared on his flak jacket. He said, 'Oh, fuck,' and worked his legs to get further into cover. Before he got to the dip in the ground that Sonny was using, he stopped. He was panting like a man hyperventilating.

Sonny rolled sideways, making ten metres, and grabbed Dutch under the arms; he scooted backwards towards the dip and tumbled them both in. At the last moment he flipped as a round took the fleshy part of his torso just below the left rib.

Ten minutes later an attack chopper came in, giving support to a troopship. The bigger helicopter rocked around, looking for the best terrain, while the other went up the hillside, flying at nap-of-the-ground level and buzzing like an angry wasp.

Dutch had said, 'This is all wrong . . .' and 'Motherfuckers'. Then his eyes had lost their light, fraction by fraction, and he'd died, still sitting upright, making a last involuntary kick with one leg as if scuffing his boot in disgust.

Sonny knew about wounds and was waiting for the pain to start. He'd kept a string of clips going at the enemy position, but the Garbage had drawn most of the fire. As the chopper put down, two grenades came in with pinpoint precision. A man – it looked like Snaggle-tooth – came out fast, making for the troopship. At first he could run, at first he looked untouched, but then the shrapnel wounds became evident, blood leaping up on his fatigues as if someone were throwing red paint at him. By the time he'd made twenty metres he was an ambling sack of blood. Sonny went past him, low, favouring his torn side; he didn't stop to help.

He threw himself up the ramp and into the chopper. He said: 'Go, for fuck's sake.'

'Are you *it*?' The pilot was American.

'Fuck it! Go!'

The attack ship had released its Stingers and was on

the way back. Sonny watched as it veered and stalled, then broke up inside a bright ball of flame. On the ground a man was crawling to where the big chopper had once been, hit in his legs but hauling his frame over the tussocky grass like a mad swimmer. A sniper ripped him up at random – back, buttocks, arms – and still he moved forward until a bullet ploughed into the base of his skull and he leaped like a salmon and lay still.

Twenty, thirty rounds hit the underside of the chopper, making Sonny rear up: hammer-blows on an anvil. They rang in his skull, and he bellowed: 'Go! Fucking go!' Then they were clear and there was just the *thud-thud-thud* of the rotors.

36

Two generals and a spook. The generals said little, though from time to time they muttered rapidly to each other in their own language.

They're guessing I don't understand them, Sonny thought. He knew who they were. One ran the country, one ran the war. The spook was asking the questions.

'What time were you hit?'

'What was the enemy strength?'

'What were your casualties?'

'What were their casualties?'

'What was their firepower?'

Sonny eased a joint out of his leg pocket; it still hurt a lot to raise his arm. He looked the spook hard in the face while he lit it and hauled off a long toke. 'I don't know where they got it,' he said, 'but they *had* it. We really stepped in some shit.'

'Had what?'

'I've found all kindsa crap out there. BARs, Lee-Enfields, Webley pistols. Crap. Not these guys. We was gettin' stuff from AK-47s or M-16s. They had over-and-unders—'

'What?'

'That's an M-16 with a grenade-launcher fixed underneath. 'Less I'm mistaken, we was takin' fire from AR-15s, too. Really cool weapon. Colt commando. Machine-pistol if you just press a button in the stock. It's like, retractable. Very sophisticated. Plastic stock. They're mass-produced, well designed, don't need cleaning, don't need dismantling. If you do take 'em apart, you can put 'em back together like Leggo. Took the fighter and the gunship out with Stingers from a shoulder-launch. Asshole-creeper. Listen' – he pulled on the joint – 'why don't you tell me what's goin' on?'

'How's the wound?' the spook asked.

'Fuck you,' Sonny told him.

The generals were talking in a fast undertone. It wasn't the first time they'd heard this sort of information recently. It was serious; so serious that one of them had come to this meeting instead of attending mass.

The dim chandeliers in the church were only enough to give half-light. Banked candles by five small shrines drew dancing shadows on the unadorned plaster walls and rinsed the Virgin's face with a mellow glow. Her candles outnumbered those of the saints by three to one.

In the pew where the boy had prayed, a young woman was kneeling. The General wasn't there, but his mistress was. She was dark and doe-eyed and narrow-waisted and, until the General had found her, had sold tickets for the national airline. She didn't think much about her new life with the General, except that she knew she liked it a hell of a lot better than the one she'd been living before. There was good food and fine wine, fashionable clothes, big cool cars, and money. A lot of money.

She settled the lace mantle more secure atop her swathe of black hair and arranged her skirt on her calves as she kneeled.

Ave Maria, gratia plena, Dominus tecum. . . .

A car came fast round the square, then slowed as it drew opposite the church. The passenger yanked up the aerial on a detonation device and activated it at once.

Sancta Maria, Mater Dei, ora pro nobis. . . .

The driver floored the accelerator and the *whoomph* of the blast came in the same moment, dull and distant until the shockwave reached the church's half-open door and it became a crashing roar that brought debris and dust out across the stone steps and on to the street.

There were twenty-four dead and many injured. The priest was dead. The altar boys were dead. Worshippers in the pews nearest the altar were, most of them, dead. The General's mistress had been blown out of her pew and across the aisle, though one of her legs had remained kneeling. An unspeakable cavern had opened up in her midriff, and her guts had left her as she was bowled up and outwards – a thick red-blue tangle of viscera that landed with her and slopped on the stone floor. She wasn't quite dead, and she didn't know what had happened. There was no pain. She found she was looking up at the Madonna's calm fixed gaze and outstretched hands. The cheeks were smooth and speckled with unexpected colour. There was a flood of sound in the ears of the General's mistress, as if she could hear a vast choir holding a single note. The Madonna reached out to help, to help her up. Somehow, the delicate black lace mantle had stayed on her head. She moved, she tried to stand, and then she died.

When the General was told he was angry and frightened. He realized how close he had been to death that morning. More meetings were held. Phone calls were made. A unit of the Republican Army was ordered into shanty-town; they left several dead but came up empty-handed. The General didn't go to bed until the small hours. As he climbed between the sheets, he mourned the loss of his mistress. She had been a beautiful girl, full of laughter and life. She could keep a blow-job going for better than half an hour.

* * *

'Good,' said Austin Chadwick. 'Good.' He arranged the reports neatly on the broad surface of his desk. One concerned the death of Tom Buxton, the other told of the massacre of Sonny's patrol. 'Things are coming straight. What about Buxton?'

'Accident,' Steiner told him.

'His family thinks that?'

'Yes.'

'The police think that?'

'The police think what they're told to think.'

'OK.' Chadwick nodded. 'What does the Russian say?'

'We'll hear about that soon.'

'Good,' Chadwick said again. He paused. 'There are still a couple of loose ends out there, Harold.'

'Deacon.'

A quick shake of the head. 'He's back on the sauce, right?'

'That's what we hear.' Steiner smirked and smoothed a hand fastidiously over his hair. 'He's on the street, taking chances. His enemies know that.'

'Yes. . . .' Chadwick drawled the word, thinking things through. 'A drunk on a high wire. No, I'm not too worried about him right now. Allardyce, though—'

'Gone,' Steiner said. 'Disappeared.' He had a talent for saying the wrong thing.

'No!' Chadwick stood up. 'I don't want to hear that stuff, Harold. The guy's crazy, but he's not stupid. He likes what he's been doing and he won't stop. He might get caught. He might get caught by someone who doesn't report to this office, Harold. Jesus, we can't expect to control every patrol cop over there. Crazy, but not *dumb*. There are things he knows, Harold, things he can trade. I want him found! No one can just *disappear*.'

'This guy can,' is what Steiner wanted to say. He didn't say it.

* * *

In another country, in another way, someone was saying it for him.

'Not only Allardyce; one of ours, too.'

'Who?'

'Bob Gower. Mean anything?'

'Yes,' said Major York. 'It hasn't been that long.'

The house had been difficult to locate, despite the Major's careful instructions. A narrow metalled road through woodland, a cattle-grid, a rutted track, two farm gates: Martin Redfern had twice missed the turning that led to the Major's orderly front garden. It seemed the hinterland of the north. The clipped lawn and crowded flowerbeds were a startling area of management and control in the midst of all that wildness; an aberration.

The Major poured two beers and motioned Redfern outside. 'Let's go into the garden.' They sat in wicker chairs and gazed out towards trim pastureland. Bees mobbed the encircling blooms. Redfern felt as if he were in a time-warp.

'Well' – the Major sipped at his beer and set it down lop-sided on the grass – 'he was just one of many, you know.' A vague wave of the hand indicated the many. 'There was a swing in policy, and everyone started worrying less about infiltration by the Red Peril and more about the Enemy Within.' The emphasis he gave showed that he thought both notions pretty silly. 'It had always been policy to keep an eye on the lefties – CND, trade unionists, some Labour MPs, the Anti-Apartheid lot, you know. . . . Environmentalists most recently, I gather. I wonder what's so subversive about wanting to preserve butterflies. . . .' He shrugged. 'Anyway, there was a recruitment drive. A lot of people were approached – in the media and so forth. Television, newspapers. It seems some of that is coming home to roost.'

Redfern grunted. 'Disinformation.'

'Really.' The Major smiled. 'There were people who

327

were seen to be potentially of use. Stephen Ward was one such – an osteopath who treated the famous. And their wives – more importantly perhaps. You know about him?'

'Of course.'

'Yes. A handy scapegoat when the time came. Well, Allardyce was much the same. I bought several souls during that time. Each of them had important contacts in one way or another. It's a bit like recruiting a hairdresser: people feel secure; they'll say all sorts of things.'

'Where did you collect him?'

The Major thought for a moment. 'A society party in Gloucestershire. He was often at that sort of gathering. His clients would invite him; he's a charming man, as I recall.'

'Did he give us much?'

'Confirmation rather than news, I think. He'd get debriefed once in a while.'

'You?'

'Usually me. I handed him on to Grieg.'

'I know. It was Grieg who organized the Lorimer business.'

'That puzzles me. Why use Allardyce?'

'It had to be done quickly: at once, in fact. It had to look like an accident. There had to be someone who could get to her and kill her without giving her any chance to be suspicious, or struggle, or even tell a friend that she was expecting a visitor. It had to seem that she had been alone when she died. In fact she acted as if she *was* alone. What could be more convincing?'

'Grieg didn't come up with all that,' the Major said shrewdly.

'No.'

'Allardyce volunteered?'

'Coincidence. Lorimer kept an appointment with Allardyce. Later that day, Allardyce saw Grieg – just

328

one of their regular meetings. Among other information, Allardyce mentioned what he'd gleaned from Lorimer – obviously, since what he'd heard appeared to have something to do with a criminal act. There wasn't much time to think. Grieg told him that it was important. He asked whether there was some way of keeping Lorimer quiet. Allardyce said there was, but not immediately. They discussed it. The option of killing the girl got raised – just as a theory. Allardyce didn't shy away from it: he appeared interested. Grieg played him carefully, you know, flirting with the notion, making something of a joke of it. Allardyce stuck more and more to the point. In the end, he offered outright – even told Grieg how he could do it.'

'Someone else got consulted?'

'By that time, the conclusion was that the girl would have to go. Yes, questions were asked. But Allardyce was given the go-ahead pretty swiftly. It's not—'

' – so unusual. No. I remember we used a hotel porter once, then pensioned him off after a year or so. You have to be careful, though.'

'Yes.'

'And now you've got a subcontractor who's decided to become self-employed.'

Redfern was growing a little tired of hearing the obvious. 'Yes,' he said.

'Why is the bank fiddle important?'

The Major was still covered by the Official Secrets Act, and knew it, but there had been careful instructions about what he could and couldn't know. 'We badly need to find Allardyce,' Redfern told him.

'I'll tell you whatever I can remember.' The Major smiled. 'It was just curiosity,' he said. 'I don't really care what the service has got itself into. I live out here and grow flowers. It's all yesterday's papers to me.'

The Major's recollections didn't help much. Redfern hadn't expected that they would. At present, though, anything was better than nothing. Allardyce's house was being watched, and his office. In both places, the phones had been tapped and listening devices planted, all with no result. On one occasion a man wired in to the office bugs thought he heard the sound of a door being closed, the rustling and tiny noises that might mean someone was moving around. Two men went in, taking the lift to the fourth floor where Allardyce rented a small suite, but it was a false alarm. The guys staked out with cameras and field-glasses in a building opposite could have told them they were wasting their time. Thirty or more people had come and gone that morning: some who worked there, some visitors, some making deliveries. None of them resembled Allardyce.

The men who had gone to investigate returned within eight minutes and made their report. No one – a caretaker, a security guard, a few people in the corridors going about their business. One of them had been a tall woman with long black hair, wearing a peach dress. But they hadn't reported that. Why should they? They had barely noticed her.

37

Deacon found his drink; he found several. Another night passed. He spent it in a cemetery somewhere close to the river. There was no church, just a vast necropolis with tombstones in strict lines. When he came to, he was lying alongside Imogen Seymour, 1851–1935, *Only sleeping*.

'Is that right?' he muttered and pulled himself up, one hand on the stone.

The bottle he'd bought with the last of his money was lodged against the low wrought-iron rail that bordered Imogen's little plot. He took a slug and held it up: two-thirds empty, give a drink or two. A pessimist's calculation. He climbed the graveyard wall and walked south, crossing a bridge clogged with commuter traffic. The fumes seemed to crackle in his sinuses. He saw the bottle and the morning out, then slept again until the traffic was going the other way. He hadn't eaten for better than two days.

No money and no booze. Deacon solved the problem by simply walking into a small off-licence and asking for a bottle of Bell's. When the shopkeeper put it down on the counter, Deacon said: 'I won't be paying for it.'

The man's hand went out to retrieve his property, then he saw Deacon's face, like stone, and he checked the gesture in mid-air. Deacon walked out. After he'd gone, the man lifted the phone and dialled, but put it down before the ringing tone arrived. He couldn't think how to explain what had happened without looking bad.

Laura had spent most of the previous day and night driving around the neighbourhood before she realized how pointless that was. All she could do now was stay home and nurse the fear: fear for Deacon and fear for herself.

He walked for a mile or so, but didn't uncap the whisky. He felt lousy, but it wasn't just the drink and sleeping rough; and it wasn't just Maggie. It wasn't even the two put together.

A question was being asked of him. Now and then, he would flick his head sideways like someone avoiding a cuff: that was when the questioner was growing particularly persistent. He didn't want to hear the question. He didn't want to have to listen, because he knew the questioner's voice was his own.

A couple of drinks would dull the voice. A couple more would make it so faint as to be barely audible. A few more on top of those, and he wouldn't hear anyone's voice, real or imaginary.

'What are—'

He cocked his head violently.

'What are you—?'

He quickened his pace, as if he might outstrip the voice.

'What are—?'

He unscrewed the bottle-cap, then turned, all in one motion, to plant his forehead against the wall he was walking beside.

'Please,' he said. 'I don't want to.'

After a moment he straightened up and went to a nearby bench. He had simply let the bottle fall from his hand and walked away from it. He sat down and listened to the voice.

'What are you feeling?'

'Despair. Loss. Anger.'

'Are you?'

'Of course. How the hell would you feel? You

discover the woman you worshipped was cheating on you, dammit, all the fucking time you were thinking how good everything was, how fucking *special*, your whole life based on that, on that feeling, and you ask—'

'Worshipped?'

'Sure. Christ, what would you call it? Is that a soft word? Aren't men supposed to use those words? What—?'

'No, that's OK. It says how you felt. It doesn't say why, or whether that was wise.'

'*Wise?*'

'Sure – wise. This woman: this Maggie. . . . What did you expect from her? Was she supposed to take responsibility for your life? Whose fucking life is it?'

'It's . . . I'm just . . . saying that I loved her.'

'Fine. That's *your* responsibility. You loved her. Does that mean she sticks to rules you invent?'

'She was *cheating* on me, God dammit.'

'I know. So she had problems, too.'

'You don't understand. We had a perfect thing going. Perfect. It was magical. Everything about us – being together, everything – was fine. And she—'

'No, it wasn't, pal. You *thought* it was. You loved her blind. That was *your* problem, not hers. Listen, what are you feeling?'

'Loss. Anger.'

'You missed out despair.'

'I—'

'You don't feel as bad as you should, do you?'

'What?'

'You don't feel as bad as you'd like to.'

'What the fuck do you know?'

'I said you don't feel as bad as you'd like to.'

'Smart talk. What are you? Some fucking shrink?'

'Try answering the question.'

'Sure, I feel – I felt lousy yesterday. I felt as if I wanted to die.'

'Yes, I know. How do you feel *now*?'

'Listen, I can't cope with—'

'Isn't there a touch – just a touch – of something like relief?'

'Relief?'

'Sure. The burden of loving Maggie, of missing Maggie, of mourning Maggie. Maybe some of that's gone. What do you think?'

'I think you're full of shit.'

'OK, try this. If you're not feeling as bad as you think you ought to, why is that?'

'I don't know.'

'If there's something taking the edge off this, if there's a reason for dropping that bottle, if there's a consolation somewhere, a life-saver, what is it?'

'You're the one saying it's there.'

'*If* it's there. What is it?'

'I don't know.'

'*If*.'

'I don't know.'

'*If*, you arsehole.'

'Laura.'

He went to the phone-booth on the corner across the street and phoned her. He gave her the street-names. She said she'd come and pick him up. When he hung up and turned round, he was looking at four men. One of them was Marcus Archangel. The big limo was parked just down the block.

Holy Christ, Deacon thought. I'm in terrific shape for this. He started to run.

In no shape for it. Even so, he made twenty metres on them because they simply weren't expecting him to act so quickly. The story was he'd be drunk. Archangel yelled at them but stayed put. It was nine-thirty and still light; no cover of darkness. Deacon rounded a corner and looked for a bolt-hole, but there wasn't one. People on the street watched, or parted swiftly to let the runners through. No one was going to give any help; city-lore was don't get involved. Deacon's only advantage was that they almost certainly wouldn't shoot him in the street. They had expected to be able to get him into the car without much difficulty – a scuffle, a complaining drunk, a couple of wary bystanders, perhaps, but soon an incident already over and the limo disappearing. When he turned into the next street and saw that it was pretty well populated, he slowed at once to a walk. People might not want to be heroes, but they wouldn't fail to report a killing.

The four men chasing him almost fell over him. One of them said: 'Just like you goin', man – back towards the car. Don't get ambitious nor nothin'. You can die right here if you like to.' Deacon didn't believe that, but he didn't believe he could shake them, either. Sooner or later there would come a moment when they'd be able to jump him. If he kept walking, so would they, with the car following slowly for collection.

Close to the corner where he'd used the telephone – but not close enough for the men to hustle him into the limo – was a pub with some wooden benches outside. Deacon waited until he was almost there, then quickened his pace for two or three strides and sat down abruptly. The men stopped. One of them said: 'Why you bein' difficult, man? Wha' difference it goin' ta make?' They sat down with him, one alongside, the others opposite. Archangel strolled over; he was smiling.

'I don't see a way out of this for you, Deacon.'

'I could sit here for ever.'

'We'll wait with you.'

'I could shout "Copper".'

Archangel laughed. 'What would you do? Ask for protective custody? Talk about heroin loaned to you illegally and a policeman paid off with ten thou?'

Deacon didn't answer. He was trying to watch the

road without seeming to look. Ten minutes, he figured; maybe eight, maybe twelve. He wasn't far from home, and Laura was a snappy driver. He watched for a white VW convertible.

'Deacon.' Archangel spoke almost sorrowfully: a chiding note in his voice.

'Suppose I force you to take me right here?'

'You're right – I don't want to. However, I will if I must. A dozen people will say I was somewhere else – some of them rather respectable.'

A couple of minutes; maybe even less.

Deacon sank his face into his hands. 'A drink first,' he said. Through the lattice of fingers he studied the road.

'Deacon. Don't be pathetic.'

'I *need* a drink.' His voice filtered out from the bowl of his hands.

'Ah, yes. I see.' A top-up. Archangel smiled. A drink, or even three – sure. He watched Deacon's shoulders slump and saw the fight go out. He gestured, and one of the men got up.

'Scotch,' Deacon told him. 'A double.' He sat in silence until the drink arrived.

Archangel beckoned, and the glass was handed to him. He set it down carefully, by Deacon's hand. 'Don't sip,' he said.

Bad traffic; or lost car-keys. Deacon sighed and took the glass, and in that moment saw the VW turn into the road where the phone-booth stood. He got up, took a mouthful of whisky and started towards the limo as if he'd suddenly come to terms with his fate. Took a mouthful but didn't swallow. Archangel and the others were behind him, staying close.

In the middle of the road, he suddenly stopped and turned, as if to speak. The abrupt halt brought Archangel almost nose to nose. He spat the Scotch in a fine spray, going for the eyes and finding them, then pushed Archangel back into the closest man and began to run in a direct line at the VW.

336

Laura saw the scuffle, but at first couldn't decide what it was. Then she saw Deacon coming straight at her and the four men closing on him. She had to go left or right; and it was nothing but instinct that made her flip down her right-side indicator. The men didn't consider the car. To them it meant no more than an obstacle for Deacon. They divided, two going on one side, two on the other, expecting the VW to pass. He held his line until he was almost under the wheels. Laura hit the brake and hauled the wheel right. Deacon veered to the left. The car stopped.

There was a pause of a second or two. The men had over-run the car, imagining that Deacon would be hit, or be left stranded. By the time they understood what was happening, Deacon had the door open.

'Move!' he yelled.

He ran with the car as it rolled, pitchforking himself in feet-first and yanking the door shut.

'Go left!' The driver of the limo was starting a U-turn. Archangel was still in the road, knuckling his eyes, in pain, trying to focus. In a couple of seconds the limo would take the crown of the road and begin to go broadside against Laura's approach.

'Left!' Deacon shouted again.

Archangel was moving away from the limo's angle of turn, stumbling towards the roadside but still partially obscured by the big car. As Laura swooped into the narrowing gap, he emerged. There was now-here to go. The VW's bumper smashed into his legs, and he flew up and sideways, flipping off the wing, somersaulting, then going under the limo's bumper before the driver had time to react. One wheel crossed his ribs, staving them as if they were palings; the other went over his head. An eye popped like a trodden grape.

Laura was shaking so hard that she couldn't keep her foot steady on the accelerator. It hopped like a drummer's. Deacon yelled instructions at her, and she made the turns as he dictated them, driving entirely by instinct while he navigated them back towards the busier streets.

When they parked, he checked the front of the VW. Nothing, really; a shallow depression on the wing and the bumper was slightly misaligned. They went into the flat, and Laura spun round in the centre of the living-room to regard him. Two days solid of boozing, not eating, sleeping rough.

'You look like hell,' she said. She started to cry.

Deacon shaved and bathed and washed his hair. By the time he emerged, Laura had made spaghetti, a green salad, with bread: the best she could come up with from the limited food-supply. It was the first time she had cooked for him in his flat. He ate the meal in silence. When he'd finished, he stood up to take his plate and the rest of the dishes into the kitchen. Laura intercepted him – 'Put them down' – and held herself against his chest, arms wrapped tight.

She said: 'I'm sorry.' Not an apology, but sadness for what he'd learned.

'It's all right,' he said. 'It's all right.' And clapped her on the back with his hand.

It wasn't the truth, though he hoped that, in time, it might become true.

38

Oleg Volkov's car pushed up a dirty white wind-sock of dust on the minor road. A three-year-old sedan from the pool; he was driving it himself and had the luxury of neither plush upholstery nor air-conditioning. The air sucked in through the open window slapped his face like a damp cloth. If he shifted his position, he could feel the patches where his clothes were staining.

The drive took ninety minutes: it always took about that long – ten minutes either way perhaps. Volkov preferred to be late rather than early: it gave him less time in the place. The township was strung along half a mile of road, a haphazard line of buildings that extended both ways from what had once been a village-centre. The place had pretty much emptied out now: workers migrating to the cities to find work, leaving behind only the buildings, amenities and a vague sense of community. It had become an outpost, used mostly by the loggers, the cattlemen, the labour force that grew and shipped coca. The new buildings were bars, game arcades, video stores, a couple of whorehouses. A ramshackle movie-house was show-ing *Death Wish* dubbed in Spanish.

Volkov parked outside one of the bars, went in and ordered a Cuba Libre – a not very funny private joke – then played pinball for a while. He was red-hot at pinball and had already decided to install a games-room in his New England house. His mind's-eye picture had real substance now: a house built on the colonial model, half-shingled, pillars by the front door, large Georgian-style windows; a view of the mountains, maybe, and a parcel of land belonging just to him; trees and a small lake. He saw himself entertaining in the large drawing-room; himself and a girl who, as yet, had no face but was tall and slender and classy and blonde. Very, very classy. Or else he stood by one of the broad windows and played pinball while the wind made the birches on the lawn shimmer and show their gold.

A man came and stood at Volkov's shoulder and watched the score rack up. 'Pretty damn good,' he said and took a mouthful of beer. Volkov didn't reply or look round; he played out the game, then followed the man to a booth.

'You want another of those?' The man gestured at Volkov's drink.

'No.'

'OK. I'm being asked how long.' They were there for business only; Volkov had never known the man's name.

'A month; maybe less. The weapons – the ordnance and explosives, all that – have made the difference. The war's coming into the cities much more.'

'I heard about the thing in the church. They missed the Man.'

'Ill-luck. It'll happen again. The Government's ready to go. The people out here, the people in the cities – they've had enough. It was ripe a year ago; now they've got the strength to shake the tree.'

The man Volkov was talking to knew all that; he'd been working for Am-Daw on clearance projects for a long time and he knew the country, its poverty, its corruption. He also knew diplomats: especially those who could be bought, so he listened and made no comment. 'There will be another shipment next week,' he said.

'Good.'

'You'll let Los Libertadores know that?'

'Yes.'

'The consignment's coming in from Germany via Israel, labelled machine-parts. It looks like mining equipment. With luck, it'll be ready for distribution in two weeks.'

'Good. The pick-ups as usual: at night, over ten kilometres of road. You truck them there.'

'As usual,' the man agreed. 'They're not uneasy? I've been told to ask about that.'

'Uneasy? No. They think they know where the arms come from; they think what I tell them is true. Don't worry. Listen, let's talk about me.'

'What?' The man was puzzled for a moment; Volkov had sounded almost coquettish.

'About me.'

'OK.'

'I have decided I'd like to go to New England.'

'Oh, sure.' The man smiled. 'I see, yes. New England.'

'It can be arranged?'

'Of course. Whatever you like.'

'When the capital falls, there will be confusion – celebration, killings, looting, processions in the streets.'

'Yes.'

'First, I mine the embassy; a device timed to explode when the largest complement of staff is in residence. After I've primed it, I drive to the edge of the city. The roads will be clogged, so I won't be able to go further. At junction nine I wait for a helicopter. It brings me here. From here, a Lear jet from the strip.'

'What are you worried about?'

'Nothing. Nothing. Just that there'll be a lot of' – he searched for a word – 'disorder. I want to be sure we have this right.'

'No sweat. It's all arranged. Be at junction nine.'

'There'll be time—'

341

'There'll be plenty of time,' the man broke in. 'No one will know what's *really* happening for hours – a day, maybe more. The rebels think they're covered; they won't question it at once. By that time, you're long gone.'

'Yes,' smiled Volkov. 'Long gone.' He paused. 'Are you from New England?'

A wry smile; a shake of the head. 'Chicago, then Texas. Then here.'

'But you've seen it? You've been there?'

'A couple of times.'

The man offered no more; Volkov had to prompt: 'What is it like?'

Tame woodland, neat fields; people with flat accents and English suits, acres of trimmed lawn, avenues of pollarded trees; that was what the man summoned up.

'I d'know,' he said. 'I guess it looks like what God would have done with nature if only He'd had the money.'

39

'It's too early to tell. Things are quiet, and we don't
really know what that means. A bit like a phoney
war. It looks normal, but it doesn't really feel that
way.' Phil Mayhew was talking about the effect of
Archangel's death. His voice over the telephone was
clear, but sounded a long way off. 'It's bad he's dead;
but, then, again, it's not. At least he didn't get
busted. At least he's not banged up down here,
directing troops from a distance like an emperor in
exile. Christ, at least it wasn't us who saw him off. I
wouldn't mind betting that one of the reasons for all
this silence is that they don't know what's next.
Waiting for the coronation.'

Deacon said: 'I don't care an awful lot.'

'No. Well. You're not doing the coppering.' There
was a pause. 'Clearly you're back on your feet.'

'So it seems.'

'I looked in a lot of places – you know; Laura
wanted me to.'

'I know. Thanks.'

'I haven't the first idea whether she did the right
thing. But I could see, when I talked to her, you
know, she couldn't avoid it.'

'I know that, too.'

'I really think. . . .' Mayhew broke off like someone
who already had the words but was looking for better
ones. 'I'm sure she doesn't know who it was. The
man. . . .' There was no response at first. 'I think that
if—'

343

'So am I.' Deacon's reply smothered Mayhew's unfinished remark. They both waited. 'So am I.'

'Look,' Mayhew said, 'I've had a whisper. I couldn't get it all straight. It might be horse-shit.'

'Where from?'

'Your guess.' The shrug was evident in Mayhew's tone of voice. 'A call. Here at the nick. Four calls in fact, over the course of two days. I wasn't here to take the first three, so one of the other jacks left a message.'

'Which said what?'

'Not a lot, except that it mentioned your name. At first, I thought it was *from* you; then I realized it was *about* you. Just to expect a call. Eventually, it came while I was here.'

'And?'

'A voice; no face.'

'Saying what?'

'Not all of it makes sense to me. If it makes sense to you, maybe we're looking at something interesting.'

'Go on.'

'In a way,' Mayhew said, 'I hope there won't be things you know that I don't. As I recall it, the idea was we'd trade.'

'I didn't have time to tell you about Archangel; you might have heard I was on the batter for a few days. Don't fret. If what you say makes sense, I'll tell you why.'

'OK. I got three names: Lorimer, Buxton and Am-Daw. Lorimer I know about. Buxton, if I remember right, is the guy who runs the bank that she worked for. Laura works for. Right?'

'Right.'

'What's Am-Daw. Is that right? *Am-Daw*?'

'Yes.'

'What is it?'

'A multinational. American, but tentacles most places. It owns the bank.'

'Which means?'

Deacon thought it was probably time to come clean, and looked for a way of doing that without letting it be seen that he'd hedged in the past. 'I'm sure there was some sort of financial chicanery going on. A scam. Sure of it. I'm sure that Kate Lorimer found out about it and was killed.'

'Not the only one.'

'How's that?'

'This Buxton – went off the road out by the Sussex Downs.'

Mayhew waited ten seconds for Deacon's reaction. 'Is that right? Not an accident?'

It was a rhetorical question, but Mayhew answered it anyway. 'Shouldn't think so, no. He had no real reason to be there, the brakes were up to snuff and there were enough cans of petrol on the back seat to fly a Boeing. I checked it out. The family – his family – has been told it *was* misadventure, and that's what the inquest will say, too. Someone cleared up. I remain puzzled, though.'

Deacon tested himself for remorse, but nothing happened. 'OK,' he said, 'so whoever called you knows *something*.'

'Am-Daw?'

'I think the bank was stealing from itself.'

'From its customers.'

'In effect.'

'You think. . . .'

'Some of it's guesswork, some of it's not.'

'Laura helped out with that?'

It was a question, though for a moment Deacon wasn't entirely sure. While he'd been on the street, Laura and Phil had met; her desperation had drawn him in. How could she remember everything she'd said? Deacon didn't really want to box clever with Mayhew; he was simply anxious to keep Laura's profile low. 'She helped me put two and two together where that was possible; neither of us knows a hell of a lot.'

'Well, someone knows something, it seems.'

345

'A man's voice?'

'Sure.'

'Tell you anything?'

'Just a voice; not one I recognized.'

'Saying—'

'Asking for a meet.'

'Ah.' Deacon pondered. 'Why you? Isn't it D'Arblay's case?'

'Officially, it's no one's case. Don't know. Someone who knows about our connection. Knows about the bank.'

'The ghetto?'

'Not unless it's a renegade. A guy with something to sell.'

Deacon's mind flashed to Ambrose Jackson. He said: 'What do you want to do?'

'Well, let's go.'

'Where?' Deacon asked. 'When?'

'This evening. I made the place and time provisional on a call.' It was usual: you look for the high ground, then try to hold it. Stake your man out by a phone and call to give him a route and a destination. From there send him on to another place; from there to another. You don't have to follow him, just be watching when he arrives and leaves. It isn't perfect with modern wire-ins, but it gives you the edge.

'What name did you get?' asked Deacon. Mayhew laughed. 'Robinson,' Deacon guessed. 'Jones.'

'Yes,' Mayhew agreed, 'it might as well have been.'

'OK. Where first?'

'Who?' Laura asked.

'We don't know.' Deacon had wrapped the string of a pull-through round his hand and was hauling the wad upwards from the breech of a 9-mm Beretta.

'The man. . . .' She looked at the gun. 'The phone calls – him?'

346

'I suppose it might be. I don't think so.' He checked the firing pin. 'Where will you be?'

'Here,' she told him.

He glanced up, then went back to the gun. 'All right.' There was something at the back of his mind that he couldn't quite get a grasp on. He knew what it was like, but not what it was: a shape, a direction. . . . Something he already knew that refused to yield itself. 'What did you talk about with Phil – while I was getting pissed?'

'Nothing. I mean, practical things – where you might be.'

'Maggie?'

'Not really.'

'Maggie and me?'

'No. John, I wouldn't. . . . I don't know Phil. It was just . . . how to find you. What we could do.'

'About Kate? About the phone calls?'

'No. He was here . . . oh, ten minutes. Fifteen? It was tactics: what to do.'

'Did he tell you that Buxton's dead?' She hadn't been to the bank, and Deacon didn't know yet when the man had died.

'No.'

'Buxton's dead.'

Her face grew small. 'How?'

'In his car.'

'He—' Laura gestured vaguely, her hand in front of her face as if it might go to her mouth. She laid her fingertips along her brow, delicately, as if testing a wound. 'He did it to himself?'

'Yes.'

She nodded and looked at the floor. Deacon smacked the clip to seat it in the butt. 'I wish you wouldn't go.' She meant *didn't have to*.

'One thing leads to another.' He smiled ruefully. 'This appears to be the next thing.'

* * *

The weather hadn't changed: the sun still set each evening in a sky unsmudged by cloud, a dull flood of red deepening through shades of rose to oxblood and blinding west-facing windows with vermilion cataracts. The sky was sea-green glass, then amethyst, then suddenly obsidian. Mayhew had chosen the hour between the dog and the wolf: the almost-dark. Deacon parked close by a pub called the Prince of Wales Feathers. Mayhew loomed up out of the dusk. He opened the car door and got in.

'I had him staked out in there and called', he jabbed a thumb at the yellow glow from a pay phone, 'from over there. He set off two minutes ago. Your timing's perfect.'

'Alone?'

'So far. I've sent him to the Golden Gloves in the Fulham Palace Road.'

Deacon started the car. 'Let's hope he's not a drinker. How's he getting there?'

'By way of Chelsea.'

'Will he do that?'

'He'd better. If he skips the route, the meet's off. He knows that.'

Deacon made a right turn and started south. 'How many calls?'

'Four. That should let us know. Take an hour, maybe.'

'After that?'

'The docks, east of Limehouse. Just warehouses. Empty this time of night. Then we'll see what he's got to say for himself.'

'What am I looking for?'

'A red Saab.' Mayhew gave him the number.

'He could be on CB. Short-wave radio. Personal link.'

'I know. We're doing the best we can. When we get to the docks, we'll take him off a half-mile or so. Better than nothing.'

'Sure.'

They found the pub and waited. After ten minutes, the Saab arrived. A figure got out and went into the bar.

'OK.' Mayhew climbed out and walked to a nearby phone. When he returned, he said: 'Get ready.'

The figure emerged. The Saab pulled away.

And three times more, Deacon driving more or less in silence, tension building in the car as they dog-legged towards their destination.

At one point, Mayhew said: 'He's solo all right.'

'Until he gets the final instruction,' Deacon warned.

'He won't know it *is* final. We're leading him after that. He can give the area, not the meeting-place.'

'That's close enough for me.'

'You've done this before.'

'I didn't like it then.'

Mayhew laughed. 'You're kidding,' he said. 'We had some times, John. Didn't we? Some times.'

It nagged at Deacon. A feeling, a recollection that refused to step into the light. What? *What?* Laura. Phil. A connection that split and reassembled and changed its form like amoeba under a microscope, never keeping a single shape long enough to become identifiable. He gave up on it and concentrated on driving the final leg.

After Mayhew had made his phone call at the final contact-point, the figure emerged and got into the Saab, then waited. Deacon pulled ahead, blipping his lights momentarily as he passed, and the red car eased away from the kerb to follow. Mayhew twisted in his seat, looking back to make sure contact wasn't broken.

'I prefer to be where he is,' Deacon said.

'It's less than a mile,' Mayhew told him. 'He doesn't know where we're going to stop. Even if he's wired up, his contacts would have to get to the place; then they'd have to find us. Don't worry.'

They drove along Commercial Road towards Lime-house Basin, then right into the network of roads just below the East India Dock Road.

'Towards the dock pier,' Mayhew said; then, after five or six minutes: 'Stop here.'

Deacon pulled over and cut the engine. At first, there seemed to be the sort of silence so intense that it's perceived as a monotonal hum, but when he climbed out of the car Deacon could hear the distant murmur of engines and an occasional patter of back-wash where the river sucked at steps or the stern of a barge. The dock was gantries and warehouses, loading-ramps and head-high stacks of pallets. The Saab had stopped a cautious fifty feet away.

'I'll lead him off,' Mayhew said softly. 'You follow. We'll take him away from the cars, just in case some of his friends are on the way.'

The man got out and stood by his open car-door, a dark shape in the muzzy light shed by a quarter moon. Although Mayhew scarcely lifted his voice, it was enough for the man to hear. 'I'm walking off – going right. Follow me, but stay twenty feet back.' He went towards the Saab, skirting it by taking a semicircular path, making for a warehouse trellised with catwalks. The man allowed the correct distance, then started walking. Deacon knew the routine. He began to track them both, pacing himself so that he would gradually close on the man and be up to him by the time they reached cover. He could see that Mayhew had chosen the lee of the warehouse wall on the blind side of the dock, wanting open ground between himself and the cars.

White, Deacon thought. Under six feet, dressed in dark clothing. It wasn't possible to tell more. The dim moon-glow seemed to consist of swarming grey particles, distorting the shape of the man he followed. The procession moved diagonally across the dockyard. Mayhew passed a loading-crane, lost for a moment

350

against its dark outline, then emerged. The Saab's driver dipped in and out of the same blackness, keeping the same pace. Deacon shifted his gaze, checking Mayhew's direction. He was still making for the warehouse wall. Again he evaporated, this time in the gloomy overhang of a roped and tarpaulined stack, then reappeared close to the wall. The follower kept the line and was swallowed by shadow. Deacon went five paces, then stopped. His eyes were on the outer line of the stack where the man would reappear. Another three paces. Nothing broke the dark vertical.

'Phil!' Deacon's voice was sharp in the silence. He looked beyond the stack, but no one was there. 'Phil!'

He went left, putting distance between the stack and himself, intending to circle towards the warehouse. He assumed that Mayhew had rounded the corner of the building. There was a *click-hiss* and a funnel of light cut him off from his objective. He turned and started back towards the cars.

The white disc of the spotlight flowed over the stack, grounded, then slid like a vast puck over the dockyard's concrete floor. It flicked past, clipping his heels, and he dodged out towards the apron of the wharf. It circled, like something on the prowl, and he ran in a crouch, trying to stay under the beam. It quartered the ground, washing up his legs, travelling on as if carried by its own momentum then back-tracking sharply to swamp him with brilliance. He checked, hoping to lose it, but it stayed with him; the star of the show taking a curtain-call. There was a sound like someone hitting a table with a newspaper and a bullet ploughed chips out of the concrete five feet ahead of him.

He leaped out of the spotlight, hitting the ground and rolling right, away from the cars. The spot travelled left, further left, then back, and found him running towards the stack. One shot went behind him, another whined over his shoulder, opening a star-shaped rip in the tarpaulin and ploughing through the pallets. Then he was behind the stack, with the light feinting right and left like a boxer looking for an opening, sometimes washing the ground beyond the stack to let him know he couldn't retreat. He could hear a soft metallic after-sound as rubber-soled shoes hit the treads of the catwalk-ladders. Two coming down for him; maybe three.

He glanced at the corner where Mayhew had disappeared. And maybe, he thought, one already here.

Once they were off the catwalk it would be over quickly. A pincer movement would bring them round the stack; if there were three, one would come over the top – the shape of the pallets through the tarp gave perfect footholds. He watched as the spotlight switched to and fro: left and pause, right and pause, left. . . .

He came out at the run, heading to the right and the warehouse wall. The spotlight continued its pattern for a few more seconds, bracketing the stack, until someone yelled – hearing Deacon's footsteps – and the beam danced crazily, searching for its prey. The catwalk gave three feet of dead ground. Deacon flattened himself to the wall and watched the light run along the area directly in front. It couldn't reach him. To track the wall, the man operating it would need to be standing on air and angling the beam backwards.

Deacon was wearing a linen jacket. He'd put it on only for its pockets, never having owned anything as fancy as a shoulder-holster. Now he took the gun out and started towards the light, moving backwards some of the time to keep the stack in view. The light went back there for an instant, and he caught a profile that went out of sight, heard a voice that started then stopped. A few more paces took him directly under the beam. He waited until it angled away then stepped out and looked up. The peripheral glow showed him a silhouette. He crouched, bringing the Beretta up

352

two-handed, squeezing just like the textbooks tell you to, so that the shot is almost a surprise.

There came a yell of shock and pain. The operator pitched forward, grabbing at the rail of the catwalk as the slug took him in the meaty part of the shoulder. His body stopped some of the light and cast the magnified shape of a man across the dockyard floor like a vast shadow-play in an empty theatre. Deacon resighted and emptied half the clip. There was a shrill scream. The shadow jerked and dropped. The light went out.

Deacon stepped back under the lip of the catwalk. From above came a breathy gurgling sound like someone sucking the last of a drink through a straw, and the uneven spatter and drip of wetness on the metal stairway. A man yelled from over by the stack, and a dim shape moved into the open. Deacon levelled his gun and, as the shape paused, fired; then he fell to the ground expecting return fire.

There was silence. He made a brace of his elbows and kept the gun trained on the stack. Nothing moved. He heard the sound of feet running away.

He stayed put for a good five minutes. Out on the river a barge hooted and a pleasure-boat went by with a string of coloured lights from stem to stern, churning a wake that hit the wharf again and again, hollow pauses between each flat percussive slap. When the river settled, the hoarse drool from the catwalk had stopped.

As he ascended the steps, Deacon put each foot down carefully, soundlessly. On the second turn of the stairs, where it levelled out to a shallow landing, he felt the crunch of glass. A man lay just in front of the third flight of steps, his arms through the iron banister. As Deacon turned him, he kept the barrel of his gun against one temple, but there was no need. It was dead weight he lifted and turned over. He crouched by the body and fetched out his cigarette-lighter, glancing towards the stack for a moment. It was just a nervous reflex; he knew they had gone.

The flame was steady in the still air, a fuzzy circle of yellow light. He stared at the face. The metal case of the lighter grew hot in his hand, but he kept it burning. He realized, as he looked, that he wasn't surprised.

'D'Arblay,' he said; a scarcely audible whisper.

He remembered, at once, what it was that he'd always known about Phil and Laura. Known as you know something you've heard, but have failed to interpret.

40

What Deacon did next was simple, because it was the only thing to be done. He drove to Mayhew's flat, parked outside and rang the doorbell. When Mayhew opened the door, he stood there wordlessly for a full ten seconds, then he laughed.

'Shall I come in?' Deacon asked.

Mayhew backed off, leaving Deacon to close the door, and led the way to his second-floor flat. 'I won't offer you a drink,' he said. 'You'll understand if I have one.'

'Sure.' Deacon was looking round.

Mayhew took a long pull at his Scotch. 'I didn't know,' he said.

'Sure.'

'I really didn't know.'

'What?'

'Until I heard—'

'Didn't know what?'

Mayhew flopped on to a big cream-coloured couch: a way of showing the throat. 'I was told to get you there. A warning, I thought. You'd been sailing too close to the wind. A few threats. Or maybe it would be enough to tell you that things had gone too far. You might have been persuaded just to stop.'

'Is that right?'

'What are you going to do?'

'Nothing.'

'John. . . .' Mayhew threw up his hands in exasperation. 'Damn it, you told me little enough. If I'd known more, I could have told you myself that you were trespassing.'

355

'On whose ground?'

'Special Branch.'

'Which means MI5.'

'Probably.'

'D'Arblay.'

'Yes.'

'Well, well,' said Deacon, 'they do like to shuffle the pack, don't they? If they'd all stayed in one place, we'd know where the smell was coming from. What was your role?'

'Role?' Mayhew looked offended. 'I didn't have a fucking *role*. I was reporting back, that's all.'

'To D'Arblay.'

'Christ, John, I'm a copper. Whose side am I supposed to be on?'

'Someone tried to kill me tonight, Phil. Someone shot a gun at me in the hope that I'd die.'

'And I've told you I didn't know it was going to happen.'

'Horse-shit.'

A silence. Mayhew said: 'Get you there; disappear; leave them to warn you off. That was all. Do you think they asked me if I'd mind? When I heard the shots—'

Deacon cut in. 'You didn't come back.'

'No,' Mayhew said. He looked into his glass, then finished off the drink. 'No, I didn't do that.' He got up from the couch and gave himself a refill. While his back was turned, he asked: 'Did you . . . do you think I agreed to take you there so someone could kill you? Is that really what you believe?'

'I don't know.' Deacon's tone of voice made it mean *Sure, probably, why not*?

'Look, when I heard—'

'You didn't,' Deacon interrupted. Mayhew looked puzzled. 'Whoever was shooting at me was using a silenced weapon. The shots you heard were mine.'

'Ah.' Mayhew's eyes flickered over Deacon's torso, travelled to his pockets, then swivelled away.

'D'Arblay's dead.'

Mayhew sat down slowly. 'Oh, shit.'

'So you'll need to make a phone call quite soon, won't you? Unless the intrepid spooks who were with him decided to go back. In which case, you'll be *getting* a call.'

'Yes.'

They sat in silence for a while. Finally Deacon said: 'Nice flat.'

'What?' It seemed to Mayhew that Deacon could scarcely have said anything more odd.

'This is a nice flat. I like the way you've fixed it up.'

Mayhew looked round as if seeing the place for the first time himself. He nodded. 'Yes,' he said, 'it's. . . . I'm pleased with it.' The conversation was surreal – calm and commonplace, and insane.

Deacon took himself back in time, knowing, now, what waited for him there. He and Mayhew were sitting in the pub – in no man's land, close to the ghetto's fringe. He had just said Laura's name.

'A friend of Maggie's,' Mayhew had said. 'Gossipy evenings at the Turkish baths.'

He should have noticed at the time. He should have noticed when Laura had told him that the story wasn't true, but his distress had been too great for that kind of subtle recollection to make an impression. It had taken Mayhew's betrayal of him that evening to bring it to the fore. One betrayal pointing to another.

If the Turkish bath alibi was a lie, how could Mayhew have known of it? How could he have offered it as a truth? Deacon was half-smiling, gazing at Mayhew, at the cream sofa, at the clever *mélange* of photos and prints between the sitting-room's two tall windows, the gilt mirror, the Indian prayer-table, the unobtrusive halogen lighting. Her taste was all over the place. Maggie's second home.

'It's a long time since I've been here,' Deacon observed.

'I suppose it must be.' Mayhew was looking for Deacon's reasoning.

'It didn't used to look like this.'

'No.'

'When you call,' Deacon said, 'or if they call you, tell them to stay away. If that's not possible, at least stay away yourself. If I see you again, I'll kill you.'

'John, for God's sake!'

'I don't care,' Deacon told him, 'I don't care much whether you're telling the truth or not. Whether you knew what would happen or not. I don't want to see you again.'

'If you'd told me more. If I'd known more about what was happening. John, I thought it was just – just someone closing a file and wanting it to stay closed. Then Archangel and the guy at the bank. . . . *They* fed me things: D'Arblay gave me Am-Daw. I didn't know what it meant. All I know now is that it's important enough to kill for.'

'You knew D'Arblay was MI5-recruited.'

'An MP's wife was killed. The wife of a peer of the realm. I wasn't surprised to find spooks involved. Listen.' He put down his glass and leaned forward. 'I still don't know what you know.'

'That's right, Phil; you don't.' Deacon paused, then smiled. 'You don't know what I know.' He got up. 'Stay away. Tell whoever you speak to the same.'

'You know I can't guarantee anything.'

'Neither can I.'

'I didn't know,' Mayhew almost shouted it.

'I'm tired of hearing you say that,' Deacon said.

Mayhew sat still and waited for the phone to ring. Deacon's remarks about his flat had meant nothing to him, except that he'd found them strange; the bizarre upshot of tension, perhaps. Just as Deacon hadn't seen the connection between Mayhew and Maggie because his mind had been too full of hurt, so Mayhew hadn't

358

picked up on what Deacon had said because his thoughts were with D'Arblay and the evening's events.

In truth, he had half-forgotten how Maggie had picked out the furniture, suggested ways of decorating the place. He had liked Maggie, liked going to bed with her, liked the excitement and danger of the affair. From time to time, he'd felt bad about the fact that she was married to John Deacon, but not bad enough for it to matter much. He was fond of Deacon; he was enjoying Maggie. He never allowed the feelings to cloud each other. He hadn't expected that Maggie would leave Deacon for him – hadn't wanted it – and he'd been surprised, though pleased, that the affair had lasted as long as it had. Ten months. Mayhew had been sad when she died. Sad for Deacon. Sad because she was dead. Not really sad for himself. A little bereft maybe.

He sighed and walked to the telephone. The white rug that Maggie had chosen was printed with fragments of bloody footprints where Deacon had walked.

He was trying out nightmares. Maggie arriving and ringing the bell. Mayhew answering the ring, taking her in his arms before the door was properly closed. Up to his flat. Into the bedroom. Maggie undressing, being undressed, so urgent in her passion that clothes were shed across the living-room, across the bedroom floor, his hands on her breasts, her legs opening, the urgency of it all, lying beneath him, bracing him on her back, gasping, urging him on. . . .

But it wouldn't work. It should have been easy, but it simply wouldn't work. The images fragmented, the actors wouldn't behave. And, if he did manage to keep a scene going, the tangle of limbs, hands, lips, he couldn't make it hurt the way he wanted it to. He tried again. Maggie naked; he knew what that looked like. Mayhew with her. Himself at home. Maggie lying down, kneeling, straddling. . . . The figures rearranged themselves, refused to take direction, went out of focus. He felt like someone editing a blue movie with bad equipment. Eventually, he decided that he couldn't make it work, couldn't make it hurt, because it wasn't very important. He cast about for what, in that case, it might be. And realized that it was achingly, atrociously sad.

In all those forced imaginings he'd found no one to blame. He'd found no one – though he had tried as hard as he could – to hate. But still he was conscious of a deep difficult anger. It was there not for the treachery, but for the folly and waste.

It came to him, suddenly, that in imagining Maggie's stolen evenings with Phil he hadn't been able to reconstruct the features that made her face unmistakably her face.

When he returned he went straight to the bedroom and got rid of the gun. Laura watched him from the door, her eyebrows raised.

'Nothing,' he told her. 'The guy didn't show.'

'It's all a mess, isn't it?'

'Look,' he said, 'there's only one route to take – the same as the money. We know where it's going, even if we don't know why. The alternative is to stop.'

'Somewhere out there', Laura observed, 'is someone who killed Kate; and is probably trying to kill me. A man called Archangel died when I ran over him. Tom Buxton committed suicide. We know all this. I don't think it's possible to stop, is it?'

'Not unless you're prepared to make a lot of changes in your life.' She looked at him. 'Go away, live somewhere else, another country perhaps.'

'Alone?' She didn't wait for a response. 'I'd always be afraid. The things I don't know – they're what really frighten me.'

'Yes,' he said. 'I feel the same.'

They walked out of the bedroom. Deacon removed his jacket and tossed it on to an armchair. He stood by the window to smoke – a habit he'd got into for her sake. The night air was so still and so hot that he had to rest his hand on the sill to direct the smoke out of the room. He looked out at the scatter of lights, thinking things through.

Laura took his jacket back into the bedroom, but instead of hanging it up she folded it, seams outermost, and dumped it under some other clothes on a shelf where he probably wouldn't notice it. It bore two splashes of blood on the back just below the left shoulder: irregular spatter-shapes – the dripping sound he'd heard after he'd shot out the light and stepped back into cover.

Laura decided to let Deacon protect his lie; she didn't think the deceit would injure her, or put her at risk. She surprised herself – she wasn't used to trusting people much.

Later, she asked: 'The same route as the money. You mean America?'

'Yes.'

'You intend to go there.'

'Yes.'

'To do what?'

'Am-Daw is there. Chadwick is there. Everything that's happened was directed from over there. Some questions need answering. It seems logical to suppose that the answers are there. I can hardly put the CIA on the case.'

'What can you do on your own?'

'I'll find out.' He paused. 'I hope I won't be on my own. I'm going to phone Maggie's brother.'

'Will he help?'

'Yes.' Deacon nodded. 'Yes, I think so.'

'I'm coming, too.'

'No,' he said. 'All right.' Then: 'No.'

'Which is it?'

'No.'

41

Edward Henderson met them at Kennedy and drove them into Manhattan. There was genuine warmth in his voice when he said; 'It's really good to see you, John.' He shook Laura's hand, and smiled at her; there was nothing in the smile of regret or of censoriousness. She knew that Deacon had told him something of how they had come together, and of what had developed between them; because of that, she'd half-expected that Edward might be a little frosty towards her. He simply said; 'So you're Maggie's friend.' The way he said it meant *And John's, and that's all right with me*. She liked that; and she liked the way he drove his car through the freeway traffic with a real sense of adventure.

Deacon had explained some things on the phone; not everything, *some* things. At the mention of Am-Daw, Edward had said: 'Really? You don't surprise me.' He'd promised more.

They drove downtown on FDR Drive and took the Canal Street exit, then turned towards TriBeCa. When Edward stopped the car, he said: 'It's just the way it was. Someone's been in to clean.'

'Thanks,' said Deacon. He checked his watch. It was still on London time.

'Five-thirty,' Edward told him. 'Sleep. Come to dinner.'

Deacon nodded. 'OK.'

As Laura was opening the door, Edward said: 'You mentioned Austin Chadwick.'

'That's right,' said Deacon. 'Buxton gave me his name. Buxton was—'

'I remember. He didn't mention anyone else?'

'No. Why?'

'There's a guy called Harold Steiner. He's the Vice-President of the outfit. For some time now he's been making it clear that he'd be glad if we'd offer him a job.'

'Why?'

'Well, he's good at what he does. Probably wants more money. Feels like a change. Likes the look of our outfit.'

'And—'

'And I gather that he's had enough of Chadwick.'

'You talk to him?'

'Have done. Could do again.'

'OK,' Deacon said.

'Eight-thirty too early?' asked Henderson.

Deacon looked at Laura. She said: 'Eight-thirty's fine.'

She looked around the apartment – went on a short tour, leaving him standing in the large central room with its wooden floor and pillars. 'Maggie's place,' she said.

'No. My place. It's mine now.'

They got into the king-sized bed and lay like effigies, more space between them than it seemed possible to bridge, until Laura moved across and lay on her side, one hand on Deacon's chest, her knee drawn up slightly to rest against his thigh.

'I'll sell it,' he said. 'It's ridiculous. No one uses it.'

'Yes,' said Laura, 'sell it,' and drifted into sleep.

42

Elaine unbuttoned her dress, fingers stiff with anger, and hurled it on to the bed. She went to the mirror and tugged off the wig. His hair, combed straight back, was slick with sweat. Like something half-made, half-unmade – her overdone blusher, mascara and bright lipstick, his stubble of sideburn at the top of the ear; her bra, padded out, his tracery of chest-hair; her satin panties, his bulge beneath. Not him, not her; they.

'It isn't possible.'

'I saw them,' she said.

'It isn't *possible*.'

'They had cases. They got into a taxi.'

'Going where?'

'I don't know. How could I know?'

Stupid! *Stupid*! He wrenched off the underclothes and flung them across the room. 'You were there. You should have *done* something!'

'Don't be angry with me.' Her voice faded to a whisper.

Allardyce lay on the bed. He was trembling with fury, muscles bunching at the points of his jaw, his fingernails digging into the fleshy pads on his hands. It was different now. Once he would have come to this room and waited for Elaine to arrive. Piece by piece, she would enter, stroke by stroke, garment by garment; his secret sister. Her demands, her fantasies were also his – they never disagreed. All in private, a conspiracy. It was Myles who would emerge into the world; it was Myles who would control things out there where he was respected, well known, important. Now he must hide while Elaine lived in the world outside. But that was no solution. Her expeditions were risky and fruitless. It was only safe to send her out after dusk or in a crowd; when no one would look too closely. On the occasion when he'd sent her to the office to collect his address-book and the coded notebook he kept in a secret place, her edginess had soon become palpable fear. She'd never had contact with people before; now she was forced to talk to cabbies, or tourists who asked directions of her in the street. She had arrived home fizzing with anxiety.

What was worse, her appearances made nothing happen. It was Myles who had the profession, Myles who made the contacts, Myles who was liked and flattered and invited away for weekends in the country. It was Myles who had influence in the outside world; Elaine's was a dark inner potency. Now everything had become twisted. Their roles were reversed. Neither had the power to feed the other's need.

Allardyce snapped on the lights. In the room's half-light, behind the shuttered windows, the shadows sprang up. They seemed to crowd above the blotched and bloated figure of Bob Gower, as if intrigued by the livid putrifying form. He took the notebook from a table beside the bed and lay down to thumb through the pages. Everything was there, every detail, in the cipher he'd invented: dates, names, the information he'd gleaned and passed on to Major York.

He hadn't been York's most important informant by any means, but his eagerness to be involved – an almost boyish fervour – made him a perfect candidate. It was clear to York that Allardyce liked the idea of secrets, of a covert relationship with an older man who, in some small way, depended on him; he liked, too, the idea that he and York were conspiring together against heathens and lesser mortals. York knew a little of the psychology of dependency, and played on it when the opportunity arose. More than anything, Allardyce was a good bet because, although he rarely came up with anything of great importance, his methods seemed foolproof.

Myles Allardyce never had any intention of dedicating his medical career to the greater good of mankind. He'd been a qualified house physician at the age of twenty-three and a junior medical registrar four years later. On his thirty-eighth birthday he'd resigned his 9/11 post for private practice. His speciality was in respiratory complaints; his technique, while not entirely orthodox, achieved consistently good results. He wasn't the only consultant to treat patients with hypnotherapy – it was uncommon, though by no means unheard of; Myles's advantage was his charm, an indefinable air of authority, and an ability to put people quickly at their ease. He was also astute enough to extend his area of operations to concerns that the poor endure but the rich pay often and well to have treated. For the poor: painkillers, tranks and wrinkles; for the rich: osteopaths, shrinks and tucks. Myles most often found himself using hypnotherapy to wean smokers from cigarettes, provide insomniacs with rest and soothe the fretful executive.

Clients – especially women – came to trust him and depend on him. They regarded him as a friend. Many went further than that. Since he was treating them largely for complaints that had to do with tension and its symptoms, they talked to him as if he were an analyst or a counsellor. And that was before the hypnotherapy session. Under hypnosis, all sorts of things could be learned. The people Allardyce treated were – some of them – important figures in society; or they were the husbands and wives of those figures. Diplomats, politicians, society hostesses, professional gossips, financiers, owners of large companies. They all swam in the same sea. They all had secrets that York was interested in.

There were less grand clients, too, of course, but Allardyce was endlessly vigilant for any kind of related information that he might glean. That's how he'd learned of Kate Lorimer's dilemma about the computer-trace. Some of it she'd told him anyway: like many others, she treated him as a confidant. The rest had been gained while she was under hypnosis. If it hadn't been the case that Kate's appointment had coincided with Allardyce's contact-day, things might have been very different.

It hadn't been difficult to bring forward her next appointment. Allardyce simply told her he was going away and wanted to consolidate the progress they'd made – she'd reduced her smoking by half. It hadn't been difficult to detect his contact's concern when he'd passed the information on – there had been three phone calls that same evening, and that had never happened before. It hadn't been difficult to find a way of doing what they wanted: Kate hadn't seen him in her flat because he'd told her, under hypnosis, that she wouldn't. And it hadn't been difficult to kill. No, that wasn't difficult at all.

But it had been difficult to stop. With the other two women, Lady Olivia, Jessica Meredith, the same technique. Post-hypnotic suggestion working like a blindfold over their eyes. Myles in their rooms, moving about, watching them, being close to them while they did all the things that people do when they believe themselves to be alone. And Myles anticipating the moment, storing it, savouring it, until the excitement was too great and he'd strip, put on their clothes, and Elaine would enter the rooms of those women, enter their lives, trembling with need and with hatred.

Not difficult to stop. Impossible.

* * *

The knight, the bird, the flute-player, the squat toad-like figure of the sheela-na-gig. They drifted to and fro on the walls as if they were leaving and re-entering by hidden doors, or they gathered by Gower's corpse, their forms darkening as they approached it. Somehow it was a source of radiance, a source of strength. The awful totem still sat in the chair, a grotesque fetish, hideously changed. The clothes held together some of what was left, but the hands were gnarled and the fingers were tipped with spikes; the face had taken on a lop-sided look, ragged and mismatched. One eye gave a piratical leer, the other was the dark bore of a lampless tunnel. A wet grin fell off into space. There was a glisten of pearly bone from ear to nose. As Allardyce watched, a rat scampered over the half-eaten head. Others were working beneath Gower's clothing, making it seem, from time to time, as if the body were jerking spasmodically.

The shadows were restless. Allardyce closed his eyes and summoned a vision of Jessica Meredith's death. It wasn't enough. Not enough. His face hot, his body hot, teeth chattering feverishly. He heard Elaine's voice. She was there with the needle, the spoon, their cache of heroin. A little of that: yes. A little; just enough to summon the flute-player's eerie tune, the bird's lordly flight, the furious strength of the knight.

'It's all right,' she said. 'It's all right. Here's what we'll do. . . .'

And she came together moment by moment, touch by touch, garment by garment. Elaine. And locked the door in the thickening dusk, ascending into the street, the lights, the warm air, the dim noise. And walked in the shadows, walked with the shadows, wearing a dark dress, carrying a black shoulder-bag of soft leather, her pace neither slow nor quick, watchful and eager.

She went by parks and gardens, along the embankment, not seeking but anxious to be found; not choosing, but waiting to be chosen. Waiting for the moment to arrive; for the person to arrive.

She wanted to take her time. Now the decision was made, she wanted to let the anticipation grow and feed off itself like a beast devouring its young. She walked for three hours, burning with expectation, finding streets she'd never been to before, happy to be lost with her terrible purpose.

When the moment arrived, she recognized it: a girl coming out of a subway; she seemed a little drunk. A blonde in a dark green dress that rustled slightly as she walked. Her arms were bare, and the low neckline of the dress showed a pale skin decorated by a necklace of small irregular gold rods like the rays of a minor sun.

They walked together to the end of the street. Perhaps the girl would be lucky. Perhaps she would get away – her house might be nearby; she might meet someone she knew. That uncertainty was part of the thrill. But no; she turned the corner and continued to walk: past a row of shops, past showrooms, the awnings of restaurants, and then towards one of the city's commons. Two acres of grass and shrubs and an avenue of broad-leaved trees. A pathway across one corner of the common.

The girl wasn't stupid. She half-turned, wanting to decide whether to skirt the common and take the long route home or risk the short cut. There was no one about. Just another woman some twenty feet behind, also looking as if she were intending to risk the pathway. The fellow-feeling helped the blonde girl make up her mind.

In the deep darkness halfway across, she heard the hurrying feet: the other woman, she thought, feeling edgy and wanting companionship. She slowed her pace, happy to share the walk. When the footsteps were at her heels, she turned her head and was about to speak. Perhaps 'It's spooky, isn't it?' or just 'Hello'.

Then the hand on her shoulder, making her jump, though the knowledge that it was a woman behind her was enough to make her more puzzled than afraid. The hand moved to her throat, and she said, 'What?' – a purposeless word that she scarcely knew she had spoken.

After that, she was clear about nothing. A dark figure that moved in front of her, fingers biting under her jawline and bearing her backwards off the path, her indrawn breath trapped like a stone in her chest. It seemed that she ran backwards for a long way, driven to do so but also trying to escape, her fear merely aiding the other woman's strength and intention. Then she struck a tree-trunk, and the breath burst in her nose and ears. Her head sang. She thought she was floating – one moment upright, the next flat on the ground. Her senses fogged as she drifted in and out of a dream of falling. Her eyes grew blank, focused, grew blank again.

Elaine reached into the shoulder-bag and took out the knife. A thin curved blade that fishermen used for filleting. She tore the dark green dress, using the knife to help the tear until the material opened up and fell away. The girl's breasts and belly were pale patches against the blackness.

For that brief time when the pressure was released from the girl's throat, her senses began to return. She started to rise, getting an elbow to the ground, lifting a knee. The hand took her again, ramming her back, and her skull banged the base of the tree. A dark wave swamped her. Her arms rose and fell, like someone waving from a hill-top, then were still.

Elaine brought the tip of the blade up to the blonde

girl's throat. She would take as long as she dared. She drew her wrist in a long arc. The girl's heels drummed on the ground, the light swift patter of someone running for home.

43

New York, as always, was a city of extremes. Inside, the light icy chill of air-conditioning; outside, a thick, furry, oppressive heat that smothered people, making clothing wilt, making breathing a conscious effort.

Edward Henderson paid his entrance fee to the Museum of Modern Art and went at once to the upstairs gallery – to a room pretty much taken up by the vast Monet 'Water Lilies'. He turned his back on the painting and looked out of the large windows that gave on to the sculpture garden. A small group of children were making notes for an assignment. A couple in jeans and T-shirts ambled through, glancing incuriously at Picasso's goat. A man in dark-blue cotton pants and a short-sleeved shirt was reading the *Times*.

Henderson had spoken to Steiner on the phone on a few occasions, though they had never met. He took a moment or two out to study the man: short, dapper, a narrow intelligent face, a head of dark curly hair that could easily grow unruly. He had a good reputation in city business circles as the person largely responsible for keeping Am-Daw running on a week-by-week basis. He had a less favourable profile as Chadwick's yes-man. Edward went back downstairs and joined Steiner on his bench. Steiner neither looked at him nor folded his paper. The children had gone back inside.

'Henderson?'

'That's right.'

'You look older than the picture I see in the city pages.'

'Taken a while ago. Laziness rather than vanity.'

'You know a lot of stuff.'

'Do I?'

'The things you spoke about on the phone last night.'

'Can we talk about them?'

'Deep throat, huh?' Steiner's eyes were still on the page, but a tight smile twisted his mouth.

'Up to you.'

'I get—?'

'I didn't know this was a deal.'

'Everything's a deal.'

'I thought you were eager to talk to me.'

'I'm eager to know how much *you* know. And how you know it.'

'I can see this conversation growing irritatingly circular.'

Steiner was silent for a while. 'We've talked about a job.'

'In the past. You've talked about it to people who work for me.'

'Well, what do you say?'

'It's possible.'

'How possible?'

'You're an experienced man. Good track record. We could find a place for you.'

'On the board.'

'Goes without saying.'

'Is John Deacon in town?' Steiner asked. Edward didn't reply. 'Come on.' Steiner sounded impatient. 'Who else are you doing this for? Did he call you, or is he here?'

'Why?'

'If he's here, he could be in trouble. There's your first piece of information.'

'Chadwick,' Edward said.

'Sure, Chadwick.'

'Who's reporting from Britain?'

'Well, it isn't the Boy Scouts.'

'What's known about him? About Deacon.'

'Pretty much everything. About the girl, too. Laura Scott?'

'Who killed Kate Lorimer?' Edward asked.

Steiner sighed. 'I don't know you well enough for that. Not yet.'

'Where does the money go?'

'Where does money ever go? Switzerland, Florida, the IOR . . . you know.'

'There's a fund, though. A special fund.'

'Sure. But money is best if it's nimble. Remember last year, for Christ's sake. Baker hoists a finger at the Bundesbank, Reagan zaps a couple of drilling-platforms in the Gulf – *pow*! Damn near seven hundred billion dollars kissed off in a day. That's the danger of programmed selling – demon of the green screen.'

'OK. Try where does it come from.'

'Here and there. That's the truth. Several contributors.'

'How many?'

'Fifty, last time I looked.'

'Jesus.'

Steiner smiled and turned the page of his paper. 'I thought you'd be impressed.'

'All big?'

'All big.'

'What in hell is it for?'

'It's called Nimrod. The fund.' Steiner paused. 'I guess the best way to describe it – it's a war chest.'

Edward could feel the threads of sweat spreading from his neck, trickling down his chest and back and shoulders. He resisted the urge to shift position, not wanting to disturb the rhythm of his exchange with Steiner. 'Where's the war?' he asked.

374

'You're going too fast.' Steiner folded his paper.

'At least give me that.'

'No,' Steiner said. Then: 'Ollie North isn't the only guy to have an interest in Central America. He's not the only fund-raiser, either.'

'Nicaragua?'

Steiner shook his head. 'I have to go.'

'We'll meet again.'

'We'd damn well better.'

'Here?'

'Why not?' Steiner stood up. 'I like it here. I like to wander round the exhibits.'

'An art-lover,' said Edward. 'When?'

'I'll call; leave a message. Stay here for ten minutes, OK?' He put the paper on the bench, leaving it for Edward. 'Not an art-lover. I like to total the paintings. All that fucking money.'

'I'll come to you,' Edward had said. 'I'm bringing someone with me.'

When he arrived, Deacon and Laura were making hamburgers, sharing the task at the kitchen work-bench, like two kids modelling with plasticine. Edward used his key as he'd said he would, and when he walked in they looked up from the task with smiles ready on their faces. Then the smiles faded a little, because Edward hadn't told them about the person he had with him.

Peter Danzig was a surprise to most people. He'd been a surprise to his mother. He was blessed with a beautiful face: heart-shaped, almost feminine, with a smooth and flawless skin, a straight nose, a soft mouth that was almost too full, and a mane of glossy blond hair swept back from a broad forehead. Most arresting of all were his eyes. They were heavy-lidded with long curving eyelashes; the irises were a deep liquid violet. Women would have fallen in love with Peter for his eyes alone, had not God decided to redress the balance and compromise his looks by arresting his growth when Peter was seven. He stood only just over three feet tall. Peter had become accustomed to the initial reactions of people he met. He walked over on tiny, slightly bowed legs and reached up to shake hands when Edward introduced him.

'Peter advises the company from time to time. He's also a good friend.'

'You're a business consultant?' Deacon asked.

Danzig shook his head. 'Economist. Professor of, in point of fact. I'm really a teacher; sometimes my students are well beyond college age.' His voice was a soft tenor.

Deacon poured some drinks, giving himself an orange-juice and Club soda, then led the way to a couple of large couches under a window at one side of the loft-space. Danzig was wholly unembarrassed. He scrambled on to the big squab cushions and perched on the edge, cross-legged.

'You saw Steiner?' Deacon asked.

Henderson nodded, and reported what he'd learned. 'I've already told Peter this, on the way here. I hope that was OK.'

Deacon nodded. 'He wouldn't say how he knew about me? About Laura?'

'No. I assumed Buxton.'

'Yes?'

'But not just Buxton, I think.'

'Phil Mayhew?' asked Laura.

Deacon nodded. 'But indirectly. D'Arblay was Special Branch; also a Security Services recruit.'

'D'Arblay?' queried Danzig.

'A spook.'

'Ah,' he nodded. 'All the best administrations have them.'

'What did we get from Steiner?' asked Deacon.

Edward Henderson took a pull at his beer, then set the glass down and leaned forward. 'Well, there's a

376

cartel operating, that's for sure. Fifty or more contributors. What Buxton told you about his bank's part in it probably applies to the others: sums of money with no traceable history are raised as specific contributions to a fund called Nimrod. He described it as a war-chest.'

'Other contributors?' said Laura. 'Do you mean other banks?'

'Banks, companies, individuals in one guise or another. Clearly, the fund supplies working capital for some joint venture or another.'

'Administered by Chadwick,' Deacon suggested.

'Yes, I think we should assume that.'

'Which means he originated the scheme.'

'Very probably.'

'Tell me about him.'

Henderson grimaced. 'Over the past ten years, Austin Chadwick's become the Howard Hughes of the financial world. It's difficult to say where he started in the corporate world, though it seems he ran a couple of brokerage houses early on. He was a fund-raiser for Goldwater, but there don't seem to be any other blots on his escutcheon. About twelve years ago, he surfaced as a top exec at General Motors, but didn't tread water for long. Then Am-Daw. Soon after his arrival there were a number of excessively bloody boardroom coups. Since when, he's become a recluse – therefore a legend. The only thing sexier than lots of profile is no profile at all. Rumours abound: he's agoraphobic, he was hideously scarred in an auto crash, the usual nonsense. What's known for real? Well, he came up the hard way, so he's streetwise, but the roughneck image is long gone. It's true he doesn't socialize or get seen in smart places, but he certainly has important contacts in government. I mean, they all do, but Chadwick more than most. He's tough as hell. Politically, he's a little to the right of Genghis Khan. It's also true – or it seems to be – that he lives in a penthouse suite at the Am-Daw building. Unmarried – in case you hadn't guessed.' Henderson paused. 'That's Austin Chadwick.'

'Age?'

'Early fifties.'

'Still ambitious?'

'Does the Pope wear a funny hat?'

'For what?'

'Ah – you'd have to ask him.'

'Politics?'

'Very likely. Who knows?

'What about the company?' Laura asked.

Henderson waved a hand towards Peter Danzig. 'Here's your man.'

Danzig smiled and held out his glass as Deacon offered him a refill. 'Listen,' he said, 'I won't bore you with a company report. Multinationals base their growth and success on this or that product, special operation, manufacturing process – whatever. In fact they're a means of capital-holding. The only real trick is to make money make money. Am-Daw's capital is vast. The important connection we got from Steiner is that remark he made about Ollie North. For some time now, Am-Daw's principal interest has lain in Central America. Timber, minerals, coca. No one says coca but, if you're down there, that's one of the things you do. The particular country they're' – he looked for a word – *'plundering* has a military government that the West has been shoring up for some time. It also has a thriving revolutionary movement that has made some pretty startling advances just recently. They're beginning to win the war. OK, Steiner *mentioned* a war. If I had to make a guess about what Nimrod means, I'd suppose it was a fighting fund invested in that country. And I'd be aware of the fact that Am-Daw's almost certainly in collusion with the Central Bank; and that the company's foreign-exchange holdings are likely to rival those of the country itself. I mean, to some extent they're one and the same.'

378

Laura asked: 'So what would Am-Daw want?'

'Well, concessions. Logging, mining, the rest of it; you know.'

'Which they'd stand to lose if a popular revolutionary government took power.'

'Yes.'

'So Nimrod is a fund that in some way arms the present government in that country.'

Danzig nodded. 'That's what you'd think, isn't it?'

'Not so?'

'That's what's interesting. Puzzling. There's no sign of that happening. The reverse, in fact.'

'The weapons are going to the guerrillas?' Laura sounded incredulous.

'I'm not saying that. I'm saying that the guerrillas are winning. Where the firepower comes from is another matter. Russia. China. I don't know.'

'But they're – the freedom fighters, whoever – they're getting help.'

'One man's freedom fighter, another man's terrorist. Yes, they are.' Danzig smiled. In the room's gathering dusk, his violet eyes seemed to glow like points of fire. 'In such a country, with such investments at stake – such concessions to be won – the only crime is to back the loser. I confess that I'm confused. We need more from Steiner.'

Deacon looked at Edward Henderson. 'You're seeing him again?'

Henderson smiled wryly. 'Sure. I've virtually had to offer the son of a bitch a job.'

Danzig chuckled. 'A cosmetic exercise.'

'Probably,' Henderson agreed.

Laura looked puzzled. 'I don't understand. He needs somewhere to go after Am-Daw, right?'

'Yes and no,' Danzig told her. 'If he's been managing this Nimrod fund and has been disaffected and resentful at the same time, which we know to be the case. . . .' He shrugged. Laura shook her head.

'He'll have been plundering the account.' Henderson picked up Danzig's truncated sentence. 'Some here; some there. Against a rainy day which – despite what the weather's doing – has arrived for Steiner.'

'Then, why does he want the job?' Laura asked.

'Ah. . . .' Danzig grinned over the rim of his glass. 'Greed and fear – the two ruling factors in corporate life. Greed makes you rich; fear keeps you rich, and safe. The financial world isn't too tolerant of Judases. He wants the job as cover.'

When Steiner phoned again, it was the first thing he mentioned. 'I need some guarantees,' he said. 'I'm out on a limb here.'

'What are you looking for?' Henderson had been in bed when the call came through. The phone flex stretched above his wife's sleeping head. Late-night calls no longer woke her.

'I want to see a draft announcement: my appointment to the board of Henderson, Gray. I want to see it set up in type – a printer's proof. It runs the day after we next meet.'

'When's that?'

'Tomorrow.'

'Really tomorrow? Or do you mean later today?'

'Yeah – that.'

'Well, you're not giving me a hell of a lot of time.'

'It's enough.'

'What else?'

'An immediate vacation – a month.'

'Not in America,' Henderson guessed.

'Damn right.'

'Look, Steiner, just how much shit is heading for the fan with this?' Henderson felt a sudden chill of unease.

'Don't start travelling backwards now, man.'

'I'm not.' Henderson glanced at his wife's face. She was sleeping easily, her lips slightly parted, a lock of

380

dark brown hair across one eye. 'I'm not. Like you, I prefer to be prepared.'

'A lot.'

'Government?' The word fell from Henderson's mouth as if it were part of a sentence that had otherwise gone unheard.

'What?'

'I'm asking you: is the Government involved?'

There was a brief silence, then slow knowing laughter. 'Yeah. . . . You've got a few federal contacts, haven't you, Henderson? More than a few.' Another pause. 'Well, not really. Indirectly.'

'What does that mean?'

'It means that they've heard about some activities, but they're not going to *say* they've heard. Listen, I'm not—'

'I'm asking because it seems more than likely that the British MI5 is—'

'Jesus!' Steiner's voice snapped in like a circuit-breaker. 'I'm not going into this shit on the goddam phone.'

'OK, OK. . . .' Henderson's voice took on a soothing tone. 'The announcement is OK. But I need to know things you haven't told me yet. Maybe you don't know them yourself.'

'Don't worry,' Steiner told him, 'I know where the body's buried. You're talking to the guy who drove the fucking hearse.'

Henderson waited for the dialling tone and phoned Deacon. 'I'm meeting Steiner later today,' he said. 'It might be our last chance to trade.'

'What time?'

'At noon. Why not come to my office around one-thirty? I'll have someone call Peter Danzig.'

Laura put her head close to Deacon's to eavesdrop on the conversation. Deacon said: 'Ask him who killed Kate Lorimer.'

'I did.'

'Again.'

'Yes. There are other things on that shopping-list. I'll get what I can.'

Laura lowered her head slightly. 'There's something I want, Edward.' She took the phone from Deacon. 'It's important, I think.'

Henderson listened. 'I'll try,' he promised.

A different production of the same play. The school-children weren't there, nor the young couple in T-shirts, but a group of Japanese tourists ran half a reel apiece before retreating inside and a young woman in a print dress made a slow circle, consulting her catalogue from time to time. Steiner had played this part before and had decided to stick to the *Times*. He and Edward Henderson occupied the same positions on the bench.

'The last time,' Steiner said.

'Fine. Then, let's make sure we both get what we want.' Henderson passed over a slip of off-white proofing paper. The announcement was two short paragraphs: sixty words or so; restrained, formal – the usual thing. 'You manage the Nimrod fund.'

'Yes.'

'Where's the money?'

The girl in the print dress had wandered into range of their voices. Steiner paused, his eyes flicking between her and the open pages of his paper. She found a Maillol in her catalogue and read the short description, then gave thirty seconds or so to the sculpture itself. Finally, she drifted back to the terrace and through the glass doors.

Steiner said: 'Florida.'

'How much of it *used* to be in Florida?'

'What?'

'How much have you taken for yourself?'

'What makes you think I've taken anything?'

382

Henderson knew it was better than a fifty-fifty bet. He sounded authoritative. 'Don't bullshit, Steiner.'

'Well. . . .' Steiner seemed to read a paragraph from his paper; there was a short silence. 'How much is none of your damn business.'

'Who's your contact? In the Miami bank.'

'Please.' Steiner sounded offended.

'All right, which of you makes the switch?'

'I do. He's not an operative.'

'But he gave you the systems code? That's what he's paid for.'

Steiner shrugged. It meant yes. A simple enough scheme while Steiner had control of the account. A sum shaved here, another there; the money sent to a couple of laundromats then directed to numbered accounts – one Steiner's, one the accomplice's.

'I want the systems code. It's part of the deal.'

Steiner looked up sharply for an instant. 'Go to hell.'

'It's no good to you. As soon as you're out of Am-Daw someone will notice the discrepancies. Your only fail-safe is that the fund's a secret. No one can blow the whistle.'

'You're dealing with some heavy-duty stuff, Henderson. Some Cubans down there are just making a buck while waiting to go home. In the mean time, I don't think they'd like the idea of someone like you fooling with their money. Aren't you rich enough already?'

'Part of the deal.'

'Go on.'

'Reports are that Los Libertadores are close to the capital. It seems they're winning the war.'

'Well,' Steiner smiled, 'you picked the right place. Wouldn't have been difficult, I guess; Am-Daw's been there a while.'

'Are they expected to win?'

'Yes.' Steiner smiled again, guessing at Henderson's confusion.

'Who tells you that?'

'A Russian.'

It was Henderson's turn to be silent. Finally he said: 'You don't mean some itinerant logger whose grand-parents skipped with the family jewels.'

'No, I don't.'

'A Russian.'

'That's right.'

'Tell me about Nimrod.'

'Like I said: a war-chest; a fighting fund. Nimrod itself is the name Chadwick gave to the group who contribute.'

'Who are they?'

'Bankers, businessmen, you know. People who like to protect their investments. Chadwick decided it would be a good idea to be able to have a little more say in international affairs than the usual pressures and lobbying systems would allow. It's OK to be able to wave a big financial stick; sometimes it's not enough.'

'He wanted armies.'

Steiner nodded. 'Armies, assassins, weaponry, whatever it took. It wasn't tough finding like-minded people. For some of them, Nimrod is just one of several private clubs. There's P-2 – Freemasons, you know – there's home-grown Mafiosi, the Vatican. . . .'

'Governments?'

'You asked that once. No. Government agencies, though, so government money.' Steiner had taken a pen from his pocket and was writing on the proof-slip.

'OK,' Henderson said. 'Why—'

Steiner cut him off. 'This is what you're getting now.' He handed the slip back to Henderson. 'I know what your next question is. I'm trading in futures here and I want to trade on the inside. When I see that ad in the press, you'll get the rest.'

'No.'

'Look' – he gestured at the slip in Henderson's hand

– 'that's my collateral. The ad itself *and* what's written on it. I've given you most of what you want. I'm not risking more. When you place the ad – not before.' He looked directly at Edward for a moment. 'You surprise me, Henderson: wanting the systems code. Still,' he laughed, 'old money is just new money that's served its time, I guess. Don't fish in that sea too soon. There are sharks. I want to get out of the water first.' He walked away.

Edward looked down at the slip. A word; a series of figures.

The woman in the print dress moved away from the window, preparing to leave the room that housed the Monet. She had been so engrossed in the view that she hadn't noticed the other spectator standing a couple of paces back from the glass, his eyes still fixed on the bench and Edward Henderson. She checked, uncertain for a moment, then stood still while her fellow-observer approached. Henderson was leaving the sculpture garden.

'Go outside and call a cab,' the man said. 'I'll follow in a minute or two.' At first the woman was too taken aback to move. 'I had to see for myself,' Chadwick told her. He turned towards the painting, though it was clear he wasn't seeing it. He didn't look back at her. His voice was soft. 'Call a cab.'

44

They rode in the cab in silence. They took the private
elevator in silence. In silence, they entered Chadwick's office. Chadwick sat behind his desk, the
woman in the smaller and straighter of the two facing
chairs. She waited. Chadwick looked slightly dazed,
as if his trip into the world had disorientated him:
the bustle of everyday events, the heat and noise, the
astonishing, unlikely event of people.

His eyes cleared and focused on the woman. 'Last
night was the only time.'

'No' – she shook her head – 'we can't know
that. It was just a random check – that's how we
run them; not sequentially, not at any given time
or on any special day. We're maintaining – let's
see – eight taps in all. A few members of your
board are engaged in activities that aren't exactly
legal, but nothing against the company's interest.
It was a loose brief: we just plug in from time to
time and see what we get. Sometimes we hear of
something a little dubious, though I gather you've
been happy just to file our reports so far. Mostly
it's humdrum stuff, but we keep listening anyway.
That's how we found out that Steiner's wife is
having an affair. Trivial matters. Until this, of
course.'

'The tap's on full-time now.'

'Oh, yes; of course.' It didn't surprise her that
Chadwick had organized surveillance on his fellow-
directors. It wasn't her business and, anyway, she'd

heard of stranger things. A lot stranger. Her company made its money from other people's paranoia.

'Who's listening to the tapes?'

'Myself; my partner. We're handling it ourselves.'

'Keep me informed. It doesn't matter what time – day or night.'

'Glad to.'

Chadwick nodded and tapped his fingers idly on the desk. 'Bring all the tapes to me. The master-copies. Make no duplicates.'

She looked shocked. 'We *never*—'

'You know how to be discreet – you and your partner?'

'Mr Chadwick, I assure you—'

'There are no log-books, no records, diary-entries?'

'None.'

'Will you strike a bargain with me?' The woman waited. 'Your side of it is: you forget all of this forever. No matter what happens.'

'Yes.'

'No matter *what* happens.'

The emphasis didn't trouble her. 'Yes.'

'Tell your partner you just got rich.'

Steiner kept his meeting-time ten minutes later. He was never late for meetings. He had with him a folder that contained some balance-sheets and print-outs. It was a regular meeting – an update on several matters – and there wasn't a lot to discuss. Chadwick hadn't moved from his desk.

'There isn't a lot to discuss,' Steiner told him.

'OK, Harold. Leave the papers with me.' Steiner pushed them across. 'And Nimrod?'

'Nothing new; nothing bad. The consignment arrived and it's been distributed. If past performance is anything to go by, that'll make a considerable difference. From what I hear, give it ten days; two weeks, maybe. The cracks were appearing a while

387

ago. A lot of money has already found somewhere else to be. A fair part of it belongs to the guys that run the country.'

'Good.' Chadwick smiled briefly, then lifted a hand – a dismissal.

He continued to look at the door for some time after it had closed. There was nothing on his mind but immediate matters. No thoughts of the past, no regret, no memories. He made a short telephone call then got up to gaze out at the skyline: at the towers, at the sun-splashed walls of glass. His eyes had the look of someone scanning horizons. Under his breath, he said a name.

'Deacon.'

They sat in a circle round Henderson's conference-table on tall-backed red-leather chairs, apart from Peter Danzig who sat cross-legged on the table itself like a shoemaker from a Grimm fairy-tale.

'It didn't go that way,' Henderson was saying. Kate Lorimer – who had killed her. 'I got what I could. I'm sorry.'

Laura was holding the proof-slip. They had already listened to Henderson's account of what had been said in the sculpture garden. Danzig had spent part of the time with his eyes closed like someone silently repeating a mantra. He said: 'The Russian clinches it.'

'Clinches what?' Henderson wanted to know.

'I've done some rapid research – talked to some people – but I was pretty much there already.' He smiled at Henderson, the gentian eyes half-masked behind long lashes. 'Do you *want* to employ Harold Steiner?'

'What the fuck do you think?'

'Yes . . . well, I don't think you have to. Because I think I've got it figured.'

Danzig looked pleased with himself. Henderson pretended irritation: 'You want to share it?'

'We know there's a fund. We know where it's going. At least, we know where geographically. What doesn't appear to make sense is *who*. Right? All the signs are that the people who are getting help are the people least likely to qualify as friends of Am-Daw.'

'Los Libertadores,' Deacon offered.

'OK.' Danzig brightened, as if the name were a clue to the conundrum he was posing. 'Am-Daw has considerable interests in the country – logging, mining, almost certainly a large part of the coca traffic. The peasants make, like, a thousand per cent better on a coca crop than on anything else they might grow. It starts out as rarefied cabbage, gets refined in Colombia, Pakistan, wherever, and winds up being honked through a ten-dollar bill in some Wall Street men's room. The forests are felled for citrus and beef. It's been open season down there for a long time. But it can't last. However corrupt the governments, there are forces at work against them. Conservationists, narcotics squads; not least, the people themselves – the peasants. You should excuse the term. And governments. Schemes' – he said it darkly – 'are afoot. Just for starters there's a debt-for-equity theory that threatens to pull the rug out from under the big investors. The idea is that conservation groups buy discounted debt in exchange for trees.'

'I don't under—' Deacon began.

In the same moment, Laura said. 'Yes.'

Danzig smiled at Laura. To Deacon, he said: 'All Third World countries are in debt. You can trade that debt, just like you can trade anything. The important factor is that you can buy it real cheap. So a conservation group will buy part of a country's debt at – I don't know – say eighty, ninety per cent write-down; they then give the debt-note back to the country in return for an agreement that the country declares part of the rainforest, say, as a conservation area. They're buying trees at discount.'

Deacon nodded. 'All right.'

'Right. It's just one thing. There are – this is the point – there are any number of growing constraints on the freedom that foreign companies used to have in those countries. Am-Daw is one such company. Like the others, they want concessions. Now, it's not nearly as easy as it was to slip some bureaucrat a bribe. Like I say, the people themselves are taking a hand in things: invoking land deeds and titles that are valid, but have been ignored for years. Sometimes they take direct action; wreck bulldozers and sawmills, close roads that developers have constructed. And, at the same time, foreign political influence is being contested. The region's politicians and leaders are beginning to get together. So' – Danzig spread his hands, offering the logical outcome – 'while there are still concessions to be got, companies are busy devising ways to get them.'

'And that's what Am-Daw's doing?' queried Henderson.

'I think so.'

'How?'

Laura added: 'Since they seem to be arming the rebels.'

Danzig gave a slow wry smile. 'Yes; that's what I couldn't figure out. I'm not an expert on the area by any means, but I've got a couple of friends who are.'

'Economists or politicians?' Henderson wanted to know.

Danzig looked rueful. 'Impossible to be one without being the other these days, unless you've got the sand-loving tendencies of an ostrich. Anyway, I put the thing to them as a kind of exercise: a puzzle. The crucial part of the puzzle was Steiner mentioning a Russian involvement. An individual.' He closed his eyes once more, briefly, as if marshalling the facts. 'There's a war going on which the rebels appear to be winning. If they do, it ought to be bad news for any multinational with a large stake in the country. Likewise, other investors. The strong possibility is that, with every mile the rebels advance, more flight-capital leaves the country. It's the usual pattern – hot money off to a happier home. OK: let's suppose that Nimrod is buying arms for the rebels; someone sure as hell is. How does that help Am-Daw? It doesn't unless they find some sort of control. The only control is money.'

'How do they use it?' Deacon asked.

'Well' – Danzig glanced at Edward Henderson – 'it seems that Los Libertadores have hinted that if they come to power they're going to renege on the country's foreign debt.'

Henderson's brow cleared. He said: 'Jesus.'

'Exactly,' said Danzig. Deacon looked at him. 'It's simple,' Danzig continued, 'and it's clever. They do that; the West pulls aid and influence. The only place they can turn is Russia – which I imagine they're happy enough to do.'

'And a Russian is telling them that they have no worries,' said Henderson.

'Right. But he's lying. Of course he is. *Glasnost* is about retreat, not advance. Not of that sort anyway. Russia's out of Afghanistan. Gorbachev's worried about domestic problems. I'm sure Los Libertadores are getting the information from what appears a good source – the embassy, I'd guess – but, yes, he's lying to them.'

'Why would he do that?' Laura saw the answer to her question in the moment that Danzig answered it.

'Money; and a ticket to the West, I expect.'

'OK.' She leaned forward in her chair. 'And then—'

'And then the country finds itself between a rock and a hard place. Russia says: "What? Who told you that? Forget it." The new government's already in bad with the West. The investors have taken away their money and their influence.'

'Except Am-Daw,' Henderson observed.

'Right. The country's strapped for foreign exchange and desperately trying to restore a relationship with the West. Am-Daw's foreign-exchange holdings are vast – bigger than those of the country; always have been. They offer to step in and bale out: money and influence both.'

Deacon nodded. 'In return for concessions.'

'Sure' – Danzig smiled brightly – 'they'd have the country sewn up before things could straighten out. Shit, for a while there, they'd damn-near own the place.' He recrossed his legs and shuffled to get comfortable. 'Easy, you see. Take the problem, look at the constituents, apply logic, you get the answer. Why a Russian? Only one solution.'

Henderson leaned back and lodged his feet on the table. 'Damn,' he said. 'It's clever, isn't it?'

'People have died,' Laura told him. Then she got up. 'I want some time on a computer with a modem link. Can you arrange that?'

'Sure.'

'And a typewriter,' said Deacon.

Henderson swung his feet down and went to his desk. 'Can you type?' He pressed an intercom button.

'Well enough for this.'

'For what?'

Danzig knew what he meant. 'I'll dictate,' he said. 'Slowly.'

The kid was edgy and excited. More excited than edgy, di Vito could see that. He stripped the wrapper off a strip of gum and handed it over. 'Chew on that, Joey.'

'OK.' Joey slid the strip halfway into his mouth and folded it by working his lower jaw. He was trying to get people to call him Joe; he was twenty now and found his childhood name an embarrassment. 'You know this guy?' he asked, and peered through the windscreen into the false dusk of the underground garage.

'I've seen his picture,' di Vito said. 'Don't worry.'

Joey sang a fast lyric under his breath and bopped his shoulders in and out to the rhythm. 'Madonna,' he said. 'You know her?' He sang another phrase.

'Only from mass.' Di Vito was looking at the elevator lights.

'Great tits.'

'I never noticed.'

'Yeah,' Joey said. 'Terrific. Ass, too. Terrific all over.'

'No kidding.' The elevator doors opened. 'Here we go,' said di Vito. 'Stay there.'

He opened the door silently and pushed it half-closed behind him, then strolled across the rough concrete floor as if making for a car in the opposite bay. The man who had left the elevator was rummaging in his pocket for his car keys as di Vito came up to him. They had moved to the far side of the pillar. Di Vito reached under his jacket and came up with a silenced .38. He tapped the man on the shoulder; then, when he turned, showed him the gun. 'Shout, you're dead; run, you're dead. OK?'

Steiner staggered backwards in shock, half-falling against his car. His mouth opened and closed. He wet his lips with his tongue. He said, 'Hip pocket,' and swivelled his body to give access. His wallet made a bulge in his pants.

'I don't want your fucking money, man.' Di Vito grabbed Steiner's shoulder and heaved him off the car, then walked him past the pillar. 'The black Chevrolet over there. Just walk, not too quick, not too slow.'

Steiner walked, looking left and right, looking towards the elevator. There was no one else in the garage. When they got to the Chevvy, Joey fired the engine.

'In,' said di Vito. Steiner got into the back seat. Di Vito slid alongside, the gun under Steiner's armpit.

Joey looked over his shoulder. He said. 'Hi, man. Good you could make it,' and laughed at his own joke.

'Drive the car, asshole,' di Vito told him. He was smiling, though. The kid's humour was infectious.

'What is this?' The syllables seemed to stick in Steiner's throat before coming clear.

Di Vito's smile faded. 'Shut up,' he said.

'Kidnap? What? I've got money. There are people'll raise money for me. Whatever you want. OK?' Di Vito didn't respond. 'OK?' Steiner asked him.

Di Vito would have liked to rap him in the mouth with the .38, but the contract was leave no marks. He said: 'Shut up or die.' Then, imitating Steiner's accent: '*OK?*'

Steiner looked out of the window as they came out on to Sixth. There were people in the streets. He felt sick.

After they'd crossed the Triborough Bridge, di Vito had made Steiner get down on the floor. There was no other reason for this than to make Steiner believe that he was, in truth, being kidnapped. Like all good kidnap victims, Steiner timed the journey and tried to listen for sounds that might later be seen to have some significance. He didn't manage to come up with any good sounds, but he still had his watch, and he knew that the journey had taken one hour, ten minutes. So where did that put him? Westchester County, maybe. Bedford? No, more likely Armonk. There was no way he could tell really. Joey parked the car in an alley, and they ran him to a side-door and through two empty rooms to some cellar stairs.

In the cellar, they all paused a moment, like people who have reached their objective and are taking a breather before getting down to the business in hand. Di Vito had brought a sports-bag in from the car. He dumped it on the floor and gave a sigh, looking round as if he hadn't seen the place before.

Steiner said: 'Listen—'

'Shut up,' di Vito told him. Then: 'Take your clothes off.'

'You don't have to do that. I'm not going to try to—'

Di Vito turned away impatiently. 'Help him, Joey.'

There wasn't much: shirt, pants, shorts, socks and shoes. Joey made a game of it, slapping Steiner's hands away from his shirt buttons. 'Don't be shy, man. I ain't gonna laugh at your dick.' He tapped Steiner's ankles with his foot, and Steiner stepped out of his shorts, leg by leg.

'There you go,' Joey said. 'Man, you could stand to lose some weight, you know that?' He stepped back a couple of paces and looked Steiner over. Then he laughed. 'Jesus, man, I'm sorry. I know I said I wouldn't but, hell. . . .' He whooped and slapped his hands together and laughed louder. 'Your old lady ain't got much to come home for, does she?'

Di Vito was unzipping the sports-bag and taking out some equipment. He was laughing, too. He couldn't help it. The kid was a fruit, but he had the kind of laugh that set you off. He looked at Joey and started to speak, but the kid's face was too much and he turned away, shoulders heaving, trying to compose himself. Eventually he managed: 'Bring that chair over, Joey, and shut the fuck up.'

It was a wooden armchair with a bow back. They sat Steiner in it and used dog-collars to fasten his wrists and ankles. Di Vito spread the equipment on the floor. He brought a small crate from the back of the cellar and put it close to the chair, then fetched a tape-recorder that had been in the bag and set it on top. To Steiner, he said: 'Tape-recorder, OK?'

Steiner thought that he might be in shock, though

he also considered that the coldness he felt might be due to the cellar's dankness. It was impossible to feel more exposed, more vulnerable than he felt, naked there and tied, his little smudge of chest hair damp with sweat, his genitalia flopping loosely on his thigh. He shuddered, and a bead of salty water dropped from the end of his nose.

'Goose walk over your grave, man?' Joey asked him.

Steiner thought he should be reasoning with them, but couldn't think of anything to say. 'Why—?' He stopped and began again. 'What—?' The sentence he wanted wouldn't form.

'Say what?' Joey raised his eyebrows as if encouraging Steiner to find the words.

Di Vito pushed a plug into a wall-socket and held up the small box attached to the lead. 'Transformer,' he said. 'OK?'

Joey chuckled as he watched the terror inch across Steiner's face. 'You gettin' there man.' His laughter never quite died: a trickle, a flood, or sometimes it dried to a smile; but always there. He took something that di Vito passed over to him, then walked to Steiner's chair.

Di Vito spoke to Joey, though he looked directly at Steiner. Steiner looked back, too frightened to focus on what Joey held in his hand. 'OK, let's get him wired up. Don't get fresh.' The quip brought on Joey's laughter again. He cupped Steiner's scrotum in his hand.

Di Vito switched his talk directly to the man he was looking at. 'Here's what's going to happen. Joey there's putting some electrodes on you – little smear of gel to help the contact, you know? Then we're going to talk. I'll be asking you some questions; you'll be giving me some answers. Now, I don't want you to be slow answering, so I'll tell you what we're discussing here. You had a meet with a guy, Henderson. Just tell me what you told him – like, everything you told him, you got it? Do it quick when I ask you, and that way maybe we won't barbecue your balls.' He nodded, as if satisfied that he'd given Steiner the fullest description of what was required of him, then turned away and made some adjustment to the box.

Steiner had been shaking feverishly. Now he froze. He could feel the coolness of the gel that Joey dabbed on to him. The boy's hands were like a doctor's: soft and competent. 'Barbecue,' Joey said under his breath; his head bobbed with restrained mirth. He bent to his task, and Steiner could hear the gentle continuing snicker close to his ear.

Di Vito waited patiently until Joey finished and stepped back, eyeing his handiwork critically. 'I think that's got it,' he said. He started the tape running.

Di Vito fingered a switch on the box. 'OK?' He nodded at Steiner as if all three of them were engaged in some task that would take careful co-ordination. Steiner stared at him like someone waiting for a critical clue.

'OK,' di Vito said. 'Well, listen, we'll just give you a little jolt here to let you know what's involved.'

No time, no time at all. Steiner's words came in a torrent. Di Vito hadn't flipped the switch more than half a dozen times, and then only to keep Steiner going, much as you might kick a horse. After ten minutes, Steiner was repeating himself, babbling the same sentences over and over like a communicant. He was telling them things they didn't want to know. He was offering everything he had – everything he could think of: information, money, possessions, his wife. Di Vito prodded him a couple more times, to be sure, but it was clear that they'd emptied him out. He set the box aside.

'Let me have that,' Joey said. 'Come on, man.'

Di Vito glanced over at the boy and shook his head. 'I got what I want,' he said. 'You're gonna have to get what you want somewhere else.'

Steiner's mouth was gaping, taking in tiny hard

gulps of air; he was sitting still and straight like someone posing for a portrait painter. His eyes were wide but seemed to be looking nowhere. Di Vito took something from the sports-bag and went to one side of the chair. To Joey, he said: 'Hold his head.' His voice was soft and laconic.

Joey stood behind the chair and wrapped his forearm round Steiner's head, his hand over the staring eyes, elbow pulled stiffly into his ribs, bracing the man. The other arm he put over the top of the skull, grasping his own wrist, keeping that elbow tight to his own body, too.

Di Vito nudged Joey's biceps, lifting it slightly to expose Steiner's ear. He was holding a steel knitting-needle. He crouched slightly to get a better angle on what he was doing, then slid the needle into the ear cavity, drew back his free arm, and slammed the butt of the needle with the heel of his hand. Although Steiner was sitting, his body seemed to fall – a sudden shock of dead weight.

Joey said: 'Wow!' He kept hold of the head, feeling the drag of the lax body beneath it, and looked sideways at the needle.

Di Vito withdrew his hand. He tapped Joey on the shoulder. 'We gotta clear up.'

They disconnected the terminals and stowed their equipment back into the sports-bag. Di Vito took a towel and wiped some blood from Steiner's jaw and shoulder, then refolded the towel to take care of the dribble that had arrived on his chin and dropped to his paunch. Working together, he and Joey dressed Steiner and sat him back in the chair.

'Did you see that?' Joey asked. He was tying Steiner's shoelaces. 'The way, like, all his muscles cranked up when you hit the switch.'

'Sure,' said di Vito. He zipped the bag.

'Yeah,' Joey breathed. He started to laugh. 'Oh, man.'

Di Vito snorted. He could feel the laughter rising in him to match the kid's. 'Let's get this guy back to Manhattan,' he said. 'There's a doctor downtown's gonna call this a heart-attack.'

45

It was seven-thirty when Steiner died. At ten o'clock,
Deacon was preparing to leave the TriBeCa apartment.
Beyond the big windows, the streets glowed; they
hummed with people eager to keep the evening going.
Like London, he thought. Street-life in the heat. There
were no swallows.

'What time did he say?'

Laura looked at her watch. 'He'll be here soon.' She
was circling the large room, listening to the click of her
heels on the boards and sipping from an ice-laden gin
and tonic. 'I wish you wouldn't do this.'

He nodded in acknowledgement but didn't answer;
they had already talked about it. Laura began another
circuit, arms linked loosely under her breasts, the
glass canted at an angle from the uppermost hand.
Deacon watched the line of her back under the flame-
red silk shirt she was wearing, the way her waist was
cinched by the waistband of her blue jeans, her hips
rocking softly as she walked. He knew what he felt. A
half-heard voice, a voice he hadn't time to listen to
now, asked him if the feeling had come too late.

The fact that they had been preoccupied since
they'd come to New York, or the sudden acquisition of
allies in Henderson and Danzig, or maybe the knowledge that they were a long way from whatever –
whoever – threatened Laura had allowed an ease and a
warmth into the relationship that hadn't been there
before. Laura's revelation about Maggie, and Deacon's
excursion into a city of dreadful night, had been

something they'd survived. They touched more, now; they saw each other more clearly. But what they shared was not easy or uncomplicated. They both felt its cumbersome drag, like a fouled net.

Laura stopped and turned and gave Deacon a level solemn look. 'It isn't as if—' The door-buzzer cut her off. Deacon lifted the entryphone, then blipped the button that would release the catch on the street-door and admit Danzig. Laura shrugged and nibbled a shard of ice. She'd had her say.

Danzig had brought some names – a list of addresses to go with them. He handed them over, and Deacon addressed twenty envelopes; another he left blank. Then he inserted a document in each and handed all but one to Danzig. 'You can take care of this?'

'Sure; right now.' The dwarf's eyes went from Deacon to Laura, then back again. 'Listen, you could just mail them all. Why not?'

'I know.' Deacon was wearing a light cotton blouson. He put the unaddressed envelope into a pocket.

'OK,' Danzig said. 'That's what you want.' He handed over a folded slip of paper. 'Here's the number. It's no secret.' To Laura he said: 'Can I get a drink?'

'Sure.' She started towards the side-table that served as a bar.

'I'll do it.' Danzig moved fast – a rolling sailor's gait. He reached up for the vodka-bottle after scooping a glass into the bucket of crushed ice, working more by feel than by sight. 'Well,' he said to Deacon, 'roll with the punches.' The astonishing eyes seemed darker than the twilight.

There were sidewalk tables in the Village, and a neon-lit promenade of people whose moods matched their clothes: colourful and light. A constant spillage of music swamped the roadway. Everyone was having some sort of good time.

The cab took Deacon across town and up. They

pulled into the Hilton forecourt where Deacon suffered the doorman to usher him out of the cab. He went to the lobby payphones and dialled the number that was no secret. He was answered on the third ring and spoke for ten seconds: maybe less.

Austin Chadwick put down one phone and lifted another, thumbing a button in the handset. He said: 'A man called Deacon – John Deacon – will be at the penthouse entrance in a few minutes. After you've checked his ID, show him which elevator. Make arrangements to have him followed when he leaves.' The voice at the other end of the phone asked a question. Chadwick pondered a moment. He said: 'It's possible.' Then: '*If* it's possible. Understand? But wait to hear from me on that. I'll call you when he leaves.' Another question. 'I don't think you need worry about that. I'll use the tread-alarm if I want you.' He cut the connection and went into the small lobby where the elevator let out. On a coffee-table in the room he'd left was a tape he had been about to play.

The walls of the lobby bore two small Dufys and a Renoir drawing. A bust stood on a fluted plinth. A narrow bookcase held morocco-bound first editions. The area offered modest but significant hints of greater riches within, like the antechamber to a Pharaonic tomb. Chadwick waited among the least of his possessions feeling curious and oddly elated.

When Deacon stepped out, he stayed close to the elevator doors. The two men regarded one another in silence until Chadwick said: 'They told me you were a drunk. No one to worry about.'

Deacon said: 'Is that right?'

Chadwick turned his back and led the way into the glass-walled living-room of the penthouse. Thin blinds were drawn across the northern and western walls. East and south, the lights of the Pan-Am and

402

Chrysler buildings glowed in the city's polluted darkness. 'Do you drink now?' Chadwick asked.

'No.'

'Coffee, orange-juice, mineral water?'

'Nothing.'

Chadwick hovered over a drinks-table, his hand moving uncertainly among the bottles as if he were suddenly surprised and delighted by the profligacy of choice. 'I think I'll have. . . .' The words spoken ruminatively, under his breath. Finally he settled on a brandy, then sat down, waving Deacon to a chair on the other side of the coffee-table. 'I'm glad you've come here,' he said, 'though I'm not sure I understand why you have.'

'For the same reason that makes you glad.'

Chadwick smiled. 'Of course, yes. I suppose I did know, if I'm honest. We seem to have been through a lot together one way and another, don't we?'

The closeness of adversaries. Deacon didn't feel it. He was contemptuous of those cosy conventions where strength is intrigued by strength and power fascinated by power, whatever its purpose. Such conventions, he knew, salute money and fame for their own sake and become a conspiracy of egos. They fund a good intention until it becomes a lost cause. He looked at Chadwick and saw a man who would trade virtue like a commodity.

'I've wondered, of course I have,' said Chadwick, 'why you should have pursued me so relentlessly. And whether you know what you've become involved in.'

Deacon chose to ignore the second question. 'You?' he said. 'It wasn't you. I started to look for reasons why a girl drowned in her bath. One thing led to another; one of the *things* was you.'

Chadwick affected a wince. 'I can't decide', he said, 'whether you're intelligent and brave or dogged and lucky.' He swilled brandy along the side of a crystal balloon. 'I've thought about you a lot, you know. And I've allowed myself to believe that from time to time you might have thought about me.' He sipped his drink. 'I gave orders that you should be killed. Were you aware of that?'

'You're an influential man', Deacon told him, 'if you can make dogs in MI5 roll over.'

'Well. . . .' Chadwick canted his head to one side modestly. 'You talk as if that were unlikely. I suppose people might think so. A simple-minded view of the world.' He paused. 'Perhaps you're brave and lucky. That sounds right. No' – he picked up the train of thought he'd been pursuing – 'the world operates on power and money. The powerful, the rich, they're always connected. And, by and large, they share the same interests. What's good for General Motors. . . . You know the saying? We all work hand in hand: governments, financial interests, companies, wealthy individuals; we fund each other, trade information and influence. Our advantage is that, while other people rely on newspapers or TV broadcasts to tell them what's going on in the world, we *know*. We know because we make it happen. Of course' – he took another sip of brandy and waggled the glass to demonstrate life's variousness – 'there are times when we go up against each other. The world's pickings are rich, but they're distressingly finite. At such times the trick is to win; it doesn't matter how. Sometimes', Chadwick mused, 'agreements go into abeyance. Someone has to lose.'

'Sometimes people die.'

'Yes, that's true. Who were you thinking of? The girl?' He tapped his temple with a finger, summoning the name. 'Kate? Surely not.'

'Why?'

Chadwick looked at Deacon in mild astonishment. 'But that was so long ago. Months.'

'Who killed her?'

404

'The important thing to remember is that conflict shouldn't be wasteful. A battlefield strewn with corpses, the land devastated: no, we shouldn't think in those images. Better to *consume* one's enemies. The concept of the takeover – it's a particularly pleasing one, I've always thought. There's a slang term – *waste*; to waste someone: to kill him. More useful, don't you think, to *swallow* an enemy? To take his strengths for your own. To waste nothing. In Papua New Guinea, the headhunters used to believe that to eat your foe's heart and brain endowed you with his courage, his cunning; to eat his balls gave you his potency. Apparently, human flesh tastes a lot like pork, so they called enemies "long pig". That's what my opponents are to me, Deacon. Long pig.'

Deacon nodded. 'I believe you.'

'Yes.' Chadwick peered out at the lights of the city for a moment. 'Now tell me why you're here.'

And what you know, Deacon thought. *What you know.* He said: 'I came to listen to you. I came to hear about long pig.' Chadwick smiled and closed his eyes for a second. 'I came to find out who killed Kate Lorimer and two other women.'

'Oh, Deacon, Deacon. . . .' Chadwick sighed and got up to replenish his drink. 'I think I overestimated you. I'm coming back to dogged and lucky. I wondered whether you might be a little like me.'

'I'd still like to know.'

Chadwick shook his head sadly and let his glance travel round the room like a man grown suddenly bored. 'Do I know who cleans my car?' He was convincing; Deacon believed him. 'Look over here.'

Chadwick rose from his chair and went to the southern wall where he waited with his back turned for Deacon to join him. They stood side by side and regarded the sharp city lights: the brilliance of lit windows, the tributaries of neon. 'What do you see?' Chadwick asked.

'Pig-pens.'

'Yes,' Chadwick laughed. 'Yes, I hadn't thought of it. Sometimes, pig-pens. But most often I see a generator. A vast generator. So with the world, Deacon – deals, agreements, the transfer of power, the manufacture of money. Men in offices, men in boardrooms, in government departments, in banks, in stores, in liquor chains, fast-food chains. Wall Street and Chinatown. The UN building and Little Italy. Small deals and big; some that affect families, some that affect nations. Out there – across the country, across the world. What does it all make? Enormous energy, enormous wealth, enormous power.' He had brought his brandy-glass with him, and drank from it slowly as he looked out over the city, his gaze fixed, like a roulette-player assessing the run of the numbers before making a substantial bet.

'Too random, though,' he went on. 'If I could have it so, I would limit the world's controls to a single console. Things are uncoordinated; events occur at the wrong time, or in the wrong way. The management is poor, do you ever think that? The important thing is to organize as much as you can as well as you can for as long as you can. To own the power. To make straight lines of a maze; to bring order out of chaos.'

'There are people out there, too,' Deacon said.

'People. Well. . . .' Chadwick sounded as if he were conceding a minor point. 'Three hundred Chinese die in an air crash – do you care? Ethiopians starve – do you really lose sleep? Of course – people; there have always been people. They are an infinitely renewable source. History's bystanders. There are famines, there are wars – what's new?'

'There are revolutions,' Deacon said.

Chadwick turned towards him and took a step closer. 'Yes,' he said, and went closer still, as if proximity might provoke an intimacy. Deacon could feel the flicker of brandy-hot breath on his own lips.

Chadwick inched forward again, claiming Deacon's body-space, imposing his body as he might impose his will. They were close enough to kiss. 'Why are you here, Deacon?'

'I came to give you this.' Deacon removed the envelope from his pocket, but held it at his side. Chadwick looked down at it, then stepped back like a dancer hearing the music begin. He returned to his seat, and Deacon brought the letter to him. It was as if some formality had to be observed: Chadwick seated, Deacon stooping before him to hand over the envelope. They kept those positions, Deacon continuing to stand like a messenger waiting on a response or an order.

There is a war going on in Central America. . . .

Chadwick took time with the text of the letter. Though it was concise, it missed nothing. Eventually, he laid it aside with infinite care, lowering it on to the coffee-table like something brittle. He said: 'What can I offer you?'

'Nothing,' Deacon told him.

'That isn't possible.'

'Why?'

Chadwick looked as if he'd just been told that the world is flat after all. 'There's nothing you *want*?'

'Lots of things. Nothing you can give me.'

'I can make you so rich that it'll take you the rest of your life to get over it.'

'Even if you could think of something,' Deacon said, 'it would be too late.'

'I could have you killed – you must know that.'

'You could try. You might succeed. In fact I'm prepared to agree that you probably would. It makes no difference. I've told you – it's too late, whether I die or not.'

Chadwick touched the letter with a fingertip as if he were stirring a flake of ash in a fire-gutted building. 'Who?' he asked.

'You'll find out who. Not from me; though it doesn't matter now.'

'Other letters,' Chadwick said, 'already mailed.' He fingered the letter still; his voice was level and soft. The tone and gesture of a man attending a deathbed.

Newspapers in America and England; television stations; in each case specific reporters known for investigative work. Senators. Members of Parliament. Men who valued truth over expediency. Conservation groups in Germany, America, England, France.

'Yes,' Deacon said, 'already mailed.'

Chadwick stared at Deacon, a look of utter incomprehension. He said: 'Trade. . . .' His voice clogged in his throat a moment and he gave a weird gargling little cough. 'I was sure that you'd come here to trade.'

'Yes,' Deacon said. He smiled. 'Of course you'd think that.' He went to the elevator, pressed the button and waited. There was no reason not to turn his back.

Chadwick lifted the phone. 'Don't bother,' he said. 'Let him out. Let him go.' Just beyond the letter lay the tape that Steiner had made under di Vito's tutelage. Chadwick knew he didn't need to play it now.

Deacon stepped on to Sixth and lifted a hand for the cab that was cruising towards him. He would take it to the Village and walk from there. A needless precaution, he thought, but why take chances? The cab pulled over, and he got in, slamming the door. It started to move before he could give instructions. Sitting on the floor, way below window-level, was Danzig. He was holding the biggest handgun Deacon had ever seen.

The two men regarded one another a moment, then Danzig reached on to the seat for the shoulder-bag he'd brought with him.

Deacon said: 'Peter?' His mind was electric with possibilities.

Danzig stowed the gun away. 'We were worried about you.'

'I thought you were an *economist*.' Deacon tested the weight of the gun by hefting the bag.

'It's as economical as hell,' Danzig assured him. 'You can take three guys out if they're standing in line.'

Deacon looked through the glass partition at the cabbie's disinterested back. 'You know this guy?'

'No. But he's well acquainted with a fifty-dollar bill I used to own. Tell me what happened.' He sounded eager.

Deacon laughed, shaking his head in disbelief. He looked again at the bag.

'Listen,' Danzig told him, 'it's a big world out there. Little guys need to even the odds.'

Deacon's laughter grew. 'Here's to the little guys,' he said. Soon they were both laughing. The cab swung south through cooling streets towards the Village where there was bustle and music and other laughter.

46

Henderson took them to Kennedy, his driving as cavalier as on the trip into town.

'What will he do?' Deacon asked.

'I don't know.' Henderson grimaced. 'His lawyers have lawyers. . . . Even so, you've connected him with so much. He can hardly expect to ride out the storm.'

'What would you do?'

'Collect whatever I could – the Nimrod fund, probably – send the money on a trip and go with it.'

'He can't do that,' Laura said. 'Not with Nimrod anyway.'

'So I gather. Well. . . .' Henderson pipped his horn and took a cab on the inside. 'He's linked with frauds, deaths, funding a left-wing guerrilla force. Christ, whatever happens, he's through. Anyone who so much as passed the time of day with him in the last five years is going to be running for cover. That's the least of it.'

'The company?' Deacon wanted to know. 'Am-Daw?'

'He *is* the company. There'll be others get burned. The ones who were just obeying orders – you know?'

'Steiner,' Laura observed.

'Among them, yes.' Henderson paused. 'I've tried, but I can't feel too guilty about him. His hands were as dirty as anyone's.'

It was sixteen hours since Steiner's wife had heard about her husband's heart-attack. A girl who said she had known Steiner for some time had called a doctor

410

to her apartment. Steiner was naked in her bed. The doctor had prepared the necessary papers. Steiner's wife had checked the insurances. Dry-eyed, she dealt with her children's grief and phoned some close relatives. No one knew about the event apart from those most concerned with the death, and Edward Henderson's guilt had a little further to go. Though not much.

'I'll call you,' he said. 'And watch the front pages.'

Deacon said: 'There's only Steiner – to make the connection.'

'Don't worry. He won't want any of us to turn up in a law-court. There'll be enough action without that. There are people who've been standing in line for Chadwick for years.'

'Long pig,' muttered Deacon.

'How's that?'

Deacon smiled. 'Nothing,' he said . 'The biter bit.'

Laura slept through the meal and she slept through the in-flight movie, coming to only briefly from time to time to use her inhaler. Flying was always a problem for her, and sleep was the best way to defeat it. Deacon watched in concern as she thumbed the pump and gasped the spray into her lungs. If he settled to sleep himself, placing his head close to hers on the seat-back, he could hear the faint persistent wheeze of her breathing above the drone of the plane.

During one of her wakeful moments, she asked the stewardess for a glass of water. Her face was drawn, but she smiled at him and took his hand. 'It's usual,' she said. 'Don't worry. Nothing dreadful's going to happen.'

For the first time for a long time, he thought that could be right: nothing awful would happen. He said: '"Not with Nimrod" – you said that to Edward.'

She drank some of the water and gave it to him to hold. She was getting ready to go back to sleep. 'That's right.'

'You used one of the computers at Edward's office. With a modem?'

'Yes.'

'What did you do?'

'Steiner had been easing the Nimrod account – he and some guy at a bank somewhere.' She remembered. 'Miami, right?'

'That's right.'

'I might have been able to hack in if I'd had time and help. As it was, Steiner had given Edward the systems code. Same as at my bank – Buxton's bank . . . Chadwick's. Whoever's damn bank it is. The God-word. It lets you into the mainframe. I had the account number. I just gave the computer an instruction.'

'What?'

'Well, in simple language it said: "Report all accounts as they stand except *this* account; report *this* account as containing one dollar."' She pressed the recline button on her seat and eased backwards. 'I emptied the account.'

'How much?'

'I don't know. Millions, I expect. Whatever Chadwick's friends had contributed. The Nimrod fund.' She smiled sleepily. 'Here today, gone tomorrow.'

'Where did you send it?'

'Nowhere. It isn't money; it's just a bunch of figures. I made it disappear.' Her eyes closed, opened again, closed. 'Isn't science wonderful?'

Chadwick didn't know about the one-dollar account, because it hadn't occurred to him to go anywhere with or without the Nimrod fund. It hadn't occurred to him to wonder about the fund at all, or those who helped build it. He had almost forgotten about Volkov and Los Libertadores and Steiner. Deacon was still in his mind, though less as a man than as a symbol of ruin. He could have issued Deacon's death-warrant, but since there would have been no purpose in that, no gain, the knowledge held no pleasure for him. If it had been profitable to kill Deacon, he would have given the order without a shred of remorse. But it was as Deacon had said – too late. He didn't think of revenge; he thought only of himself and what had happened to him.

He spent the night and half the next day sitting in the penthouse apartment. No one would approach him there; for a while, at least, business would continue as normal. Not for long, though. He knew that.

The lights of the city had burned through the night like beacons signalling from hill-top to hill-top. Then came the deep pre-dawn blue. And still he sat, hands folded in his lap, listening to the tick of his own pulse. The half-empty brandy-glass was at his elbow, but he made no move to lift it. For a while, his mind had gone this way and that, a trapped animal running the coop, looking for a way out, sniffing the air beyond the bars; then it had quietened and retreated to the darkest part of the cage.

The sky had lightened, hot pearl chased by primrose, then the first shafts of silver struck the city's peaks. In the streets, the earliest stirrings of daytime life had eddied around the nightlife's remnants. Garbage-trucks, thin lines of cars, hotel workers trading shifts, people who had woken half an hour ago, people headed for their beds. There had been a trace of freshness in the air that disappeared almost immediately.

As the noise built, as the streets filled, as the triumphs and disasters of that day had begun to take shape, Chadwick sat unmoving and undisturbed. It was a day like the day before: hot and lacking any breeze. By noon there was a blaze that scorched the city. Fumes eddied off the streets. Four men walked into a Third Avenue drugstore, herded the customers and staff into a backroom, shot the manager, raped two of the women, and took what cash there was to

413

hand. In a West Side apartment a teenage boy, who had been too often beaten by his father, stabbed him as he lay drunk in bed. The city went about its business.

A circular staircase leading up from the penthouse brought Chadwick on to a roof garden: large terracotta urns full of colourful plants, Astroturf, weatherproof tables and chairs. He went to the parapet and looked down. Cars, buses, people moved in a random pattern like animated graphics obeying a program that allowed them infinite chance.

He looked out over the pinnacles and towers, the invisible, imperishable gridlines of power. What lay below was a life he no longer understood. Patterns. Yes, patterns; an ebb and flow of people and events that were there to be manipulated from above. Strength always came from above. Nero looking down on Rome. The flash of the Aztec priest's knife. The soft noiseless flowering of bombs as they bloomed on the target. He saw the great empires reflected in the gold-struck windows that confronted him: Nineveh and Thebes. He saw Carthage burning.

The sun dazed him, molten in the vast planes of glass. Standing there, above everything, he remembered a moment in his childhood: a hot day, like this one, his hand in his mother's hand, walking from a low picket fence to the church door; the minister's head bowed over the lectern.

Cast thyself down . . . the kingdoms of the world and the glory of them . . . all these will I give thee . . . .

Chadwick laughed at the memory. He felt a strange sensation that he couldn't isolate at first; then he realized that he was hungry. He caught, as if on a breeze, the fragrance of coffee. He imagined the after-taste of eggs and muffins.

It hadn't once occurred to him to run for cover. A team of smart lawyers could have held things at bay

414

for a while. Not for ever, of course; money and influence – even the closed ranks of Wall Street – weren't enough to deflect justice these days. How long had Boesky held out? It would have been possible to buy time, though. The idea had barely passed through his mind. It had been his way never to take prisoners, and he had no taste for becoming one. The emperor in chains, hauled through the streets, jeered at by the mob – no, not that. It was for the Emperor to fall on his sword. Not defeat, but glory.

A step took him to the railing. He straddled it and latched his heels to the outer parapet, one hand locked on to the knee-high bar behind him. The street seemed to leap into his vision: crowded with people and vehicles, its din a faint susurration like the sea heard through a shell.

His fingers loosened and he fell. So high, he was flying. So high, he never expected to come to earth. He turned and turned, falling through a golden glow, his body reflected in the endless mirrors of the sun-shot windows, an eternity of falling until the blue and white light that shimmered on the tall buildings engulfed him completely.

47

It was like watching a river in spate. The guerrillas had cut a channel towards the capital, submerging opposition or sweeping it away; now their forces spread like a delta and swamped the ground, held in check here and there by a patchy rearguard action that broke and re-formed and broke again like a faulty dam. 'Give it ten days,' was what Steiner had said to Chadwick. It was happening a lot sooner than that.

The General was travelling light. Six suitcases had already been loaded into his limousine: four contained clothes, two others contained a million dollars in cash. It was cab-fare compared to the holdings in his numbered account in Zurich. Other items had been shipped out days ago: paintings, gold statuary, some Fabergé trinkets. The walls of the presidential palace were patched with faint rectangles where the canvases had once hung.

It was 1 a.m. Beyond the city's outskirts were sheet-lightning flashes of mortar-fire and the short white rods of tracer bullets that seemed to lengthen and quicken as they gathered on a target. The percussion of the fire-fight was ceaseless: dull bass-sounds overlaid by the rapid snare-drum riffs of automatic weapons. Two mortar-shells whistled in nearby, shaking windows and starting fires on the south side of the city square. The girl squealed and hopped sideways in fear, wobbling on her high-heels. The General was loading papers into an attaché case. He chuckled and patted the girl's arm reassuringly, but went back to transferring the documents with renewed speed.

Soon after his mistress had died in the church, the General had begun to miss the particular compensations of female company. This girl was just as skilful, just as willing; it was as if the first girl were still with him. She tottered alongside as he strode down the long corridor leading to the courtyard, her heavy breasts swaying as she strove to keep pace, her eyes wide with anxiety. In her silk dress and fashionable shoes, she looked as if she were going to a garden-party. She click-clacked along on the tile floor, stumbling occasionally, and finally linked her arm through the General's for support. Her ungainliness was fear.

There were five vehicles in the convoy: two jeeps ahead of the limo, two following. They drove south for eight miles, moving further and further away from the flashlit sky and the sound of gunfire. One end of the airstrip was a blaze of dead white halogen flood-lighting where the plane had already taxied into position. While the cases were put aboard, the General stood close to the loading-hatch door, his face made chalky by the beams.

The plane lifted and circled, heading back over the city and gaining height. The General looked down, beck-oning to the girl and pointing. She scrambled over him to gain a view, kneeling on her own seat but leaning her head on the window at his side. Safe above it all, she could enjoy the spectacle: the sparkle of shell-blasts and muzzle-flashes, the sudden rhom-boids of brilliance that collapsed to a fist, the ruby glow of blazing buildings. She giggled with relief and delight.

The General tested the weight of a breast with one hand, while the other slid up the back of her thigh and under the silk dress. He spoke softly, teasingly into her ear, mistakenly calling her by the name of the girl who had died, though she didn't mind that. He lifted the skirt to her waist, then slipped his fingers between her thighs. She smiled absently and muttered an endearment, but continued to watch until the noiseless, flickering lights mingled and shrank and were swallowed by the dark.

Dawn made the fighting seem to recede – sounds no longer magnified by night, gunfire no longer cast on a black backcloth. In truth it grew closer each hour. Pockmarked buildings smouldered. Soldiers of the Republican Army retreated through their own lines, retreated further, deserted. Stores were looted. The civilian population looked for cover.

There was nothing about Sonny Moreno to let you know he'd been in combat recently: he was wearing jeans and sneakers and a Snoopy T-shirt; his few belongings had been thrust into a battered rucksack. The only weapon he had about him was a .38 short-barrelled Colt taped to his shin underneath the jeans. The spook was debriefing him in a hotel room close to the main route south – Sonny had made it clear that he didn't consider it healthy to be found in any official residence.

The conversation had gone pretty rapidly, the spook's questions receiving clipped replies from Sonny, who was standing, rucksack-strap over one shoulder, all ready to leave and resenting every minute of delay.

Finally, the spook said: 'How long would you give it now?' He shut off his dictaphone.

'An hour. Less. Man, they're already *here*.'

'Where are you headed?'

'Out.' Sonny threaded his arm through the second rucksack-strap. 'Another war, another time.' He started for the door.

'You want company? There're three of us; with transport.'

'You're leaving?'

'Does a bear shit in the woods? Twenty minutes, tops.'

Sonny hesitated. 'What transport?'

'Red Subaru four-track.'

'Going south.'

'For sure.'

Sonny went to the door and opened it. 'Look for me on the road,' he said. 'I'll be the guy with his thumb out.' He nodded a farewell. 'I'd shift ass, I was you. Twenty minutes ain't as long as you think.'

Oleg Volkov was jumpy. He'd have been happier to travel south like Sonny, but Junction 9 was due east and he was driving close to the fringe of the combat zone. At some points the road was badly churned by mortar-fire, and he'd been forced to slow to a crawl, taking the big car round the worst of it by mounting pavements or, later, negotiating the rutted slope at the roadside. Three or four times, as he'd inched round the potholes, people had clung to the door-handles of the car, their faces pressed to the darkened glass pleading with the invisible driver. He'd speeded up when the road surface cleared, and they had run with him as far as they were able, yelling and beating on the roof. One man had stood in the roadway to flag him down, arms held high and crossing in a desperate semaphore. Volkov had driven at the man, but he'd held his ground until there was no leeway. Volkov had tramped on the brake, twitching the car right, then heard the thud and clatter as the man was struck and lofted and thrown away.

The fighting was almost at hand: lines of smoke, gunfire – though less and less as the rebels came closer to shanty-town and the roads that controlled access to the capital. That, at least, was working out for him.

They would be in the city within the hour, he reckoned: say, by noon. He'd set the device in the embassy cellars for twelve-thirty – a chain explosive with intermittent incendiaries. No one would be able to say quite what happened or who was responsible, but it would certainly hold up any friendly chat between the rebels and any survivors from the embassy. He hoped there wouldn't be any: he'd take all the advantage he could get.

Once he hit the open road, he relaxed a little. The timing was good. The rendezvous with the chopper was for eleven-thirty, which gave him half an hour for the remaining fifteen miles. He took the first ten faster than he needed, to push beyond the line of the advance, then dawdled over the final five. . . .

He was standing on the porch of a big colonial-style house, flanked by elegant pillars. It was summer, and a light breeze was blowing as neighbours came up the driveway to join the barbecue. He was at the back of the house, chopping cordwood for the stove; the nearby hillsides were flanked with trees, their leaves glowing russet and gold in the late-afternoon sun. He was lingering by a big bow window, whisky-glass in hand, and watching the slow thick fall of snow as it settled in his orchard. Sometimes he put the girl into that last picture: she was pretty, blonde and slim; she had an intelligent face and green eyes that lingered on him invitingly.

He arrived early and waited in the car. He knew just where the chopper would put down and had parked about thirty metres from the spot, listening for the noise of the rotors, but going on with his dreaming. He was cross-country skiing; taking the shuttle to New York; furnishing the house. He was in bed with the slim blonde girl on an afternoon of soft rain.

After fifteen minutes, he got out of the car and watched the sky to the south. It was clear. It stayed

420

clear. For another ten minutes he supported belief
with increasingly wild theories. Mechanical problems
with the chopper; a pilot running late; a bad map-
reading. But soon he'd see the dot in the southern sky,
closing fast, and watch it grow, and hear the chug of
the blades.

He knew that no one was coming for him. It was
past noon; the rebels would be in the city, among
them the Indian who had travelled with him to the
bridge on route 18 and listened to promises that could
never be kept. He didn't want to meet that man again.
In twenty minutes, step-explosives would trigger the
incendiaries. Even if he'd dared, even if he could
think of a way, there was no time to go back. Nothing
to go back to.

Volkov shook his head violently, like a dog emerging from water. Madness; madness to think such
things. Soon they would be here, the chopper tilting to
land, the downdraught plucking at his clothes as he
ran towards it. Some small mechanical fault. A mis-
read map.

He stood beside the car, his head lifted, staring at
the sky – a man looking at a blank screen. Thirty
minutes; fifty minutes; an hour. His gaze never
wavered. Projected on the screen were the house, the
orchard, the girl, the silent, drifting, unhurried
descent of snow.

48

The flute-player went on tiptoe, not to wake the dead.

Elaine was excited. She came into the room eager to share her news but went to the mirror first, wanting to tease the moment out. She removed the wig and set it aside, then began to work at her make-up with cold-cream and a cotton-wool ball. She dragged at her lips to wipe the redness off. He could tell from her face that something had happened, but she cocked a shoulder and grinned, playing a game of Won't Tell. When his pleading finally pleased her, she let him in on the secret.

'Back?' he said. He sat beside her, looking at her reflection and his own. They were both smiling wildly.

'Back.' She nodded furiously. 'I saw him today.'

'And her?'

'No, not her. But they're back.'

'How long? When did they arrive?'

'I don't know.' She was cautious, not wanting to earn his displeasure. Things had changed since she had forced them into hiding. Myles was confined to the room while she went out, and the altered roles had given him control. When she was his secret he had indulged her; now he was the hidden one, and she sometimes felt his rage. He'd wanted her to go to Deacon's flat every day – to watch for them, to wait for their return; but the dark streets had drawn her fantasies and her desire. She had paced them like a predator inventing kills.

'Last night?'

'Yes, I think so.' Three days, she thought, maybe four. 'What shall we do? We could phone – we did before.'

He shook his head. 'We'll watch for a while. You can watch, follow her perhaps; I'd like that. Just for a while. She'll come to us soon enough. She's bound to come to us.' He put a hand to her cheek. It was burning.

The sheela-na-gig's dark obscene little face was sharp with laughter. The chasm between her legs gaped, promising harvest.

49

For days a break in the weather had been forecast. It wouldn't come. In truth, few people wanted it to; the round of baking purple nights, and life lived outside, had become almost usual. The city had loosened up, and it was likeable.

Within a day of being back, Deacon was sharply aware of a restlessness in Laura. It communicated itself, making him jumpy, too. They moved about the flat, trying to avoid one another but trying, also, not to make a point of it. They made love, but it seemed only to increase the tension. On the third night, Deacon woke to find himself alone in bed, and went through to the living-room where Laura was sipping tea and reading, swathed in his bathrobe.

'It's jet-lag,' she told him.

He sat on the sofa, not close to her. 'No, it's not.'

'No, it's not.' She didn't look up from her book. Neither spoke for about five minutes. Laura continued to stare at the open page, but didn't turn it. Finally, she began to cry, softly. 'I'm sorry,' she said. 'It's. . . . There's been no *time*. Everything that's happened; what I told you about Maggie; nothing seems really resolved.' As she said that, she glanced at the phone, as if it might ring on cue, bringing back the voice. Somewhere . . . somewhere out there still . . . whoever had murdered Kate. It was as if they had come full circle.

Laura cuffed her jaw, taking teardrops off with the heel of her hand. 'It's not that. . . .' She shook her head at the impossibility of finding just the right way of saying things, and gave in to weeping. Deacon put a hand on hers; otherwise he made no move to touch her.

Eventually, she looked up. Her whole face was wet, but she had stopped crying. There was only one way to get it said. 'I love you. I've loved you for a while, now. I want everything to be right between us, but it's not. So many things. . . . I hurt you. I didn't want to, but I did. We came together because of violence and fear, and. . . .' She shook her head. 'It just went on like that. I still feel frightened. I feel bruised and unhappy and uncertain. If I could make it all different, God knows, I would. I don't know whether we're in a relationship or a fortress. I want to be with you, but it's as if I were trapped. Not by you, so much; by what's happened to us. If I think back to that first time I came here, after Kate died, then think of everything since. . . .' She freed her hand a moment, then returned it to clasp his. 'The reason why we came together; the reason for our closeness; the reason why we first made love. . . . It's scary and odd. I don't know what can come of it. I know what I want; I don't know if I can make it happen.'

'You're going away,' Deacon said.

'For a while. For a while, at least.'

'Where?'

'Norfolk. My friends up there.'

'You've already phoned them.'

'This afternoon,' she said.

'I'll drive you. In the morning.'

'No,' she said.

'Will you call me?'

'After a while,' Laura nodded. 'After a while.'

'I love you,' Deacon told her.

'I know. It makes it better. It makes it worse.'

He moved closer, and she folded into the crook of his arm, resting her head on his shoulder. Within a minute or two, she had fallen asleep. Deacon held her like that for what was left of the night. He didn't sleep. He sat still, like a statue.

50

And now it was dark again, well, not quite dark; a deeper darkness, though, than the half-light of the shuttered room, a rich, bruised, damson blue, with pockets of furry blackness in doorways, in parkland shrubbery, in alleys. Not black, no, not quite black, but dark enough, yes, dark enough.

And now it was time, almost time, soon, yes, soon enough, there was no real hurry, that was part of it, that was how it should begin, with time to spare, a little time to spare, to follow this one or that, to think perhaps this one or that, maybe her, or maybe her, not to move too soon, but make sure it was right, make sure there was time, time to spend with her, time to spend on her, yes, time enough.

And now it was here again, the excitement, the feeling of power, Elaine moving through the darkness, gliding through the darkness, dressed in dark clothing, over her shoulder the bag, in the bag the knife, yes, and everything yet to happen, everything to come, the glory still to come, as she walked slowly in the night-time streets that were thinning of people, finding the shadows, walking with the shadows, a stroller, a woman alone, quite harmless for that, it made her want to laugh – how harmless she must seem, the laughter bubbled in her throat, she touched the bag, people passed, not knowing, yes, and someone, some-where, not knowing, yes, that person, this person, maybe her, or maybe her, the one she would choose.

It was late. The last trains were running. The last buses. Elaine walked softly on light, flat-soled canvas shoes. She had been out for almost two hours. Her face was flushed, as if she were running a mild fever. She liked the feeling. It gave her a sensation of lightness, as if her feet were not quite touching the ground. Myles would be cross. He wanted to wait for Laura – wanted Elaine to watch and follow and wait until Laura came to them. But that would happen; it would happen before long. He said it was a risk – to go out like this. He was wrong. No one knew her. No one could possibly guess. A woman walking alone. It was safe. And she remembered the last time – the girl on the common, the fury of that, the wonder, like an endless dream of falling.

She kept away from main roads, walking the side-streets where only a few people passed on their way home. Her route was a wide circle that kept her, always, fairly close to the room and refuge. Each circuit took about forty minutes, though she varied it a little, in order to walk down a new alleyway, sometimes, or to skirt a dark square that she hadn't passed before.

As time passed, there were fewer people. It didn't worry her. She knew that somewhere, that night, she would meet the person she was meant to find. Maybe this one . . . maybe that one. When the fever was too great to bear. When the time was right.

And, as if the thought had summoned her, suddenly the person was there. Elaine almost cried out. Just ahead, alone, coming out of a side-street and turning to walk ahead. Impossible. Elaine picked up her pace slightly, getting a little closer to be sure. And, no, it wasn't impossible. Of course it would be like this. No such thing as chance. No such thing as coincidence. She had delivered herself up. Laura.

428

They walked the length of one street, Elaine quickening her steps to get closer still. Twenty metres ahead, the road crossed a small iron bridge over a railway line with hoardings on either side, and a dirt bank shelved down steeply to what seemed fathomless blackness.

Closer, almost close enough to touch as they reached the near side of the bridge. Elaine smiled, a genuine smile of pleasure, the kind of smile anyone would give at meeting an old friend in the street. The delight was plain in her voice when she said: 'Laura!'

The girl turned. The tall woman was advancing on her, smiling, her arm extended as if for a handshake. A moment's puzzlement, then the girl said, 'I'm sorry, I—' but stopped, because the woman just kept coming, knocking into her, putting her off balance, pitching her sideways behind the hoarding, arms bound round her like a lover's as they fell down the bank into the dark. The girl was too shocked, too surprised, to call out at once. The moment had all the suddenness and ungainly violence of an accident. If it had been a man approaching her, she would have been wary. She might have tried to run, or at least have cried out. As it was, there was a woman, an instant's surprise, a jarring tumble that allowed no time for thought.

When they came to rest, the girl half sat up. It was all she had time for. Next, there was a hand across her mouth. Her head was slammed against the ground, and the *crack* of the impact rang in her ears, as if she had heard the sound of something vital breaking in her own skull. Everything swam away. There were fingers at the buttons that ran down the front of her dress.

Elaine pulled the garment off and threw it aside. The girl's body seemed to glow, like a pale icon. She stirred as Elaine took out the knife and brought its tip to the hollow of the girl's throat.

'Laura,' she whispered. 'Oh, Laura. There's time. There's plenty of time.'

51

Deacon had spent a day roaming the perimeters of his flat. He drank coffee and made snacks. He played music, but didn't listen to it. He was waiting for Laura to phone, and even admitted that fact to himself from time to time.

He'd made his own calculations about their relationship, just as she had, and examined his own motives. It was clear that there was dangerous ground – areas heavily mined with memories of Maggie, with the secrets Laura had kept from him, with a closeness that had been forced on them, and with fear in the guise of passion. None of these considerations, though, seemed to count for much when weighed against Laura's absence and the way he felt about that. He missed her, and he wanted her back. That simple knowledge overpowered all caution. It provoked in him a fear of loss combined with great urgency, as if he'd realized, for the first time, that no one lives for ever. It scared him that she couldn't match his certainty, even though he knew how essential it was to allow her the time she'd asked for. Impossible to wait; impossible to force the issue.

It was growing dark, but he hadn't bothered to switch on the lights. The dimness was soothing. To bring the room back into sharp focus would have exaggerated his restlessness. He finally settled in a chair opposite to the window, where he smoked obsessively and watched the last of the daylight fade – a slow irregular reduction, like something being gradually crumpled. When the phone rang he checked his hand a moment, as if impatience might bring disappointment.

'It's me.' Her voice sounded distant and strained.

'How are you?' His question meant *How are we? What have you been thinking about? When will I see you?*

She said: 'Not well. I'm coming back to London in the morning.'

Strange to have his question answered with such literalness. The fact that she had a severely practical response to offer made him feel cheated. Her urgency seemed dismissive. But he could hear the breathy wheeze behind her words – the now familiar way she used short sentences to conserve energy. He asked: 'How bad?'

'All right.' There was a brief pause, and he guessed she was using the inhaler. 'Well, not desperate; not great, either.'

'I'll come and get you.'

'No – really. I'm OK. OK to drive. I'm better on my own.'

'What will you do?'

'See Myles.'

A moment's incomprehension, then he said: 'Oh, yes. Then what?' He meant: then *where*?

'I was thinking of coming straight back here.'

'Laura—'

'No,' she said. 'I was *thinking* of it. I won't, though. The pollen's awful. Or it might be house-mites. I'm reacting badly to something.' Mixed in with the sing-song of her breathing was a lightness of tone, close to laughter.

'That's the only reason?' He knew he sounded like a supplicant, but didn't care much. Pride didn't seem one of the things at issue.

'No,' she told him. 'I want to see you.'

'What time is your appointment?'

'I haven't made one yet. There's always a free hour,

432

though. Myles leaves a gap for emergencies. I'll make it as early as possible and go straight there.'

'Let me know what time you fix and I'll meet you. Bring you back.'

'No, I'll have my car.'

'I'll take a cab.'

Laura managed a husky laugh. 'I'll be there soon enough.'

'Will you?'

'I'll try to be with you around lunch-time. Listen' – she blocked further argument – 'I've talked for too long. It's tiring. I'll see you tomorrow.'

'Yes,' he said.

'Because I want to.'

He didn't ask what would happen after that, mostly because he guessed that neither of them quite knew.

After the phone call, he felt suddenly tired. He sat in the darkness – complete, now, apart from the faint false dawn of the city's sodium lighting – and smoked a cigarette. Its glowing tip left a snaky trace of orange, like a firefly's dance.

That night, he dreamed a river-bank, a hot land, though not arid, everything washed in a clear white light. Palms and trees gravid with fruit grew beside the river, and there were creatures, in pairs, lying on the bank, or drinking from the shallows. A pair of lions, except that their coats were a dusky coral-colour. A pair of wildebeest, except that they were striped with muted greens and ochres. A pair of buffalo, except that their hides were a startling cobalt blue and glowed in the sun. Though the colours were odd and extreme, they struck Deacon as entirely harmonious; and a quiet harmony existed between the animals.

He and Laura were strolling beside the river. He turned to her and said: 'This is the Peaceable Kingdom.' He saw it as a place he recognized, as if a fabled map had drawn them in, like dream-children, to the world that lay beyond its contours and symbols. All that worried him was that the light seemed too concentratedly bright, as if arc-lights were trained on a film set. The animals were, perhaps, posed too carefully. His remark sounded too sculpted and pat, like a line from a script. Still in the dream, he began to puzzle this out. The telephone scrambled his thoughts and the scene simultaneously. He fished for the receiver while fragments of the vision rushed through his memory and were lost.

The first words eluded him, and he didn't reply. The caller spoke again.

'John, it's Phil Mayhew. Don't hang up.'

Deacon had supposed it would be Laura. He glanced at his radio-alarm and saw that it was too early for her to phone from London – and probably too late for a call from Norfolk. He felt disappointed and angry.

Mayhew said: 'John?'

'I'm here.'

'I'm not— I'm only calling for one reason. This isn't to mend bridges.'

'Go on.' Deacon hauled himself up and sat cross-legged on the bed.

'You've been away.'

'Yes.' Deacon was wary and anxious at the same time. There was something in Mayhew's tone.

'I tried to call you. A week ago?'

'Yes. . . .'

'I tried more than a few times.'

'What is it, Phil?' He felt strange using the name.

'A week ago – eight days, now – a girl was killed in a west London park.'

'The same man,' Deacon said. It wasn't a question.

'Without doubt.' Mayhew hesitated.

'And . . .?'

'And last night, another.'

'What do I need to know?' Deacon asked.

434

'I owe you one, John. Owe you this phone call, at least.'

'I'm not sure debt comes into it.' Deacon didn't want to offer the notion of repayment. He knew there are some things that can't be made good. 'What happened?' Laura outside his protection became, at once, a frightening thing.

'She was found early – at first light.' His next remark came quickly. 'She'd been disembowelled. This guy – he's lost control, now. He can't stop. He wants more victims – and faster, you know? More often.'

'It's a pattern,' Deacon said.

'Yes, I know. Slow start, growing frenzy. Newspapers are using the "Ripper" tag. They're on to the connection with Meredith – speculating anyway.'

'What are your lot saying?'

'Refusing to comment, you know. Pursuing a line of investigation. That stuff.'

'Thanks for telling me.'

'No, John. . . . Look, I don't know what the hell's going on any more. I can see there were things you didn't tell me. The D'Arblay business was simply buried. I expected a grilling: it didn't happen. Just told to keep my mouth shut. Since then there's been a wall of silence. I've stopped guessing. In fact I don't want to know.' Deacon stayed silent. 'I'm not asking you where you've been, what's happened, anything like that. OK?'

'OK.' Deacon could tell there was more to come.

'The girl,' Mayhew said. 'Last night. I saw her at the scene of crime. Then we got photos from the family: the usual thing.' Deacon waited. 'The thing is, John, it's unmistakable. She looks a hell of a lot like Laura. Same build, same height; colour of hair, the way it was styled. Facially, very like. It shocked me. For a moment, I thought it *was* her. I mean, the connection with Kate Lorimer and all. . . .' A coldness

435

started up in Deacon's gut, and began to spread. 'I thought you should know,' Mayhew said.

'Where was she found?' Deacon seemed to hear his own voice coming from an impossible distance.

'Railway embankment. Half a mile from you. Less. She'd been bundled under a bridge where the road crosses the line. She mightn't have been spotted so soon, but the guy had stripped her dress off and thrown it to one side. Eventually, someone decided to go and take a look. Poor sod; he won't forget in a hurry. A number of people have reported seeing it, though. Workers on early shift; and someone saw it from a train. Couldn't miss it, really. It was bright yellow.'

Deacon called Norfolk, but Laura had left. On the pad by the telephone she had scribbled *Paul and Moira Yarnall*, then a phone-number but no address. It was Moira he spoke to.

'She made an appointment from here . . . oh, just past nine; then went immediately. She has to be there at noon.'

'Noon.' He repeated the word like someone learning by rote.

'I'm sure she's all right – to drive and so forth.' She thought Deacon's anxiety had to do with Laura's asthma attack. 'I've seen her a lot worse. She was just uncomfortable, you know? The pollen count's pretty dreadful up here. I expect it was that.'

'I expect so.'

'Don't worry.' Moira chuckled. 'She'll be with you in three hours or so.'

She was out of reach, and the feeling made him insecure; but, he reasoned, it was needless worry. She was driving – safely in motion. She would go straight to Myles – what was his name? – Allardyce, then directly to the flat.

Because he needed something to do, Deacon went from room to room, tidying the place. In the bedroom, Laura's suitcase lay on the floor, only half-unpacked. She had taken the minimum of clothes with her. The fact cheered him; it seemed to suggest that she had never meant to stay away for long. On the other hand, she hadn't put the remainder of her things away. Because they had never agreed to live together – because it had been an event forced on them – she hadn't been able to take the wardrobe-space she needed. It was a token; an unanswered question.

A name was tapping at his mind.

He felt, now, like a man who has been standing on the crown of a bridge. For a while, he had been unable to do more than stay in the middle and watch the water. Maggie had been on the side he'd left from. To have continued would have required a choice, and he hadn't been ready for that. But he had stopped watching the water; his eyes were on the opposite bank. New ground. He wanted it. Deacon drew the bedroom curtains and picked up a water-glass from the bedside table, and the name asserted itself. Myles Allardyce. A connection somewhere that escaped him.

Places, he reflected, were supposed to be more difficult than other things. He knew people whose break-ups had effectively closed down for them whole areas – sometimes countries. They couldn't bear to go back. He knew, though, that it wasn't places but times, and that times only remained potent because people elected to live them through again and again. He had done that. But those times with Maggie had lost the power to obsess him; they existed where they should – in the past. No, not times; and certainly not places. He remembered how readily he'd taken Laura down to the beach-house where he thought she would be safe. Even then, and without knowing it, he had been gaining little victories.

The recollection brought him back to the name.

Laura had gone to see her hypnotherapist then – the only sure way of relieving her asthma attack. *Allardyce*. The name flickered like a flame, then died down.

He spent another ten minutes or so on delaying tactics, cleaning the coffee-jug, reading a page or two of a book without retaining a single word, then went back to the bedroom, as he'd intended from the start, to hang Laura's clothes in the wardrobe.

The blinds were always drawn. They lived in half-light with the shadows. They lived with memories and plans. They lived with dreams that were stored in the barrel of a syringe.

So like her. . . . So like Laura. But it hadn't been her. The phone call had been a shock. 'Who?' he had asked, 'Who?' and she had sounded puzzled until he recovered himself and pretended that they'd had a bad line. Now he saw the symmetry in it all. The other girl's death was part of a pattern of power that had now drawn Laura to him. His belief had been so strong, his desire so great, that it had manipulated events and delivered Laura up to him.

Allardyce laid Elaine's clothes out on the bed, folding carefully, smoothing; he put her make-up in front of the mirror. Soon Laura would arrive. Allardyce put a hand to his mouth and bit hard against the rising excitement. Laura. . . . And then Elaine, entering the room as she always did, greeting the shadows as they scurried on the wall. He loved her now as he'd loved her when they were children. Sister and lover. Her darkness dizzied him.

He set a chair in readiness and looked round the room like a nervous host, gulping on his laughter.

Deacon had pushed Laura's empty suitcase underneath the bed, then gone back to the living-room and spent a couple of hours with old ghosts. Places and times. It was necessary to remember them – it was also fine. He felt sad, but knew that it was proper to do so. Now and then, the name nudged him, irritatingly. It wasn't a memory – something else. An instinct. He checked his watch, and saw that Laura ought to be arriving for her appointment in ten minutes or so. Again, the nudge; a blurred understanding. He felt like someone who has turned to a task and instantly forgotten what it was he'd intended to do.

He went to the pad by the phone and riffled the pages. *Myles Allardyce*: a flat-number, a street-name, a phone-number. That wasn't it. He'd expected to find the information there. It looked oddly familiar, though. The name in Laura's handwriting – long loops on each 'y', the way she fashioned a Greek 'e'. But not here. Not this.

And then he had it clear.

He saw the moment: Mayhew handing over the slender blue book. 'Lorimer's diary' he'd said. 'In a drawer – someone's out-tray. . . .' Deacon saw, as if he were looking over his own shoulder, his fingers turning its pages. *Myles Allardyce*.

He went to the desk and took the whole drawer out with one pull, grabbing the book and flipping through. Usually once a week; sometimes every other week. *Myles Allardyce*. Kate's attempts to stop smoking: probably as much for Laura's sake as for her own. And then, as the weeks went on, just the initials: *MA* for each appointment.

He heard Laura's voice, 'I don't understand . . .,' and then 'The bird was real'. It wasn't the name alone that had prompted his instinct. She *believed* in the phone. She *believed* in the voice.

He chased the dates, crumpling pages. The day of Kate's death. His eyes flicked back. *MA*.

439

52

Deacon was running. He'd driven as far as he could, but the traffic build-up had balked him half a mile from the address. Vehicles were backed up where a road-gang had brought the flow down to one lane. The side-streets were clogged with drivers trying to beat the trap. He abandoned his car where it stood.

The phone calls. Oh, Christ, the phone calls. He had told her what he wanted to do to her. Deacon remembered Mayhew's description of Jessica Meredith's death. The mirror and the word *Glory* written in blood. He was crying as he ran, saying Laura's name.

He found the street. He found the shuttered windows. The door wasn't locked. He simply opened it and walked into the nightmare.

Coming in from hard sunlight, Deacon was near-blind. He screwed his eyes up and opened them again. Through a swarm of yellow amoeba, he saw a passageway – three doors leading from it. He listened. From the far door, there came the sound of voices: a man's and a woman's; neither of them Laura's. He went the length of the passage and opened that door.

The room was dim. His eyes still hadn't adjusted. There came a stench that brought bile rushing to his throat. Two shapes, one seated, one standing, the standing shape leaning forward as if in attendance, hands raised and busy. Then the shapes separated and he could see more clearly. In the chair, arms rigidly at her sides, a naked woman he didn't recognize. And

440

moving towards him another woman, tall and raw-boned, her face livid with make-up. She was wearing a peach-coloured blouse that glowed in the semi-dark. Her hand was drawn back.

Their arms clashed: the downward blow of the knife and Deacon's instinct to ward it off. He stepped back. The edge of the bed took him behind the knees, and he fell. Allardyce fell with him, striking again. The blade rode over Deacon's collarbone, slicing his shoulder. He caught Allardyce's wrist with both hands and held it. Then he reared, jack-knifing his knee hard into the other man's breastbone.

Allardyce roared on a violent indrawn breath and fell away. Deacon turned, kneeling over the man, still clutching the wrist. The painted face was wrenched with pain, the lips a ragged red gap, but Allardyce's free hand was reaching up, searching for Deacon's nose, his lips, anything that could be crushed or torn. His voice filled the room – Elaine's voice – howling and snarling with effort.

Deacon ducked the outstretched hand and bore down with straight arms, turning Allardyce's wrist. He felt the ligaments pop, then the joint went with a wrenching crack, like a wet stick. Allardyce screamed, showing his teeth. Deacon felt a nail score his cheek, the finger looking for his eye. He took the knife two-handed and drove down, finding the hollow just below the thorax.

Allardyce put his tongue out. A gusher of blood rose past his lips, bubbling like a spring. He seemed to be trying to speak. Deacon leaned on the knife, unable to move. He started to shake.

Eventually, with infinite slowness, he inched backwards from the body, first one foot on the floor, a pause, and then the other. He looked round the room, turning his entire body like a man at exhaustion's edge.

*　　*　　*

441

Two figures in chairs. One unrecognizable for what it had once been; putrid, decayed, a sack of pus topped by a chewed death's head. The other, he now saw, was Laura. The shape of her face had changed because her mouth was stuffed with rag and taped. But it was more than that. Allardyce had started with her hair; and that was all he'd had time for. It was hacked off above her ears and close to her head. There was blood on her face where the knife had nicked her. A thong round her neck kept her head against the chair-back, but her cheek was canted over against one shoulder; not slackly; her entire body was rigid.

Deacon stripped off the tape and took the wadding from her mouth. She looked at him, and her eyes were bulging, her body leaping with spasm. The asthma and the fear. The plug in her mouth. She had almost stopped breathing completely. Deacon freed her and took her into the passageway. He brought her clothes. Garment by garment, slowly, she put them on. She didn't let him help. She didn't speak.

53

It took days. He cut her hair as best he could, clipping away the ragged edges until it lay close to her skull, downy and childlike. He brought her food at unscheduled moments in the hope that she might eat it. He talked to her without expecting replies. He lay awake at night, the cut in his shoulder stinging if he turned the wrong way, and waited for her nightmares. The bedside light was always on, but she slept like someone drugged.

Even now, Deacon wasn't sure what it was that they had left in the room for someone, some time, to find. He guessed, he came up with some likely answers, but in truth he didn't care. At one point, he took a call from Edward Henderson. He listened to what Edward had to say, told him things were fine, hung up. Laura stayed in bed, sleeping most of the time. It occurred to him that he might be trying to cope with something beyond his means.

He read and played music and waited, but without knowing what he was waiting for. Because he watched over her at night, he napped during the days.

It was a dragging sound he heard, and a muffled thump. When he got to the bedroom door, he found Laura standing in front of the wardrobe. Her suitcase was on the bed. She was removing her clothes. He watched as she folded some jeans and a light sweater and stowed them in the case.

She said: 'Let's go away.'

The drive west took them into changing weather, the air soggy, the sky bearing a sickly yellow tinge.

When they got to the beach-house, Laura made him wait outside while she went in alone. After five minutes, she emerged. As if reading Deacon's mind, she said: 'It isn't places.' And then, more to herself; 'It's just a house.'

They took the cliff-path to the beach, wanting what little breeze they could find. The sea was low, opaque like the sky, and almost noiseless.

'The bird was real,' Laura said.

'Yes.'

'But the phone – the voice – all of that. . . . He'd told me to hear it. He'd sown the idea in my mind.' She made it sound like a species of poisonous plant.

Deacon could see that much, and some of the rest: how Chadwick had found the man. There was a line of connection: Am-Daw, Nimrod, D'Arblay and the security service.

Laura said: 'He used it, somehow, post-hypnotic suggestion, when he killed Kate. When he killed those other women.' It was a question she was asking of herself.

Just as Laura had been instructed to hear, so Kate had been instructed not to see. *You'll hear a phone, you'll hear a voice saying. . . .* Allardyce's voice. *It will be as if no one's there. You'll see nothing.*

'In some way,' Deacon said. 'I don't know. . . .'

Laura traced random lines in the sand. 'It's why her clothes were tidy,' she said. 'He put them on.'

'I think so. I think that's what he must have done.'

Heavy cumulo-nimbus was building on the skyline and moving shorewards: big anvil-shaped clouds, their undersides purple-black.

Laura said: 'I think so, too.'

A sudden wind brushed them and died, then

444

quickened again, raising whitecaps off-shore, making loose sand hiss among the rocks. There was a clatter of raindrops like a handful of flung pebbles. Then the light seemed to go all at once, and the outer line of the rainstorm dragged up the beach to engulf them.

By the time they reached the path, their clothes were saturated, their hair slick as paint. They started back, unhurried, with Laura leading the way. From time to time, Deacon almost lost sight of her in the downpour, but when he lengthened his pace she was still there, a dim shape in the hanging rails of rain.

THE END

THE FOURTH PROTOCOL
by Frederick Forsyth

'A triumph of plot, construction and research. As good as any Forsyth since the Jackal'

The Times

The Fourth Protocol is the story of a plan, dangerous beyond belief, to change the face of British society for ever.

Plan Aurora, hatched in a remote dacha in the forest outside Moscow, and initiated with relentless brilliance and skill, is a plan that in its madness – and spine-chilling ingenuity – breaches the ultra-secret Fourth Protocol and turns the fears that shaped it into a living nightmare.

A crack Soviet agent, placed under cover in a quiet English country town, begins to assemble a jigsaw of devastation. Working blind against the most urgent of deadlines, and against treachery and lethal power games in his own organisation, MI5 investigator John Preston leads an operation to prevent the act of murderous devastation aimed at tumbling Britain into revolution.

The Fourth Protocol is outstanding – for sheer excitement, for marvellous storytelling – a mighty entertainment and a superlative adventure.

'Forsyth's best book so far'

Washington Post

0552 13195 4

CROW'S PARLIAMENT
by Jack Curtis

Simon Guerney plies a lonely trade. He specializes in the rescue of kidnap victims; his unrecognized skills the last resort of the rich and desperate.

At first the disappearance of David Paschini seems a straightforward abduction case and Guerney joins the boy's mother in New York to play out the usual waiting game. Once there he begins to sense inconsistencies in the pattern of events – but it is not until the unknown kidnappers demand that he travel to London that Guerney realizes the game has turned and that suddenly he is the prey not the hunter . . .

Strikingly original in its combination of power politics, the growing menace of kidnapping and the disturbing but very real world of ESP, *Crows' Parliament* will take its place amongst such classics of the genre as *Rogue Male* and *The Third Man*.

0552 13081 8

A SELECTED LIST OF FINE TITLES
AVAILABLE FROM CORGI BOOKS

THE PRICES SHOWN BELOW WERE CORRECT AT THE TIME OF GOING TO PRESS. HOWEVER TRANSWORLD PUBLISHERS RESERVE THE RIGHT TO SHOW NEW RETAIL PRICES ON COVERS WHICH MAY DIFFER FROM THOSE PREVIOUSLY ADVERTISED IN THE TEXT OR ELSEWHERE.